ILLICIT

THE AGENTS

BRYNNE ASHER

Text Copyright
© 2024 Brynne Asher
All Rights Reserved
No part of this book may be reproduced, scanned, or distributed in any printed or electronic form without permission from the author. It is not legal to scan any part of this work into artificial intelligence. Please do not participate in or encourage piracy of copyrighted materials in violation of author's rights. Only purchase authorized editions.

Any resemblance to actual persons, things, locations, or events is accidental.

This book is a work of fiction.

ILLICIT

The Agents

Published by Brynne Asher
BrynneAsherBooks@gmail.com

Keep up with me on Facebook for news and upcoming books
https://www.facebook.com/BrynneAsherAuthor

Join my reader group on Facebook to keep up with my latest news
Brynne Asher's Beauties

Keep up with all Brynne Asher books and news
http://eepurl.com/gFVMUP

Edited by Hadley Finn
Cover Design by MSB Design - Ms Betty's Design Studio

ALSO BY BRYNNE ASHER

The Agents

Possession

Tapped

Exposed

Illicit

Killers Series

Vines – A Killers Novel, Book 1

Paths – A Killers Novel, Book 2

Gifts – A Killers Novel, Book 3

Veils – A Killers Novel, Book 4

Scars – A Killers Novel, Book 5

Souls – A Killers Novel, Book 6

Until the Tequila – A Killers Crossover Novella

The Killers, The Next Generation

Levi, Asa's son

The Carpino Series

Overflow – The Carpino Series, Book 1

Beautiful Life – The Carpino Series, Book 2

Athica Lane – The Carpino Series, Book 3

Until Avery – A Carpino Series Crossover Novella

Force of Nature - A Carpino Christmas Novel

The Dillon Sisters

Deathly by Brynne Asher

Damaged by Layla Frost

The Montgomery Series

Bad Situation – The Montgomery Series, Book 1

Broken Halo – The Montgomery Series, Book 2

Betrayed Love - The Montgomery Series, Book 3

Standalones

Blackburn

CONTENTS

1. Illegal Versus Illicit	1
2. Pipe Dream	19
3. Deal	29
4. Cussing	43
5. Governmenty	53
6. Panties	63
7. Get Over Myself	79
8. Fictionally Fucked	89
9. Control	105
10. Vagina Stats	117
11. Goth Girlfriend	127
12. Good Grovel	139
13. Hang Meat	147
14. At Least Three Fucks	159
15. The Secret	169
16. By Blood	179
17. Orgasm Terms	189
18. Jealous of My Toes	199
19. Ghost	209
20. You'll Pay	219
21. Before the Obsession	225
22. A Watermelon and A Bagel	233
23. Teach Me	243
24. Emotional Diatribe	253
25. Figurative Orgasm	259
26. Under Duress	269
27. Unbridled	279
28. Bloody Chuffed and Badass Shit	289
29. Messier	303
30. Fairytale	317
31. Boy	325
32. Hell	333

33. I See Myself	341
34. Normal	349
35. Russian Roulette	353
Epilogue	359
Acknowledgments	369
About the Author	371

This book is dedicated to found family.

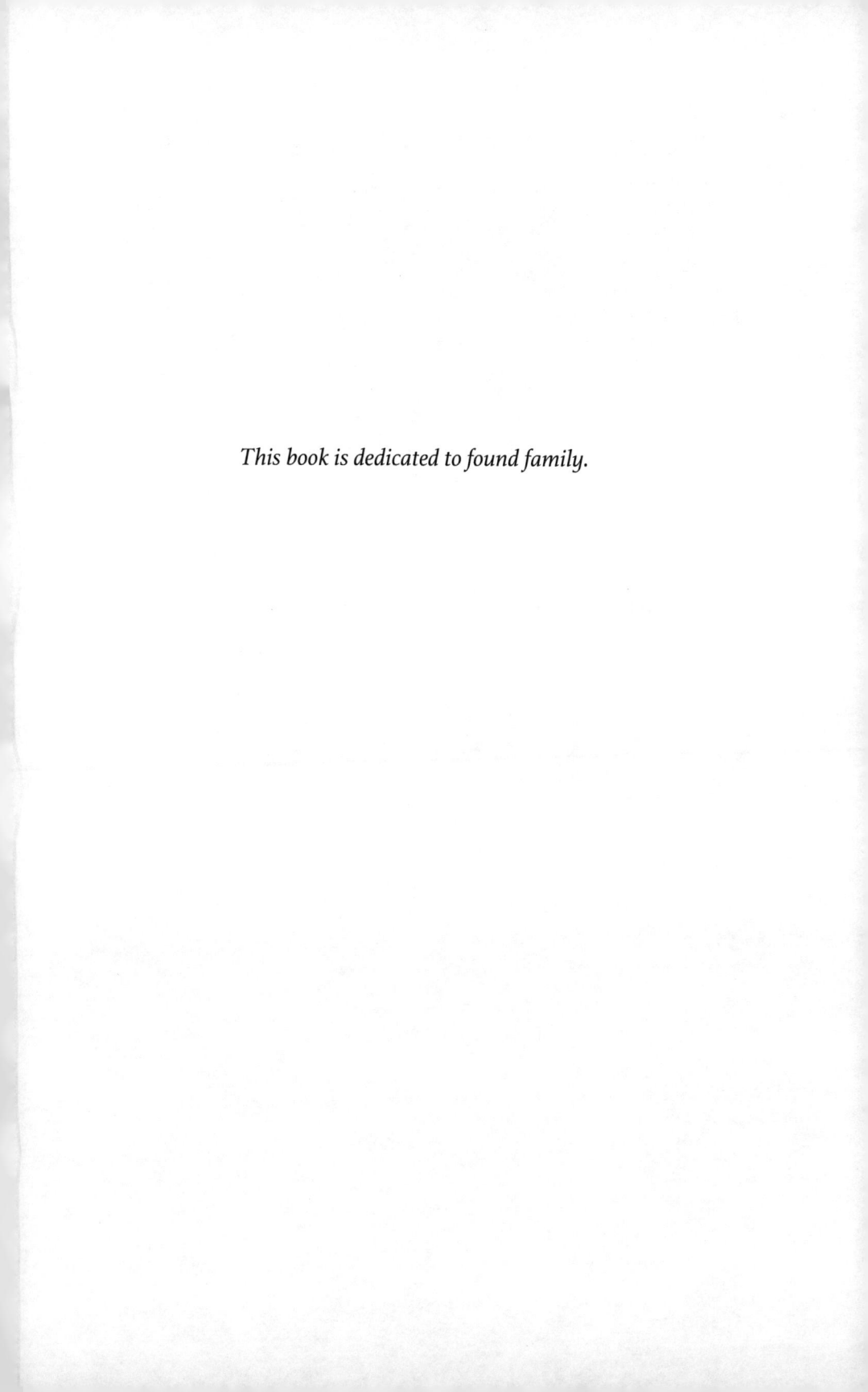

1

ILLEGAL VERSUS ILLICIT

Rocco

It never fails.
　　I can't not see it.
　　Me.
In someone else's skin.
But not really me.
The me that could've been.
The me that, without a doubt, would have been had I not been dragged out of the life I was born into.

Every time I'm like this—working a case, sitting surveillance, or hearing the metal click around wrists when I make an arrest—I see it.

Because every path I was on led me to be on the other side of the law than where I currently sit.

"Dude, are you even paying attention?"

I look over at Taylor. "When will you get it through your head that I'm not a skater. Do not *dude* me."

Taylor is not a skater, but he was a snowboarder in his previous life before joining the DEA. That's close enough to a skater in my book. If I didn't know he was an agent, I'd think he was a target. He's been in New Orleans longer than me. He's originally from Vermont, which makes him more of a fish out of water than me in The Big Easy.

But we're both fish out of water in our current surroundings—him because he looks like he could shred a half-pipe at a moment's notice, and me, because I don't belong anywhere posh no matter how I look.

The Hotel Monteleone.

One of the most historic spots in the French Quarter.

But if there's anything I've learned in my three years working for the DEA in New Orleans, no place is off limits when it comes to drugs, crime, or filth.

And this proves it.

Filth is everywhere.

"I'll *dude* you all day long. Fuck, man, I know you have one foot out the door, but you might as well be checked out. Jules Robichaux just entered the building. Get your shit straight, or I'll go in myself."

"No offense, Taylor, but if you walk into the bar of The Hotel Monteleone you'll attract more attention than Robichaux."

I slide my cell into my pocket and turn back to the monitors focused on the Carousel Bar and Lounge.

Jules Robichaux has been on my radar for over a year. His name comes up from time to time in my cases, but that's it. I have nothing solid to prove he's doing anything wrong other than having shit friends. But when a guy associates with distributors, dealers, and pimps on the regular, it puts him under the microscope.

Hanging with the wrong crowd isn't against the law. If anyone knows that it's me. But this guy is popping his head above water in public, and he never makes an appearance. Not like this. He called one of my targets I'm listening to on a wire to let him know he was taking a meeting at the lounge of the Carousel.

Out in the open.

In public.

For all to witness.

Namely ... me.

And Taylor is right. I have one foot out the door. I've done my time in New Orleans. My transfer back to Miami was approved three months ago. To say my days are numbered in the Big Easy is an understatement. I can count them on one hand. The only reason I'm here is because curiosity runs hot through my veins. I've worked on this case for over a year and am about to hand it over to Taylor.

Hell, I don't need to be here today.

But a rare appearance from Jules Robichaux is enticing. The saying that curiosity killed the cat is spot on, because I'm here instead of back at the office transitioning my cases, or at home trying to get my shit together. Not that I have much to my name, but it is more than I've had in my entire twenty-nine years.

"He claimed the booth at the side of the room. Private ... *ish*." Taylor motions to the monitor where we're watching from the security room of the Monteleone. Businesses don't always cooperate, but places like this don't want drug deals going down in the corners of their establishments. The management was happy to open their security cameras to us, which means I don't have to mess with warrants. "The booth behind him is open. I'm not sure what you'll hear, his back will be to you. I'll have the perfect view of whomever meets him."

I adjust my duty weapon so it can't be seen and slip my badge into the breast pocket of my sport coat since I can't exactly walk into The Carousel to eavesdrop looking like a government agent. "I can't wait to see who sits down across from him. Between my ears and your eyes, this is an opportunity we've never had. We might just learn something about Jules."

"Hell yeah." Taylor slaps me on the back like we're watching a football game. "This is like old-school shit. No warrants. No wires. Just good old investigating. It's time we outsmart this asshole once and for all."

Robichaux is no different than the kind of filth I grew up around. My friends are different, my address is a major upgrade, and my closet is from a different universe thanks to the women in my life who enjoy bossing me around.

I might've carried a badge for the last six years, but I'll never forget where I came from. I don't get outsmarted by people like Robichaux. And when I do arrest people like him, I've got to do it by the book.

I exit the surveillance room, move through the back offices of the hotel, and make my way through the lobby.

I'm lucky this meeting didn't go down in the height of Mardi Gras. The Carousel is busy, but not like that. It's also four o'clock in the afternoon. It'll be hopping in a couple hours.

Robichaux took the seat in a booth facing the door. I don't make contact as I pass him and claim the one behind him. My ass barely hits the seat when a server is at my side and places a cocktail napkin on the low table in front of me. "What can I get you?"

I lift my chin as I pull my cell from my pocket. "I'll stick with water until my girlfriend arrives. Thank you."

I don't touch my drink as I pretend to scroll on my phone. The server moves onto other tables while I pretend to wait for the fictional woman in my life. Hell, there hasn't been anyone in my life in a long time—not casually and definitely not serious. I've given new meaning to throwing myself into work.

I fucking buried myself in it.

Returning to Miami has always been the end goal, even if that goal was put in place by people who think they know what's best for me. I have more strings at my disposal than most agents in the whole damn DEA, but I've refused to pull them. No one gets a transfer before putting in three years. The last thing I want is people whispering behind my back that I'm not pulling my weight.

I've done my time and earned my spot.

I'm also more than ready.

A text comes across my screen.

> Taylor – His meet might be a no-show.

> Me – I'm willing to wait.

> Taylor – Wait. He's got his eyes set on a woman who just entered the bar. This might be it.

A woman.

Not what I expected.

Ty's next text confirms my thoughts and more.

> Taylor – She's looking around. Fuck. It's a good thing we're not profiling. She doesn't fit the bill as someone who would sit down with Jules. Young and hot as fuck.

Interesting.

Maybe I was wrong about Jules. I thought for sure he was dabbling in distribution, but he might be playing in prostitution instead.

But meeting a prospective girl at The Carousel?

It doesn't jive.

> Taylor – They made eye contact. I think we have a match made in hell. It's go time.

I pick up my water and take a sip before turning back to my phone when the conversation starts to play out behind me.

"Jules Robichaux?"

I freeze, not seeing anything scrolling across my screen.

Fuck.

"That's me," Jules grunts. "You Stella Hayes?"

"Yes, Stella," the female confirms. "Thank you for meeting me."

Stella Hayes.

I exhale.

I have no fucking clue what triggered it, but my mind is fucking with me.

I type the name into my phone ... not that I'd forget. I have the memory of bad screenshots that live forever and haunt the worst of nightmares.

"I don't normally take meets like this, but your email caught my eye. You're five minutes late, by the way. That usually pisses me off. Get to it, cher."

Interesting. Robichaux's tone doesn't match his words. He doesn't sound at all pissed. He sounds exactly like a man who's talking about a hot piece, just not to her face.

There's an awkward pause before the woman clears her throat. "I'm here about my grandfather. I'm trying to find him. One of his last forms of communication was with you."

I ignore the uncomfortable feeling that settles in my gut as my phone vibrates with a text.

> Taylor – What I wouldn't do to be listening to this play out live. I'd be surprised if this chick is even twenty.

Fuck that. I'd give anything to have eyes on what's going on. It shouldn't matter, but I need to see the face that voice is coming from.

"Who's your pawpaw?" Jules demands.

"Heath. Heath Hayes," the woman says. "Surely you remember. You and he had a business meeting. We haven't heard from him since."

"I know Hayes. How old're you, cher?" Jules drawls in his deep Cajun accent. "That old man looked old enough to be your great-granddaddy."

"I'm older than I look. My aunt and I are so worried. My grandfather basically raised me. I've read through his emails from you. My aunt and I know he accepted your proposition, got on an international flight, and the last we heard from him was when he touched down in Spain. His itinerary said he was supposed to travel through to Africa, but we have no idea if he got there. We don't even know why he left to begin with. He's never traveled outside of the south. I need your help. My family needs to find him."

There's nothing I want more in life than to turn around and get a look at the woman who just admitted she's willing to do anything for fucking Jules Robichaux. And that's saying something because I want a shit ton out of life.

My blood pumps way too fast for my age, my physique, and my mental well-being.

I need to know who she is.

Hell, I need to know who she *isn't*.

My mind is playing tricks on me. This is like a sick fucking joke or cruel and unusual punishment.

This is a nightmare playing out in the light of day.

I glance down at my phone.

> Taylor – What the fuck is going on with this woman?

That's what I'd like to know, but for a much different reason.

"You don't look like you belong anywhere near old-man

Hayes," Jules mutters. "In fact, you look like you're from a whole different world."

I don't like his tone. My curiosity has taken a big fucking leap off the skyscraper. It's replaced with an almost undeniable desire to turn around.

I'm plagued with it.

Her voice creeps under my skin as every desperate word pleads with the asshole sitting behind me. "Please, Mr. Robichaux. My grandfather isn't young or healthy. I have a feeling whatever he did, he did it for me. I can't handle the guilt if something happens to him. I had no idea what he was doing. He acted before I could stop him."

"Hayes was desperate. Nothin' you coulda done woulda stopped that old man." Jules does nothing to make her feel better, but he does throw her a bone. "But I can look into it for you."

"You will?" A tinge of hope hangs in the woman's voice.

Hope with a hint of sincerity.

And...

Familiarity.

"I'll do anything." The words rush from her mouth with desperation. "*Anything*."

Fuck me. I can't take it another moment.

I put my fingers to the screen of my phone.

> Me – Send me a pic of the woman. I want to see her.

> Taylor – You looking for a last-minute New Orleans hookup on your way out of town?

"Anything," Jules echoes as if he's tasting the meaning of that word on his tongue. "I might be able to help you for ... *anything*."

> Me – Just fucking do it. Now.

"I'm desperate," the woman confirms. The tone of her voice causes my skin to defy science as a chill ripples down my spine in the heat of NOLA. "Please."

Please.

That word slithers into my soul like a ghost at the same time a picture appears on my screen.

A snapshot of the monitor.

The man behind me who just became my number one target for no other reason than he's leering at the woman sitting across from him. I want to carve his eyes out and throw him into a swamp as the next meal for some lucky gator.

Because what in the actual fuck?

This can't be happening.

> Taylor – What's wrong?

> Me – I'm going in.

> Taylor – You're what?

> Me – I don't know how this is going to go. Be prepared to have my back.

> Taylor – We don't have an op plan. This wasn't approved. You can't do this.

> Me – Watch me.

I take a gulp of water to calm my nerves, though I'm not sure anything can cool my red-hot anger until I drag her out of this place and maybe tan her ass for even thinking about meeting up with a guy like Robichaux. Hell, I don't know how she knows of his existence.

But I'm about to find out.

In about two minutes when I have her all to myself, I plan to learn everything.

I unfold from the booth but don't turn to the patrons behind me. Instead, I take one lap around The Carousel. When I make the final turn, I see in the flesh what Taylor confirmed digitally.

It's her.

It's fucking *her*.

Not that I questioned it but seeing her for the first time in almost two years in a position like this fucking pisses me off.

How can someone be one of the most familiar people in my life yet look like a complete stranger?

Her hair doesn't hang down her back like I'm used to. It dusts her shoulders and falls around her face, framing the deepest and darkest eyes I've ever experienced. Her warm skin is fairer than I'm used to, which confirms what I already know. She hasn't had time to laze in the sun.

It also confirms what's been relayed to me by more than one person—she's too busy to go home.

Or, what no one knows but me, she's avoiding home.

Because of yours truly.

I should feel like an ass, which I usually do, but right now I'm too pissed.

The rest of her is the same. The same slight build. The same long, toned legs from years of running track through high school and on scholarship to help pay her way through her high-priced private university. The same curve of her hips, her small tits, the column of her neck, and darkest hair I've ever touched.

All things I've become obsessed with in my mind.

And shouldn't be.

Because she's off limits.

She's like an illicit drug formulated just for me.

That's the difference between illegal versus illicit.

Illegal is forbidden by law.

Illicit is just forbidden.

Improper.

It goes against social norms and values.

So, unlike the rest of society, she's only illicit to me.

"Please." Watching those dark eyes beseech the monster across from her makes me want to tear the fucking place apart. "I need to find my grandfather, and I need your help."

"Stella." The name rolls off my tongue as smooth as a rusty hacksaw.

It takes a second, but when those dark eyes shift to me, it's her turn to see a ghost.

Her pink lips part as she sucks in a breath. I narrow my eyes and give her one quick shake of my head, allowing my hardened expression to be enough of a warning before I ease into a fake smile when Jules turns to see who she's gaping at.

"Who're you?" Jules goes on the defensive when he turns back to her. "You said we were meetin' alone."

"I ... yes, um..." Her meaningless words trail off as I get closer and don't look at the man sitting across from her.

I have two goals.

One, for Robichaux to understand the beauty sitting across from him isn't up for negotiations in any way, shape, or form.

And two, to get her the fuck out of here.

I'll deal with the repercussions from what I'm about to do later.

As in for the rest of my fucking life, most likely.

Her shocked gaze never leaves me when I put one hand to the back of the booth and the other cups her cheek to tip her face to me.

"What are you—" she starts, but I shut her up.

With my lips.

And my tongue.

This reminds me of the last time we were together. Though there wasn't a nefarious government target as our witness, and it was angsty as fuck for entirely different reasons.

The circumstances couldn't be more different.

This is for show.

But when my tongue reunites with hers, it's no less real than it was before.

I never thought this would happen again. In fact, I swore to myself, and to her, it wouldn't.

That it couldn't.

But here we are.

I slide my hand into her thick hair to cup the back of her head and hold her to me.

I move my lips on hers.

I taste her.

No, I fucking lap her up like I'm parched and stranded in the desert.

Now that I'm right here, that feels like a reality rather than a metaphor.

And the way she's reciprocating, she might actually miss me instead of hate me.

If that were only the case.

Still, I don't regret this decision.

My only regret is the circumstance.

"What the hell?" Robichaux bites.

Fucking Robichaux.

Fucking reality.

I pull in a breath and savor the last moment of our kiss before I pull my lips from hers and watch her thick lashes flutter open to gape at me.

"Missed you," I tell her the truth.

"You did?" she whispers.

I nudge her nose with the tip of mine and give her hair a slight tug. "I always miss you when we're apart. I know I'm early, but when you told me you'd be in town and to pick you up here after your meeting, I couldn't wait another second. You about done?"

The spot between her brows crinkle. "Done?"

I nod. "Did you find out anything about your grandfather?"

She sucks in a surprised gasp, but only loud enough for me to hear. She knows I know.

And, in reality, I don't know shit.

"No," she admits and finally catches up. "Mr. Robichaux and I were just getting to that when you interrupted us. You're being rude—as always."

"The way I see it, you're being rude for not introducing me." I lean in and give her lips one more peck before sliding into the booth while shoving her sweet ass over far enough to make room for me. I stretch my arm behind her and settle in so I can make sure Jules Robichaux understands Stella Hayes is not going to do *anything* he wants in exchange for information. "Robichaux. I'm Stella's boyfriend."

"I see that," he drawls.

I smile when her hand grips my thigh with a firm squeeze.

It's meant to be a warning, but I enjoy it too much to take it as one.

I focus on the man across from me. "So where are we at? Consider me a new part of the negotiations. Stella wants her grandfather back. I want Stella happy. And you're the guy at the table with all the answers. What can I do to speed this along?"

Robichaux leans forward, rests his forearms on the table, and stares at me. "No offense, but what the hell can you offer me?"

"Whatever you want. I'll make it happen."

She tenses at my side. "Maybe this was a mistake—"

I glance down as my arm constricts around her. "No mistake, baby. I'm here to help."

"I don't like this." I brace when Robichaux moves. He digs into his pocket and pulls out a business card like he's selling us homeowners' insurance rather than keeping information about a missing person. He tosses it on the table between us and stands. Then he proves he's the person I thought he was all this time.

Someone who likes to play in the shadows and stay out of the public eye. "This is too much attention. I don't do business in public. If you want to meet, I'll do it in private. Call me, don't call me, it's no skin off my back. The old man knew what he was getting into."

I feel like a sitting duck and want to get the hell out of here as much as he does, so I grab his card in one hand and claim hers in the other.

She struggles out of the booth after me in that damn dress and tries to ignore the fact I have her in a death grip.

"Wait," she calls. "Don't leave. You have to tell me something. Why were you and my grandfather doing business in Africa?"

Robichaux's jaw goes taut as he turns his glare from her to me. "I don't give information for free. It comes with a price. If she's not willing to pay it in the only way she can, then it's going to cost you. Call me if you're willing to do business. Otherwise, I don't want to see either of you ever again."

Before she has the chance to beg him to stay, or worse, agree to what he wants, Jules Robichaux is out the door.

And I'm left standing here with a direct line to the man I haven't been able to pin down for over a year while holding the hand of a woman who refuses to give me the time of day.

Neither one of us moves, and I do my best to ignore the phone vibrating my ass. It reminds me of the tanning the woman next to me deserves.

She tries to pull her hand from mine, but I won't allow it.

"What the hell do you think you're doing?" she hisses.

I give her a yank so her front is glued to mine and wrap my arm around her waist. With her hand in mine, I have her arm pinned behind her back, and I lean down to put my lips to her ear. "I'd like to know the same thing about you. What the hell do you think you're doing meeting with someone like Robichaux?"

Tension bleeds through every inch of her body that touches me. "No way. Tell me why you're here."

To anyone else—meaning Taylor who's probably taking this in over the surveillance cameras—we probably look like lovers having a hushed conversation instead of hissing angry words at each other. "I have reasons of my own. Reasons I can't tell you."

She pushes far enough away to stare up at me through angry, dark eyes. "You have the worst memory, Roc. You know how I grew up. You're here on a case, and you just fucked up what I was trying to do."

I stare down at her, not wanting to let her go, even though I know the smart thing to do is to get the hell out of here. I make myself do the right thing, since that's what I do ninety percent of the time, and peel myself away from every curve of her body. With her hand still firm in mine, I pull her from the bar and through the lobby.

"What are you doing?" she hisses.

I push the main door open onto Royal Street. "I'm taking you home with me."

She yanks my hand and comes to a stop. "I'm not going anywhere with you!"

I have to stoop a few inches to get into her face and lower my voice. "If you don't quit throwing a fit on the street, you're going to force me to do something you won't like."

Her eyes narrow. "You wouldn't."

I cock one brow. "Don't try me. You know I will."

She shakes her head. "I don't believe you. After everything we've gone through, you wouldn't do that to me."

"To save your ass from whatever you were about to get yourself into, I fucking would. Are you going to come willingly or not?"

Her tits rise and fall with angry breaths when she lowers her voice. "I hate you."

And there it is.

I pull my phone out of my pocket with my free hand, touch the screen three times, and put it to my ear.

Her expression turns to horror. "Rocco, don't!"

I don't look away from her when Taylor answers the phone. "Dude, what the fuck was that?"

I swear, tears come to her eyes as she silently begs me not to tell her dad. Tears on her are something I can't take, and she knows it.

I let her off the hook. "Taylor, I'll call you later. And if you tell anyone what went down at The Carousel, I'll rip your balls out through your throat and fry them up like Rocky Mountain Oysters."

I lose her dark eyes when she exhales a relieved breath.

"Only if you give me the full scoop on your dark-haired little minx," Taylor says.

"Done."

He proves how much of a freak he is. "Man, I'm gonna miss you."

"I'm taking her home. I'll see you in the office tomorrow," I say.

"Taking her back to your place so fast. You were boring as hell for the last two years. I guess you're doing your last few days up big," Taylor says.

I've had enough. "Later."

I disconnect the call, slide my phone back into my pocket, and look down at her. "Are you going to come willingly, or are you going to make a scene? Because I bet we're being watched."

She mulls that over, going through all her options. Instead of answering, she states the obvious that I can't forget since I can still taste her on my tongue. "You kissed me."

It's not a statement. It's an accusation.

I throw one right back at her. "Yeah? Well, you kissed me first."

"That was years ago," she seethes.

"Not quite. Twenty-two months, to be exact," I correct her. "And I kissed you in there to save your ass."

"I didn't need saving," she spits.

I close what little distance we still have between us and lower my voice. "You have no clue who Jules Robichaux is or who he associates with. Your ass needed saving."

"I would have found out what I needed to know had you not barged in."

"What the fuck are you up to?" I shake my head and take a step back. "You know what? You can answer that when we get back to my place. I'm not having this conversation on the street in the middle of the French Quarter. Are you going to cooperate or not?"

She rolls her pink lips while glaring at me. "I'll come as long as you don't call my dad."

It's my turn to exhale as I drag a hand down my face. I turn but don't let go of her. She has to double time it to keep up with my quick pace.

She squeezes my hand. "You're not going to call him?"

I can't look down at her. She should know by now I'd never do that.

But I do tell her the truth.

"So help me, Teagan, I don't know what to do with you."

2

PIPE DREAM

Teagan

Rocco Monroe has been a constant in my life for...

Well, forever.

Okay, maybe not forever, but he has been for more than half my life.

Twelve years is a long time since I'm only twenty-two.

I was eleven when my dad got a transfer to Miami and brought all his friends with him.

Plus one stray.

That's what Sammie called Rocco back in the day.

My sister is bitchy by nature. She was then and she still is. I love her, but bitchy is bitchy. I doubt she'll ever change.

But I never thought of Rocco as a stray.

Rocco's personality is as wide and as broad and as strong as his shoulders. He lights up a room and makes everyone smile.

He even managed to win over Sammie.

Eventually.

So, no, Rocco Monroe is no stray.

He's a bonus.

Once I was older, I realized Rocco started out as a project for the tight group of agents I've known most of my life. But he turned into so much more.

Brax and Micah still treat him like a younger brother. They didn't have room for Rocco to live with them when everyone migrated to southern Florida, so he moved in with us. We went from a family of four to one of five overnight.

It didn't matter that he was officially an adult at the young age of eighteen. My parents gave him a home and a family and a place he could always come back to on summer break, between semesters, or even for the weekend.

Rocco became the son my father never had.

The project my mom gets off on since she's a teacher and loves the forgotten kids.

And an annoying older brother to Sammie.

But he was none of those things to me.

He was my friend before he was my obsession.

In fact, there's nothing about him I wasn't obsessed with.

If I'm honest with myself, I still am.

It was innocent in the beginning. I was obsessed with the man-boy with no parents, no family, and a life so different from mine, I didn't understand it.

I was obsessed with the way he spoke. How he dropped the F-bomb every other word when Mom never allowed cursing in our home. Or how he never complained about what we had for dinner, because everyone complains about something when it comes to dinner every once in a while.

And I was obsessed with the way he sat back in a room and took everything in. That was when his eyes were haunted and his scar wasn't even a scar yet.

He thought no one was watching.

But I was.

Dad always says I was born with curiosity running hot through my veins. Mom always said I was the quietest learner she'd ever seen—that once I soaked it in, I never let it go. She said I was hungry for information.

When it came to Rocco Monroe, I was ravenous.

He's been a constant in my life since I was a girl. Somehow, he fit in with the tight group of government agents and their families even though there's nothing about him that should fit.

Sure, he's changed over the years. He's even molded himself into them—a blend of Brax, Micah, and even King. He looks up to my dad and worships my mom.

Rocco Monroe is good to the bone.

But, still, he's dangerous.

I've never loved and hated anyone more. If I could unlearn everything about him, I would.

But the word obsession packs a punch for a reason. It's strong and impossible to fight.

More than anything, I was obsessed with the way Rocco always paid attention to me. Whether it was a board game he was sick of playing, movies he pretended to hate, or taking me and my friends to get ice cream when he came home from college before I could drive. He'd play Words With Friends with me when he was away at school even though he could've been doing all kinds of other college things, but he knew it was one of the only apps my parents allowed us to have. And he knew I liked words and loved to read and write.

He did it even though he hated it, and I usually won.

Rocco never said no to me.

Until the one time when he did.

And it happened twenty-two months ago when my obsession turned less-than-innocent.

That was the last time I saw Rocco.

Until today.

It seems alcohol and obsessions are a dangerous concoction for Teagan Mariana Coleman.

A *no* from Rocco was too much. It's easy to avoid another human when you're an adult and live in different states. It doesn't matter where your home base is or if they are your found family.

The day Rocco said no to me was it.

He'd never hurt me on purpose, and that made it worse.

I've only been to New Orleans a couple of times. The first was the spring semester of my sophomore year. Before my parents dropped me off in my small college town in Mississippi, we came all the way to NOLA as a big, fat family to say goodbye to Rocco when he followed in the footsteps of Brax, Micah, King, and even my dad, and became a DEA agent.

The next time was when I made a bad choice with a fake ID. That was the day he broke me.

And I'm back.

Rocco's apartment looks different today.

His sofa is nicer, his TV is bigger, and the whole place is messier.

Goodness, is it messy.

"Don't start," Rocco mutters as he slams the door behind us, locking me into the small space with him.

How the hell did this happen?

This is torture.

I'm trapped in hell with Rocco. I watch him unload his pockets along with his gun and badge. I might have the backbone to meet someone like Jules in a bar during daylight hours, but I have no desire to walk around the French Quarter at night by myself. At least he took me back to my car to get my backpack, but he didn't trust me to follow him back to his place and made me come with him.

Smart man. I would've driven back to Mississippi and broken every speed limit on the way.

I might talk a big game to keep my shit together in front of Rocco, but I was raised by Tim and Annette Coleman. They scared the shit out of us to instill stranger danger at a young age. It never wore off.

I dig deep and channel a bit of Sammie's bitchy attitude. "Look, you're the one who butted into my meeting today, dragged me out of The Carousel, and drove me forty-five minutes in the opposite direction of my car. I have the right to *start* about anything I want. And let me tell you, Annette would have a fit if she saw the state of this place. I heard you're moving back to Miami. I'd say good luck with that, but Landyn will be so happy you're there, she might just clean for you."

"Don't give me shit about this place. You know I'm in the middle of a move." Rocco has the nerve to look me up and down before shaking his head. And it's not the way a woman wants a man she's obsessed with to look at her. Definitely not the way I thought a man would look at me when I put on this dress today solely for attention. "Fuck, no wonder Robichaux was so keen on working with you until I showed up. What in the hell are you up to?"

My feet hurt from walking four blocks in these shoes. I flop down in the middle of his sofa and reach down to unclasp my wedges. "I'm in the middle of a project."

His thick brows rise. "A project? What kind of project includes meeting with a lowlife like that?"

I kick my shoes to the side and prop my feet on the coffee table, nudging a remote and empty sports bottle to the side. "I'm about to graduate, again, in case you need a reminder since you missed my first graduation. I'm wrapping up a semester-long project I need to get my masters."

"You think I don't know what's going on in your life? You might've ignored me for almost two years, but I talk to your parents more than you do. I know your every move, Teagan."

I roll my eyes. "Sucking up to Annette. Why am I not surprised?"

"They're worried about you. Everyone is. What happened to the job you had lined up in Miami?"

I aim a generic smile toward the angry man. I hate that he feels familiar ... like home. "Even though it's none of your business, I changed my mind. I'm moving back to New York."

"Your mom is upset. Like really fucking upset, Teagan. You ditched a job at one of the biggest cable news outlets in the country in the same city as your family."

I cross my arms. "No, it was the Miami office of the largest news outlet in the country. That's a big difference. And I had a better opportunity come up. It might not be the biggest or the best, but I landed a gig at the headquarters of a startup news organization in New York City. Print is dying off right along with the oldest generation, and no one finds cable news trustworthy. I couldn't pass up the chance to work in New York. Location, location, location. What can I say? I leveled up before my career ever started."

"That's not what you want," he argues. As if he has any clue what I really want. "You've never wanted that. The only person I know who values family more than you is Landyn. Moving to the Big Apple makes no sense."

"You moved to the Big Easy. What's the difference?"

He takes a step and drops his arms. "The difference is I didn't have a choice, and I'm moving back. If I could've gone back sooner, I would have. What I'm talking about is you flipping off a job that would've allowed you to stay in Miami near your family."

I hate that he knows me so well. I decide to tell him a version of the truth. "Things change."

He settles back on his heels and stares down at me. "You have interesting timing, Teag."

Oh, no. He does not get to do this. I have no desire to address the elephant in the room. "Carrying a federal badge has really made your head swell, *Roc*. Not everything is about you."

But one thing about Rocco, he always tells it like it is. "Bullshit. I'd put the very small fortune I've saved to buy a house on the fact it's all about me."

I'm not doing this. I can't. "Think what you want, I don't care. All I care about is getting back to my car. I have an hour-and-a-half drive back to school."

"You're impossible," he mutters and pulls his cell from his pocket. "And you're not going anywhere until you tell me about Robichaux."

My feet drop to the floor to stand. "Who are you calling?"

He doesn't look away from his phone. "Don't worry. I'm not calling Tim. At least not until you tell me what's going on with your buddy, Jules. I'm ordering dinner."

Even though stuffing my swollen feet back into my shoes is the last thing I want to do—and there's the fact I'm starving—I can't stay.

I grab my sandals and hoist my backpack over my shoulder. I never go anywhere without my laptop. I thought at this point I'd be amassing lengthy notes from everything I got Jules Robichaux to tell me about Heath Hayes.

But instead, Rocco scared off the one person who knows where the elderly man really is.

"Take me back to my car. Since I didn't get the information I needed from Robichaux, I have to regroup."

Rocco taps his screen a few more times before leveling his moody, whiskey eyes on me. "I'll give you two choices."

I shake my head. "Sorry, but no. We need to go back to ignoring each other for the rest of time. I much preferred that to whatever this is."

Like the invasive jerk he is, he ignores me. "One, I'll take you back to your car."

"Great. I pick that one. Let's go."

"Then I'll call your dad and tell him the whole thing. Have fun dealing with the aftermath."

My expression falls. He knows how not fun that would be.

"Two," he goes on. "You can stay here tonight, eat the kung pao chicken I just ordered you, and tell me what you're up to and everything you know about Robichaux."

I offer him the palm of my hand. "I'm a grown-ass woman. I don't need your choices or your ultimatums. If I have to call an Uber, I will."

Rocco says nothing, but he moves to yank my backpack down my arm.

"Hey! What are you doing?" I call, but he doesn't listen.

He stalks around me and disappears into a short hall behind the kitchen. When I round the corner, Rocco is stuffing my bag on the top shelf of his closet. I'd need a step stool to reach it.

"Give that back," I demand.

He turns and has the nerve to smile.

It takes my breath away.

It's been a long time since I've seen that expression on his face.

Too long.

I love it. It reminds me of simpler times. When I was young and…

We were friends.

A pang hits my chest, and something inside me dies just a little bit more. But it has nothing to do with alcohol or obsessions.

Twenty-two months, one week, and three days.

I'm so lame, but I miss that smile.

Hell, I just miss him.

"Please don't do this," I whisper.

"What? Save you from yourself?" His words are not a whisper. "You can avoid me for the rest of your life and hate me forever, but I'll never not do that."

At the worst time ever, my stomach growls.

His beautiful smile shrinks into a satisfied smirk. "And you're hungry. Just one more reason to stay when your favorite takeout is on the way."

My eyes fall shut as I exhale. I hate that he hasn't forgotten my favorite takeout.

"Go take a load off. I'll get you a beer." I open my eyes as he keeps bossing me around. "I'll find you something to wear, because you're not wearing that for the rest of the night."

"If I have a beer, I can't drive home."

Rocco moves to his dresser and yanks out a T-shirt and pair of sweatpants. They fly through the air, and I barely catch them when they hit my chest. "Get comfortable and prepare to spill everything you know."

"Rocco—" I start.

But he interrupts me when he stops right in front of me. "Teagan."

My arms fall to my sides. "What now?"

He pauses.

I brace.

And it's a good thing, because I'm not prepared for what he says next.

He raises a hand and gives the end of one of my loose curls a gentle yank. "I hate that you hate me, so you're not going to want to hear this."

I'm not sure how much more I can handle today.

His gaze roams my face before settling back on my eyes. "I wasn't lying before. I missed you. I don't care why you're here or how much you want to run away from me—it's good to see you. I promise to get to the bottom of whatever the fuck you're up to, so you're not going anywhere tonight."

And with that, he stalks out of his bedroom and slams the door.

My shoes hit the floor.

My ass lands on the bed.

And I fall to my back.

In the matter of a few short hours, all my hard work went down the drain, and I'm in Rocco's bed.

Fine.

I'm not in it. That's a pipe dream.

I'm on it.

And not in the way it played out in my fantasies.

But he missed me.

I already knew that. I've saved every text and voicemail he's sent. I even revisit them often.

That's painful enough, but this is something I can't handle.

3

DEAL

Teagan

I push the remnants of rice and bits of chicken and pepper around my plate. In the time I've put off talking, Rocco ate most of his beef and broccoli and the rest of my kung pao. He's banging around in his messy kitchen among boxes. We ate off paper plates since his things are packed.

He swipes my plate out of my hands, takes it to the kitchen, and dumps it in the trash.

Rocco changed before the food arrived. We pretty much match. We're both in T-shirts, but he threw on a pair of gym shorts. I'm the one wearing his gray sweatpants, which is a disappointment. I had to roll them over three times to keep them up. They're soft and comfortable, even though I'd rather he be the one wearing them.

I think I was seventeen when I realized the beauty of Rocco in gray sweatpants.

It's a sight to see and will forever be burned on my brain. So much so, I'm unimpressed with the phenomenon my friends fawn over. No one measures up.

Par for the course.

Fucking Rocco.

For the last two years of almost twelve he's been in my life, I've ignored him, shunned him, and blocked him. I thought going cold turkey would be the only cure. Like any addict, I cut off my obsession at the root.

But I was kidding myself.

I had no idea how strong an addiction could be.

Twenty-two months of no Rocco Monroe was barely a drop in the bucket.

I quit my sorority and immersed myself in school so deep, my parents have never been prouder. I had two mediocre boyfriends who were so basic, it makes me want to poke my eyes out just thinking about the experiences. And I logged more volunteer hours than I can count.

I'm beginning to think my addiction has no cure.

The man standing over me with two fresh beers is nothing like he was the first day I laid eyes on him. I take a bottle, silently grateful, even though this means he's never going to take me back to my car tonight.

I'm stuck in my own personalized, sadistic brand of hell.

I watch him take another long pull as he plants his very fine, firm ass on the messy coffee table in front of me. His apartment isn't big, but there's plenty of space for him to sit across the room rather than sucking the oxygen between us.

With his beer in his hand, he widens his legs, leans forward to rest his forearms on his thighs, and focuses his light brown eyes on me. "Since you've gone silent on me, I'll go first and tell you everything I know about Jules Robichaux. When I'm done, you'd better explain why you're in New Orleans pretending to be someone you're not meeting a lowlife like him. Depending on your answer, I might or might not call your dad."

My blood boils. "Don't give me an ultimatum. Just because you're an agent now doesn't mean shit when it comes to me. And since when did you become so holier than thou? They handed you a federal badge and you turned into Brax and Micah. Maybe even a little bit of King. You refuse to see it, but I'm all grown up and can take care of myself. I knew I was sneaking into your backyard when I set up a meeting with Robichaux. But, statistically speaking, the odds were in my favor. New Orleans is a big place. The chances of running into you were quite literally almost none. You ruined months of hard work."

I watch him put his beer to his lips one more time before he focuses on me and ignores everything I just said. "I've kept tabs on Robichaux for the last year. He skims the surface of so many cases in this city then disappears without a trace. He's like the rat you know is there but never leaves a trail. His name is mentioned by suppliers, dealers, pimps, bar owners, and even a manager of the transit authority who was arrested last year on distribution."

I swallow a sip of my beer before wiping a drip from my bottom lip and mull that over. "Huh."

Rocco narrows his eyes but proves he's on a roll and keeps talking. "I'll tell you what he's not known for. Volunteer work, track and field, journalism, or sorority parties. Though I wouldn't put it past him to dive into the last one if the opportunity presented itself. Which means the two of you shouldn't be in the same city, let alone the same room together. I want to know why you left the small, southern town you love so much, dressed like you're auditioning at strip bars in the French Quarter, and pretending to be someone you're not."

I hike a brow. "For your information, I dropped out of my sorority my junior year and haven't been to a party since. That goes to show you don't know what you're talking about."

"Teagan, who is Stella Hayes, and what the fuck are you up to?" he demands.

I set my beer next to him and wipe the condensation on his sweatpants that I'm considering not giving back. If he's going to hold me here against my will, I think I deserve a souvenir from being subjected to his cruel and unusual punishment.

When I say nothing, he sits up straight, and his bottle lands with a thud next to mine. Tension hangs between us—a mix of his frustration and my sheer determination to not be pathetic.

But he doesn't give up, and this time I know he's serious. His next threat isn't empty. I know he can and will follow through. "If Heath or Stella Hayes are real people, I'll know everything about them two minutes after I get to work tomorrow morning. If you think that won't happen, you haven't been paying attention for the last twenty-two years."

I roll my eyes.

"You know I'm right, Teagan. Tell me, or I'll figure it out on my own. Either way, I'll know exactly what you're up to in approximately ten hours."

I cross my arms. "And what are you going to do when you figure it out? You can threaten to call my dad all you want—I wasn't doing anything wrong."

"Jules was looking at you like you were his last meal before he pimped you out to the underworld of New Orleans. You weren't doing anything illegal, but you were treading in dangerous waters. You know it."

"So you do think I'm an idiot. Thanks for your confidence. I already told you I wasn't going to go anywhere with him."

Rocco drags a hand down his face. "I'm moving in a few days and have a shit ton to wrap up before I head back to Miami. I do not have time to investigate you too."

It's not lost on me that telling Rocco might work in my favor.

That's a heavy *might*, but I could talk him into it.

There's no way I can ask my dad without my parents freaking out on me. They're already upset that I ditched the job in Miami to go to New York City. My mother hovers, and my dad is overprotective. Even so, Sammie is a shit show on normal days. In the past, they were too distracted by her to worry about me.

Until I announced my job change. You'd think I was the one who got knocked up and ditched by her deadbeat boyfriend who made a million empty promises to love and cherish her forever and ever. Sammie is unemployed and on her way to being a single mom. My parents have enough on their plates. Aside from one rogue semester during college, I'm boring. My sister is the one who keeps them up at night.

"There's no way you can find out everything in two minutes." It's a stretch, but it's my only leverage at the moment. And it doesn't matter what happened two years ago. I know Rocco is the only one in my life who won't shut me down and might actually help.

There's that might again.

"Don't underestimate me, Teag."

"Don't underestimate the work I've put into this project."

He shakes his head. "I've never once underestimated you, taken you for granted, or doubted what you can accomplish, but I am the one with access to government files."

"You won't find anything on Stella Hayes," I tell him the truth. "She's never been processed, arrested, or fingerprinted. You'd have to put in the time the old-fashioned way."

"Oh, yeah? Google or Facebook?"

"Seriously? So you do think I'm an idiot. There's no need to be an asshole."

A million memories flood my heart as a playful smirk kisses his lips.

More proof.

Once an addict, always an addict.

Gah.

I hate him.

"I'm just fucking with you ... sort of. Teagan Coleman, Private Investigator is all new to me."

Goosebumps prickle my skin as I think about all the ways Rocco could fuck with me. I want to tell him everything I've done since I blocked him. The urge to impress him overwhelms me. He might think he's kept up on my life through Mom and Landyn, but the only thing they know is that I zipped through my master's after getting my undergrad a semester early. I might spend my extra time volunteering, but not at the dog shelter like they think.

"I'll make you a deal," I offer.

That wipes the smirk clean off his face. "Why do I not like the sound of that?"

"I'll tell you why I'm in New Orleans and why I met with Robichaux. Hell, I'll tell you everything I know about him. You might be the big, bad government agent, but from the sounds of it, I know more than you."

He cocks his head. "What do you want in return?"

"You can't tell anyone. That includes your friends, their wives, and, especially, my parents."

He studies me as he contemplates my offer.

"Good luck doing all the groundwork yourself. You've known about Jules for a year and have nothing on him. Your time in New Orleans is waning. You said it yourself—you only have three weeks. That's not nearly long enough to build the relationships and trust that I have."

He shakes his head. "Why do I have a feeling that you're right and this is going to bite me in the ass?"

"Trust me, you can't take the heat. But, if we're careful, no one will find out." I do everything I can to entice him. "You don't realize it yet, but you need me, Roc. I'll prove it to you."

Rocco

The heat.

She's right about one thing.

The heat will do me in.

But visions of Robichaux leering at Teagan and my curiosity get the best of me. "It's a deal. Tell me everything."

She smiles, and it even touches her dark eyes. Hell, it reminds me of better times.

"Do you promise?" she demands.

I narrow my eyes. "When have I ever lied to you?"

I might've pissed her off or hurt her, but I've never lied to her. She shrugs because she knows that's the truth.

"Fair enough. Stella Hayes lives in southern Mississippi, close to school. She's in her thirties, married, and has two little kids. I met her through the nonprofit I've been volunteering for, A Life of Justice."

I huff an exhale. "You and your unsolved crimes obsession."

"Always and forever," she confirms. "Anyway, poor Stella has been snubbed by the State Department and the FBI, not to mention her local police department, not that they could do much. They're made up of four part-time officers and don't have jurisdiction outside of their little town, let alone outside the country."

"Wait." I sit up straight and hold out a low hand. "The State Department and FBI? What the hell have you gotten yourself into?"

She frowns like I'm an idiot. "Our own government turned its back on her. Someone has to help her."

"I do work for that big, bad nemesis, remember?" I deadpan.

"But for drugs." She emphasizes the last word, like that makes any sort of difference when it comes to the U.S. Government turning their back on poor Stella Hayes. "This is different. This is about humans. One in particular that I'm trying to help Stella find."

I stand and stretch. "I can tell you right now, you're in over your head. You need to step back and be grateful I was there today to extract you from the situation."

Teagan looks up at me from where she's made herself too comfortable on my sofa for the current conversation. She crosses her legs and looks proud of herself. "I'm not stepping back from anything. You might've fucked up my day, but I promised Stella I'd help her. And you promised me you wouldn't tell anyone. We are where we are. But I'll admit, this might go faster with your help. A Life for Justice can do a lot, but we don't have access to the systems you do."

"Are you talking human trafficking?" I demand. "Because the way Robichaux was looking at you today, I see it. And I'll tell you, I don't fucking like it."

"See, that's the thing. I don't think this is officially considered human trafficking. I mean, it was consensual, but it's still fraud."

I pick up my beer and start to pace. This whole thing pisses me off, and I have no fucking idea what I'm dealing with yet. "That makes no sense."

She claims her own beer and stretches her legs out in the space I was sitting. "I'm not sure it's a thing, but I'm calling it elder fraud."

I stop and look down at her. "Elder fraud?"

She nods. "Heath Hayes is Stella's father. He's seventy-seven and owns a small farm in central Mississippi. Farming isn't what it once was—he's been behind on his property taxes for a few years. The only thing he wants in life is to leave his farm to his family."

"What does this have to do with human trafficking or fraud?"

"Heath has been missing for months," she says.

I take another drink and fight for patience since I've finally got her talking. "Has she heard of a missing person's report? Not that any missing person isn't important, but it doesn't involve the State Department or the FBI. Well, maybe the FBI, but only in certain circumstances."

She leans forward. Gone is the person who's pissed at me and shut me out for the last two years. Who I see in front of me is the old Teagan. The one who's passionate about everything.

In fact, if she's not passionate about it, she doesn't give a fuck.

That hasn't changed.

All in or …

Nothing.

The last two years should not surprise me. Teagan gave new meaning to being all in before shutting me out for good.

But she's back. And I just made a deal to help her with something that I have no fucking clue what it's about other than my employer is on her shit list.

And I'm just a DEA agent with barely three years under my belt.

I have a feeling I'm fucked.

"This isn't some story about a man who drove to the store and disappeared or wandered off and doesn't know who he is because dementia set in. Heath Hayes is healthy and is of sound mind. He was still running his farm on a daily basis when he disappeared. He left the country when he's never traveled outside the southeast region of the red, white, and blue. The red flags are endless, Rocco. Heath was issued an expedited passport. He left the country and didn't tell his family. When Stella hit a dead end with the government, she got desperate and came to A Life for Justice. I was assigned to her case with a local attorney who also volunteers his time. I even made it the subject of my thesis. We traced Heath Hayes all the way to Nigeria. After that, he disappeared."

I set my beer down again and cross my arms, because this just went from zero to sixty. "Nigeria?"

She nods. "And he's gone. Just … gone."

"I'm not going to lie. I had no idea what you were up to, but I never thought it would end in Nigeria. The State Department makes sense now. Not the FBI, but I've got to give props to Stella for effort." I sigh. "But I give—where does Jules Robichaux come into the picture?"

A satisfied expression settles on her face as she gives me a little shrug. "Jules was the last person Heath Hayes communicated with before he disappeared. He even arranged the expedited passport. I have a feeling he paid for Heath's plane tickets, but I haven't confirmed that yet because I can't trace the money transfer back to Jules. I do have the email from him with instructions for which flights to book—the same string of flights that ended in Nigeria."

I shake my head. "You put yourself on Robichaux's radar for volunteer hours? You're about to graduate, and I know your thesis passed with flying colors—Annette told me. What the hell are you thinking?"

Teagan stands and downs the last swallow of her beer. She proceeds to lick a drip off her bottom lip before shoving the empty bottle into my chest. I have no choice but to take it. "I'm doing what I love and helping someone in the process. Despite what you and everyone else thinks, I can take care of myself."

I point the bottle at her. "You have no idea what someone like that is capable of. Don't underestimate him."

She shifts around me, and I'm forced to watch her walk her fine ass to the bathroom. The same ass that I know is fine even if I can't see it because it's hidden in my sweats that are a million sizes too big for her. Giving her those to wear was no accident. I could barely focus while she was in that damn dress.

She turns at the threshold of the bathroom and levels her eyes on me. "I know exactly what he's capable of. Jules is responsible for the disappearance of a sweet, old, desperate man. I pretended to be his granddaughter, there's no way he knows who I am. But you're the one with his phone number who promised to make it worth his while to give me the information, and I'm not giving up. I need that number, Roc."

I cross my arms and think about the direct line to Robichaux that I have no plans to share with Teagan. "You expect me to give you his number so that you can meet up with that shithead again? Because that'll only ever happen over my dead body."

She shrugs like the thought of my dead body doesn't faze her in the least. "It might not be as fast as a phone call, but I can still contact him. I emailed him the first time—I'll do it again. In fact, I have access to all the correspondence between him and Heath. You can't stop me, so you might as well give me the number."

I want to rip the fucking number to shreds and throw every electronic device she has access to in the Mississippi River. While I'm at it, I'll confiscate her car keys.

"You're playing with fire," I tell her the truth. Probably too much of the truth. "I don't like it."

She leans her shoulder on the jamb and crosses her arms. I barely recognize the woman standing in front of me, and it has nothing to do with her new look. Her hair is shorter and her curves are...

Curvier.

But it's not that.

It's her eyes.

Her aura.

Teagan has changed in the last two years.

I decide to call her on it. "When did you become so..." I flip my hand between us. "Like you are."

"Are you kidding? You must be dense or have amnesia." She tips her head to the side and hikes a brow. "Actually, I hope it's the latter. One less thing for me to be mortified about."

"My memory is as sharp as ever, Teag."

She rolls those eyes again that are nothing like they used to be. They're cold, angry, and audacious.

I don't like any of it.

"Two years ago, you told me to get my shit together." She pushes away from the door jamb and holds her arms out low, throwing her new persona right back at me. "You got your wish. Here I am, Rocco. At your demand, I got my shit together. I'm doing something important—something I love to do and something that matters. I have a short amount of time to help the Hayes family. Then I hope to see my niece or nephew born before I move to New York. You won't have to worry about me again because you'll be kicking ass in Miami, and I'll be nowhere near you."

"Dammit. You've shut me out for too long, but you're here. Let's talk this shit out, once and—"

"Stop." She holds a hand up before taking a step backward into the bathroom. "There's nothing to talk about, remember? Your words, not mine."

"For fuck's sake. It's been two years. Let's get this shit settled, once and for all."

Her expression is void of emotion even as she white knuckles the doorknob. "This is what's going to happen. I'm going to wash my face with whatever you've got in your bathroom, brush my teeth with my finger, pass out on your sofa, and ignore you until you take me back to my car tomorrow. What I am not going to do is talk to you about anything that happened before I saw you today in the Hotel Monteleone. And if you really want to squash all my hopes and dreams for good, you can be a selfish asshole and not give me that phone number. The weight of the world is on you. Goodnight."

I start to take a step forward, but she slams the door in my face. It's followed by an angry click of the lock.

"Fuck," I hiss.

She mutters something from the bathroom, but I can't tell what she said, because the water turns on full blast.

Teagan fucking Coleman.

What the hell am I going to do with you?

4

CUSSING

Teagan
Twelve years ago

"How long is he going to live with us?"

"Watch your tone, Sammie," Mom warns. "Brax and Micah don't have an extra room. We do. Rocco doesn't have anyone else. He'll be here until he gets settled at college."

My older sister doesn't watch her tone. Instead, she raises it to a level that's high drama, even for her. "All summer? How am I supposed to make new friends before school starts when some weird guy with his arm bandaged is hanging around with nothing to do. He has, like, two old T-shirts and a pair of jeans. And he doesn't even have a car. What's that about? Everyone his age has a car. Does he even drive?"

"Yes, he drives," Mom snaps, and Mom never snaps. Not even at Sammie, and my older sister deserves it on any normal day. Mom closes her eyes and exhales the way she does when I can tell she's mad but pretends not to be. When she finally opens her eyes, she shines a fake smile on my older sister. "This will be a lesson for us that not everyone is as fortunate. Not everyone has a home or a family to love them. It's a new start for Rocco, and we're going to do our part to get him on his feet. You will be welcoming and kind."

Sammie hitches a foot and cocks her head. "He's not the only one starting over. My life is ruined because Dad made us move. I'm starting over, too, and I've decided since I have no choice, I'm going to reinvent myself. From now on, no more Sammie. I'm *Samantha*."

Being dramatic and rude isn't new for Sammie, so she's easy to ignore. I allow my gaze to stray past the sea of boxes and the mess that's strewn throughout our new kitchen. There's only one interesting thing in Florida since we got here yesterday.

The boy.

I mean, I know he's not a boy even though he acts like one, but he sure isn't a man either. He's nothing like Dad or Brax or Micah.

Mom said he's going to college.

Uncle Brax dropped him off last night. Mom handed out pillows and blankets, and we all slept on the floor of our new rooms. Rocco took the guest room. Our furniture arrived today. Our new house looks nothing like our old one in New York.

We even have a pool.

We've never had a pool before.

We've also never had a live-in guest like Rocco.

As I look out at the sunny afternoon, I could care less about the pool, palm trees, or hot sunny day.

All I see is Rocco.

He's spread eagle on his back other than his bandaged arm. It's resting over his face blocking the sun from his eyes. He's wearing ripped jeans and a faded black T-shirt that's almost as abused as his denim. It's the same thing he wore yesterday when Uncle Brax dropped him off.

I bet he slept in it. He only has a small duffle bag to his name.

"Where are his parents?" I ask without looking away from our guest.

Mom busies herself with a stack of mixing bowls. "They're not in his life. He's starting over, just like us."

"They're dead," Sammie announces.

I jerk at my sister's words and gasp. "Dead?"

I don't know anyone with dead parents. That's the saddest thing I've ever heard.

"Sammie!" Mom raises her voice.

"Well, they are," Sammie drawls. "I heard Dad talking to Micah about it when they were doing something for his financial aid. He might've said something about being as good as dead, but whatever. I hope he's smart enough to stay in college, otherwise he'll never leave."

I finally speak up and shove my sister in the process. "You're so mean."

She tries to slap me back. I'm too fast and shift out of the way, and she accidentally bumps into Mom.

"Enough!" Mom puts her foot down and doesn't care that my sister wants to create a new identity. "Sammie, go to your room. Unpack and clean up the boxes. Don't come back until you drop the attitude. Teagan, why don't you go outside and ask Rocco if he's hungry?"

Sammie pushes past me. "Oh, sure, *perfect Teagan*. I have to clean boxes and all she has to do is play waitress to the orphaned houseguest. Why did we have to move here? My life is ruined!"

She runs out of the kitchen and stomps up the stairs.

Mom turns to her open box, and this time, her order isn't a suggestion. "Go, Teag. Check on Rocco. I'll help you unpack your room later."

I don't move as I stare out the back of the house toward the boy who has nothing to unpack.

Mom stops what she's doing and turns to me with a sigh that's different from the one she reserves for Sammie. She places a gentle hand on my cheek and forces me to look up at her. "I know we're starting over with school and friends. That's never easy. But this is a good move for your dad, and we can be closer to Grandma and Grandpa. That boy won't be here forever. This is a transition for him. Your Uncle Brax wouldn't bring him here if he didn't trust him completely."

Uncle Brax isn't really my uncle. Not the way my other aunts and uncles are that we hardly ever see. Brax has worked for Dad for as long as I can remember, but he moved away for two years. We didn't even see him at Christmas, and we used to see him all the time.

It seemed like he was gone forever for work. Mom and Dad think they hide things from us, but I could tell they were worried.

Now Brax is married. His wife's name is Landyn. She's young and funny and pretty. She's also friends with Rocco.

At least that's what Dad told us yesterday when Brax dropped him off.

Mom pulls me in for a hug and presses her lips to the top of my head. "I'll make this easy on you and order pizza. Ask Rocco what he likes. We'll start on your room as soon as I find the dishes. Rocco will be here with us until he goes to college in August. No time like the present to start talking to him. Sammie will come around."

I doubt Sammie will come around. Even so, I don't like it when people are sad.

Other than Sammie. She's never sad. She's just grumpy.

But the boy sprawled by our pool looks sad. He has ever since he got here yesterday. But who wouldn't be sad if they didn't have parents, their arm is bandaged, and everything they own fits into a duffle bag.

We could barely fit everything we own into two gigantic moving trucks.

Mom goes back to her box, and I force myself to go outside. Rocco doesn't move a muscle when the sliding door shuts behind me. The sun blazes so hot, I feel it through my flip flops as I walk slowly across the patio to where he's sprawled.

"Hi."

He doesn't budge.

His brown hair is almost golden, and he's tan in a way that comes from the sun—not like Sammie and me. My dad is a mix of everything, and my mom was born in Miami, but my grandparents are from Puerto Rico. Sammie is fairer than me, but our eyes are as dark as our hair.

Maybe he's asleep.

But if Mom is going to order pizza, I need to get this done. "I'm Teagan."

His bandaged arm moves so he can glare up at me through squinted eyes. "What do you want?"

I should ask him if he likes pepperoni or cheese, because that's all I like, and I'm hungry. Instead, I ask what I really want to know. "What happened to your arm?"

He holds it up in the air and studies the bandage that goes from his elbow all the way to his hand where it threads between his thumb and fingers. "I was taken by the president of my old MC, and he burned my tattoo off with a blow torch."

It's all I can do to keep my jaw from hanging open. "Like ... fire?"

He looks at me like I'm not the best reader in my class when I am. "That is the definition of a blow torch."

Despite the temperature of the pavement, I fold at the knees and sit crisscross next to him. "Does it hurt?"

"It's a third-degree burn. Yeah, it fucking hurts."

The only time I hear anyone say the F-word is on the school bus. I bite my lip and try not to giggle.

"That's funny?" he bites.

I shake my head immediately. "No. No way. Sorry, it's just that my parents don't allow bad words in our house."

He looks back up to the sky and mutters, "It's not like I asked to be here. The MC is a no-go." He motions to his bandaged arm. "And even though Brax lied to me for months, for some reason I can't say no to Landyn, so I moved my ass across the country. They're bouncing me around like a foster kid. I've avoided the foster system my entire life, but when I'm finally an adult, someone thinks they give a shit about me. As soon as I get a job, I'm out of here."

I can't take my eyes off him. I've never met anyone like him before. What I don't tell him is that I know his parents are dead or what a grump Sammie was about him. "My mom said you'd be here until you start college."

He shakes his head without looking over at me. "The only reason I agreed to college is because it includes a roof over my head and a meal ticket. I'll sit in a miserable classroom and catch a ball if it means free food and a bed."

I want to ask him what happened to his parents, but that's rude. I'm not like Sammie. But since I ask a lot of questions in general because I'm nosy, I ask, "What's an MC?"

He rolls his eyes. "Are you serious? A motorcycle club. I guess I shouldn't be surprised you don't know. I haven't even been here for a full day and can tell you have no idea what the real world looks like."

"I sort of know what the real world is like. My dad puts drug dealers in prison. I might not be allowed to curse or know anyone in a motorcycle club, but my parents warn me about everything."

My parents do warn us about everything except motorcycle clubs.

But if they gave Rocco a third-degree burn with a blow torch, I assume it's bad.

Like, bad-bad-bad.

"Teagan Coleman." Rocco mutters my name and closes his eyes as he turns his face back to the sun. "A little girl who knows the ways of the world. Well, I promise not to be a bad influence and corrupt you with my shitty life."

I bring my thumb up to bite my nail and glance back at the house. My heartbeat skips a beat when I try the word out on my lips for the first time. "The only thing *shitty* about my life is my grumpy older sister."

That gets his attention.

His eyes snap open and he looks over at me with a glare. "Thought you weren't supposed to cuss, little girl."

I shrug. "I'm not so little. I'm starting middle school this year."

He shakes his head. "Why are you talking to me? Don't you have an entire wardrobe to unpack? Dolls and shit?"

I shake my head. "I don't play with dolls or toys. I read books. And they're already unpacked. It's the first thing I did when the movers brought my stuff to my room this morning. I love my books."

"Great." Rocco spits that word like he's half-mad and half-tired. But I was up for hours before he came out of the guest room—he shouldn't be tired. "I should've known Brax would move me in with a bunch of brainiacs. I can't get out of here fast enough."

"Don't leave too fast. Mom's ordering pizza."

"I'm fucking starving," he says. "But then again, I'm always hungry."

"I'm supposed to ask you what you like."

"As long as I eat, I don't care what it is. Anything beats being hungry."

"I only like cheese or pepperoni."

He sits up and hops to his feet faster than I can blink.

I work my toes back into my flip flops and scramble to stand much slower.

"Sounds good to me. If your parents are going to feed me, I'd better do something to work it off."

Rocco towers over me and this time it's my turn to squint in the sun when I have to lean my head back to look up at him. "Why do you think you have to work off pizza? It's just pizza."

He huffs. "For you maybe, but nothing is free in my world. The last thing I want to do is piss off your daddy until I can get out of here."

"Dad is never..." I pause and do my best to make this one sound more natural. "Pissed off."

Rocco moves around me in his dirty, worn sneakers. "He will be when he hears you talking like that."

He's already at the back door, and I'm forced to skip to keep up with him. When the cool air hits us, I yell into the house. "Rocco said he likes cheese or pepperoni!"

Mom must have found her teacher patience while I was gone. She shakes her head but does it with a smile. "Did you convince him of that?"

"No. He said he'd eat anything, because it beats being hungry."

Mom's smile changes into something I don't recognize.

I've never seen this look on her face before. I didn't know a smile on my mom could be sad.

"I'm used to feeding two finicky girls. I'll order you a whole extra pizza to make sure there's enough. No one will be hungry in this house—I'll make sure of it."

Rocco stuffs his hands in his pockets. "Tell me what to do. I'll carry boxes or some shit for you."

Mom doesn't get onto him for his language. Instead, she takes him up on his offer. "There are some heavy ones in the garage I could use your help with. I appreciate the offer."

Mom turns and Rocco looks down at me before he lightly bops

me on the head with his bandaged forearm. "Don't get me in trouble with the cussing."

I smile. "I won't. I promise."

With that, he lifts his chin and heads to the garage without giving me another glance or thought.

5

GOVERNMENTY

Rocco

New York City.

That wasn't her plan until I announced my transfer back to Miami.

She did a hell of a job selling it to everyone as the opportunity of a lifetime that would open doors for her. A dream job. She couldn't pass up the chance to work in the news hub of the country—maybe the world.

So she said.

I know better.

No one loves their family like Teagan. And that's saying something with a group like ours.

Tim and Annette are heartbroken.

Sammie is pissed.

Landyn is just plain hurt and confused by Teagan's change of heart. She told me so when she called to tell me the news. I would say it's the pregnancy hormones. She and Brax are about to have their third kid, and Landyn gets like this every time she's pregnant.

But I know she'd feel this way no matter what. Listening to Landyn's tears through the phone when she lamented how she thought she'd finally have everyone together again in the same city was more than I could take.

Because no one knows.

Nor will they.

But knowing it's because of me...

That's fucking heavy. I've carried a shitload of burdens in my life, and this one ranks high on the list of things that weigh on me. And it's not because of Landyn or Annette or Tim.

New York City might as well be a deserted island when it comes to Teagan. That's how alone she'll be. It kills me that I can't do anything about it.

For now, I've got to get her out of New Orleans and put myself between her and Robichaux. Every time I tried to shut my eyes to find sleep, all I saw was him leering at her before I broke up her little undercover gig. No fucking way will he ever look at her like that again.

Me? I'm the one who's been staring at her for hours as she sleeps. I've lost track of the time I've sat in this very uncomfortable kitchen chair watching her like a creep.

I'm not proud of the creep I am, but I haven't seen her for two years. When I realized it was Teagan yesterday at The Hotel Monteleone, it all came rushing back. Since I know she sleeps like the dead and I wouldn't wake her, I decided there was no place better to figure out my plan of action than right here.

It doesn't matter how many ways I spin it in my head, none of them are good.

I glance at the clock on my microwave and decide it's time. "Teagan."

She doesn't move.

Nothing has changed ... like the dead.

"Teag," I call for her again.

This time she stirs and rolls to her side, facing me. Her dark hair is messy, her face is free of makeup, and every barrier she's built that only pertains to keeping me out hasn't been reinforced.

I raise my voice. "Teagan, wake up."

She stretches before her eyes flutter open. It takes her a nanosecond to remember where she is. When she does, she presses up to a hip. Her tone is groggy when she asks, "What's wrong?"

"A lot of shit is wrong," I announce. "But I'm going to make it right. We're going to get up, and I'll drive you to your car. Then I'm going to follow you halfway back to your posh, private university to do what you need to do before graduation. What you will not do is come back to New Orleans."

She rubs her eyes and does her best to shake off the sleep I woke her from. "Sorry, but you don't get to tell me what to do or where to be. This is my project. I'm not delusional—I know the chances of getting Mr. Hayes back are slim, but I need to try. If you met Stella, you'd do the same."

"The only thing I care about is making sure you don't do something stupid and that Robichaux never leers at you again."

She tosses the blanket to the other end of the sofa and climbs to her feet. She does a full body stretch as she makes her way to the kitchen. "You seem to have forgotten my area of study. I already have a job lined up to be an investigative journalist in New York. It might be volunteer work now, but I'm going to make a living at it. If you think you can stop me from doing anything, you'll be sorely disappointed."

She goes to the kitchen and digs through boxes until she finds what she wants to make a cup of coffee.

I cross my arms and lean a shoulder on the wall, trapping her in the small galley kitchen that I'm about to say goodbye to. "I was busy while you were getting your beauty sleep."

She doesn't look at me while she talks. "I'd expect nothing less.

Isn't that what DEA agents do—work day and night? Wait, that's until they find *the one* and start popping out babies. Then they just work every third night."

"Can we please have a civil conversation without you throwing your bitchy sarcasm at me?"

"No."

No.

That's it. Just a simple fucking *no*.

"Sammie finally rubbed off on you," I note.

She picks up the mug after the last few drops of coffee fall and stirs in sugar. She doesn't even look for creamer because she knows I drink it black and turns to me. "What can I say? I've learned from the best."

If she's going to act like a petulant child, I should be the one to rise above it.

But fuck that.

I'll throw it right back at her.

"Congrats, you've perfected Sammie two point oh. Since you don't have a desire to find out what I learned about Robichaux, do what you need to do before we leave. I'm taking you back to your car. Maybe I'll see you at graduation—maybe not. Depends on if I have a few hours to kill on my drive back to Miami."

Through my tirade, her Sammie expression dissolves into something I'm familiar with as she grips her mug. "You found out something about Robichaux?"

I tip my head, give her a slow, lazy smile, and shake my head. "You had your chance to cooperate. And if you think about coming back to NOLA, I'll put an APB out on you, your car, and your plates. I've spent the last three years getting to know local law enforcement. I'm going to be so far up Robichaux's ass, there's no way you can communicate with him without me knowing."

Her expression falls farther and her full, pink lips part.

Fucking-A.

My mouth waters.

Her mug hits the counter, and she calls for me, "Rocco!"

It's too late.

I'm on my way to the bathroom. I've got a long day ahead of me, and it all has to do with Jules Robichaux after I kick Teagan out of Louisiana.

"Tell me what you found out," she demands, but I slam the bathroom door in her face and lock it.

I flip on the shower water and strip out of my clothes as she bangs on the door. "Cool it, Teag. You're going to get me evicted in my last days here."

"It'll serve you right," she yells. "I'll quit yelling if you tell me what you found out. Seriously, Rocco. You're the most aggravating man on the planet. This is important to me. You can't just take over and not tell me anything. I have the emails. With your ability to do your governmenty stuff with warrants and shit, we could find out who Robichaux was communicating with. I need to know how he targeted Mr. Hayes and why his trail went cold in Nigeria. Please."

I toss a washcloth over the shower curtain and rip the towel off the hook. I flip it around my waist, fist it at my hip, and open the door.

When she sets her eyes on me, she's flustered, standing there in my clothes while I face her in nothing but a towel.

Her gaze drops to my chest before her arms cross over her small one hidden in my shirt. Finally, she angles her eyes to mine and glares.

So much glaring.

I rest my free hand high on the jamb and lower my voice. "Quit yelling."

She hikes a brow. "Quit being an asshole and help me."

The problem is, she knows I'll help her. There are certain people in the world I can't say no to. Most of them live in Miami.

The other one slept on my sofa last night while I spent a good part of it staring at her.

"I'm going to take a shower. Then I'm going to take you back to your car, and you're going back to school. You'll send me the emails and put me in touch with the Hayes family."

Her brows pinch. "No. You can't cut me out. I won't allow it."

"The last thing I want to do is call your parents. They have enough shit to deal with right now with Sammie. And you're finally speaking to me. I'm not anxious to fuck that up."

Her dark eyes flare and she starts to yell again. "I'm only speaking to you because you basically kidnapped me yesterday!"

I smile down at her. "You know what? Yell all you like. I'll take it. Yelling is better than nothing."

"Fine. I'll go back to school and regroup. You can't stop me." She drags her hands through her messy hair and fists it with frustration before giving up on begging me for help. "And you know what? Go ahead and tattle to my parents. They can't do anything to stop me either. Everyone in my life seems to forget I'm an adult. I've worked damn hard. I'll have my master's in a matter of days and will be on my own a few weeks after that—literally and figuratively. Good luck trying to control my life from Miami."

With that, she turns on a bare foot, and I lose sight of her around the corner. I slam the bathroom door and take the fastest shower I can. I doubt she'd leave on her own, but she's also not the same Teagan I've watched grow up since she was eleven.

I've known it for a while, but after the last twelve hours, nothing is more apparent than the new and less-improved Teagan Coleman.

Teagan

The drive back to the French Quarter has been long, silent, and miserable.

Rocco didn't even turn on the radio.

Pure hell.

I'm also still in his big, baggy clothes and helped myself to a pair of flip flops from his closet. The thought of cramming my feet back into those heels from yesterday gave me a figurative cramp.

He's not getting his clothes back. I'll keep them as a reminder of how Rocco Monroe has ruined my life in more ways than one. Maybe, someday in the distant future when I'm in the right mood, I'll burn them in some type of ritual to cleanse him from my soul for good.

Who am I kidding? If that were possible, I would've done it long ago. I won't be able to avoid holidays and family get-togethers for the rest of my life. Rocco will forever haunt me.

"It's fucking busy today," he mutters as we enter the heart of The Quarter.

I pull my backpack to my lap, dig my keys out, and am ready to bolt. "Feel free to drop me here. I'll walk. The sooner this day is over, the better."

"You're not walking. I don't trust that you'll actually leave."

"You're impossible. I promise to go home. It's not like I have anything else to wear anyway."

He takes the last turn as I contemplate how this may be the last time I'll see him until I'm forced to be tortured again. I must be a masochist, because I take this opportunity to steal a glance.

I've always loved his profile. Probably because I've spent way too many hours staring at him without him knowing.

His hair is shorter than it used to be, but his lips are just as full and his lashes just as thick. He must not plan to go into the office, because he's wearing a clean T-shirt, workout shorts, and running shoes.

Apparently, the only work on his agenda today is making my life miserable.

I must be in a trance, because it barely fazes me when he hits the brakes and mutters, "What the fuck?"

"What-the-fuck what?" I snap out of it and turn to see what caused him to hit the brakes. I gasp. "Holy shit."

I don't waste any time. I scramble for the handle and throw open the door.

"Wait—" Rocco calls for me, but I ignore him. He catches up with me and we meet in front of his car.

We stand silent as we stare at the sight in front of us.

My car.

The one I worked two jobs to save for. The one I negotiated for by myself. The one that's all mine. It's registered to me and me alone. It was my first step in being independent from my parents. It wasn't new, but it was new to me.

I love my car.

And it's trashed.

"Fuck," Rocco growls. I take a step closer to evaluate the damage, but Rocco tags me around the waist and pulls me back. "Don't step on the glass. It'll go right through those shoes."

"Shit," I mutter. He's right. There's glass everywhere. Every window is smashed, and the passenger door stands wide open.

I try to remember what I had stored in my car that's probably gone.

Rocco pulls me with him as he sidesteps the glass and moves onto the sidewalk. "This isn't Bourbon Street, but it isn't a ghost town either. Whoever did this was ballsy."

"It probably happened in the middle of the night." I yank on his arm, and he looks down at me. "This is your fault. Had I returned to my car last night when I wanted to, this never would've happened."

Rocco turns back to the mangled mess in front of us. "What's in the back seat?"

"My gym bag. I can't believe it's still there."

I realize Rocco is holding my back tight to his front. I try to twist out of his grip to get a closer look, but he holds tight and digs his cell from his pocket. "Wait. We need to make a report and get it towed. I'll see if any of these businesses have surveillance cameras."

As I stand flush to Rocco in the bright morning sun, I realize what this means. "This is unbelievable. I'm stuck here until I can get my car fixed."

He describes in detail the damage to my car to the dispatcher. The call is quick and the moment he hangs up, he juts his chin back to my car. "Your glove box. It's empty."

That's when my phone vibrates with a call in the deep pocket of Rocco's sweatpants. I dig it out and read the screen. "It's my apartment complex." When I answer, it's the office manager. "Oh, Teagan. Thank goodness. Are you okay?"

I frown. "I'm fine. I had to make a trip to New Orleans. What's wrong?"

"Your apartment—there was a break-in right before dawn. Your downstairs neighbor reported it when she left for work this morning after she saw your door ajar. We called the police and pulled surveillance video. They were in and out so fast, we couldn't ID anyone. They were wearing full face masks."

My eyes fall shut, and I feel myself lean into Rocco for the mere reason I might collapse into a puddle of tears. "Did they clean me out?"

"What happened?" Rocco demands.

"My apartment," I whisper.

His jaw tightens.

The manager keeps detailing the downward spiral of my life. "Your TV is missing, and the place is a mess. You need to come home and assess the damage. There's no way for us to know what else was taken. Maintenance will fix your door and replace the lock right away."

Well, joke's on her.

I don't own a TV.

But I don't tell her that, because something catches my eye. My brain clicks with the realization of what's playing out in front of me. "Thank you for letting me know. I'll be there as soon as I can."

I disconnect the call and realize what happened as I stare at my empty glove box.

"My registration and insurance," I mutter. "They were the only other things in there."

Glass crunches on pavement as I feel Rocco close in. The sun beating down on us is nothing compared to the heat from his chest pressed once again to my back. "Fuck."

I turn to look up at Rocco and ask, "Do you think it was Robichaux?"

"Teagan, you've never had a break in until you pretended to be someone you're not and met with a criminal connected to the underbelly of New Orleans. Now you've had two in the same day. You do the math."

Shit.

Robichaux knows my real name.

And where I live.

"You're fucked," Rocco mutters my thoughts out loud.

And for the first time since Rocco Monroe rammed back into my life like a force, there's something we can finally agree on.

I'm no idiot.

But I am, indeed, fucked.

6

PANTIES

Teagan

I work hard.

I save my money.

I've even been financially independent from my parents for the last year. And in a matter of weeks, I'll have two degrees under my belt.

Besides carrying around the emotionally traumatic baggage from being rejected by the one and only Rocco Monroe, I feel like I'm a pretty put-together kind of gal.

I'm not sure what other women do when their life shatters into a million pieces within a matter of twelve hours, but for me, there is only one option.

Retail therapy.

Though, in this case, it's less about therapy than it is necessity.

As soon as we made a police report, my car was towed. I might normally have my shit together, but having my property and privacy violated in two different cities—hell, two different states—is too much.

I need a shower, a clean set of clothes, a real pair of shoes, and maybe a nap. And not in that order.

Rocco proves he will continue to come through for me even after I cut him out for as long as I have.

He informed me I wasn't going home until he had a chance to at least look for a surveillance video to see who may have broken into my car.

I told him I needed real clothes, a decent conditioner, and a toothbrush.

He might've rolled his eyes, but he drove me straight to the big, red bullseye with the cute dog.

My home away from home. I could live in this store.

That doesn't mean he lets me shop in peace.

Rocco grabbed a cart and has followed me around the bright, clean mecca like he'll get fired from the DEA if he lets me out of his sight.

I toss a pair of shorts in the cart along with a tank and T-shirt. I haven't stopped flipping through racks and Rocco hasn't stopped talking.

"Taylor is calling businesses up and down the street where you were parked to see if they'll give us surveillance video. He's also making calls to businesses between The Hotel Monteleone and where you were parked. Robichaux was not working alone. If it was him or someone who works for him, then they were watching and followed us back to your car and have your home address. You're not going back to your apartment anytime soon."

I can't think about Robichaux or going back to my apartment. Rocco is right—I'm in over my head, but I'm not about to admit it.

I toss in another pair of shorts and flip through a rack of sundresses as if I'm shopping for a girls' night out rather than being held somewhat against my will.

I'm saving face by giving Rocco the silent treatment.

Not that it's working. He's filling the dead space that hangs between us just fine on his own.

"And when we get back to my apartment, you're calling the Hayes family. I want to talk to your contact. I can't just cold call Robichaux without information about your so-called grandfather. That's assuming he'll answer. If it was him or his people who broke in, they know you aren't who you said you are. He'll never answer my call. Even so, add a prepaid phone to your list of shit we need. I can't exactly ask the DEA to provide me one. This is on my own time."

I don't argue, agree, or add to the conversation. Instead, I move two aisles over. Shopping for panties and bras in front of Rocco should give me top-tier anxiety, but I don't have the energy today. Maybe it's because I'm used to him being around for long spurts of time in between semesters or all summer.

Why does it matter anyway?

Everyone wears underwear and most women wear bras. I'd only be embarrassed if I cared.

And I definitely don't care. Not today, anyway.

"But you were right," he goes on without any encouragement from me. "If the Hayes family can log me into Heath's email, I won't need warrants. I can run the IP address. We'll see where that takes us."

I flip through a rack of bralettes and hold one up to myself before tossing it in the basket with the rest of my new wardrobe. A shopping spree is not in my budget. I need work clothes appropriate for New York City, not shorts and sundresses. I want to be taken seriously.

"Then I'm going to call your dad."

That gets my attention.

I spin on my heel and point at him with a butter yellow thong clipped to a hanger. "Whoa. Stop right there."

Rocco crosses his arms and leans back on his heels. "You're not listening to anything I say. I had to get your attention."

The thong and hanger become one with my agitated soul when I poke him in the chest with it. "You promised. I did everything you asked. You can't call him now. This will…" I pull in a deep breath and try to convince myself of my next words. "Blow over. I'm moving after graduation anyway. I just need to get through the next couple days."

Rocco narrows his eyes at the panties hanging between us before pushing them to the side and lowers his voice. "Your car was busted up, and they have your address. Let me clue you in on a little fact, Teagan—most criminals are lazy by nature. The fact that whoever did this took the effort to drive over an hour east across the state line to break into your apartment says a lot. They're committed to the task."

"It doesn't sound like they took anything." Now I'm standing up for the shitheads who broke into my car and apartment. That's a new level of lame, even for me. "You know what would be really nice? If I could see my apartment. Let's go back to your place, I'll get ready, and we can go. I'll need to come back with you anyway because of my car. I'll even give you the emails, and we'll call Stella Hayes. See, there? I was listening." I take a step back to put some space between us and wave the panties around again. "Look at me—I'm a cooperative participant in our fight against crime."

The whiskey eyes that have haunted countless sleepless nights stare me down before he shifts his gaze and fists the panties between us. "Are you buying these or are you just going to taunt me with them for the rest of the day?"

I shine a fake smile up at him, snap them out of his grip, tossing them in the cart with the rest of the clothes I can't afford. "I'm buying one in every color."

When I turn away, his exhale is loud and frustrated. "Speed it up. If we're taking a trip to Mississippi, we need to get going."

I leave him and the cart behind me and head straight to the cosmetics section. "I need a few more things. If you're nice, I'll buy you something for all the trouble I'm sure to put you through. Your cleanser sucks and you don't even have a bottle of lotion, let alone a moisturizer."

He follows while complaining. "I live in a swamp. I don't need lotion."

"You'll age prematurely. Between my mom and Landyn, I'm disappointed they haven't raised you better."

"You seem to forget I was plenty raised before I met them," he mutters.

I pick up a box and read the ingredients. "Hardly. I remember the day Brax dropped you off. You were emotionally stunted, and that's saying something because I was only eleven. If you think we weren't basically raised together, your memories are playing out as fiction. But don't utter those words around my mom. You'll hurt her feelings."

Finally, something that shuts him up. He might love my mom as much as I do.

But I'm as anxious as I am nervous to see the state of my apartment, so I toss a moisturizer, mask, and toner into the cart. "There. I'm done. Had I known we were going to make a trip today, I wouldn't have spent the time shopping for all this stuff. But I like it, so now I want it. If they didn't take my clothes, I'll pack a bag."

He pushes the cart past me as sarcasm bleeds from him. "So, you're saying you don't need those scraps of material in every color of the rainbow?"

I shuffle faster in his flip flops and have to squeeze my toes with every step to keep up as he heads to an empty checkout line. "They're panties, Rocco. And, yes, I need them all. A girl can't have too many pairs of panties."

He refuses to look at me as he fists panties, bras, and the rest of my new clothes with his big hand and tosses them on the conveyor belt before pulling out his wallet.

I put my hand out to stop him. "You're not paying for any of this."

He waves me off. "Tim tells me how you work long hours. And if that car is registered to you, you're going to have a deductible to deal with. Consider this an early graduation gift."

I cross my arms over his big shirt. I'm still not wearing a bra. "Panties from Rocco Monroe. Is this what you buy all the girls for graduation?"

I ignore the checker who bites her lip as she quickly scans my mini shopping spree. Rocco swipes his credit card before turning his back to the checker. The next thing I know, he leans down, and I'm almost nose to nose with the man who just bought me a week's worth of thongs and multiple outfits. When I inhale, he smells like home. He uses the same body wash my mom stocks in all the bathrooms, and his fabric softener is a scent from my childhood.

So many memories. Even my nose can't escape this man.

Rocco is tied to every single one of them, dammit.

"Just so you know, I've never bought slips of fabric that you consider underwear for anyone. Not for a woman, and especially not for a girl."

I lean in closer and lower my voice. "Good. Because I haven't been a girl for a very long time. Thanks for the rainbow of thongs. I'll think of you every time I wear them."

With that, I side-step him, snatch the bag, and stalk for the door with my head held high. I need all the courage I can gather if I'm going to be stuck with Rocco for another day.

Rocco

I've never been more disappointed that a burglary resulted in not one thing stolen.

Teagan's studio apartment is smaller than my living room. She wasn't kidding when she told me she had nothing that anyone would want. And it's not lost on me that we're living parallel lives, both packed and ready for new things, even if we are going in opposite directions.

Her place was tossed—it was a fucking mess. She was packed to move right after graduation this weekend, but whoever broke in undid her hard work.

Boxes were dumped and bags were ransacked. It was easy to see what the intruder was after.

Information.

Unfortunately for them, Teagan Coleman is not only a lover of information and obsessed with cold cases, but she's also a tree hugger and a minimalist.

There was no connection of Teagan Coleman to old man Hayes in her apartment to be found since she keeps everything on her laptop. Who knew her inner environmentalist would save the day. She didn't even have any pictures out to incriminate herself. There might still be a chance that Jules will take my call. There's no evidence she isn't the fake granddaughter she claimed to be at their meeting. Thank goodness there aren't photo IDs on registrations.

We didn't take the time to clean up the place, but she did pack a small bag for another day with me. She may have had one wayward semester in college, but Teagan is smart and always has been. She might have met with Jules Robichaux by herself, but she did it in a public place. She knows she's not safe in her apartment by herself. She didn't even argue.

It's one small miracle since this shit show started yesterday, but

I'll take it. Arguing with Teagan sits near the bottom of my list of things I enjoy. It barely ranks above buying her sexy underwear, which I didn't know I hated until today.

We're back at my place, and together, we annihilated a large pizza.

Teagan tosses the last pizza bone in the empty box, picks up her phone, presses a few buttons, and leans it on the greasy pizza box.

I gulp down the last of my water. "Who are you calling?"

Her eyes angle to mine as she leans forward. "Stella Hayes—the real Stella Hayes."

I barely have a chance to claim the spot on the sofa next to her when the caller immediately pops up on Facetime. The woman looks older than me. She's also anxious as hell. "Teagan! Are you okay? I was so worried when I didn't hear from you last night. Were you able to meet Robichaux?"

The woman who feels like a stranger to me compared to who she used to be, rests her forearms on her knees, and I swear the old Teagan makes an appearance. It brings back years of memories with the Colemans while doing some weird shit to my insides.

I choose to ignore the weird shit and focus on the stranger on the screen as I listen to Teagan be downright sweet.

Something she has yet to shine my way in the last twenty-four hours, let alone two years.

"I'm fine." She smiles into the camera. "Yes, if you can believe it, Robichaux actually showed up. I'm so sorry I didn't call you last night, Stella. Things got hectic after the meeting."

Stella glances at me then back to Teagan. "Did you find out anything?"

"I'm sorry. The only thing he verified is that he communicated with your dad, which we knew. We do have a new avenue to explore though." Teagan pulls in a deep breath before tipping her head in my direction. "Stella, this is Rocco Monroe. He's with the DEA."

"Good to meet you, Stella. Teagan has filled me in on your dad. I know you're worried. I'll do what I can to help." What I don't say is that I'll do just about anything to keep Teagan speaking to me. "I think we should start with the emails. If you're willing to share them, I can subpoena the IP address for records of other communication being sent and received."

Stella's hesitant stare lingers on me for an odd amount of time before she looks back at Teagan. "I'm not sure. Why would the DEA help me when I didn't have any luck with the State Department?"

Teagan opens her mouth to say something, but I beat her to it. "I can't speak for the State Department, but Robichaux has been on my radar for a while. If this leads to a drug case, great. If not, I'm willing to help Teagan—especially if that means she'll retire her undercover hat."

When I glance over, Teagan is rolling her eyes. I'm not sorry, and I don't give a shit. What I do need is for her not to perform any more sting operations.

"I was worried about her too," Stella adds for good measure. "Heck, she's young enough to be my daughter."

That's the farthest thing Teagan Coleman feels like to me, so I say, "Then we can agree that it won't happen again. But if you give me access to the emails, I can take it from here."

Teagan sits up straight and puts a hand out. "Wait a second. I've logged so many hours on this case, I feel like Heath is my grandfather. You can't cut me out."

"I can," I refute before adding as I give her the side eye, because I'm tired of this argument. "And I will."

Teagan glares at me. "You said we'd work on this together."

I shrug. "Let's see where the emails take us before we chart the course for the rest of the case."

Tension rolls off the woman sitting next to me, but Teagan stays focused on Stella. "Can I give him the emails? He can get the subpoena started. This is going to make a huge difference. We can see who Jules is communicating with—maybe even find out something about your dad."

That's all it takes for Stella to come around. "Okay, I'll do it. I trust you, Teagan. No one has cared about finding my father as much as you."

It's like Teagan forgets all about me. Her smile is genuine and from a simpler time.

Before we fucked it up.

"I wish I could give you a hug," Teagan says. "I had some car problems, so I'm stuck in New Orleans for a couple days until I can get that sorted. I promise we'll get together before I move. But even after that, I'm not giving up on you or your dad. I promise."

Even over the small screen, it's easy to see Teagan's friend get emotional at the mention of her dad. That's something I can't fathom.

Don't get me wrong. I've gotten emotional about my father. But more like the *I'd kill him if I could get away with it* kind of emotional. And since he's doing time in prison for manslaughter, that's saying something.

There's a ruckus in the background and Stella says, "I'd better go. The hellions are getting hungry. I don't want them to hear me talking about their grandpa. We'll talk soon?"

"Very soon," Teagan promises with another warm smile.

She disconnects the call, turns to me, and warns, "Did you see that woman? She trusts me. I've developed a relationship with her whole family."

It's my turn to make a connection, even though I've been dreading it all day. I made a stop on the way home from Mississippi and bought a prepaid phone. This shit isn't an official case. There was no way I could go into the office and ask the tech group to set me up with a phone that wouldn't connect me to Uncle Sam. This needs to stay under the radar. I lean back to dig the phone number out of my pocket as I fire up the burner phone.

"Are you calling Jules?"

"Yes. I'm following through on my promise to you, Stella, and maybe building a case for myself. Just don't tell my boss where I got the lead."

"This is so exciting!" Teagan's face lights up with more pleasure than I like for the topic at hand.

"Temper your expectations. Let's be real, I doubt he'll answer. I don't know many bad guys who answer unknown numbers."

"He might." When she beams with excitement, I realize this makes her so happy, she lives for this shit. "He answered my email right away. He had no idea who I was."

I type in the number from the card Robichaux gave me but pause before I press go and look at Teagan. "Even if he answers, it'll be me. Not a young woman who excites him in ways that make me want to commit felonies."

"Stop being so negative, Roc," she admonishes. "Think good things. He's going to answer. I mean, he might. There's a good chance he might."

I sit back and realize exhaustion is setting in from not sleeping last night, dealing with broken windows, burglarized apartments, and buying panties in every color under the sun that I'm trying my hardest not to think about at the moment. "I'm not negative. I'm realistic."

She bops me on the shoulder with her fist. "We're doing the right thing for good people. If we manifest it, it will happen. Or it might."

I shake my head and look down at the screen. Right after I press go on the call, I put it on speaker.

Teagan pulls her feet up and tucks them under her ass in anticipation.

"Relax," I say. "He's not going to answer."

With every ring, I'm ready to kill the call and try again tomorrow.

After the fourth ring, I'm about to hang up when the call connects.

Teagan's gaze shoots to me as a voice over the line is as sharp as cut glass. "What?"

From that one simple word, I can't decide if it's actually him and pause before asking, "Robichaux?"

He does not pause. "Who's asking?"

I narrow my eyes when Teagan starts to open her mouth and intercede. "Name's Mack Crowder. We met yesterday at The Hotel Monteleone. You had a meeting with my woman, Stella Hayes."

Teagan rolls her eyes.

It's all I can do to keep the smile out of my voice.

"Mack." The fake name that came out of nowhere and means nothing rolls around his mouth like he wants to bite me in half. "I remember your woman. Sorta remember you."

"I would hope so. I'm memorable." Teagan's head falls back as she contemplates the ceiling. I keep talking. "Told you I'd make it worth your time to tell us where Stella's grandfather is. I'm following up and ready to make that happen. What do you want?"

The chatter in the background fades as I hear the phone shift. "Gotta say, this is unusual. If you've got the cash to pay for information, old man Hayes wouldn't have been so desperate for money."

"I wasn't in the picture then," I offer even though I have no fucking clue of the timeline that Hayes made a deal with Jules. "But I am now. I want to know where Heath is, and you're the man with the information."

The click of a lighter sounds over the phone before he pulls in a sharp breath. "I trust very few people, and I have no fucking clue who you are."

"You trusted Stella enough to meet with her," I say without taking my eyes off Teagan. All I can think about is the way Robichaux was targeting her that day in the hotel bar. "You don't give a shit about Heath. If I'm willing to pay for the information, what do you care?"

"I care a fuck ton about my business," he bites. "And no offense, asshole, but your woman was an interesting meet. You are not. Now, if Stella is involved, I might be willing to talk."

"No fucking way," I snap. "You can deal with me and me alone."

"Looks like Pawpaw's location will continue to be a mystery. No skin off my back," he mutters. "I've got real business to take care of. Don't call me again."

I'm about to offer a sum of money that I have, but definitely one I'm not willing to part with, when Teagan blurts, "Jules, wait! I'll meet with you."

"No," I growl as I shoot Teagan my what-the-fuck glare and do my best to fix what she just did. "Stella isn't a part of the deal."

All of a sudden, Jules sounds interested. "Smart little girl. Now we're getting somewhere."

My blood boils as it pumps through my veins. "No fucking way."

"He's my grandfather," Teagan argues. "Please meet with us again. You, Mack, and me. Tell us what you want in exchange for information about my grandfather."

Before I have the chance to shut this shit down, Robichaux proves he's willing to negotiate with a beautiful woman. "I'll text this number when and where. It'll be on my terms and not in a fucking hotel lobby in the middle of The Quarter with an audience."

"Great." I try to keep the irritation out of my tone and wonder how I'll get this done without Teagan by my side. "We'll be there."

Robichaux proves he wants to talk less than I do and ends the conversation with one word. "Later."

The call goes dead.

Dead.

Which is what we could be if we meet with someone like Robichaux without an operational plan or backup.

I toss the prepaid cell next to the empty pizza box before leaning back on the sofa to stare at the ceiling.

I close my eyes and drag a hand down my face, but don't say a word.

"Um…" Teagan breaks the silence. "I'm sorry about that."

I don't open my eyes. "Don't lie. You're not one bit sorry."

"Okay, you're right. I'm not." I lift my head to look at her. She at least has the decency to look guilty. "I had to do something. He was going to hang up and never take your call again. And it's not like I agreed to meet him by myself in some dark alley. I'm not an idiot. You'll be with me."

"I don't have the energy to argue with you." I lean back on the sofa and kick my shoes off before propping my feet up on the coffee table. "It's late, Teag. I barely slept last night and drove you all over the south for most of the day. I'll get the subpoena going first thing. If Robichaux actually texts me a location, I'll figure it out, but you won't be a part of it."

She doesn't give up and nudges my leg. "Please don't do that."

I sigh and scoot deeper into the cushions. "You know I won't, but I don't like any of this."

She exhales and flops back on the other end of the sofa. "I know I can't do this without you, but that conversation was proof that he won't meet with you alone. You need me if you want to get to Jules."

I rest my head on the back cushion and close my eyes. "No more than you need me."

She grabs the pillow she slept on last night, stuffs it under her head. "It kills me, but I agree."

I don't have the energy to open my eyes when I keep talking. "It's been a long fucking day. Can we just sit here for five minutes without you busting my balls? You know, for old time's sake?"

She rolls to her side and takes up two-thirds of the sofa by tucking into herself. "Okay. Just for five minutes."

I yawn. "I appreciate that."

"I graduate on Sunday. You know my—"

"I bought you underwear for every day of the week as your graduation gift. Don't ask me for anything else."

She kicks me lightly. "That's not what I was going to say. I was going to say that I need my car. My parents will be there. They can't know what happened."

I roll my head to the side to look at her. "It's just glass. I'm sure it'll be done in plenty of time for you to keep all the secrets from your family."

She yawns. "Rocco?"

"Five minutes, Teag. Am I asking for too much?"

She doesn't give me a warm smile that lights up her face like I'm used to. She pulls her lip between her teeth and hesitates before finally saying, "I'm sorry I dragged you into this."

I don't take my eyes off her. "The last thing on earth I want is for something to happen to you. You should've called me in the beginning when you hit a dead end."

She shakes her head but says nothing.

Exhaustion takes over, and I close my eyes. "Someday, you'll get it."

She moves and shifts to get comfortable. "Right back at you."

That cuts through the long day, the sleepless night, and the drama I just inserted myself into. I open my eyes and stare at the ceiling.

I feel that comment down to my bones.

And it doesn't feel good.

7
GET OVER MYSELF

Teagan

Light peeks through the drawn blinds from across the room. I stretch, or try to, but unlike last night when I slept on Rocco's sofa, something stops me.

A grip on my thigh.

Warm.

Firm.

Heavy.

When I roll to my back, I realize why my sofa is smaller than it was when I woke up yesterday at this time.

Rocco never went to bed.

He's taking up more than the corner he claimed last night when he begged for five minutes of peace.

Rocco is six feet, three inches, and two hundred and ten pounds of solid muscle.

At least he was when he played college football. I memorized his stats, because that's what one does when they're obsessed.

That's a lot of real estate of a man to have to sleep in the corner of a sofa. He must have been exhausted. There's not one thing on him that looks comfortable.

Other than his hand gripping my thigh.

It seems we battled for space during the night. My legs are stretched over his lap. One of his made its way onto the sofa and is tucked tight to me.

We're all arms and legs and hands and angst. It makes me equally sad and anxious and petulant.

I'm basically living out every pop song that hits the top of the charts because it makes teenage girls all up in their feels as they listen on repeat until they've memorized every lyric, melody, and dramatic pause.

I used to be that girl.

But like I told Rocco last night, I'm not a girl any longer. I'm shocked he came the same realization when he agreed with me. Seeing me as anything other than the gangly eleven-year-old whose room was across the hall from his has never been on his radar. There was no doubt when he made that fact abundantly clear the moment he shattered my dreams.

And still, I don't move.

All I can do is stare.

Rocco's wide chiseled chest rises and falls with every even breath he takes. His thick lashes fan below his eyes and full lips are slightly parted.

I hate that he's familiar.

I hate that he's so tightly laced into my life, I can't escape him.

But more than anything, I hate that I hate him.

He doesn't deserve that.

There's too much to love about Rocco Monroe. The fact he's still single is a miracle. And it's not from a lack of trying on Landyn's part. Every time I'm home and hear her talk about it, it's another twist of the rusty knife in my gut that slowly kills me from the inside out.

It's time for me to accept the fact there's no cure. Rocco isn't going anywhere. He'll be a part of my life forever, even if it's not the way I want it to be. I can't avoid him any longer since he's moving back to Miami.

I miss my family. And as much of a shit show as Sammie is, I love her and want to be in her child's life.

I'm going to be the best aunt on earth.

So, it's time.

I'm so pathetic, I can't even stand it. I need to get over myself.

It's definitely time to get over Rocco Monroe.

Mind over matter, and all that jazz. If anything, I need to do it for Rocco. Even if I didn't love him in my own secret, tragic romance, I'd love him the way the rest of my family does. There's nothing not to love about Rocco.

But there's no way I'll be able to get over myself sleeping next to Rocco with his hand wrapped around my thigh.

This is just plain painful.

It's also time to let him off the hook. This rift between us is crashing down on my shoulders.

No more pining.

No more dreaming.

Reality is a bitch and a dream killer.

I have no choice but to embrace her in all her depressing truths. Because the truth is, Rocco doesn't want me. Not the way I want him.

I'm an adult and need to act like one. There's no better time than the present to rip off the bandage.

When I nudge his abs with my toe, his grip on my thigh tightens. His head rolls to the other side as he stretches.

Seriously. I'd give anything to experience this under different circumstances.

More salt in the wound, but I force myself to do what's necessary to live a not-so-depressing life.

"Roc," I whisper.

His head rolls back in my direction, and a delicious low groan rumbles from his chest. I can even feel it from where we're connected. When I finally get a peek of his sleepy whiskey eyes, he doesn't move. And he definitely doesn't take his hand from where it's plastered high on my bare thigh.

I die a little bit more when I feel wetness pool in the new panties he bought me.

I'd rather die a slow, painful death than do what I need to.

I need to get this done.

"I'm sorry." My apology comes out hoarse and sounds as painful as it feels.

He swallows and lifts his head, but he doesn't let go of me. His words are groggier than mine. "For what?"

I pull in a deep breath to address the stubborn elephant in the room that's been sitting fat and heavy between us for far too long. I was the one who invited it in, so I need to be the one to kick it out for good, no matter how much it hurts.

"I'm sorry for messing things up."

His eyes narrow. "Is this about Robichaux? If so, I'll figure out a way to get him to meet me alone—"

"No, it's not about that," I interrupt, but I don't move. I don't want to. This will be my last memory of Rocco's touch that's anything more than friendly. Or, kill me now, even brotherly. I refuse to give it up sooner than I have to. "I'm sorry for what I did two years ago. It was a boundary I should not have crossed. I made things weird and messed everything up between us. I was angry even though you did nothing wrong. You even tried to make things right between us. It was my fault. I'm sorry."

My apology acts as a five-alarm fire. Rocco is fully alert and shifts toward me. But instead of accepting my plea for forgiveness and letting me off the hook so we can pretend the last couple of years never happened, something smolders behind his beautiful eyes. "If you're going to apologize for anything it better be for cutting me out of your life for so long."

My jaw goes slack in pure shock. "I was mortified and embarrassed."

And more than anything ... hurt. Though I'm not about to admit that.

I thought he'd say *thanks*, bump me on the shoulder like a normal guy, and move on like any emotionally unattached man would.

That was my plan.

I counted on him doing his part.

But instead of doing any of that, Rocco's stare on me intensifies. So much so, my heart speeds in my chest to a point my pulse echoes in my ears.

I panic.

"It was stupid," I blurt and think back on the night that acts as a demon I just can't shake. "No, I was stupid. Stupid and tipsy. You set me straight, and I'm over it. I'm over you."

I didn't think it was possible for his grip on my thigh to tighten further, but I'm wrong.

"You turned cold on me for two years, and now you're over it? Just like that?" he growls.

"I am." I swallow over the boulder in my throat and continue to lie. "Stupid and young and on the path to self-destruction. You didn't mince words and called me on it. I should thank you. It was what I needed to get my shit together. In fact, I'm seeing someone."

His eyes narrow. "That's interesting. Because Annette gives me the lowdown on everyone, and she didn't mention it. I bet I talk to your mom more than you do. She gives me so much information, I know how wide Sammie's vagina is dilated. And that is shit I do not need to know."

"My sister is pregnant, not a porn star," I bite. "There's nothing wrong with knowing that. The fact that pregnancy details give you the ick proves you are emotionally unattached."

"Since when am I emotionally unattached?" he demands.

"Since you're weirded out by my panties and Sammie's vagina. Which, by the way, it's not her vagina, it's her cervix. It's a good thing you're moving back to Miami. Landyn, Evie, and Goldie have their work cut out for them. It's no wonder you're still single," I state firmly. "I can't believe we're talking about this. I'm done."

"We are not done."

"I am." The torture is killing me. I yank my leg from his hold and shift off the sofa.

He juts to his feet just as quickly to grab my arm. "Who the hell are you seeing? You're moving to New York."

This is a new kind of panic—one that can only stem from a Jenga tower made of lies. "Jed."

"Jed?" His brow furrows. "That guy you dated in high school?"

I force a satisfied expression on my face and hope it doesn't look as anxiety ridden as it feels. "Yes. We reconnected a few months ago when I was in Miami for a visit. We rekindled our old flame. Jed is..." I struggle for words and am forced to settle on being pathetic, which is nothing new. "Great."

"Jed is great," Rocco echoes and finally lets me go, but he doesn't let me off the hook. "I don't believe it. You're full of shit."

I wave my hand around. "And you're still full of yourself. Nothing has changed."

He shakes his head and keeps at me. "You didn't kiss me like you're seeing someone else."

My eyes go wide. "You kissed me. And right in front of Robichaux. If I reciprocated, it was out of shock. What was I supposed to do?"

"That kiss was just as intense as the first one. Nothing has changed in two years. If you want, I'll prove it to you."

I gasp. "How on earth are you going to do that?"

The eight inches that separate us on bare feet makes me feel small. He towers over me when we're like this. Wide and powerful. The veins in his arms are more distinct than ever.

He shifts closer. "Maybe I'll kiss you again. We'll see how *great* Jed really is."

My mouth waters.

Damn him.

I want that, even though he has nothing to prove. Jed and I are friends and have been since he broke up with me right after our junior prom. But if I took him up on a kiss, that would make me a cheater. A fictional one, but still a cheater.

"Don't you dare," I warn.

He studies me before shaking his head. "Everything has changed ... yet every fucking thing is the same. If our lips ever meet again, it'll be because you beg me to kiss you."

I huff an exasperated breath. "That will never happen."

"Never say never, Teagan. Just when you think you're on a path, life fucking obliterates the road in front of you. You're forced to offroad until you can get that shit back on track."

I know he's talking about his younger self when he was a motorcycle club prospect and met Brax and Landyn, but his metaphor means something else to me. I feel like I've been wandering offroad for the last two years. I need to get back on the highway and fast track myself to a new normal.

My apology was supposed to do that, but instead, I've found myself in the middle of an ugly lie and a game of Truth or Dare.

I'm about to push him out of my way and lock myself in his bathroom for longer than necessary, but there's a vibration on the coffee table.

A text.

On the prepaid cell.

My gaze jumps to Rocco. "Is it Jules?"

He bends to pick up the phone and mutters, "Since no one else has this number but him, I'd say the chances are good."

"What does it say? Will he meet with us?"

Rocco unlocks the phone and reads the text.

He exhales before dragging a hand down his face.

"Oh no. Is it bad?" I grab the cell and read the screen.

> Unknown Caller – Tonight. Location and time to come. Be ready. The girl better be there.

I smile for the first time since I opened my eyes after sleeping tangled up with Rocco. "This is great."

Rocco snags the cell from my hands. "Do you mean *great* like Jed, or *great* like a lowlife who arranged for an old man to disappear who also has a fascination with you has agreed to meet with us? Because both make me irate."

"*Great* that he agreed to meet us. See, I manifested this. You're welcome." Now I really need to get away from him. "I'm going to take a shower. When the message comes in, we need to be ready to hit the road."

I turn for my bag, but I'm stopped once again by Rocco's warm grasp on my skin. He turns me to him, and his focus is lasered in on me. "If he doesn't want to meet in a public place, I'm not going without backup, and you're definitely not going at all."

When I look up at him, there's something smoldering behind those light brown eyes that I don't recognize. It's not playful or easy natured. It's not even angry, though I've rarely seen Rocco enraged.

Whatever it is, it's intense to an extreme. I'm not sure what to do with it. I definitely don't know how to handle it. But there's one thing I know for sure, I'm going to this meeting.

"Please. You saw Stella with your own eyes yesterday. If that were someone you loved, you'd do everything you could to find them. I'm not stupid. I can't do this by myself. I need you."

His jaw goes taut before he gives in. "I have phone calls to make. I was going to do this shit off the record, but I also want both of us to live to see next week. I need an op plan and backup."

He didn't argue the fact that I'll be by his side tonight, so I smile. "Tim would be proud."

He shakes his head. "Tim is going to kick my ass. There's no doubt in my mind."

"I won't allow it." I don't ask if it's because Rocco is allowing me to meet Robichaux or because he kissed me. "You do your agent thing. I'm going to take a shower. This is exciting stuff."

I grab my things off the floor and head to the bathroom as he mutters, "This is not exciting. This is hell."

8

FICTIONALLY FUCKED

Rocco
Twenty-two months, one week, and four days ago.
But who's fucking counting?
Me, that's who.
Because that's what you do when you're in hell.

This is the last fucking place I want to be at three in the morning. This might be New Orleans, but the city finally starts to settle down around this hour.

But not this place. This place is just getting going for the night.

I pull out my badge and pass my creds through the window to the attendant. "I'm here to post bail."

The woman pushes her cold cup of coffee to the side as she looks from my ID to me and frowns. "DEA agents usually put people in jail, not pay to get them out."

"Yeah," I agree. "This is a first for me. I'm here for Teagan Coleman. She was processed a couple hours ago."

She turns to her computer and starts to type away. "Ah. Underage. Wonder what she did to get the full treatment in the middle of the night?"

What I don't admit is that she probably dropped my name. Not every cop extends professional courtesy to government agents. It's par for the course—Teagan has been on a string of bad luck for a while, even if it is by her own doing.

She needs to get her head out of her ass. There's a point of no return. If anyone is intimately familiar with that concept, it's me.

"Oh, I have a note for you," the clerk says. "You're supposed to call the lieutenant on duty. Here's his number."

She slides a piece of paper my way. "What's this?"

"It's about the girl. I'll start her paperwork while you make that call."

I don't know what I'm more anxious about—getting Teagan the hell out of here or knowing what Lieutenant Boyd has to say about the girl I'm about to post bail for.

The call barely rings a second time when a man answers. "Boyd."

"Lieutenant. My name is Rocco Monroe. I was given your number at booking when I got here to bail out a friend's daughter."

"Ah, the girl."

I tense and wonder what the hell is going on. "Teagan Coleman. What about her?"

"She told me she was a friend of yours. I wanted to see if she was feeding me a crock of shit. You can imagine what underage drinkers come up with to get out of being arrested."

"I was Miami PD for three years. I get it. But I can vouch for Teagan. I've known her half her life. I haven't talked to her yet. What happened?"

"She and her friends were at a shady joint a few blocks off the main drag. They either don't card, or they let in the young pretty ones. I think the latter happened with the Coleman girl. There was a fight, and my guys were called out. She claimed her friends scattered and left her behind. She has shit friends. Is this normal? You bail her out often?"

I have a feeling Boyd is trying to do me a favor, so there's no way I'm going to let on that I've had a feeling this has been Teagan's new normal for the last semester. "Never. This is not normal for her."

"I wondered. She has no record. Not even a parking ticket." When he pauses, all I hear is his comm radio crackle in the background. "Look, I've got three kids. It's like they lose their fucking minds and do stupid shit at some point. I told my guys to take her to the station and hold her until we heard from you. She swore on her own life you'd come for her. She's yours now ... if you want her."

Teagan Coleman.

The thought of that in any form is fucked up.

"I'll make sure she gets home safe. And I'll make damn sure she doesn't do this again."

"I'll make the call to have her released to you. No record. But no shit, if I see or hear of her name again, I won't be so nice."

"Point taken. I appreciate you," I say. Teagan had also better appreciate me. Her birthday is next month. She couldn't wait thirty days to hit the bars.

When I go back to the desk, the clerk looks up at me and slides a manilla folder through the plexiglass window. "I know, I know. Boyd is a softy. Your inmate will be out in a minute. Here are her things."

The next thing I know, a security tone sounds, and the heavy door to my right pushes open.

There she is.

The last time I saw her, we were both home for Christmas. I took off enough time to spend the holidays in Miami and she was off between semesters. I've been close to her family for over a decade, so I'm not a guest in that house. When we weren't opening presents or toasting a new year with the only family I know, Tim and Annette were on their daughter's ass for her choice in friends, pathetic effort, and low grades. They usually have to reserve that shit for Sammie.

It seems tonight has been a long time in the making.

If her skirt were shorter, it'd be nonexistent. She might as well be wearing a bikini top with as much skin as she's showing. And the shoes she chose for the night prove to be a shit decision since they're dangling from her hand where she stands barefoot.

I can't imagine how she looked a few hours ago.

I mean, I can. She's almost twenty-one. It's impossible to not appreciate everything about her over the last couple of years. The person standing in front of me is no girl.

There's also nothing about her that shows she's ready for a good time now. Her makeup is smudged from tears, and her hair is a mess.

Fuck.

Boyd is right. She has lost her mind. The shit that could've happened to her tonight is not good. She's lucky she's standing here in one piece.

And that pisses me off.

But I don't have a chance to tell her any of that. The dried tears on her face aren't dry anymore when her expression screws up, and she comes straight for me.

She faceplants in my chest. Her arms wrap around my waist, and she holds tight as she cries, "I'm sorry. I'm so sorry. Thank you for coming for me."

I want to shake her and tell her how stupid she is, but I don't.

I can't.

If this were Sammie, I'd do that in a nanosecond.

But this is Teagan.

I wrap my arms around her and tip my face to the side of hers that's planted in my chest. "Let me get you out of here."

She nods against the old T-shirt I threw on when I got the call that woke me out of a dead sleep. When she looks up at me, her eyes are bloodshot, and her expression is a mix between terrified and relieved.

I hardly recognize her, and I don't fucking like it.

She says nothing but nods.

I keep her tucked under my arm and move for the door. The last place on earth Teagan Coleman belongs is the Orleans Parish Jail.

Teagan

THE BOND FOR LIFE, my ass.

Sorority sisters. I'm done with them. They swore the drive across the state line wasn't a big deal because they knew of a bar that would let us in no matter how bad our fake IDs were.

And mine is bad. So bad, this is only the second time I've had the nerve to try it. I was basically laughed at and sent on my way in my small college town the only other time I had the nerve to use it.

But they were right. We got in, but it had nothing to do with my fake ID. The bouncer barely glanced at it. He was too busy leering at me from top to bottom.

We had drinks. We were hit on. We danced. The bar was a dive and the whole place smelled. But once I had a few drinks, I didn't care.

Things were fine … until they weren't.

A good time and a warm buzz turned south in a heartbeat. The two sisters who pulled me into a new social scene I'm not used to over the last few months were on the dance floor with two guys. I was feeling light-headed and stayed back to hold the table.

That's when the fight broke out.

The moment the cops hit the door, everything turned to chaos.

I was in cuffs and my sorority sisters were nowhere in sight.

I'm on thin ice with my parents as it is for my grades. If they find out about tonight, they'll drag me back to Miami without a second thought.

My phone vibrates constantly on the vanity as I squeeze the water from my hair. Texts roll in from my so-called friends asking where I am and if I'm okay.

They didn't give a shit about me when they were doing everything they could to save their own asses.

Well, they can sit and wonder where I am until tomorrow. They weren't handcuffed, thrown in the back of a sticky police car, and held in a cell for over two hours.

My buzz burned off somewhere between worrying about what was so sticky on the bench of the cop car and wondering when I'd get to the fingerprinting and horrible picture part of the night.

But that never happened. The moment I heard Rocco's voice after I was given one phone call, I knew he'd come for me.

He was pissed, but I knew he'd come.

Maybe that's why I let them talk me into coming to New Orleans to do something so stupid.

And, quite honestly, dangerous.

I knew Rocco was close if I needed him.

I pull the big T-shirt over my head and roll the boxer shorts over twice so they stay up on me.

"I know you're done. You can't hide in there forever."

I look at myself in the foggy mirror. The moment we got back to Rocco's apartment after the silent car ride from the police station, he shoved clean clothes into my hands and ordered me to take a shower to wash away the filth.

I've never been so happy to follow someone's orders.

Rocco might've saved my ass tonight, but he's not patient. I owe him an explanation after he saved me.

When I open the door to the bathroom and flip off the light, the apartment is dim. A single lamp in the corner doesn't come close to flooding the space. Rocco stops his pacing in the middle of the room and crosses his arms. "What the hell were you thinking?"

I mirror his stance and cross my arms as I stand swallowed whole in his clothes. "I didn't set out to get arrested tonight. I'm not happy how the night ended either."

He cuts the distance between us in half. "The best thing that happened to you was getting arrested. It probably saved you from a worse fate. This is New Orleans, Teag, not your sleepy little college town. I don't need to spell this shit out for you, because I know you're not naïve, so don't act like it. It's not a good look on you. You're smarter than that."

I hug myself tighter. "I said I was sorry. I messed up, okay? It's not like you have an uncheckered past."

He narrows his eyes. "There's no comparison, and you know it. For one, you know better. And two, you have a fucking family who loves you. Hell, you have a whole tribe of people who aren't your family who love you. What is so hard about your life that you're willing to throw it all away for some shits and giggles in college, not to mention put yourself in danger the way you did tonight?"

I can't argue because we both know he's right. Everything he's saying is true. I can't justify it with any type of rationale, at least not that I can admit to him.

Or anyone else, for that matter.

"You're about to lose your scholarship, aren't you?"

I roll my eyes. "Great. Nothing is private. Who doesn't my mom talk to? It's not like I'm flunking my classes. I had a couple bad grades last semester. It dragged my GPA down. I can't be perfect all the time."

Rocco holds out a low hand. "There is a difference between perfection and what you did tonight. None of this is like you."

I bring my hands up to fist my wet hair. "My parents' expectations are bad enough. I can't take it from you too. I'm doing my best."

"Tonight was your best?"

Tears flood my eyes. I can't make them stop. As much as I want to be right here, I can't take it from him and whisper, "Please don't do this."

"Tell me what's wrong."

I shake my head.

His whole demeanor changes. It's like I didn't wake him from a sound sleep and make him pick me up from the police station. He's like he's always been with me—patient and sweet.

"You can talk to me, Teagan. You always have. Nothing has changed. If you need me, I'm here."

I huff out a ridiculous, exasperated laugh as I swipe my cheeks. "Yeah, I don't think that's going to happen."

He tips his head and shoots me the same smirk I've become obsessed with over the years. "Is that a challenge? Don't tell me there's something I can't do."

I shake my head. "Can and will are two very different things. I know better than anyone not to get them confused."

The smirk disappears. "It's me. Do you really think there's anything I wouldn't do for you?"

"Yes. I know without a doubt there's one thing you won't do for me." More like one line he won't cross, but I don't dare utter that aloud.

"You wound me," he utters.

The thing is, I think he's serious. He really will do almost anything for me.

I tell him the truth. "That's the last thing I'd ever want. You don't deserve that."

The little space remaining between us disappears. Just like earlier in the police station, I'm in his arms, but this time it's not me running to him. It's him pulling me there.

It's no different than the countless other times he's hugged me.

Saying hello...

Saying goodbye...

Or just being playful.

It feels good and hurts all at the same time.

And he has no clue how strong both feelings surge through me.

With one hand pressed to the middle of my back and the other on the side of my head, he drags a hand down my hair. "You're off. You have been for a while. If you don't want to talk to your parents, I get it. I don't even have parents, and I get it. But you have me."

I shake my head against his chest and wrap my arms around him. If I'm here, I might as well enjoy it. "Trust me, it would be a burden on you."

His hand on my head moves. I feel a tug on my hair. That little tug shouldn't excite me, but it does. My heart pounds as I clench my thighs, but it doesn't keep me from feeling the wetness it causes between my legs. And since I'm commando in Rocco's boxers, the feeling is more extreme than ever.

Especially since *ever* only lives out in my wildest dreams. This is very, very real.

He forces my head back, looks down into my eyes, and demands, "Tell me what's going on with you."

I fist his T-shirt at his lats as my heart skips a beat.

I lick my dry lips and swallow over the lump in my throat.

His gaze drops to my mouth before his eyes find mine.

A small frown touches his brow.

"Teagan." My name is a whisper on his lips, exactly the way I've fantasized.

This is too much.

I may never have this opportunity again.

Maybe it's the exhaustion or the drama of what happened at the bar or almost being arrested. I don't have time to think or contemplate the ramifications.

I don't think about anything other than what I've wanted since I was seventeen. Hell, maybe sixteen.

I'm sure it's never crossed Rocco's mind.

I surge to my toes and barely catch his shocked expression before my lips touch his.

Every muscle in his body tenses.

My kiss isn't epic or romantic or sexy. It involves no tongue or roaming hands. I'm nervous and awkward. It doesn't help that I don't have a willing participant.

But I did it.

I hold my uncomfortable kiss for as long as I can before his hold in my hair pulls me away.

I'm breathless when I open my eyes.

But Rocco isn't.

He's holding me close. His hand, which was light on my back just moments ago, is heavy and strong through the shirt. His breath is hot and heavy on my skin, warming me from the inside out.

And his eyes.

Those eyes that I've come to love—there's something new in them I've never seen before. They sear me through his gaze, roam my face, and settle on my awkward lips.

"Teagan." He bites my name on a warning.

"I..." I can't form words. I should apologize, but that would be wrong. I've never been less sorry for anything I've ever done.

I feel my skin flush from the neck up as heat floods me below the waist.

But before I can pretend that I had a seizure or was possessed by some horny demon, his grip on my hair tightens and my body becomes one with his.

And wow.

This experience couldn't be more different.

His mouth crashes to mine.

Lips.

Tongue.

Our teeth scrape in a way that I never imagined. Who knew that could be sexy?

When his thick arm wraps around my waist and lifts, that's when I realize my daydreams suck.

My legs wrap around his waist instinctively. And they've never done anything other than walk on instinct. I don't feel him move, but when my back slams against the wall, and he pins me with his hips, I wonder if I've died and gone to heaven.

I grip his neck to hold on and do everything I can to get the full experience. He tastes better than I imagined—he's stronger and more forceful. There's a desperation about Rocco Monroe I never knew existed.

And it's for me.

Talk about a one-eighty. An hour ago, I was in jail.

But the best part is what's going on below the waist. I have no trouble feeling all that is Rocco between my legs.

He's long, hard, bigger than I dreamed. His hand slides into the boxers and becomes one with my bare ass. When his fingers grip me, there's no doubt he feels how wet I am.

For him.

This is it.

Every dream I've ever had is going to come true, and all

because I was pseudo arrested for drinking underage with a fake ID.

When I sink down for the only friction my clit has ever had other than my own fingers, his groan vibrates on my tongue.

He presses his cock harder into my sex as his tongue delves deeper into my mouth.

Every nerve ending in my body is hyperaware. Our moans sound sharper. His scent smells sweeter. And he feels...

Like a fantasy.

But a fantasy is just that ... fictional.

When my cell dings from across the room with another text, everything stops.

We freeze.

One moment I'm living out my dreams, and the next, I'm dropped to my bare feet on the floor. I have no idea what I look like, but from the sight of Rocco, I can only imagine. His lips are swollen, he's breathing hard, and when I look down at his cock through athletic shorts, the evidence is clear that I'm not hallucinating.

"Teagan." My name is sharper than ever before on his tongue. I don't like it. It's not at all like it was a few moments ago when he sounded like he wanted to eat me up in one bite.

My gaze jumps from his erect cock to his piercing, angry eyes.

"Why did you stop?" I ask. If I sound desperate, it's because I am. It's the only thing in the universe I want the answer to.

"Why did you kiss me?" he growls.

"Because I wanted to." This is no time for games or lies. I tell him the truth. "I've wanted to for a very long time."

Like since before I got my driver's license, but I leave that part out.

He has nothing to say to my admission of pining after him for eons, but he does turn on his tennis shoe and begin to pace. He drags a hand down his face and mutters under his breath, "What the fuck did I do? I'm as good as dead."

"Wait, why?" I demand. "You didn't do anything. That was all me."

He turns to me and points to the spot on the wall that should be a shrine if I have anything to do with it and raises his voice. "That was not you. That was all me, dammit. You're Tim's daughter. Not only that, the baby. I am so fucked, I can feel it into next week."

I cross my arms to cover my hard nipples that are no doubt cutting through his T-shirt, because unlike him, I am not at all fucked and never have been. I was quite looking forward to the experience, too, but only with him. "No. It's fine."

He drags his hands through his hair and fists it on top of his head. After turning in a slow circle, he stops and glares at me. "This is the least fine thing I've ever done. And I've done some pretty bad shit."

I take a step back and hug myself tighter. "What are you saying?"

He stops and turns to me. "I'm saying that was a mistake. It was my fault, and it will never happen again."

"But—"

"Never," he bites and raises his voice. "I'll never allow it to happen again."

Tears burn my eyes and threaten to spill over. I bite the inside of my cheek to keep them from humiliating me one more time today. I move to my cell and ignore every text message coming in from my so-called friends and go straight to the Uber app.

"What are you doing?" he demands.

I shake my head and can't look at him. "I'm going home."

"You're not going anywhere," he states, as if he has any say about where I go.

"Thank you for getting me out of jail. I'm sorry about tonight.

You know, jail..." I wave my hand around and sniff, doing everything I can to keep it together. "This. But I know where I stand. I get it."

Rocco tries to get between me and the door. "It's the middle of the night. You can't leave."

I grab my heels that hurt my feet before we left the state of Mississippi and skirt around him. I don't worry about my clothes. I never want to see that outfit again, anyway.

I open the door and am down the stairs of his apartment building on bare feet even though he's hot on my heels. "You're not leaving. We need to talk about this."

Damn, how many times can a girl cry in one night. Maybe the shroud of darkness will hide my fresh tears. "No, no. You've said plenty."

"Teagan," he calls as he catches up. "Dammit, wait."

I check my app to see where the driver is. A mile. I guess it pays to be in a big city. There are maybe three Uber drivers in my small college town. It takes forever to get a ride.

I ignore Rocco and stare down at my phone, willing the driver to speed as I try to memorize how I felt right before I was rejected. I need to hang onto that feeling until I can get far, far away from Rocco.

I flinch when his hand touches my shoulder.

"Fuck," he whispers as he pulls his hand away. "Teagan, please. Come in and talk to me."

I'm forced to sniff back my tears but can't form words. I shake my head as headlights round the corner.

"You can't leave in the middle of the night and drive off with a stranger," he growls.

I swipe my face and look up at him. I'm past hiding my feelings or my hurt. "I'll take the chance. There's no way I can stay here."

The driver rolls down the passenger window and frowns at me. "Coleman?"

I nod and move for the back door. "Yes, that's me. It's a bit of a drive. Thank you for accepting it."

He frowns and looks between me and Rocco. "You okay, lady?"

"Stay. I'm begging you."

I look back to the driver. "I'll be fine. Please, just drive."

"Teagan," Rocco calls for me, but has no choice but to move when I slam and lock the door. The driver does as I ask and pulls away. Unlike my current statistics grade, I have an impeccable Uber score, after all.

"Mississippi, huh? You get in a fight with your boyfriend?"

"Not a boyfriend. That door has been nailed shut." My tears flow freely now as every painful memory sinks in to stain my soul. "But I will miss him with all my heart."

9
CONTROL

Rocco
Present time

I walk into the bar with my hand plastered to the small of Teagan's back. My fingertips press into the swell of her ass like they spend a great amount of time there on the normal even though this is new real estate for me.

When Robichaux texted the address for the meet, I had to do a double take. It's not what I expected from the lowlife who likes to diversify his income.

We're out of New Orleans proper, toward the lake and skirting the burbs. This isn't a place I would go on any Saturday night for a burger, but it's also not the worst joint in this area of town. Since we just did surveillance on Robichaux, my supervisor wasn't surprised when I put in an op plan, though he was surprised since I move in a couple days.

Unlike before, our tech group got involved. A special cell acts as my mic and tracking device. And since I'm here, we might as well harvest phone numbers. If Jules is hanging here, I guarantee there are others we need to look into. I might be on my way out of town, but Taylor was basically drooling when I filled him in on the latest developments of the case that will soon be his.

Teagan is more excited than a kid on Christmas morning, not that I'd know what that feels like. Those memories were not a thing in the house I grew up in. But they were for Teagan. Hell, she's an adult and nothing has changed since the first holiday I spent with the Colemans.

It's like she forgot how we woke up this morning. She's been nonstop chatter all day about the meeting. She doesn't give a shit that we're newly reunited and every memory that's been marinating under my skin like a simmering flame has all of a sudden burst into a four-alarm fire.

When we make our way through the crowded restaurant to the bar, I slide my hand to her hip and pull her front tight to my side. If I could cuff her to me, I would. I lean over the sticky surface and wave down the bartender.

He barely looks up at me from where he's pouring vodka into a highball. "You gotta wait your turn, buddy."

"I'm here to meet Jules." That gets his attention and focuses his gaze across the sticky bar, so I add, "*Buddy*."

"Name," he demands.

"Mack Crowder. He's expecting me."

He glares at me before turning to the side and lifting his chin to a waitress. "Go tell Jules he's got a visitor. See if he wants to take the meeting."

She wipes her hands on a rag and tosses it to the bar.

I look down at Teagan. We might not be in the worst part of town, but she looks oddly comfortable in her skin.

Older.

Confident.

Cunning.

Shit. I cannot think about her moving to New York.

The thought causes me to tighten my arm around her and dip my face into the loose waves she spent too much time perfecting when she took over my bathroom. "You okay?"

When she tips her face to mine, all I can think about is my threat to kiss her again. As if the memory of her for the last two years wasn't painful enough, now it's no longer a memory. The reality of Teagan standing here in my arms is a million times better.

Also, a million times more frustrating.

She's like a diamond being dangled in front of me, reminding me of her perfection and beauty, and my burning desire to obliterate every relationship that's more important to me than my own life.

Tim and Annette love me. I can say that with confidence.

Annette says it. Tim shows it.

But loving a stray because you're good people and loving that same stray for your youngest daughter are two very different things.

Teagan slides her hand up my abs, pec, and brings it to a stop over my heart as she shoots me a private smile. "I'm good."

Too good. I feel it plastered up against me, even if it is for show. There was nothing normal about my morning wood after sleeping next to her all night. Just the simple touch of her leg was too much.

The only reason I didn't jerk off in the shower was to prove to myself that I have the self-control to be this close to her and not cross the line.

Because crossing that line would be the easiest thing I've ever done.

You know, as soon as I convince her not to hate me.

The waitress breaks into my forbidden thoughts and talks more like we're meeting a Fortune 500 CEO rather than a man suspected of human trafficking. "Mr. Robichaux said he's expecting you. Follow me."

Too eager, Teagan shifts out of my hold, but I catch her hand and hold tight. The chatter of the bar becomes muted as we walk down a dark hallway and up a set of narrow stairs. Our footsteps echo off the old wood while the scent of stale alcohol and hints of smoke permeate the air.

Undercover hasn't been my thing since I moved here. I've done buys here and there, but there's something about me that criminals don't trust, which is fucked, since I was raised by them and skirted the line of becoming one myself.

The waitress knocks on the door at the top of the staircase. A few moments pass, but when it finally does, the hint of smoke is gone. When the door opens, we're hit by chatter and music through a cloudy room.

The three of us file in. As soon as I get a look around, the urge to get this shit done and get Teagan out of here overwhelms me.

Jules is sitting in a leather chair across the room from what looks like a high-stakes poker game. The waitress goes straight to him, runs her fingers across his neck, and says, "Can I get you anything, baby?"

His gaze hangs on her tits while his free hand runs up the inside of her thigh and disappears under her short skirt.

I think it's safe to say her number one job is not to serve drinks, which also confirms my suspicions that Robichaux dabbles in more than one crime.

He finally looks up at her and exhales a lungful of smoke. "Later, when the boys are done with the game."

She leans down and presses her lips to his temple.

He smacks her ass before she saunters back to the stairs.

I don't take my eyes off Jules even though my entire being is focused on the woman plastered to my side. She might've been good just a few moments ago, but this is not her scene.

Every ounce on her lean body is tense and glued to me.

That shouldn't give me this much satisfaction, but I can't help it. The asshole in me wants to tell her I told you so, and another part of me—one that I do not recognize—wants to throw her over my shoulder and get her the hell out of here.

"Sit down." Jules lifts his chin, motioning to the single chair across from him.

Teagan fists my shirt at my back to hold on, as if I'd let go.

We have a part to play, and I intend on winning a fucking Oscar.

I claim her hand again and do as Jules says. Before I lean back, I pull Teagan between my legs.

When her fine ass hits my thigh, I wrap an arm around her waist to pull her into me. It's so faint, I don't know whether I hear it or feel it, but she sucks in a surprised breath when her hip becomes one with my dick.

It's been two years. There's no way she could have forgotten. The time I had her pinned to the wall is burned on my brain, and my dick isn't interested in anyone but her.

It's been a long two years.

Normally I would claim that I'm unforgettable, but the fact is, the two of us together were pure fire. So much so, it's haunted me.

A memory to last a lifetime.

She's wearing cutoff shorts, a tight-ass tank, and a bra with more straps than seem necessary—and I know that because I can see every one of them. I've tried not to think about the new panties she's probably wearing, but the fact I bought every stitch she has on is more satisfying than I could've imagined.

I, on the other hand, decided to dress like I have more money than currently sits in my mediocre bank account. I'm in a crisp dress shirt and black dress pants, and I broke out the leather shoes Micah and Evie brought me straight from Italy when they were there last year on vacation. At the time, they seemed like the most useless gift on earth, but now I'm grateful.

I look older than I am, and she looks younger than she is. It's not lost on me that I probably fit in here better than I planned—a slick older man with a young girl.

I mean, fuck. I am older and she's younger even though she isn't a girl any longer.

I wrap my hand high on Teagan's thigh and settle my gaze on Jules. "I've got shit to do tonight that doesn't include this. Talk."

He takes a pull on his smoke and narrows his eyes on me. "You wanted to meet with me. Tell me what you wanna know. I'll decide what it'll cost ya."

When Teagan shifts in my lap, I feel it against my dick. I give her leg a squeeze so she'll keep her mouth shut. "I want to know where Heath Hayes is. And then I want to know how he got put on your radar in the first place."

"Those are big wants." He exhales two rings of smoke before tapping his ashes to the floor. "I wanna talk about something else first. I have no fucking idea who you are, and I know everyone. Why is that?"

I tip my head. "Because I'm new to town. Moved here to be with Stella. My business can be conducted from anywhere." I take the moment to shift my gaze to Teagan but continue talking to Jules. "Who can blame me, yeah?"

"No cunt is worth moving for," he drawls.

I shrug and reach for Teagan to pull her close enough for me to lean in and give her a slow kiss on the jaw before running my nose down the column of her neck. She goes taut as her breath shallows. When I lean back enough to look her in the eyes, hers are heavy. "Mine is."

Teagan's face flushes, but I don't have time to enjoy it. I need to get this done.

I turn back to Robichaux. "Nothing is too good or too much for

Stella. If she wants it, she's going to get it. Name your price. I'll make it happen."

"See, the thing is, this is a slippery slope. I'm gonna need you to make it worth my while. I'm not the only one at stake here. In fact, I don't own the information or whereabouts of Hayes anymore. I gave that up when I sold him to the next guy."

"Interesting." So he creates the contact, hooks them in, and sells the information—or in his words, the human. That adds another level to my investigation, but I also have it on record from the mouth of the trafficker. "I have a flight number I can start with. If I have to follow every breadcrumb from here to Nigeria, I will, but that doesn't mean I have that kind of time. Stella wants her grandfather back, and I'm determined to make that happen sooner rather than later so we can get on with our lives."

"That's gonna cost you some cash, Crowder. I just find 'em and sell 'em. I can't afford to piss off my clients."

"Please," Teagan pipes in. Her sweaty hand wraps around the top of mine that's still gripping her bare leg. "He's not well. We need to bring him home. Tell us what you want."

Jules hikes a brow and looks her up and down. "Oh, I know what I want."

My grip on Teagan tightens, and I growl, "A dollar amount, fuckwad. Stella is here because it's the only way you'd agree to meet with me."

"Possessive," he mutters. "Even more interesting."

"Wouldn't you be?" I throw back.

"The only thing I'm possessive about is cold, hard cash. Pussy can be replaced. If you want, I can prove how easily. You can have your pick of the litter."

I'm not sure how much more bullshit I've got in me to give. Bringing Teagan here was a mistake. No case is worth this, and definitely no stranger is worth it either. Not when I just got her back.

I feel my cell vibrate in my pocket. I have every notification on silent other than one. The only one that matters.

Phone numbers are captured and downloaded. We can get the hell out and hope that we can find Heath Hayes the old-school way. Nothing will make Taylor happier.

"I'm done." I put my hands to Teagan's slim waist and we both stand at the same time. "You know what we want and how to get hold of me. I'm willing to pay, but I'm also a busy man. Don't waste my time, Robichaux. It pisses me off."

Jules juts to his feet, dumps the butt of his smoke to the floor and twists the toe of his boot on it. "Twenty grand."

Teagan is smart enough not to gasp or agree and lets me negotiate. But she does fit herself to my side as she keeps her mouth shut.

"Fuck that," I bite. "I'm not asking you to fly him home in a private jet. I'm asking for a location. Five Gs."

For the first time since I laid eyes on him, Jules actually smiles and huffs a laugh. "You don't fucking know who I am."

"Everyone knows who you are," I spit. "But handing over a location on the globe is easy shit. Take the cash and move on."

He crosses his arms and is lasered in on me now. "You're right. Everyone knows who I am. Why is it that no one in my circle knows who you are? I've asked around."

The cell vibrates again. Teagan feels it too since it's sandwiched between us.

I need to get this shit done. "Open your eyes, Robichaux. You think a lot of yourself, but your circle is not that big."

A commotion comes from behind me. Someone just won big, and someone else just lost bigger. Everyone wants to know when the girls will be back so the party can move to the next level.

If I've ever had a cue to exit, it would be that.

Jules rolls his eyes at the poker table. All of a sudden, he looks like he wants to wrap this up as much as I do. "Ten. That's my last offer. You put up the cash, I'll tell you where your woman's pawpaw is. Take it or leave it. I don't want to ever see you again."

I lift my chin. "You'll hear from me tomorrow with a time and address. I'll have your cash."

"Get out," Jules demands.

As if he'll get an argument from me.

I turn Teagan, and we head for the door. She never lets go of me. When we make our way through the crowded bar and hit the front door, fresh air has never tasted so good, which is fucked because that doesn't come close to the tensest situation I've ever been in.

I shift Teagan to my other side and grasp her hand so I can get to my cell. She has to double time it to keep up with me but stays close.

"Ten thousand dollars?" she hisses. "How are we going to come up with that amount of money?"

"Not now," I order in a low voice.

Taylor answers on the first ring. "We've got eyes on you. You're good. No one's following yet. But we're curious how you're going to get the boss to fork over ten K for something that isn't a drug buy."

I look around and pull Teagan into a mass of people who were waiting on traffic to cross the street. "I've got a plan. Just make sure we're not being followed."

"You're good," Taylor says. "I've got two cars ready to follow you. Take the long way home just to be sure. We'll meet first thing in the morning. I can't wait to see how you're going to talk the boss into this."

"I'm not worried," I lie and disconnect the call without saying goodbye. Teagan picks up her pace as we cross to my car.

I beep the locks and open the passenger door for her, but she doesn't get in. She turns to me. "Is everything okay?"

Is everything okay?

No. Very little is okay at the moment.

Control is something I value and pride myself on, because I had to work fucking hard to change back in the day.

I've had no issue keeping my shit tight until it comes to the woman standing in front of me.

And that pisses me off.

I put a hand to the hood of the car and lean in to get in her face. "Let's see... I've got to figure out how to convince my boss to assign ten K in cash in exchange for the location of a man he didn't know about before I submitted the op plan for the little party we just attended. I move in a few days, you graduate the day after that, and this case isn't going anywhere fast. But really the kicker in all this is I just took Tim Coleman's daughter on an undercover operation to meet with a man who looked at you like you were a juicy steak. I respect your father. The fact that I can't say no to you is a problem I need to get under wraps. I'm not even going to get into the other shit that's wrong, the first being that you're moving to fucking New York. So, no, Teagan. Everything is not okay."

Her dark eyes widen as she stares up at me.

I lean in farther, there's barely a breath between us. Her tits rise and fall in quick succession way too close to me. The hairline crack in my control just splintered a hair farther.

I lean in and put my lips to her ear. "So help me, if you don't get in the damn car so I can get you the fuck out of here, I will not be held responsible for my actions."

She puts a hand to my dress shirt and fists it to push me back far enough to look at me but close enough that our noses brush. Instead of being freaked the fuck out by the undercover meeting I just took her into, her expression is down-right smug. "I'm not who I used to be. If I looked or acted scared in there, it's because I was playing the part. That was exciting, and we're one step closer to finding out where Heath is. So don't make threats you're not willing to follow up on, Rocco. I might just call you on them."

Ever so slowly, she casually sits her fine ass in my car. As I slam the door and stalk to the driver's side, it's impossible not to think about it pinked from my hand while still wearing the panties I bought her.

Control.

I don't even recognize that word anymore.

10

VAGINA STATS

Rocco

"Let me get this straight. Tomorrow is your last day in the New Orleans Division, and you want me to allot ten grand for you to find out the location of an old man who the State Department doesn't give a shit about?"

"That's right," I answer with conviction even though I'm not at all confident. "I've got the proof from harvesting numbers last night Robichaux is connected to no fewer than eight of the biggest targets on active cases in the division. This guy might not be moving product, but he's a part of the pipeline in a big way. Taylor is writing the wires as we speak since he'll take over the local part of the case, but I plan to follow the trail from Miami. This is good shit. Or it could be, but we won't know if we don't try, and this is my way of continuing the communication with him."

"You could've just coasted out of town." He drags a hand down his face. "Fine. I'll put the order in. This had better lead to something. Monroe, Tim Coleman fought hard to get you to Miami. I hope he knows you're twenty percent pain in the ass along with being a hard worker."

"I'm sure he'll figure it out soon enough," I mutter, since there's a fifty-fifty chance he'll find out eventually what Teagan is up to and that I am aiding her, even if it is only to keep her safe. "Now that you know where Robichaux hangs, I have a good feeling this will pad your stats for months to come."

"It better." He slaps me on the shoulder. "I'll miss you, Roc. Send me that op plan before you make the drop."

"Will do." I wait until he's down the hall and out of earshot before I turn to Taylor. "I've got to get home. Teagan is still there. I threatened her within an inch of her life not to leave."

"Dude." He pauses and looks around. "Tell me your cold spell is over."

I frown. "Just because I don't announce every detail of my personal life doesn't mean I've had a cold spell."

"You work circles around everyone. And don't give me that shit that you're pressured into making a name for yourself. You're friends with the biggest wigs in the DEA. You're even going to work under their wings so their greatness can either rub off on you or you can ride their coattails. I get it. I respect it. I'd do the same thing if I were friends with Cruz, Emmett, and Jennings. They're the shit."

It's everything I can do not to roll my eyes. "That's my plan."

The DEA is not a small organization, but I swear I can't turn around without anyone throwing it in my face that I'm tight with the fab three of Miami. Brax, Micah, and King have made names for themselves in career-making cases.

And they've made it no secret that I'm their little project.

They visited me in the academy.

They attended my graduation.

They've been to New Orleans more times than I can count since I started my time here three years ago. Whenever they do, they find reasons to visit the office. I'm basically the golden retriever in their fictional family.

But I'm no pet and riding coattails isn't my jam. If anyone in this world has something to prove, it's me.

More like I have to prove what I'm not. I have the scar to remind me day in and day out.

The thing is everyone knows I'm tight with the Miami clan. What they don't know is they're all I have. And Taylor doesn't know that I've known Teagan since she was eleven. She was right when she said I was emotionally unattached back then.

I gave that shit new meaning, and the Colemans gave me a family.

And for that reason alone, I will not be *hitting* Teagan, even though the thought has eaten away at me for the last two years. It's gnawed away so long, Taylor was spot on about a cold spell. There's been no one since my first kiss with Tim Coleman's daughter.

I look up at him. "Good luck with the paperwork. This could be your breakout case. I can say I knew you when. I'll contact Robichaux and set up a meet. Let me know if you need anything else."

Taylor gives me a shove on the shoulder. "Go get her, Romeo."

"Fuck you," I mutter.

His grin spreads across his face. "No, fuck her."

With two days left in New Orleans, I don't need the drama of an OPR investigation, so I choose not to punch him in the face.

Look at me ... in control. It doesn't seem to be an issue with anyone but Teagan.

My cell vibrates in my pocket, and when I look at it, I know it won't be a short conversation no matter how hard I try to make it one. But this is my chance to escape a conversation with Taylor about Teagan.

Even if it is with a phone call from her father.

Karma is hitting me from every direction.

I look to Taylor before I leave. "I've got to take this. See you later."

The moment I connect the call, Taylor yells, "Good luck!"

"Good luck with what?" Tim asks in lieu of a greeting.

"The move," I lie. "Just wrapping things up before I head out of town."

"Gotcha. About that. I need a favor." He sounds busy and distracted, which he should be. He manages five enforcement groups.

"Seeing as how you pushed my transfer through to get back to Miami, I owe you."

"You'll never owe me for that, but Annette and I are in a predicament. Sammie is ... well, she's always been an energy suck. You know this. But she's single and dilated to an eight."

Again with the vagina stats. It's like Saturday morning Game Day during football season. This can't be normal.

I try to keep the wince out of my tone. "Yeah, I heard."

"And Teagan graduates this weekend," he adds. "FYI ... doesn't matter how old your kids are, they can still be needy as fuck."

"I'll keep that in mind," I mutter as I push out the door and head to my car.

"We don't want to be away from Sammie for long. I've got a flight in and out just long enough for us to see Teagan walk across the stage. Annette is too busy fussing around Sammie and spending money on baby clothes to worry about details, so I told her I'd call you. I know you're heading south anyway. We need you to help Teagan get loaded up and follow her so she's not on the road by herself."

I start my car and crank up the AC. What I want to say is that Teagan has no problem flying solo when doing sketchy shit, no matter how bad of an idea it is.

When I don't answer, he adds, "You know Teag. She hardly has anything. Her studio apartment came furnished. Everything she has should fit in her car.

Her car with no windows, but that's beyond the point.

"Look, I know you two aren't close like you used to be. If it's a problem, I can ask Micah if he can fly up and do it—"

I stop him right there. "Sorry, I got distracted. You know I'll do it. I planned on going to her graduation anyway."

It's his turn to pause. "We didn't know you'd be there."

"I wouldn't miss it. I even got her a graduation gift." I'm forced to adjust my junk when I think about her rainbow of panties. "And we're both headed to Miami, anyway. Might as well caravan."

What I don't add is that she'll have to pack for a second time since her shit was tossed two nights ago.

Do I feel guilty keeping everything that's happened in the last few days from Tim?

Hell, yes.

I feel like a teenager, digging myself in deeper every minute I don't fess up to the parents.

But at this point, Teagan and I are in this together, even though I'm the one aiding and abetting Tim and Annette's youngest child and taking her on undercover deals.

My only defense is that she started it, which makes me sound like a crabby pre-teen. Not to mention I'm getting more and more comfortable touching his daughter in ways that would make him lose his shit.

On the bright side, I can keep her under my thumb with the full permission of Tim Coleman.

In fact, it was his idea.

Even better.

"You can count on me," I say. "I'll make sure she gets home safe."

Tim lets out a sigh of relief. "I knew I could count on you. Can't wait to have you home, Roc."

"Me too."

"Your room is ready for you. Annette insisted on holding off making it into a nursery until after you close on your house. Teagan doesn't have to be in New York for a few weeks. I'm still pissed about that. But it'll be like old times. You know, with the addition of a grandbaby."

Like old times, my ass. It's been years since I've been back to the Colemans with their whole family. Teagan was barely eighteen.

"I feel bad about that. Brax and Landyn are bursting at the seams with my godchild on the way. I'm sure I can bunk at King and Goldie's or Micah and Evie's. They've got extra room."

"Not unless you want to hurt Annette's feelings. She's emotional enough with the baby on the way. I wouldn't recommend crossing her right now."

Even better. Teagan won't have a chance to avoid me if I'm sleeping across the hall from her.

Even though we haven't slept that far apart the last few nights. My back is a fucking pretzel to prove it. We had a repeat of the night before on the sofa.

She didn't ask me why I didn't go to my room, and I didn't think about why I refused to go to bed and leave her the whole sofa.

My actions and intentions are in a civil war at the moment.

"I guess we'll see you at graduation. Appreciate you. Here's to new beginnings," he says.

"New beginnings," I agree as I reverse out of my parking spot as another call comes across the line.

Speak of the woman who's testing my control.

"I've got another call. Tell Annette and Sammie hi for me."

"Will do."

Tim barely has time to say goodbye when I click over. "Please tell me you haven't run away while I was gone."

"What are you going to do if I did?" There's a smile in her tone that reminds me of times when she didn't hate me.

"I'd have no choice but to chase you down." I don't add that I'd do it with permission from her father since I've been tasked to keep an eye on her.

"I have good news." She moves the conversation on, so I assume she's not on the run.

"You found Heath Hayes and are saving me from having to meet Robichaux again?"

"Hardly. Uncle Sam is going to have to pay up for that one. My car has windows! I can pick it up anytime!"

"That's good since we need to get you back to school to walk across the stage."

"There's no we, Roc. I'm going home as soon as you pay Jules. I need to clean up my apartment and pack."

"You're not going back there by yourself. I'm coming with you. I just got off the phone with your dad. He asked me to chaperone your way home to Miami. Looks like you're stuck with me a while longer."

"Of course he did," she mutters. "I have two days until graduation, and I need to be out of my apartment the next day."

"Then the timing is perfect since I have to be out of mine before then. I already promised your parents. They're stressed enough about Sammie as it is. And, honest to God, does she know your parents are updating the entire world on the size of her vagina?"

There's a pause over the line before she says, "You know, now that I think about it, it is sort of weird."

"The baby's coming, it's not coming—that's all I need to know. And don't call me emotionally stunted or unattached. I'm completely in tune with my feelings."

"Whatever. I'm just happy my car is done. If it weren't for my mom insisting I walk for graduation, I'd go straight to Miami. I want to get back before the baby comes."

"Despite the fact I know the size of your sister's vagina, I still have no clue when that might be."

"Again, it's her cervix. You need to brush up on the female anatomy."

"I can promise you, I do not need lessons on the female body."

She laughs.

I actually made Teagan Mariana Coleman laugh.

I can't remember the last time that happened. It used to be a normal occurrence. One I took for granted. Now that it happened again, I had no idea how much I missed it.

I pull in a deep breath and decide she needs to know. "Missed that, Teag."

She's banging around doing who knows what in my apartment. I don't give a shit because I have nothing tangible in the world that means anything to me. But when she answers, there's an echo of a smile in her tone. "Yeah? What's that, Roc?"

As opposed to hers, my tone is sober. "Your laugh. Almost forgot what it sounded like."

It's her turn to sober, or at least that's what it sounds like. The banging stops too.

"You didn't run away, did you?" I ask.

"No," she whispers. "I'm here."

"Good. I'll be home soon. What are you hungry for?"

I know what I'm hungry for. Yesterday at this time, I wasn't willing to admit it.

"You've fed me the last two nights. But I've been going through your kitchen—there's nothing here even if I wanted to cook for you. I'll buy dinner tonight."

"You're not buying me dinner. Tell me what you want."

She sighs. "Okay, thank you. You know I'm not picky."

I flip my blinker fast and change lanes, making a last-second decision. "It usually takes a few hours to process that much cash for an undercover buy. We'll eat and play the rest of the night by ear."

"And get my car," she adds.

"I just got you back. You're so anxious to leave," I say as I pull into the parking lot of my favorite restaurant.

"I'm just..." Her thought trails off. All of a sudden, she sounds exhausted. "I don't know what I am these days."

"Whatever it is, you'd better be hungry. I'll see you soon."

"Mmm, a surprise," she hums. "You know I don't like surprises."

"Touché. I felt the same way when you showed up to meet with Robichaux."

"The surprise of the year," she notes.

I turn off my car, grab my cell, and climb out. "Teagan, you might as well be the surprise of a lifetime. If you keep this up, it won't be good for my heart."

"I'll, ah, see you soon?"

"Soon," I confirm.

"Oh, Rocco?"

"For someone who didn't talk to me for almost two years, you're chatty on the phone. I like it."

"I was just going to ask for beignets—if they have them at your mystery restaurant."

"Thanks a lot. I've known you for half your life. I know what you like. You just ruined the surprise."

She doesn't sound the least bit sorry she ruined anything. "I can't wait. See you soon."

I end the call and as soon as I open the door, the old woman greets me by name. "Rocco! I thought you were moving to Miami!"

"I couldn't leave without having your gumbo one more time."

She beams. "The usual then?"

I stuff my hands in my pockets as she takes my order. "Yes, but double it. And I need a box of beignets."

"Look at you," she exclaims. "Gonna go out with a bang, aren't ya? Lemme go box those up for ya. Be right back."

That makes me think of the fuse that's flickered too many times in the last couple days. If I tiptoe closer to the line of no return, it'll explode with a bang. And it won't have to do with gumbo or baked goods.

And as the moments click on, I care less and less that she's off limits to me.

11

GOTH GIRLFRIEND

Rocco

"Your last hurrah in NOLA. You good to go?" Taylor asks.

I look into my rearview mirror to straighten my collar. "I'm ready to get this shit done. Can you hear my mic?"

"Loud and clear." Taylor is in the tech van on the next block. More agents are on standby in case this goes to hell. But every muscle in my body isn't tense tonight like they were last night.

Teagan is nowhere in sight.

It took about two minutes for her to realize she didn't have a choice. By the end of the night, I'll have the information she's looking for whether she's there or not. This is my last-ditch effort to explain to Tim that I did everything I could to protect his daughter. The way this case is turning out, he'll know about it sooner rather than later since he'll be my supervisor soon.

I might've taken her in with me once, but not twice.

I'm counting on that to save my ass.

Not that he doesn't know what Teagan will do for a living

when she gets to New York. But being an investigative journalist is very different from going undercover with someone like Jules Robichaux.

When Tim and Annette find out, they'll never sleep again.

When I texted Robichaux when and where to meet me, he didn't like my location and said the deal was off unless he called the shots. This wasn't unexpected, but it did require a new op plan for backup.

So here we are, only a mile from the bar where we met last night, though this isn't a restaurant or a high stakes card game.

This is a warehouse.

Nothing good goes down in a warehouse. I've got the scar and six years under my belt in law enforcement to prove it.

"I'm going in."

"See you on the other side, dude," Taylor says.

"No need to be morbid, asshole," I mutter.

"Shit," Taylor bites. "I didn't mean *that* other side. You know what I mean."

"Just watch my ass," I say.

"Dude, we've got you."

I disconnect the call from my Bluetooth, kill the engine, and grab the bag of money.

It's Friday night. Teagan and I didn't even get to the beignets when Jules got back with me. She vowed to wait for me and then wrapped her arms around me in an embrace that lasted longer than it should have and made me promise her I'd be careful.

I jog up the steps in another business casual outfit. I'm glad this shit will be done soon. I'm running out of clothes nice enough to play the part of Mack Crowder much longer.

I bang on the door three times.

Unlike last night, they don't make me wait. Two men stand behind the open door.

The short, stocky one lifts his chin. "Crowder?"

"That's me," I confirm.

"Get in." Once I step into the dim and dusty building, the door slams behind me. "Gonna need to frisk you, man."

I don't let go of the bag, but I do hold my arms up. The tall lanky one pats me down. Even though all I have is a cell that's secretly my location and ears, he does a shit job and would be fired if he worked in the jail.

"My-my! He really showed." I look over and Jules comes out of the small office to the left. "You've got balls, man. We were taking bets."

"He's clear," the tall one announces.

Jules looks surprised. "You're not packin'?"

I lower my arms and grip the money bag. "You've been a man of your word so far. I have people who know where I am. There's no reason for me to fuck with you."

Jules cocks his head and his cheek twitches. "I don't know anyone who wouldn't come in here packin'."

"I'd tell you to expand your horizons, but that's none of my business, and I'm not up for talking. Tell me where Heath Hayes is, and I'll hand over your money."

He motions to the bag. "Open it. I need to make sure you're not trying to fuck me over."

My stare is heavy and never shifts from him. "You think I'm going to walk in here surrounded by your people and try to fuck you over?"

"Open it," he stresses.

I rip the zipper open and spread the bag to prove I came with actual cash. The short guy reaches for the bag, but I'm quicker and put a hand out low to stop him. "What the fuck kind of deal is this? I've got your payment. Give me the information, and it's yours."

Jules crosses his arms and rocks back on his heels. "She must be the sweetest pussy in the land. No one I know would do this."

"She is," I confirm. Hell, I don't know that for a fact, but in my most erotic imagination she is. My thoughts run wild when it comes to Teagan. "Consider me whipped."

"I'll say," he drawls. "Have you even met her pawpaw?"

"Nope," I tell the truth. The more truths I can tell, the more I can keep my story straight. "He disappeared before I moved here. I know he's old, has health issues, and Stella wants him home. Is this an interrogation or a deal for money?"

"Trying to see if I trust you as far as I can throw you."

The lanky guy laughs.

I do not.

I don't take my eyes off Jules. "Are you backing out of our deal? If so, I'll take my money somewhere else."

Jules scoffs. "Fuck, man. You're standing unarmed, surrounded in a dark warehouse by men who are very fucking armed, and you're carrying ten Gs. You're desperate enough to be here. You've got no one else to turn to."

I shrug like it's no skin off my back, which it fucking is. I've had my skin burned off once. It's damn important to me. "I've got the name of the travel agent who booked his ticket. I've got airport security in Nigeria that has footage of him deplaning. And I've got a hotel in Mozambique confirming he was there the day before he disappeared. Guess how far the US dollar goes in Africa? A long fucking way. But you're my fastest option. This is your last chance. Do you want my money, or should I take it elsewhere?"

He narrows his eyes and massages his jaw like he's contemplating his choices.

"Your call," I demand. "I don't have all night."

He must have thought he was my only option. I mean, it's not like my supervisor is going to approve an op plan in Mozambique, so he is my only game in town at this point.

But he doesn't know that.

Finally, the thought of me giving the money to someone else must be too much for him. "The old man is in Nigeria."

"Don't fuck with me, Robichaux. I know his plane landed in Nigeria. Where exactly is he in Nigeria."

"Last I heard, prison," Jules says with a tip of his head like he delivers this news all the time. "He got caught."

I narrow my eyes. "Caught doing what?"

He looks at me like I'm the idiot in the room. "What do you think? Transporting product. Sometimes they get through, sometimes they don't. He fell into the wrong category."

I'm here and plan on getting my ten grand worth. "You paid Hayes to mule drugs for you?"

"Nah, man. I don't work that shit over there. I make the contacts here and sell the information. I did my job. Not my fault he got caught."

From what Teagan told me and listening to Stella, I cannot imagine this old man went out on his own to look to make money transporting drugs.

"How did you find him?" I ask.

Jules throws his arms out like he's exhausted. "I told you where he was. That was the deal. If you don't hand over the money, my guys will take it. Because you haven't tried to fuck me over, I'm going to do you a favor and suggest you do that because you don't want to experience the other."

"How did you meet him?" I push.

This time both the skinny and the stocky guys close in at the same time.

"Fuck, man, do I look like I'm out networking? I don't meet people. I pursue them."

"Then what made Heath a target?" I demand. "Answer me, and I'll toss the bag."

I'm not worried. Jules doesn't look frustrated, he looks bored. "You know what happens when people can't pay their taxes? They get desperate. Hell, the older they get, the more desperate they are. The older they are, the riper the target. You're from out of town, but it pays to be local. I've got friends, everywhere across the south—even the Parish Tax Office. Now, toss the money, or else be prepared to have your shit tossed."

And there it is. I knew Jules Robichaux was no ordinary dealer.

It all fits. He's preying on the elderly. And from what Teagan said, Heath had a lien on his property and was about to lose everything. He was desperate.

I know where Heath is. Jules is tied to drug mules, and he revealed his pipeline. Once I uncover his contact at the tax office, I can go from there. There's no way I can ask who he sold Heath's information to without looking like this is an interrogation.

I'm about to toss the bag to Jules when the sound of a switchblade sounds from my side.

Stocky boy thinks he's tough.

I don't take my eyes off him. "Settle down, man. I was about to toss the money."

"You're asking too many questions," the guy grits.

"I'm asking the same questions he knew were coming." I played football long enough, tossing the money to Jules without taking my eyes off the knife is easy. Jules must not have played sports, because he misses the bag when it hits him dead in the chest and has to scramble to pick it up off the floor. "There's no need to be dramatic. Put the fucking knife away."

He doesn't put it away. He flips it around and around, showing off a dumb-ass, useless skill.

"Call off your dog, Robichaux," I demand. "We both fulfilled our sides of the deal. I'll go, and you'll never have to see me again."

"Not so fast," Jules mutters as he flips through the money. "I helped you. I want to know how you can help me."

I shake my head. "We don't run in the same circles. You got

your cash, and I got what I need to help Stella. There's nothing else we have in common."

"I don't know about that." Jules zips the bag and lets it drop to his feet. He kicks it behind him, as if I'm going to lunge for the cash that a drug dog would hit all day, every day. Who knows, they might just get that opportunity ... if I ever get out of here. He focuses his gaze back on me. "You know about me. I know about you. You know what they say, keep your friends close and enemies under lock and key."

I shrug and start to wonder if I'm going to have trouble getting my ass out of here. "I'm neither to you. We had a business transaction. I don't give a shit what you do after today. I got what I wanted and appreciate the information. Enjoy your money."

I turn for the door, but the skinny guy steps in my path.

"What now?" I ask, as if I'm as bored as Jules was a few moments ago. I could take both these guys if a gun weren't in play. The knife depends on their skills, which I doubt there are many with these two.

The skinny guy tips his head behind me. "Mr. Robichaux has one last message for you."

I turn to the side and look over at Jules. Having my back to anyone right now is a bad fucking idea.

Jules takes another step toward me. "I need insurance."

"I don't sell insurance. Call Jake," I deadpan.

Jules is not amused. "I don't like funny guys."

"And I don't like to be held against my will. I told you, my people know exactly where I am. I might not sell insurance, but my name holds power in circles bigger than yours. If I don't report in soon, they'll be here to get me." I look down at my watch. "In fact, you're almost out of time."

Robichaux's jaw goes tense as his cheek muscle jumps.

My head jerks when the switchblade clinks and clangs—metal on metal.

"Do you understand what'll happen if this comes back to bite me in the ass, Crowder? I don't give a fuck who you have at your back. They won't find you if you cross me. There are so many places in New Orleans to get rid of a body." He pauses and looks beyond me to the guy with the knife. "Maybe we should just do it now. Sweet Stella would be back on the market."

The hair rises on the back of my neck at the mention of Teagan. It doesn't matter how much I know I should keep my cool. I can't keep my mouth shut. "If you think I won't come for you, you have no fucking clue who you're dealing with. You'll never touch her."

When Jules lifts his chin a mere centimeter, my mouth turns to cotton.

I hear it before I see it.

A shuffle at my back.

I whip around.

He's lunging at me, the knife angled straight for my neck.

"Fuck." The word barely slips through my lips when I put an arm up and dodge to the right.

I was an all-state receiver before I dropped out of high school.

I played D-1 for four years. Granted, it was a small D-1.

But I've got three inches and at least thirty pounds on this guy.

He might not be fast, but he's not slow. The blade grazes my arm. I grip his wrist and twist.

He cries out in pain when his arm is pinched up his back in a way God did not intend. I slam his face into the wall.

"Drop it," I growl at the same time I feel hands on me from behind.

Fingers squeeze around my neck like a noose.

I gasp for air

I keep hold of the guy's hand with the knife and let go with the other. I swing my elbow back and hear the crack the moment I connect with his jaw, but he holds tight.

I do it again.

And again.

Just when I think I'm going to have to focus on the guy behind me so I can breathe, I swing my arm around. He howls and lets go immediately.

I've been in tight situations before, but never one where oxygen felt like a gift.

I rip the knife from his hand and push him to the floor with his friend, who's writhing in pain. Blood is seeping from his face where he's holding his eye.

I thought that felt like an eye socket.

Jules Robichaux is standing there watching the whole thing like this is his favorite spectator sport.

It probably is.

His arms are crossed, and he's wearing a smirk on his ugly mug. He unfolds his arms and starts to slow clap. "If I didn't know better, I'd think you were trained."

I back up to the door, and for the first time, feel the pain in my arm.

Exactly where I wear the scar to remind me of what I could've been.

"If you consider the school of hard knocks training, then yeah. Don't fuck with me, Robichaux. You'll get it back ten-fold if you do."

He drops his arms to his sides and loses the smirk. "You're the one who needed me, fuckwad. Tonight was my JV squad. This is a taste of what you'll get if I get blow back from working with you. Get the fuck outta my building."

That's something I don't need an invitation to do.

I don't take my eyes off him or the incompetent assholes he calls the JV. I put my hand to the door and push it open.

I check my surroundings, but don't waste any time. My phone is going crazy, and I don't hesitate when two cars I recognize drive by. It's Taylor and another agent. They must see me, because they hit the gas and speed by.

That lasted longer than I planned. They didn't wait for the code word. I've never needed it. Hell, I wasn't close tonight.

Once I cut the figurative noose off my neck.

Taylor doesn't waste any time. I'm in my car and speeding out of the warehouse district that's seen better days when my phone rings over the Bluetooth.

I connect the call as I check my rearview mirror.

"Did you hear a code word?" I bite.

"Dude, you went silent for way too long. You know I get antsy. The code word is not a hard and fast rule. It's a stop sign in a parking lot. That shit is just a suggestion. We were about to come in and get you."

"The code word is a code word for a reason," I grit. "I assume you got all that. They're international mules. You're welcome. I'm definitely handing you this case on a silver platter."

"Africa. I think I need to go over there to personally investigate. You think I can scam Uncle Sam out of a work trip? I've always wanted to go on a safari."

I take a quick left. "That was definitely my last hurrah in NOLA."

"You did it up big, my man. You coming to the office or handing me the reins now?"

As I merge onto the interstate, the pain starts to seep in. I hold my arm up the way I've done so many times since I got this damn scar when I was eighteen years old.

That feels like a lifetime ago. Hell, that feels like an alternate universe.

I ditched the sport coat tonight and am only in a light blue dress shirt, so there's no missing it.

Blood.

I don't think he got me deep, but the cut in my shirt is at least eight inches.

"Fuck," I mutter and press my forearm to my chest to stop the bleeding.

"You okay?" Taylor asks. "I know you're going to miss me, but it'll be okay. We always have FaceTime."

"I'm going home." It's close to midnight. I need to see how bad this cut is and maybe sleep a few hours before I have to deal with the next drama that seems to be nonstop since Teagan barged back into my life.

Technically, I barged into hers. She'll thank me someday.

"Did you lose your glass slipper running out of that warehouse? Don't turn into a pumpkin, princess. We'll talk tomorrow."

"I feel sorry for your next partner," I mutter.

"Cut me some slack. You're going to replace me with Brax fucking Cruz. How do you think I feel right now? I'm like the goth girlfriend you dumped for Miss America."

It's all I can do to keep the wince out of my words. "Wait until Brax hears that you called him Miss America."

"No-no-no," he whispers. "Don't fucking do that to me. It was a metaphor. Please. I need the king to like me in case I ever need a favor. I mean, I guess there's the actual King, as in Jennings, but you know what I mean. You're going to be the godfather to his kid. You're my only connection to the fab three."

I glance down at my arm and decide I don't have time for this shit. The bleeding hasn't let up. This night will never end if I have to get stitches.

"I'll touch base tomorrow, Tay-Tay."

"Ah. See there? Now I know we're all good. Enjoy your beauty sleep."

Sleep, my ass. The war between needing a good night's sleep and the desire to touch Teagan is raging inside me.

And I really fucking love my sleep, so that's saying something. I guess we'll see which one is the victor when I get home. That's if I don't bleed out.

12

GOOD GROVEL

Rocco

The moment I push through the door, Teagan's face lights up. "You're home!"

Until she sees the blood.

It's hard to miss. I'm covered in it.

Her expression turns to horror.

I barely have time to shut the door when she rushes to me. "You're bleeding!"

I start to unbutton my shirt. "Jules decided to make a point. One of his guys caught me with a knife."

She gently pushes my hands away and takes over, yanking my shirt from my trousers before finishing the buttons. When the tips of her fingers drag across my chest to push the shirt away, I almost don't feel the slice in my arm.

Almost.

She gasps. "Roc, it's through your scar."

She drops my bloody shirt at our feet. Normally, I'd be pissed if I got a blood stain on the floor two days before I move out and lose my deposit, but right now I don't give a shit.

Teagan turns my arm in her hands, and we both get a good look at it for the first time.

I look on the bright side. "At least it's not gushing anymore. I'll bandage it up. It'll be fine."

Her deep dark eyes are wide when they angle to me. "We need to go to the hospital. Surely this needs more than a bandage."

I shake my head. "I know you're graduating this weekend, but not with a medical degree. I've got some butterfly bandages somewhere. It'll be fine."

She looks from me to my arm. "It will scar worse if you don't get it stitched."

"Look where it's at, Teag. Do you think my arm could look worse than it already does?"

"It's my fault," she whispers before looking up at me.

I do what I've done so many times since I've become a stray in the Coleman family. I reach up and yank the end of her hair.

Even though I want to do so much more.

I shake my head. "Don't say that."

"It is." She raises her voice and tears fill her dark eyes. "You'll have another scar ... because of me."

I shrug my bare shoulder. "A scar on a scar. At least it's nowhere else, right? What does it matter anyway?"

"Don't do that. You act like this when it comes to you. You always have, and I've always hated it. It very much matters, Roc. Especially because it's you."

I pull my arm out of her hands and move toward the bathroom. "It's late. Help me find something to clean this up with."

Teagan takes charge and rips open the box labeled *bathroom* while I drench a towel and start cleaning myself up. It's long but only deep in one area. I run it under the water and hope for the best.

"I found ointment and some bandages. Damn, the packers just threw stuff in here. They could've been more organized when they boxed your things."

"Probably because it wasn't organized before they packed it. You know me."

"I still think you need stitches. But this should get you by until tomorrow." She moves into my small bathroom. "There's no way you can do it with one hand. Do you think it's clean?"

I grab a clean towel and press it to my arm. It's stopped bleeding for the most part. "It's clean enough. I had a tetanus shot before I left for the academy. At least there's that."

She works quickly with the butterfly bandages and even found some gauze and tape I had no idea I owned. It probably came from an old emergency kit that Annette bought me.

When she's done, I hold up my arm. "Like old times."

"I feel horrible. Hold your arm up so it doesn't swell," she says before her gaze shifts to my bare chest. "Look at you. You're covered in blood."

I shouldn't let her. I still have one good hand. But it's late, and I'm exhausted. So when she starts cleaning me, I don't stop her. She's focused on her task.

I'm focused on her.

"Tell me what happened. You said this was going to be a simple meeting for a money drop. How did you get to this point?"

She already feels guilty. I'm not about to make that worse. "Robichaux tried to make a point of what would happen to me if I ratted him out."

She's thorough in her work. I appreciate it for every reason that doesn't have to do with being clean. Fighting my dick from appreciating it, too, might be the hardest task I've had all night.

When she's finally happy with her work, she tosses the towel into the sink and looks up at me. "You should probably take something."

I stare down at her. "Maybe you should've gone into health care. You would've aced the bedside-manner class. Then I wouldn't have to worry about you meeting people like Robichaux. You haven't even asked what I found out."

She doesn't hesitate. She steps in and plasters herself to me. She wraps her arms around my middle and presses her cheek to my heart. I bring my good arm around her back.

"I don't care. I know I should, but I don't. I'm too shaken up that you were hurt."

I lean my ass on the counter and hold her to me. How can something familiar feel so fucking new? I close my eyes and bury my face in her hair to keep myself from doing anything else.

Doing what I feel like doing.

Because, at this moment, everything that's wrong feels natural. I let this go on longer than I should.

I could stand here all night even though I'd rather be horizontal. I need to focus on something else.

I pull in a deep breath and pull away from her. She doesn't let go, but when she looks up, her tears slay me more than that fucking knife did.

Like it's instinctual—which it is not—I catch one with my thumb that falls down her cheek. "Teagan, I'm fine."

"But you might not have been. If something happened to you because of me—"

I shake my head. "Nothing was going to happen to me. I could've called for backup and didn't. It was just a scuffle. I swear."

Her small tits rise and fall with an exasperated breath. I realize she's in another one of my T-shirts and it doesn't feel like there's anything beneath it. She's also wearing a pair of my boxers that she no doubt had to roll to get them to stay up.

Fuck, I need to divert this. Nothing good happens when humans are tired and emotional. Common sense has a way of flying out the window. If I've learned anything from being a cop, it's that.

"Let me take something and tell you about Heath. At least Robichaux followed through on his end of the bargain."

She doesn't seem excited to hear about Heath Hayes the way she's been so focused on the last few days, but she does let go of me. I take this opportunity to move to my bedroom, and she follows.

I walk to the far side of my bed and grab a bottle of Tylenol off the nightstand. I'm surprised she doesn't give me shit for leaving my stuff cluttered, but she doesn't. She climbs on my bed, sits in the middle with her legs crossed, and never looks away from me like I'm going to pass out and die from a cut.

I down the meds with water that's been sitting there for who knows how long since I haven't slept in my own bed for two nights. I rip my belt off and toss it to the floor. "If Robichaux isn't a liar and an asshole, Heath Hayes is in a Nigerian prison."

That gets her attention. She's as shocked as I was. "Prison?"

"At least he's not dead—that we know of."

Maybe it's because I've known her for so long. Maybe it's because we've shared the same bathroom for more than a decade at her parents' house.

Who the hell knows, it might just be because I'm fucking tired. When I unbutton my pants and drop them to the floor, it doesn't seem like a big deal to either of us. Hell, she's in my T-shirt and underwear too.

It might not be a big deal, that doesn't mean her eyes don't wander.

Not at all natural for a woman who's "seeing" someone else.

I can't think about that right now.

I tell her everything I found out about Heath Hayes. It doesn't seem like much, but it does give me something to focus on. When my head hits the pillow, she doesn't move to make room for me. Just like the sofa the last two nights.

When I get to the end of the list of shit I learned tonight, she looks down at me. "Rocco?"

The thought of the sofa reminds me of the backache I've sported the last two mornings. I stretch out. "I swear, I've told you everything. The good news is this is tied to the transportation of drugs. From here on out, I don't have to try to justify the case. Taylor is going to work the local NOLA targets, and I'll find out where Heath is. I have an idea, and it doesn't include the State Department."

"That's not what I was going to say."

All of a sudden, she looks as tired as I feel. She steals my second pillow and lies down next to me on her side. I can't take my eyes off her. This feels different. Different than the sofa. Different than having her in my arms. Different than it's ever been with anyone else I've been horizontal with.

It's different because it's Teagan.

And as wrong as it is, it doesn't feel that way.

Her words come out soft. Like she feels everything that's coursing through my veins. Like if she whispers, we can keep this moment between us, and the universe won't ever know. "I was going to say thank you."

My tone matches hers. "You don't have to thank me."

She snuggles into her pillow and tucks a hand beneath her cheek. "I know I don't. But you'd do anything for me, and I was a bitch."

I can't help the corners of my lips from tipping. "Being bitchy and being a bitch are two different things. You were just the first, not the second. And since you're not afraid of blood, I can forgive the bitchy."

She fails to bite back a smile. "You have a weird way of letting me off the hook."

"Who says I let you off the hook? That doesn't touch the two years you refused to speak to me. I think I have a right to hold a grudge for at least another day. Don't rip that away from me. If we're being honest here, you've hardly groveled. You could give it some more effort. I have a slash in my arm. I deserve a good grovel."

Her bare foot comes into contact with my bare thigh for a light kick. "You haven't changed a bit."

I tell her the truth. "And it seems everything has changed about you."

She sobers and shakes her head. "The only thing that's changed about me is that I grew up. You just refuse to see it."

If she only knew.

I see everything.

Every damn thing.

And I like it all—way too damn much.

"Go to sleep, Teag. Movers will be here tomorrow, and we'll pick up your car. We'll both be out of New Orleans in no time."

She sighs. She nods. And her body relaxes deeper into my bed.

What she does not do is move.

I do a half sit up to turn off the lamp. Neither one of us reach for the covers. I don't know if it's too much or too intimate or if we're both just too tired.

But whatever the hell that's going on between us has officially moved from the sofa to the bedroom.

And in the middle of the night when common sense takes a hike, I'm not upset about it.

13

HANG MEAT

Teagan

I didn't know it was possible to be freezing and hot at the same time.

Rocco keeps his apartment the temperature of an icebox. Before he got home last night, I buried myself in blankets on his sofa.

But when he got home, and I realized he was hurt because of me, I was numb to everything but him.

It could have been worse. So much worse. And it would have been my fault.

The last thing I remember was feeling like an ice block when I rolled over in the middle of the night.

My toes might still be ice cubes, but the rest of me is not.

The only things in my vision are half the bed, Rocco's messy bedroom with boxes littered everywhere, and his bandaged forearm draped over my body. Besides my toes, I'm toasty warm and more comfortable than I've ever been.

Rocco's wide chest rises and falls against my back in a rhythm so even, there's a beauty to it. His thick thigh is threaded between my legs pinning my bottom one to the bed. In fact, his hairy leg is sort of itchy.

That doesn't seem like something that would feel good, but it does.

In fact, it all feels good.

Especially his cock.

I might not be the most experienced twenty-two-year-old on the planet, but I'm not naïve or innocent.

It's hard as a rock and pressed firmly into the small of my back.

Sure, he's asleep. And, yes, I've read that most men wake up like this.

It could have nothing to do with me.

But as I lie here in his arms, I'm going to pretend it has everything to do with me. I'm good at daydreaming. Before our first encounter, it's all I did. And no matter how hard I tried to shake the dream of Rocco Monroe after our moment at the now-enshrined spot on the wall, nothing ever compared.

And now that I've made my way back here, my worst fears have come true.

No one will ever compare to this.

To him.

That fact is totally and utterly depressing.

Like more depressing than moving to New York by myself. I don't care how amazing the job opportunity is.

The desire to roll in his arms to see what would happen is strong. Been there, done that. The last thing my psyche can take at the moment is Rocco pushing me away.

Again.

But my dream reality is about to come to an end. His rhythmic breathing is cut off by a quick intake of air. Just when I think he's going to wake up in shock and push me off the bed from the position we put ourselves in during the night, he buries his face in the back of my head, and his strong arm pulls me into his chest tighter.

Delicious.

Delicious and interesting.

My heart picks up its pace the longer we're like this.

There's one thing I know for certain, I can't get used to this.

I'm about to do something about that when a cell vibrating on wood breaks into my cherished moment.

I freeze.

Rocco jerks awake.

I start to move, but he tenses around me.

Lord, that feels good.

The cell vibrates again and again and again.

But he doesn't move for it.

Finally, it stops. My heart is no longer just excited. It's panicked. He's awake and the only move he's made is to keep me here.

I start to shift and whisper, "Rocco—"

But I'm interrupted by the vibrating cell again. Whoever's on the other side of the line isn't in the mood for being ignored.

"Fuck," he hisses in my ear.

Damn the caller. If they only knew they're ruining my once-in-a-lifetime experience.

He still doesn't make a move to answer the call or roll me off the bed.

Instead, his thigh bends my top leg higher, spreading my legs, and pressing into me everywhere.

"Morning." His voice is low and groggy. I can't control my heart, my quickened breath, or the wetness between my legs.

"Good morning," I rattle too quickly.

The cell stops vibrating.

"That was better than sleeping on the sofa."

"I guess."

I feel him pull in a deep breath as his head angles down to mine. Against my hair, he mutters, "You prefer my sofa over my bed. That hurts my feelings."

What I want to say is I just prefer him.

But his phone vibrates again.

"For fuck's sake," he mutters. He lets me go long enough to twist at the waist and tag his phone. The next thing I know, he clicks it on and tosses it on the bed in front of me.

"Hey, Landyn. What's up?"

I let out a small gasp, but he presses his index finger to my lips to shut me up.

"It's moving day!" I jerk when her screams of delight sound over the speaker. "And answer your phone when I call."

"I'm talking to you, aren't I?"

"But you made me call you three times," she spouts. "Today is a big day! You'll be back in Miami soon. I can't wait!"

Landyn is married to Brax, but she's known Rocco as long as she's known her husband. The way my mom explained it to me years ago, Rocco and Landyn bonded over cartels, the mafia, and a motorcycle gang. They were in survival mode together. Landyn might've fallen in love with Brax, but she and Rocco have a friendship unlike any other.

I'm hyperaware of every move he makes. When he exhales, my hair flutters around my face, and he hasn't taken his finger off my lips—as if I'm anxious for Landyn to know I'm in New Orleans with her best friend for life.

"I can't wait either."

There's nothing facetious about his tone, but it is a bit sad.

"Did I wake you? Aren't the movers coming today?" Landyn asks. Her kids, Brian and Bailee are chattering in the background. "Lovies, Uncle Rocco will be here in a few days. Everyone say hi!"

I've always loved how close Rocco is to Brax and Landyn's kids. He plays the part of the uncle in the best way possible. I know it's killed him to not be near them for the last three years. And him moving back now just in time for the birth of their third is everything to him. He'll even be the godfather.

When the kids yell for him in unison, I feel a smile against the side of my head.

"I'll see you next week, little rugrats," he teases.

They giggle in the background, and Landyn laughs. "I'm not sure who's more excited, them or me. I hear you're stopping at Teagan's graduation on the way home."

"I am." I feel those two words everywhere when they rumble through me.

"Tim told Brax and Brax told me. That's what I'm calling about. Maybe you can convince her not to go to New York. Annette might be distracted with Sammie, but that doesn't mean she isn't beside herself. You and Teagan used to be close. She's always listened to you. Try to convince her she can have everything she wants in a career in Miami."

"I was as surprised as anyone to hear she was moving," Rocco says as he leans into me farther, pressing me into his mattress. "Especially since she got back together with her high school boyfriend."

I couldn't gasp if I wanted to. The moment he speaks those words, he wraps his hand over my mouth to keep me from making a noise.

"What?" Landyn sounds like she's stopped what she's doing. She sounds truly perplexed as I die a little bit inside. "Are you sure about that? Because that's ... really odd."

Rocco just won't stop. "That's what she said when I called her to tell her we'd be caravanning back to Miami."

"Maybe she had a boyfriend that I didn't know about, because..." Landyn lets that thought trail off.

I use my free foot to give him a weak heel to the shin.

All I get in return is a chuckle—and a silent one at that, but I feel it everywhere.

"Because why?" Rocco pushes. "Teagan and I have both been gone the last couple years, but we'll be together for the next few days. Tell me everything."

I've never had the desire to bite anyone, but I do now. Rocco's hand is still plastered over my mouth, and he has me pinned to the bed. I'm screwed.

And not in a good way.

"Look, it's been five years since she's graduated from high school. It's completely possible I forgot she had another boyfriend."

"Another?" Rocco asks.

I close my eyes and wish someone would put me into a medically induced coma.

"Like I said, I only know of one. And I know for sure she's not getting back with him. He's my client. He has great hair."

Shit. A coma isn't permanent enough. Someone needs to put me out of my misery for good. I'll never recover from what's about to happen.

"Really." It's a statement, not a question. Rocco must be a mind reader because he's hell bent on torturing me before my death by mortification happens. All of a sudden, he lets my mouth go at the same time I lose his weight. He shifts to his side as he forces me to my back so he stares down at me where he's propped on an elbow. "It's been forever. What was her boyfriend's name again?"

"Jed."

I close my eyes. If I have to lie here and listen to this, I refuse to look at him.

"That's right." A big warm hand lands on the side of my face, and a thumb drags over my bottom lip. When he presses the pad of this thumb between my lips, my eyes fly open.

Fucking Rocco.

He's wearing nothing but boxers, a big bandage, and a wolfish grin.

"I remember Jed," he goes on. "He's *great*."

"Isn't he?" Landyn is clueless as she keeps digging my grave. "If you weren't already my guy bestie, I'd recruit him. I love him. I remember we were so surprised when he broke up with Teagan. I mean, it's Teagan—*our* Teagan. If anyone had a chance with her, they'd be crazy to turn that down."

Rocco's grin disintegrates.

My eyes flare.

"Crazy," Rocco bites.

"But you're right. Jed *is* great. Later, it all made sense."

"Did it?" Rocco digs, his eyes still boring into mine.

"Well, yeah. He's gay. It all came out later, remember? He told Teagan in high school when they broke up, but he didn't come out until later in college. She kept his secret and supported him all those years."

Rocco's expression softens, and he slips the tip of his thumb that was tormenting me in a whole different way from my lips. Instead, he brushes my cheekbone with it. "That sounds like her."

Landyn is as exasperated as I feel. "I can't believe you forgot all that. Seriously, Roc. You never pay attention. You are definitely not gay."

Hmm, I concur.

"Thanks for confirming that," he mutters.

"Anyway, you have one job on the way from Mississippi to Miami. We're calling it *Project Get Teagan to Stay in Miami*. Sammie will have a baby any day, we'll have another one next month, and you'll be home where you belong. Everything was perfect until she changed her plans. We can't lose Teagan to New York City. It's on you. Get her to stay."

Rocco's wide chest expands with a deep breath. He never looks away from me. "I don't know if she'll listen to me."

"Convince her. I believe in you."

"I'll do my best," Rocco says.

I can't do this. I break his intense stare and turn my head to the side.

"I know you will," Landyn says with a smile. "Just a few more days. I can't wait to have you home. I'm sure we'll talk a million times before then. Work your magic on Teagan. I almost have my family all together—she's the missing piece."

"I've got to go. Movers will be here soon and there's stuff I need to tie up before I leave town." What Rocco does not do is make any promises about me.

Smart man.

"Give Teagan a hug at graduation. I hate that I can't travel to be there for her."

"I'm sure she understands. Tell Brax hi."

"I will. Working with you is all he can talk about. If I wasn't so excited myself, I'd be offended since I'm about to have his third child. Good luck with the move."

"Thanks. But I'm really hanging up now."

"Fine. Love you."

"Yeah," Rocco agrees. "You too."

He reaches over me to disconnect the call.

And, with that, my life is over.

Of course, his hand returns to my face where he forces me to look at him.

He licks his lips as his gaze roams my face before he states, "Jed is great."

My face warms. "He is. I mean, he is now. He wasn't for a long time. I'm happy for him. We're good friends."

"Is he the kind of friend who knows you're meeting people like Robichaux by yourself?"

I frown. "No way. I don't tell him things like that. He'd kick my ass over FaceTime."

"Then Jed *is* great."

I don't want to talk about Jed. It only reminds me of my lie. But I was desperate. If I explained the whole thing to Jed, he would have wholly supported my lie. He's the only other person in the world who knows everything about Rocco.

Rocco doesn't say anything else or ask why I lied about Jed. He contemplates me like I'm one of his cases and he's trying to make two and two equal four, but the math just won't math.

"I need to get up," I blurt.

He narrows his eyes and changes the subject. "For being so small, you're a bed hog."

"I can't help what I do in my sleep. I was freezing. You could hang meat in here."

He hikes a brow and smirks. "I do ... hang meat in here."

I roll my eyes. Men will always be boys when it comes to penis jokes.

But he doesn't stop. "You practically pushed me off the bed. I was hanging on for my life. It was scarier than sparring with Robichaux's men last night."

My expression falls. "That's not funny. I feel horrible about that."

"You should," he keeps on. "I had to wrestle you in the middle of the night with my bad arm. I had no choice but to pin you down."

I need to change the subject. "Your movers will be here soon, and we need to pick up my car."

He shakes his head. "This is just getting interesting. I wish I'd known last night that you were lying to me about Jed. I felt fucking guilty with you in my bed. I know we haven't talked in almost two years, but I'm not that kind of guy. Don't expect me to be the other man. I respect myself more than that."

"You said yourself I was full of shit. I was having a moment, okay? Can you blame me? I'm not normally a liar."

"I'm not letting you off the hook. And I'm standing my ground on the kiss."

My eyes widen. "What's that supposed to mean?"

His expression goes dead serious and causes my heart to speed. I might be a young, healthy woman, but my body can't take the whiplash this morning. "I'll remind you—it means the next time we kiss, you'll have to ask for it. And from the way we woke up this morning, I have no doubt that will happen."

I shake my head. "Stop it."

He frames my chin in his hand to hold my head still. "I'm not going to bullshit you—what happened two years ago fucked me up. And you know I'm already fucked up in the head, so that's saying something."

"Don't say that." I defend Rocco to himself. "You're not fucked up in the head."

"I am," he argues. "The only thing I could think of after it happened was that I could lose everyone in my life, when in reality, I lost you."

"I told you that was my fault."

He ignores me. "I had two years to let that shit fester. It ate away at me. Crawled under my skin in a way I couldn't get away from it."

"What are you saying?" I whisper.

"I'm saying, I'm ready to figure out what this is. Just the two of us. No one knows."

I shake my head and put a hand to his chest. He finally allows me the space to get up. I scramble to my feet, but he's right on my heels. Taking a step back, I put as much space between us as I can in his room full of boxes. "No. No way. It's taken me two years to get over you rejecting me once. There's no way I can live through that twice."

He's standing there almost naked in only his boxers as he

frowns at me. "You can't deny there's something between us. Not after the last few days."

"It doesn't matter. I refuse to go through that again. And there's the fact I'm moving to New York." I shake my head and put my hand up. "And you're not talking me into anything. I love Landyn as much as you do, but I can't. I've got a job that I'm looking forward to. I'm going."

I turn for the door. I need to get through the next few days. Once we get back to Miami, there will be no more alone time with Rocco, and I'll be mesmerized by my niece or nephew.

Life will be easy again.

"Teagan, we need to talk about this." He follows me out of the bedroom, but we're interrupted by a banging on the door. "Fuck. It's the movers. My head is spinning. I have no concept of time when you're around."

He turns back to his room to get dressed, and I go straight to the bathroom. Once I'm locked inside, I pull in a deep breath and flip on hot water. When I catch a glimpse of myself in the mirror, I pause.

Hell.

I just slept in Rocco's arms.

Rocco Monroe.

And he wants to see where this is going. I drag my hands through my messy hair and sit on the closed toilet.

What's happening?

And why could he not have come to this realization two years ago when it mattered?

Two whole miserable years.

My heart can't go through that again. If it doesn't end in some fantasy happily ever after, I'll never recover.

I hear the movers shuffle through the apartment. I've moved with the government, I know how it goes. And Rocco doesn't have that much. They'll be done soon, and we can pick up my car.

Then it's back to school, call Stella, and get through graduation. Rocco might be following me home, but at least I won't be in the same car as him.

I've done harder shit than this.

But there's one thing I refuse to do.

And that's ask Rocco to kiss me.

That ship has long since sailed.

14

AT LEAST THREE FUCKS

Rocco

Today has been like a laundry list from hell.

Movers ... check.

Hand in the keys to my home for the last three years ... check.

Pick up Teagan's car ... check.

Tailgate Teagan all the way to Mississippi ... check.

Make a shit ton of promises to Stella Hayes that I hope I can keep ... check.

Get Teagan Coleman to say more than five words to me at the same time?

Nope.

That would be a big, fat fail.

All fucking day.

We've been back at her apartment—if you can call it that—for an hour. The moment she unlocked the door, she turned on one of the only electronics in the place, a Bluetooth speaker.

It's not even a good one. No wonder the thing wasn't stolen. I bet Robichaux's people confused it for a large dice.

When I told her this, she corrected me that the singular for dice is die.

I told her that I might die if she doesn't talk to me soon.

She turned up her lame excuse for a speaker.

The more time I spend with the new Teagan, I realize there were so many other things I could've gotten her for graduation other than the pile of damn underwear that she's no doubt going through daily.

The same underwear I can't stop thinking about.

I just finished boxing up the small collection of antique poetry books she's amassed since she's been at school. And I don't know that because she told me. I read the inside covers where she wrote the date and place she bought them.

I smack tape on the box, toss the roll to the floor, and turn to the woman I allowed to ignore me for far too long. I've decided I'm going to rectify that. She's not getting the choice to ignore me any longer.

I thought I was doing the best thing for both of us and her family when I pushed her away. But I'm done.

"Since when have you embraced angry-female music?"

She stops what she's doing in the kitchen and glares at me. "Read the room, Rocco."

"Four words in a row. You haven't done that for at least two hours."

She rolls her eyes and goes back to her box.

I grab a duffle lying on the floor and start to go through the dresser that normal people would put a TV on. One more thing I could've gotten her for graduation.

I pull out the first drawer and freeze. It's a sea of silk and lace.

I grab a handful and hold it up to her. "You're telling me I could've bought you a real speaker system or a TV, but you wanted a cart full of underwear when you have all these? Do you have a penchant for these things, or what?"

She puts her hands on her hips. "Put those down."

Well, lookie there. Three more words. She's talking to me. "No."

"Dammit, Rocco. Can't you just pack the shit that's already on the floor?"

I roll her panties around in my hand and enjoy the feel of the lace on my skin. "No. I want to pack your panties."

She puts her hands up, palms out. "You know what? I don't give a shit. Pack what you want. I'm tired. When you're done with those, my tampons are under the sink in the bathroom. Have at it."

I open the duffle and start to drop them in one by one. "Very colorful, Teag. Pink, blue, yellow… It's like my own easter basket of panties. Remember when Annette used to make us dye eggs? Hell, she'd make me come back every Easter when I was in college. I'd never once touched an easter egg before I moved in with your family. Dying eggs was for people on TV. I had no idea everyone in the world did it but my fucked-up family."

She throws shit in a box with more force than necessary.

"Careful over there, angsty girl," I say, as I inspect every piece of lace before I drop it in their new home to travel south. "The music is getting to you."

She mutters something that I can't make out, but I'm pretty sure it includes at least three fucks.

I focus on my task. "If I thought Easter was a culture shock, you can't imagine how it felt to experience my first Christmas with the Colemans. I've never been more uncomfortable in my own skin. And remember, Brax forced me to live with the cartel back in the day. A Coleman Christmas was an out-of-body experience."

She turns back to her box.

I keep talking.

"One year in middle school, my parents didn't even come

home for Christmas. My mom claimed she was at work, but you never really knew if she was telling the truth or just escaping our shit life. The asshole stumbled in drunk and high the next day. Your mom spent months planning for the holiday. It's like I was on an alien planet, when really, I was the freak from another world."

She pauses throwing stuff in her box for two seconds.

I move onto bras, which aren't nearly as interesting as the panties.

"That first year was like the *Twilight Zone*. I couldn't figure out why anyone did anything they did for me. That someone would buy me a present? And not just someone, but everyone. I felt like a fucking charity case."

Teagan peeks up at me from under her thick lashes but doesn't say anything.

Jokes on you, Teag. I can talk until I'm blue in the face.

"I never understood Sammie. She'd rip through everything your parents gave her and never be content. You, on the other hand, would curl up for the next month and read every book they gave you."

"That's Sammie," she mutters.

"She infuriated me. She had no idea how good she had it."

Teagan opens the last drawer and isn't careful when she tosses what few kitchen tools she has into the box with a clank. "I love my sister, but nothing has changed."

"From packing your apartment, I can see nothing has changed with you either."

She shakes her head. "Lots of things have changed."

"You might be ballsy in a way I never expected, but that's it. Other than that, you're the same. You graduate tomorrow. There's no reason for you to give a shit about a man you don't know imprisoned in Nigeria, but you do."

She tosses a stack of measuring cups in the box and leans a hip on the counter. "He was taken advantage of, and no one was helping him. I had to do something."

"And that's why you're still you. Or you are with everyone but me."

Her arms fall to her sides, and she looks exhausted. "Can we please not do this? I have just about everything packed. I'm tired and tomorrow is going to be the longest day."

"I couldn't agree more. And tomorrow we'll celebrate you. You're done with school for good."

She presses her lips together and scrunches her nose. "Is it weird that I'm going to miss it?"

"Yes," I bite. "That's really fucking strange, you weirdo."

She can't hide her smile any longer. "I know. I'm a freak. I'm really going to miss this small southern town. The little main street. The shops. The diner."

She's actually speaking to me, so I cut the distance between us and go to the so-called kitchen—if you can call it a kitchen in this studio. We ate on the way out of New Orleans and got a box of beignets to go.

I open the box and hand her one. She doesn't argue, and I mirror her stance as I pop it in my mouth. "Not as good as when they're hot and fresh, but fried bread is fried bread."

She tears hers in half and eats it in two bites as I have a second. "My favorite diner in town has the best bread pudding. They don't put raisins in it." She pretends to shudder as she licks the tips of her fingers. I wish I could do that. "The caramel sauce is to die for."

I don't lick sugar off my fingers. I bop the end of her nose. Sugar-covered Teagan. Another dream.

Before she has a chance to roll her eyes or yell at me, I grab her hand to pull her away from the kitchen counter.

"What are you doing?"

The song changed. It's not angry-angsty like the others. It's not fast and not slow. It's about a familiar love and not giving a damn.

And it's about the end of innocence.

"You're pissed, and it's because of me. I don't like that."

I grip her hand in mine and swing her around in the small space before whipping her back under my arm. Her dark hair flies behind her, but she doesn't miss a beat. When she spins around, it doesn't look like she hates me. "I'm not pissed. I'm frustrated."

"If you're going to miss school that much, I can assign you homework."

"Really?" She mocks surprise. "You think that's why I'm frustrated?"

I flip her around one more time before pulling her straight to my chest where I wrap an arm around her waist and pick her feet off the floor and spin. "I'm as confused about your frustration as you are. There's too much good in the world for you to be anything other than happy."

She slides down my body until her bare toes hit the top of my feet. I don't let go when gravity takes over. There are no complaints when I slow the pace to the chorus. We're pressed together as one from our chests to our thighs. I hold her firmly to me, like she'll slip through my fingers if I let go.

She plays along as our bodies sway as one and looks up at me. "I didn't say I was unhappy. I know I have plenty to be content about. I'm not Sammie."

"Content?" I frown. "Damn, you can do better than that. Content is fucking depressing. Don't settle for being basic, Teag."

"Since when are you the expert on emotions?"

"You, of all people, know I'm no expert when it comes to that. I am an expert in other things."

"Right," she drawls. "Rocco Monroe and the female species. I was forced to watch it play out over the years. It was…" She rolls her eyes. "So fun."

I shrug a shoulder unapologetically. "Back in the day, sure. But you have no clue what I've done for two years."

She comes right back at me as we slow dance amid boxes and chaos. "Oh, trust me, my parents and everyone else we have in common made sure I was updated on Rocco Monroe. Ignoring you was not easy."

I push her away for a quick spin before bringing her right back to me, but this time, I don't let go of her hand and pin it at the small of her back. "You forget that the people we have in common are the only people I have."

That sends a crack through the wall she's built between us. "I'd never forget that, Rocco. Ever. It's why I apologized the other night."

I press our hands that are threaded into her back and lower my voice. "Don't ever apologize for that again."

Her voice drops to a whisper. "You make my head spin, and not in a good way."

"I feel like I've been spinning my entire life in one way or another. From surviving to self-destruction to desperation."

She lets go of my other hand to grip my bicep. I take the opportunity to wrap her up tighter. I drag my hand down her spine and press in on her upper back. After the last few days, the need to be close to her is overwhelming. The moments I have her to myself are like a ticking bomb. The countdown is racing too fast.

"You're Rocco Monroe. You're larger than life. What do you have to be desperate about?"

I don't know what we're dancing to. I can't hear the music or the lyrics. I might sound like a chick, but we're swaying to the beat of hearts. I feel hers beat against my chest.

"Do you know why I started playing football?"

At this point, whatever our bodies are doing is second nature. We're laser focused on each other.

"Because you're insanely athletic?"

"No. I only played football so I didn't have to go home. I was lucky I was athletic. The coaches were desperate to get me there. They'd pick me up, drop me off, pay for uniforms. Later in high school, I played as an excuse not to be recruited by gangs. The only reason I dropped out was because I started failing classes because I had to work. If I didn't work, I didn't eat. And I was fucking tired of being hungry."

I didn't think it was possible for us to be closer, but on her exhale, she sinks deeper into my hold.

The look in her eyes makes me sick to my stomach. "I didn't know that."

My tone is gruff. "No one does. Not even Landyn. They know what's on record. They have access to that and are nosy enough to look it up. After that, they assumed the rest. I'm sure it's not far from reality, but I still wasn't going to shout that to the world. I didn't need any more pity."

"They only wanted to help you."

I turn us in half a circle and exhale. "I didn't care. Brax tried countless times to get me to talk about shit, but it wasn't going to happen. Landyn never pushed. Years later, when times weren't as weird as they were in the beginning, I asked her why she never pushed me to talk."

"Why didn't she?" Teagan slides her hand up the sleeve of my T-shirt. Skin on skin, the way we were when we woke up this morning. Blood rushes to my dick, and I don't try to stop it. This time, I enjoy it.

"She did what she still does so often—she got in my space and wrapped her arms around me like she hasn't seen me for a lifetime. Her only answer was, 'Because I love you, and it doesn't matter.' That was it. Unconditional. Just like it has been since the day I met her."

A ghost of a smile touches her lips, and my eyes drop to her mouth. Her feet stop, and we're rooted in the middle of her minuscule studio. When my gaze jumps back to her dark eyes, she asks, "Why did you tell me that when you've never told anyone?"

I tip my head and brush the hair from her face. "If you really have to ask me that, I need to up my game."

Her eyes fall shut, and she leans in to press her cheek to my chest. I let my hand snake up her back and into her hair to hold her to me.

"You deserve unconditional, Rocco. You deserve everything. I hope someday you realize it."

My chest seizes, but I don't answer.

I'm good at giving. That's easy.

Receiving makes me uncomfortable.

But *unconditional*?

That makes me itch in my own skin.

It's like she realizes it and lets me off the hook when she changes the subject. "Are you staying here tonight?"

My grip on her tightens. "I dare you to try to kick me out, Teagan. I'm not going anywhere."

She turns silent.

She doesn't argue.

And she doesn't beg me to kiss her.

All she does is nod and press into me tighter.

I have a feeling this will get harder before it gets easier.

But one thing is for sure, it'll be messy.

15

THE SECRET

Teagan

When my eyes flutter open, familiar and strange emotions hit me all at once.

I'm tangled up in Rocco.

Again.

Only this morning, I'm not wearing his clothes.

Though, I probably should have. My pajamas are thinner and smaller, which means less of a barrier between us than yesterday since Rocco is down to his boxers again.

But unlike yesterday morning, Rocco isn't pinning me to the bed. This time it's me, even though with our size difference, I doubt I'm pinning him to anything. He's a willing participant and has his hand on my ass to prove it.

Hand.

On.

My.

Ass.

That's Rocco Monroe, just for clarification. The man who ran so hot two years ago, I thought he was going to tear my clothes off, and then turned to ice when he realized what was happening.

Did he beg me to speak to him after that?

Yes.

It didn't matter how much I told him to stop or that I wanted to forget about the entire humiliating nightmare. He was relentless.

For three months.

Three whole months!

Rocco must be out for revenge. This morning he's starfished in the middle of the bed, and I'm half sprawled on him. My bed is only a full size and he's extra sized in all the best ways. I'm going to blame that on the reason I'm plastered to him for the second morning in a row.

With one hand cupping my ass cheek, his other arm is extended under my pillow. I'm not sure when we kicked the covers to the bottom of the bed, but I'm not cold.

Not at all.

In fact, I'm not only warm everywhere, I'm downright hot in certain places.

The tips of his fingers dig into my skin, and his voice is rough from sleep. "You're awake."

I turn my head to rest on my other cheek to look at him. I have no concept of time, other than the sun is rising. My one window is barely lit where the morning greets us through the drawn blinds.

I've always loved his eyes, but gazing into them this close is new. One more thing to consume me.

"Look who's the bed hog now," I say.

His grip on my bottom loosens only to stroke the skin where my cheek and thigh become one. "It's called offense. I can't let you push me off the bed. I'll lose my man card."

My bed might be small, but I have no trouble sleeping on one side. That's where I was when we didn't discuss the sleeping arrangements, but just fell into bed next to each other. I tried to pretend it wasn't a big deal, when, in reality, it ranks high on life experiences I'll never forget.

But the fact I migrated to Rocco while unconscious proves I'm no more over him than I was before the Hotel Monteleone. "The man club would have to know that I pushed you out to take your man card. If you keep it a secret, no one will know."

"A secret," he echoes as the tips of his fingers tease my ass under my sleep shorts. "I'm not sure I like the sound of that."

"What's the point of announcing it to the man club? It doesn't matter how much you want to see where this goes. I'm moving to New York, and you finally got your ticket back to Miami. I know that's where you want to be, close to Landyn and the agents. They're your family."

My heart skips a beat when his soft touch disappears. He snakes his hand fully beneath my sleep shorts where he palms my bare ass. "They're your family, too, and they want you in Miami. Maybe it's time we talk about the real reason for your plans to relocate."

It's all I can do to keep my defenses up and focus on my lie. "I'm not sure what you're insinuating. I was offered a dream job. Why should I pass that up just because my family isn't happy about where it is? You can do your job anywhere in the US. It doesn't hurt that Miami is the crème de la crème for the DEA, not to mention you'll get to work with Brax, Micah, and King. That's your dream. Why is my dream less important?"

He doesn't waste a second punching a hole in my story. "Since when is anything more important to you than your family?"

"Please, Rocco. You know I love my family. But I don't have to justify anything to you or anyone else."

He inhales a deep breath, and since I'm still half lying on him, I feel it everywhere along with his intense gaze. "I need to convince you to stay."

My eyes go wide. "Why would you do that?"

He leans in and nudges the tip of my nose with his. I think he's going to kiss me—let me off the hook for making me beg for it—but he doesn't. What he does do is blow my mind. "Because the idea of this has marinated in my fucking chest for almost two years. So much so, when I walked into that hotel lounge and laid eyes on you, I thought I was going to lose it."

"Roc, you did lose it."

He shrugs. "You're right, I did. Can you blame me?"

His fingers inch closer to my sex. It's all I can do not to shift and fidget, but I hold strong. This cat and mouse thing we've been doing has done a number on me. Everything I've done to numb myself to the thought of him—no, the thought of *us*—has melted.

I think it melted into my panties.

I'm impossibly wet. An inch or two farther, and Rocco will know just how wet I am all because of him.

I can't ignore it any longer. "Nothing has changed. My parents are still my parents. They were the sole reason you pushed me away."

He nods slowly. "That hasn't changed. If I fuck this up, everything changes."

"Rocco, you have your hand up my shorts and are daring me to beg you to kiss me. Something has changed."

He shakes his head. "The stakes are high, which means I have no choice but to not fuck this up. When I put my mind to something, I never fail."

"So cocky," I mutter. "And what if I fuck this up?"

His lips tip on one side. "I'll make sure that doesn't happen either. When I'm done with you, you won't be able to resist me."

"I'd like to refer back to my last statement. So cocky."

He shakes his head. "Confident."

I roll my eyes.

"Teag," he calls for me. When I focus back on him, the cocky is gone. His expression is dead serious. "When I say you've had a chokehold on me for two years, I mean it. I've had more time than I've wanted or needed to get to this point. There's been no one else. Not for two fucking years, and that's because of you. I don't want to think about the time wasted. All I want to do is move forward. If Tim and Annette aren't happy, then I'll just have to deal with it. We'll keep it between us. You and me. No stress or pressure from everyone in our lives. I know some will be elated and some will be fucking shocked. Neither one of us needs that pressure."

My lungs weigh heavy in my chest with labored breaths. "You keep forgetting one thing—I'm moving."

"Not for a few weeks. Give me that time." He shifts and rolls to his side. We're nose to nose sharing one pillow. His hand slides down my leg far enough to pull it high up his body, but he's quick to slide it back up my sleep shorts. And he's done teasing. My breath catches when he touches me for the first time. The tips of his fingers dance on my sex making my insides go haywire. "Give me the chance to show you how good this can be. You spent the last two years hating me. I've spent that time hating myself for pushing you away. If I have to beg, I will. Give me the chance to make up for two years."

Between his words and his fingers, I'm not sure how I can say no. "A secret? I'm not sure how we'll manage that."

His finger drags through my sex. His warmth could melt butter. "You're so fucking wet, and it's all for me. Your body is on board, baby. Let me convince your heart."

Baby.

He's right. My body is definitely on board.

I close my eyes and try to focus on the offer he just presented. Rocco and me, a secret tryout.

I press into him and pull my leg higher on his side. This is different than waking tangled up together. I thought that was intimate, but I was wrong.

I groan when he circles my clit with the tip of his finger.

"Say yes," he demands.

I exhale on a moan.

When he slides a finger inside me, I press down on his hand.

Dreams really can come true.

I lose his finger, but my clit gets another stroke.

And another.

So much love.

Until he stops.

My eyes fly open.

"Say yes." He echoes his own words, but this time they have a bite to them.

A desperation that heats me from the inside out.

I've been desperate for Rocco since I realized boys were stupid and no one on earth was as charming and charismatic or as funny as him.

As I got older, Rocco being hot was icing on the cake.

But even in my passion-induced state, I have to tell him the truth. "I'm scared."

He flicks my clit. "What are you scared of?"

"Putting myself out there. Having you. Losing you."

"Well then, we're even. I'm the dumbass who wasted two years and now you're moving to New York. You're scared, and I'm pissed at myself. It goes both ways." He strokes my clit with more pressure. I feel it everywhere right before he pulls his hand away. "Edging you is better than I ever dreamed. I could do this all day. If you want more, you're going to have to say yes."

I lick my lips and find it hard to form words. "I don't have all day. It'll make things weird if we're still like this when my parents get here."

"I agree. But I like where I am. I'm not letting you go."

This will either be the biggest mistake of my life or the decision leading to a happily ever after I never thought I'd have.

"Okay. As long as it's a secret. I don't need everyone in my business or feeling sorry for me when this doesn't work out."

His fingers continue to tease my sex as if they're getting to know me, they like where they are, and have settled in for a thirty-year mortgage. "When did you become such a pessimist?"

I wiggle my hips to search for his touch. "You know the answer to that."

Instead of giving me what I want, his hold on me becomes firm, and I get something new. He cups me between my legs. His hand is so big, he touches everywhere and everything. It's strong and unmoving.

Possessive.

"You forgot something," he says.

I open my eyes. "I agreed. What else do you want?"

"Ask me to kiss you."

I shake my head. "Maybe later. I haven't brushed my teeth."

He huffs but doesn't argue. "I'll take that for now because I can't wait to watch you come. You don't know how many times I've jerked off to the thought of you."

This is unreal. Just last week I assumed Rocco didn't want anything to do with me. Now he's about to rock my world.

His grip loosens and the tips of his fingers return. This time he means business. Strokes are followed by circles. He sneaks his other hand up my back and into my hair as he works his magic between my legs. I move as much as he allows in tandem with his hand. He's been teasing me so long, I'm aching for it in the best way.

His hand fists my hair and tips my head back enough to expose the column of my neck. I shiver when the tip of his tongue drags up the side. He stops below my ear where he gives me a delicious suck on my sensitive skin.

The fact that I don't care if it leaves a mark when my parents will be here today for graduation is a testament to how good Rocco is and how much I want this.

"There you go." He pulls his head back far enough to look into my eyes. "Fuck, baby. You want this as much as I do. Are you going to fall apart for me?"

I can't form words, not that an answer is needed. My orgasm is creeping in and threatens to crush me.

"Please," I beg.

"Please what," he demands. His tone is rough with emotion.

My eyes fall shut. "I'm close."

"I know you are." He gives me a bit more pressure with quickened movements. "There you go."

When it washes over me, I gasp and moan at the same time. My body quakes, and Rocco holds me tight to his chest as his bare thigh presses between my legs. He has me pinned. He wrings every ounce of orgasm out of me and never lets up.

His fingers slow as I collapse against his chest, but he doesn't pull his hand away. He holds me between my legs and strokes my hair as I recover from my first Rocco-induced orgasm.

My breaths are labored as I will my heart to slow to a steady pace. Rocco says nothing as he holds me close, but all I can think about is his rock-hard cock that's pressed to my thigh.

"Roc?" I try to pull my head away to look up at him, but he holds me tight.

"Hmm?"

"Um, what about you?"

I'm satiated and relaxed. Rocco is anything but when he looks down at me. "We need to set some ground rules."

I frown. "Rules?"

He lifts his chin. "A contract. This secret between us … anything and everything is on the table, but no sex."

My frown deepens, and my post-orgasmic haze disintegrates into a depressing reality. "You-you don't want to have sex?"

"Let me amend that. No sex until I know you're all in."

"Why?"

"For the same reason you were hesitant to be right here. If you walk away from me, I refuse to sit across the dinner table from you at Christmas and know what it's like to have you but not have you. The fact that your family is my family makes this messy enough as it is. When I make you mine, you'll be mine forever. There will be no going back."

"I'm not sure what to think about that. So you'll get to touch me as you please and I don't get the same in return?"

He pulls me up his rock-hard chest and rolls me to my back. His hips fall between my legs where I feel the effects of what we just did. He rubs his long cock against my still-sensitive clit. "Who said you couldn't touch me? I said no sex. Other than that, you can do whatever you want. Are you disappointed?"

Disappointed?

Hell, yes. But I can't show him that.

"Of course not."

His smirk is more beautiful when he's leering over me. "Not even if you beg."

Being pressed into the mattress by Rocco would be my new favorite thing in the world if the orgasm he just gave me weren't at the top of the list. "I didn't know your virtue was at stake. Begging is officially off the table."

He shakes his head. "It's been so long since my *virtue* was intact, it feels like another lifetime. That's what happens when your parents don't give a shit where you are or what you do."

I shouldn't have brought that up. Not only do I not want to talk about virtues, but I really don't want to think about who came before me. Rocco basically melts the panties off women with the lift of his chin. He could have any woman he wanted.

Which is why it blows my mind he hasn't been with anyone since our first kiss.

That shouldn't give me as much satisfaction as it does.

He changes the subject from sex to reality. "Your parents will be here soon. I need to calm my dick the fuck down and pretend I don't know what it's like to watch you come. This will be interesting."

"A secret relationship with Rocco Monroe while living at my parents' house across the hall from each other. Yeah, it will be interesting."

He presses his cock into my sex one more time. "Get ready. And brush your teeth. I'm looking forward to the begging."

I lose his cock, his weight, and his smirk. I can't take my eyes off him as he walks mostly naked to the bathroom. When he slams the door, I let out the biggest exhale of my life.

I just agreed to a secret relationship with Rocco Monroe.

A trial run.

With no sex.

Yep, just as I thought. This is either going to be the best thing ever or a nightmare I'll never wake from.

There will be no in between.

16

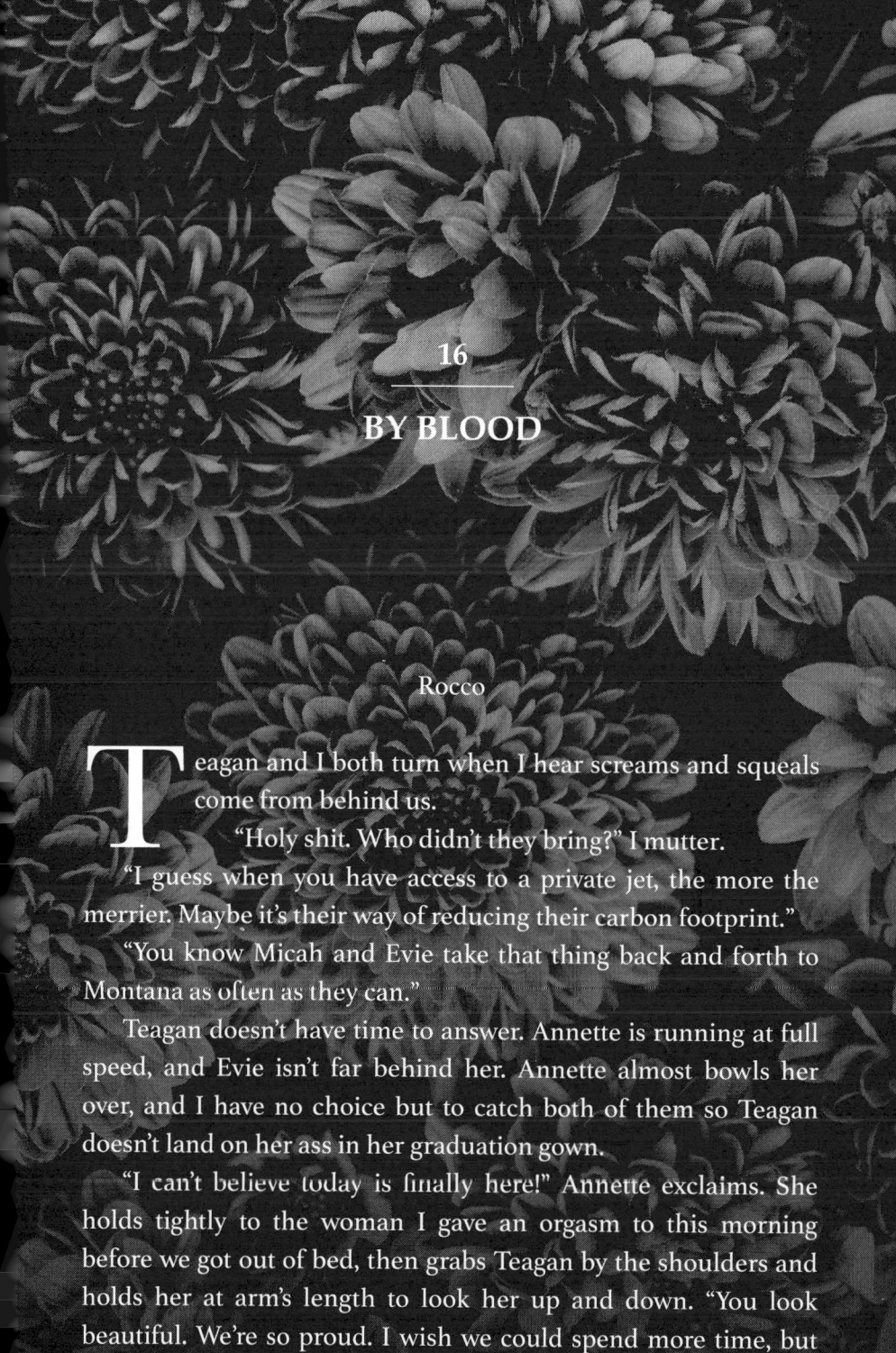

BY BLOOD

Rocco

Teagan and I both turn when I hear screams and squeals come from behind us.

"Holy shit. Who didn't they bring?" I mutter.

"I guess when you have access to a private jet, the more the merrier. Maybe it's their way of reducing their carbon footprint."

"You know Micah and Evie take that thing back and forth to Montana as often as they can."

Teagan doesn't have time to answer. Annette is running at full speed, and Evie isn't far behind her. Annette almost bowls her over, and I have no choice but to catch both of them so Teagan doesn't land on her ass in her graduation gown.

"I can't believe today is finally here!" Annette exclaims. She holds tightly to the woman I gave an orgasm to this morning before we got out of bed, then grabs Teagan by the shoulders and holds her at arm's length to look her up and down. "You look beautiful. We're so proud. I wish we could spend more time, but we couldn't leave Sammie when she's dilated as far as she is."

Again, with the unnecessary vagina statistics. It's all I can do not to cringe.

Teagan bites back a smile. "Thanks, Mom."

"And you." Annette turns to me and hugs me just as tight as she did her daughter. "You'll be home where you belong in a few days. It's about time."

"I can't wait to be back."

She kisses my cheek before she stands back and sighs. "I'm going to have everyone home for a short time. It'll be like old times. Tim told me he talked to you, Rocco. Thanks for following Teagan home. We worry."

I stuff my hands in my pockets and shrug. "I'm more than happy to do it."

"Congrats, Teagan," Evie says and leans in for a hug before doing the same to me. "It's good to see you, too, Rocco. Landyn wanted to come, but all the pregnant women had to stay home. Goldie is slammed with events today at The Pink, and King stayed home with Bale. It would just be too long of a day for him."

"You and Micah are a surprise." Teagan beams. "Thank you so much for making the trip."

"We knew your parents had to turn around and go home fast. We were happy to tag along to help celebrate," Evie says.

There's a firm slap on my shoulder. When I turn, Micah is standing there with Tim. I shake Micah's hand, but Tim knows his priorities, and goes straight to his youngest daughter. "My baby is graduating with her master's. I feel like I just dropped you off for your freshman year."

Before I came to live with the Colemans, I had no clue what family dynamics were. Tim and Annette shower both their girls with love, but Sammie is Annette's.

Let's be real, Annette has the patience for anyone.

Teagan, though, is Tim's. They've always been tight.

She hugs her father. "I missed you, Dad."

He kisses her forehead before taking one more look at her and shakes his head. "Missed you more than you know. Can't wait to have you home, even if it's just for a few weeks before you break my heart and move to Mars."

Teagan rolls her eyes. "I was born in New York. You worked in New York." She turns to Micah. "You worked there too and had no desire to go to Miami."

Evie wraps her arms around her husband's middle and looks up to Micah. "Best move ever. You'd be lost without me."

He leans down and presses his lips to the top of her dark hair. "I'd be wandering around lost and a poor excuse for a human. Thank you for saving me, Evie."

Evie bites back a laugh as Micah reaches around his wife to shake my hand.

"What's up, big man?" I say.

"Your initiation, that's what. Wait until you see what we have in store for you. You're scheduled on call for the hotline every weekend for the first six months. We've already agreed that if we run across a hoarder, it's your case. And consider yourself on coffee duty everyday but Monday."

There's no way I'm doing half that shit.

"Fuck that," I mutter.

"I agree with Rocco," Tim says, coming to my rescue. "Fuck that. I'm expecting high level cases from him. What he's not doing is running for coffee."

Micah pushes me in the shoulder. "You know I'm fucking with you. We can't wait. Brax even broke up with me. I'm teaming up with King for a while so you two can work together. Personally, I think it's because Mama Landyn wants him to keep an eye on you."

"He could do worse than have Brax Cruz as a partner, right?" Annette chimes in.

"As much as I appreciate everyone planning my career for me,"

I say as I reach over and give Teagan's graduation robe a tug and don't look away from her. More than anything, I want to pull her to me, take her mouth, and tell her how proud I am. Graduations are boring as hell, and I'm more than anxious to get this one over with. That means everyone can get back on Evie's private jet to fly home, and I can have Teagan to myself again. "Teagan needs to walk across the stage. She said she's going to miss school. She's a freak."

Teagan smirks up at me through her thick, dark lashes before she hits me with her square graduation hat. "I'm not a freak. I like to learn new things."

"It's because you're so smart," Annette announces proudly.

My thoughts go back to her bed where we woke up this morning. I wonder what I could teach her...

As if Tim can read my mind, he makes me feel like a dirty old man at my ripe age of twenty-nine. "It feels like yesterday you graduated from kindergarten. In case anyone is curious, between this and becoming a grandpa, I'm not doing well."

"And just when we thought King was old," Micah says with a loud clap. "Let's get this party started. Teagan, if you don't do something completely offensive and off the wall when you walk across the stage, I've failed as an uncle. Do not disappoint me, girl."

Evie gapes at her bear of a husband. "This is a private university, Micah. Teagan would never do anything like that."

"You'd be surprised," I mutter thinking about her having the balls to meet up with Robichaux by herself.

"That's it. I'm going to be late to my own graduation because you people never stop talking." Teagan leans in to kiss her mom's cheek then her dad's. She turns to me and the rest of the group, finally giving us an awkward wave. "I'll see you on the other side!"

"We'll be the annoying, loud ones!" Micah calls after her. "Wave to us!"

We're standing outside the main hall where commencement will soon bore us to tears. I'm about to turn for the front doors so we find a good seat, when Annette steps in front of me and grips my hands. "When did you get here, and have you talked her out of moving to New York yet?"

Damn.

I ignore the first question and focus on the second. "Give me a minute, Annette. I'm working on it, but it's going to take some convincing. Your daughter is savage."

Annette's shoulders droop like I just crushed every hope and dream she has in life, which probably isn't far from the truth. I prepare myself for an onslaught of guilt trips until her gaze catches the butterfly strips on my arm.

"What happened to your arm?" she exclaims. I try to twist my hands out of hers, but like the mother she's proven to be since the day I met her, there are just some things that can't be stopped in life. Annette is at the top of the list.

"Just a cut," I say and look over at Micah. "If we don't get some seats soon, we'll miss our chance at being obnoxious."

Micah starts to move, but it's the doctor, Evie, who zeroes in on my wound like a laser. "That's more than a cut, Roc. You're barely holding it together with those bandages. What happened?"

I take a step back from the doctor and the only real mother figure I've ever had. "I got in a scuffle at work the other night. It's nothing. It's already starting to heal."

Annette doesn't care what I think of my own arm, she turns to the expert in the group. "Does he need stitches?"

Evie grabs my hand again and turns my arm over to inspect it closer. "How long ago did you do this?"

"The night before last. It's fine."

"The night before your move?" Micah produces a low whistle and looks over at Tim. "Your new young agent is going to give us a run for our money. He's still got the ambition of a newbie even though he's been on for three years. I'll call Brax and King—warn them that Rocco is hell-bent on making us look bad."

Micah and Tim aren't worried about my arm, only cases. Tim says, "I'm counting on it."

"I think he needs to have it looked at." Annette turns to me. "At least it's on your scar, right? You won't have another one. But I'm worried you'll get an infection."

"The mom and the doctor are hitting me hard. It'll be fine. I didn't have time to go to the ER that night. It's probably too late for stitches at this point."

Annette gapes at me. "Who doesn't have time to go to the ER when they have a slash in their arm?"

Someone who was anxious as fuck to get back to your daughter, but I can't exactly say that since we agreed to the secret trial run. "It was late. I'm sure it will be fine. It can't be worse than a third-degree burn, right?"

"If it gets infected," Annette keeps on.

Tim puts a hand to Annette's back and motions toward the door through the sea of people filing in for the ceremony. "Roc can take care of himself. We're going to miss our daughter graduating if we stand out here in the heat for you to mother him."

Annette lets her husband usher her in but turns around and points to me at the same time. "Keep an eye on it."

"Let me know if it looks infected," Evie adds.

It took me a few years, but I finally got used to Annette and everyone else. I have very few memories of my own mother giving a shit if I was hungry, let alone hurt. Those memories were before shit got really bad when she started using again.

And since you can't give a shit about your kid when you're in prison or dead, I've been taking care of myself for as long as I can remember.

Micah and Evie file in next to me.

"Tell me about the case that has you working on your way out of town that you'll have to leave behind for someone else to claim the glory," Micah demands.

I hold the door as we file through the crowd. "I'm not leaving much behind. This is international. I'm bringing it with me."

Micah's brows rise. He's impressed, and it takes a lot to impress him. "No shit? South America?"

I shake my head. "Africa."

"Impressive," Evie exclaims.

Micah looks down at his wife. "You never say that to me anymore when I talk about work."

"I'm always impressed with you," Evie croons.

"I traced it to Nigeria," I add. "There's a local Mississippi man they tricked into being a mule. He's in prison there, and his family wants him back since he was framed. I made some calls."

"You're coming in hard," Micah says. "Now I'm jealous that Brax claimed you first. Young blood with all the excitement to get your hands dirty."

"I know you're still willing to get your hands dirty," I reply.

"Maybe." He smirks. "Where'd you get the lead?"

"It's complicated and a long story. I'll brief you when I get to Miami next week," I explain, wanting to put it off for as long as possible. And there's no way I'm throwing Teagan under the bus. The agents can't keep a secret. I've known Teagan since she was a girl, but they've known her since she was a baby. If they find out what she did, they'd go to Tim in a heartbeat.

We file into the auditorium and take our seats. The women sit next to each other, and I'm flanked by Annette and Tim, who I'm usually more than comfortable with.

Today, not so much.

We're all here to celebrate the same person, though she and I had our own pre-celebration before our feet hit the floor this morning. It was just a tease of what I wanted, yet it was one of the hottest experiences I've had in my life.

I didn't even get off.

But watching her was better than anything I could've imagined. Especially after I pushed her away. That will prove to be the biggest mistake of my life if I can't make this work.

The reality of the situation has slapped me in the face today as I sit here between her parents.

Her family.

Make no mistake. They were hers first. They're hers by blood.

I'm just the charity case that grew on them.

If I didn't have two years to figure out that I want her and no one else, who knows what would've happened.

"There she is." Annette grabs my hand and points across the auditorium where the graduates are entering as the band plays.

Teagan is wearing the hat and is cloaked in every cord and stole available. Other than the one semester when she had her run in with the law and got to experience the other inside of a jail, she earned every award and exceeded her parents' expectations.

"She's going to do big things," Annette whispers. "I just wish she'd do them closer to home. I miss her so much my heart hurts."

I don't respond. There's nothing to say, other than Teagan moving to New York is because I'm transferring back to Miami.

I reach for my program so I can pretend to give a shit what it says, when she catches my eye from all the way across the space.

Annette and Evie make a dramatic exhibition of waving to get her attention, but the moment our gazes lock, I know she's focused on me.

She bites her lip. The same way she did this morning right before I gave her an orgasm.

Micah and Tim are busy talking about work. Annette and Evie are comparing how many more honors and awards Teagan has than the other graduates.

It feels safe, so I return her private smile with a wink.

Weeks.

I have a matter of weeks.

Hell, Landyn would kill me with her own hands, but I'd follow Teagan to New York if I could. That will never happen. Getting a transfer to Miami was hard enough. I'm locked in and need to do my time. Even then, I'll have to become a Brax or Micah or King to build the kind of resume to pull those kinds of strings.

I need a plan to keep her in Miami.

Failure is not an option.

17

ORGASM TERMS

Rocco

I scan the parking lot as we pull in. Management at Teagan's apartment complex pulled the video surveillance from the break in, but it gave us nothing.

They were masked.

They were also in and out in under two minutes. I'm surprised it took them that long with as little as she has in this place. I doubt it will take us twenty minutes to load her car before we leave tomorrow.

It had to be Robichaux's people. I don't trust that they won't be back.

One more night, and she won't have any ties to this place.

After Teagan walked across the stage, we went out to eat at her favorite local diner before her parents, Micah, and Evie flew home on Evie's private jet. It wasn't a long goodbye. We'll see them in a matter of days.

The moment we waved them off, Teagan fell back into investigative journalist mode. She wanted to see Stella Hayes one more time before she moved.

That was a longer goodbye. There were a few tears and so many hugs, I lost count.

None of them were for me.

Needless to say, I was ready to have Teagan to myself. I had to drag her out of there. I have my own plans, which requires alone time to work on our secret contract.

The moment we left her apartment this morning, I was forced to pretend I'm not into Teagan Coleman.

All fucking day.

I'm not well.

I knew this was going to be the case. But what I didn't know was that it would piss me off as much as it did.

Our big, fat secret hasn't even been put into effect for fourteen hours. I'm not okay and feel like a grumpy old man.

I'm still in my twenties, for fuck's sake.

At least I am for another month. I'm holding on to that for as long as I can since I've given into the temptation who's only twenty-two.

So, yeah. I'm ready to have her to myself again.

When my cell rings, it makes me even grumpier.

"What?" I bite after I put the phone to my ear.

"You know, you can drop the 'tude, dude. You didn't even bother to come and see me one more time on your way out of town."

If Taylor only knew how anxious I am to get Teagan back to Florida, he wouldn't complain about missing one last drink with him.

Who am I kidding?

He'd still complain.

"I already told you I was behind schedule. What do you want?"

Teagan frowns and whispers, "Why so hormonal?"

I'd like to show her what hormones are coursing through my body, but I was the idiot who laid down the gauntlet for no sex.

"I've got news on Jules Robichaux. Do you want it or not?" Taylor demands.

I inhale a deep breath to calm down. "Yes, I want it."

I pull into the parking lot as he talks. "It seems Jules has friends all over the place. And by friends, I mean business associates who like to make a little cash on the side. Some of those friends work at the Parish Tax Assessor's Office. He's even got people across state lines in multiple counties. These so-called friends are selling him private information of people behind on their taxes. I haven't confirmed it yet, but I'd bet my collection of snowboards that he's targeting the elderly."

I meet Teagan at the front of the car. She looks down at our entwined fingers after I claim her hand. A small smile settles on her lips.

"Fan-fucking-tastic," I drawl. Teagan's eyes dart to me when the sarcasm seeps from my tone. I shake my head and lead her up the stairs to her apartment for the last night ever. "How did you figure this out?"

"We've been tailing him since you left town. The judge rushed the warrant for a wire. Boom, bang, bamboozle—I'm the information king."

"I'm going to miss you, Taylor."

Teagan lets us into her apartment, and I lock us in for the night. I drop my keys and wallet on the kitchen counter, since it's the only space not covered in boxes and bags. I watch as Teagan goes straight to the bathroom and shuts herself inside.

"So he's buying information, hooking them, and selling off the information. We need to figure out who his clients are," I say. "I think it's safe to say they aren't in the US."

"Agreed. I intercepted the calls to the tax offices. I'll see where it goes from here. He just bought a shit ton of fresh contacts in

Jefferson Parish we're going to follow. Or I will, since you skipped town."

"You act like I snuck out in the middle of the night. Anyway, you work your end. I have an idea for mine. I'll make that call first thing in the morning."

"Do you have a smoking gun?"

"Something like that." I turn when I hear the bathroom door.

Fuck.

Teagan is standing there in a tiny robe. Tiny as in short. Like it barely covers her pussy short. She has it cinched at the waist, and the arms are so wide they hang past her hands. It lands somewhere on the scale between white and pink.

But that doesn't matter.

It's time for me to conduct a different kind of investigation. The kind to figure out what's beneath that robe.

"I've got to go," I mutter and push myself away from the counter where I was leaning. "Call me tomorrow. I'll be driving most of the day. You can keep me company."

"I can't wait. Like old times."

I don't shift my stare from Teagan where she fingers the tail end of the belt that holds that damn robe together. "It's like you forgot we worked together the day before last."

"Yep. The good ole' days."

"If you don't let me go, I'm hanging up on you."

"Fine, fine. I'll call you tomorrow. You'll hurt my feelings if you don't answer."

I'm done. I disconnect the call and drop my cell into an open box. I hope to find it later, that's how distracted I am by the woman across the room.

"This is a surprise."

She lifts a slim shoulder. "Is it? We've been dancing around each other all day. So many eyes on us."

I take two steps toward her. "I didn't say it was an unwelcome surprise. And the secret was your idea."

She winds the end of the belt around and around her finger. "After spending all day with my parents, you can't tell me you aren't grateful for the secret."

I have to roll my lips to wet them. "I'd rather shout it from the rooftops. The only thing today proved is that privacy does not suck. I was happy to not be interrogated."

"You're ready to tell the world we don't know if this is a sure thing when I haven't even begged you to kiss me?"

"I'll kiss you soon enough." I erase every inch between us until we're flush. Her tits brush my chest through the thin robe. "Do you know what I like?"

"Me?" The word is more than a guess. If a word could be a hope and a dream, that would be it.

I shake my head. "Give yourself more credit, baby. Like is not a strong enough word when it comes to you."

I feel her breathe deeply against my neck. "Tell me what you like."

I reach up and dust my fingers against her cheek. "I like that we don't have to fuck around with the *getting to know you* stage."

She hikes a brow. "So we can skip straight to *fucking around* stage?"

"I'll enjoy any stage with you ... but the getting-to-know-you stage?" My fingers play with the ends of her loose waves. I wind a curl around my finger to toy with it, the same way she was doing with the robe I'd like to rip off her. "I know you. You know me. Which is why I'm confident this won't be a secret for long."

"That's pretty presumptuous of you. We're not even on kissing terms," she teases.

"But we are on orgasm terms." As opposed to hers, my words are dead serious. "A little out of order, but the kissing will come."

"It's like you assume I'm a sure thing." This time it's her turn to touch me. Her hand comes to my side, and she drags her fingers to my pec. There, she drags her nail over my nipple and looks up at me through dark lashes. "I'm not desperate like I was two years ago."

"That's interesting." I give her hair a gentle tug. "You seemed quite desperate this morning when I had my hand between your legs."

Her expression falls.

Score one for me.

"It's been a stressful few days." She tries to justify begging me to let her come. "It was ... a nice stress reliever."

"Was it?" I have to bite back a grin. "You're welcome. I'd never want you to be stressed."

"Roc—"

"What I meant was..." It's my turn to pause. I wrap my arm around her and turn her so her back is pressed to my chest. She's small compared to me, but like this she feels even smaller. It makes me want to wrap her up in my arms and never let her go. I lean my head down and press my lips to the side of her head and keep talking. "I know you here. I love your brain. How you think. Your combination of intellect and tenacity are a deadly weapon. You know, the rhetorical kind."

When I wrap an arm around her waist, she leans heavy into my chest. I drag my hand up her middle and graze her tits with my hand.

No bra.

My dick thickens in my pants as my blood rushes south.

I feel every beat of her heart as it speeds where my hand is pressed. Together, we're a storm of emotions.

"But what I really love is this." I slide my hand into her robe, so we're skin on skin. I press my hand over her heart. "You said you've changed, but you can't lie to me. I know you too well. You're the same girl who treated me like I was someone when I wasn't. You're the same one who will do anything for your sister even though she's a pain in the ass and everyone knows it. Fuck, baby. I watched you grow up. You had a heart of gold the day I met you—it only shines brighter now."

Her breathing shallows. I only have to move an inch to cup her tit.

She lets out a groan when I circle her nipple before giving it a twist. Her robe falls open above her waist, and I'm momentarily stunned. The view below me does not suck.

I could stand here for the rest of my days.

She holds onto my forearm like a lifeline, as I wrap my other arm around her to support her weight. The day I get to sink into her balls deep, pressed to the wall, will be epic.

It's what dreams are made of.

I've dreamed of supporting her weight that way—with her wrapped around me like a noose.

Until then, this will have to do.

"Rocco," she calls for me like I'm not solely focused on her since she's the center of my world.

"Yeah, baby?"

She licks her lips. "This is so good, I'm afraid to go back to Miami. I'm afraid being there will be like a bucket of cold water doused on my fantasy. Nothing will be the same."

"That will never happen. I'll find a way to make sure this never ends." I let go of her long enough to grab the end of the belt holding the last bit of robe closed and pull. It falls slack. I run the tip of my nose around the circle of her ear as I slide my hand down to her panties and tuck a finger through the slip of material at her hip. "You could've done without these. They'll just be in the way."

She exhales on a weak laugh. "I thought it was fitting to wear them to graduation. You did buy them for me."

My dick doesn't care about graduation gifts. He's hard as a fucking rock in my pants and begging to be set free.

But I need to see this better.

I step away from her far enough to pull the silk robe over her shoulders and allow gravity to take over.

She's bare other than the damn butter yellow pair of panties she taunted me with. When I take another step back to get a good look, she peeks over her bare shoulder at me. "Did I say thank you?"

I don't take my eyes off her ass. "Only dripped with sarcasm."

She turns, and I barely get a good look at her from the front before she returns to me, pressing her front to mine. "Then I owe you a heart-felt thanks. I love them."

I drag my hands down her body to land on her hips. "I'd love them more on the floor."

"But then I'd be completely naked." She widens her eyes and is back to throwing sarcasm. Shockingly, I'm good with it when she's mostly bare. "You don't want to tempt the no-sex rule, right?"

"You little minx. It seems like you're doing just that by talking about the rule. Plus, the no sex rule can be followed as long as one of us is dressed. Another rule to add to the list."

"Another rule?" she asks. "How is that fair for me?"

"Because you're going to benefit from it. It's a promise I won't break."

She looks into my eyes, and because I know her well enough, I know she's dead-ass serious. "I've never known you to break a promise."

I shake my head, and my answer is as grave as her own words. "Never. Especially to you."

She nods. "I know. Even when I made you promise to leave me alone the last two years. You agreed and you followed through."

She slides her hand down.

Down.

And farther down.

When she palms my hard dick over my pants, she gives me a firm stroke. I shift my legs to adjust myself and she cups me.

She has me by the balls.

Figuratively.

Literally.

Deliciously.

I've never been happier.

"If we get to skip the getting-to-know-you phase, why so many rules?"

"I told you why, and I'm not changing my mind. I'll do all kinds of other shit with you, but making you mine?" I shake my head. "That's for life."

"Life," she echoes and licks her lips.

Her gaze travels south while her fingers make quick work of the buttons on my shirt as she tugs. She's not patient and shoves my shirt over my shoulders as fast as she can.

She tips her face to mine. "I'm not going to lie. I'm bummed about the no sex."

I shrug like it's no skin off my back, even though I'll bet I'm more bummed than her. She drags her nails lightly down my skin and I get to watch her lean in and press her lips over my heart.

That's when I feel her fingers at my waistband. I grab her hand. "Teagan. Do not tempt me to break my own rule. You know how I feel about being in control."

"But—"

"It's hard enough sleeping next you in my boxers." I rip her hands from my pants and pick her up under the arms. She squeals but wraps her legs around my waist to hold on. My hands go to her bare ass in those sexy as fuck underwear. Her barely covered pussy is pressed to my bare abs. I turn and put her back to the bed coming down on top of her. We're nose to nose again. "I'm waiting."

She beams up at me. "For what?"

I give her more of my weight. "You know what."

"Maybe you're up for a negotiation?"

"Why are you pressuring me to have sex while we're not even on kissing terms yet?"

She drags a finger down the middle of my chest. "I'm not going to lie, I'm just happy to be on any terms with you again."

"I'd agree, but now that I'm here, I'm not settling for anything less." I dip my head and run the tip of my nose up the column of her neck. My tongue sneaks out for a taste of her bare skin before I look up. "I can wait to kiss you, but there are other things I'm not willing to wait on."

She tries to reach for my face, but I shake my head as I reach for her hips. "No, baby. Me first."

18

JEALOUS OF MY TOES

Teagan

I have no clue what I'm saying half the time when we're like this. I'm winging it and hope I don't come across awkward as hell.

The number of times I've almost begged him to kiss me is ranking right up there with the National Debt.

I want it so bad.

I get what he's doing with the sex rule. He's being pragmatic and responsible and levelheaded. I might seem like I'm teasing him about it, but I'm not. I'm dead serious. I don't care about future me at the moment. But that's what desperation does to a woman.

I want every single experience I can get with Rocco.

I refuse to think about going back to Miami. Sleeping across the hall from him. Or moving to New York.

When those times come, I'll deal.

Or I won't.

It'll just be more drama weighing me down.

The only thing I want is to focus on our secret and seeing where it goes.

That's why when I feel my panties wisped down my legs, clearing the tips of my toes, every nerve ending in my body goes on high alert.

I'm naked.

And the only man I've ever wanted is looking down at me like I'm his last meal on earth.

Dreams really do come true.

All it takes is his index finger on the tip of my knee to send a rush of goosebumps over my flushed skin.

His gaze washes down my body like a wave at high tide. Forceful, strong, and overwhelming.

He pushes one knee to the side leaving me open and bare and wanting.

Who knew there was another level of want when it comes to him?

He shakes his head as the tip of his finger trails down the inside of my thigh. "I'm not going to lie. You're like a dream I never thought would happen for me. You should be off limits to me for so many reasons."

"Are we really going to have this conversation right now? I mean, if you insist, fine. But I think it's only fair that you get naked too."

The smirk that usually makes my stomach do flips appears. Sometimes it's enough to make me wet. I'm already past that point, but it doesn't mean I'll pass up that expression any day. It's lived in my head rent free for years. I've missed the reality of it like it was a severed limb.

"I can't wait to be naked with you." He sighs as if checking his resolve. "But not yet, baby." He bends at the waist and his hands land on the bed on either side of my head. He's looming over me like he's trying to decide what he wants to do first.

I've never loved anything more than the dream of us. But in the past few days, there are things vying for that spot—this is one of them.

He leans in, and for a split second I think he's not going to make me beg for it. Our lips are a breath apart.

Then he moves.

Instead of my mouth, his lips hit my breastbone before taking a sharp turn straight for my nipple. I moan when he sucks. My hands come to his head, and I thread my fingers through his hair.

"Roc," I call for him.

He doesn't answer—his mouth is too busy. His hands join his lips for the full experience, and the sensation overwhelms me.

Tongue.

Lips.

Fingers.

Big, strong hands.

My mouth falls open as I press my head into the bed when those hands grip me between my thighs to open me.

That's when it happens.

Oh, Lord.

Rocco Monroe puts his mouth between my legs.

I call out the moment it happens. It's as if he likes my moan as much as I like what he's doing between my legs.

Impossible.

But it does spur him on. His grip on me tightens, and he pushes me higher and wider.

It's impossible to move, so I fist the messy covers beneath me to hang on.

He laps and sucks and flicks. Just when I think my orgasm is about to take over, he pulls back, and kisses me everywhere but my clit. He traces me with the tip of his tongue and kneads my ass and thighs where he's holding me in a vise. It's only when my breathing evens out that he starts again.

"Rocco." I pant his name. "Please. I can't take this."

He lifts his head and lightly nips the side of my thigh with his teeth. "That's funny, because you don't seem to have a choice."

I start to groan a complaint, but that's when he pulls my clit between his lips again. Another flick followed by a firm circle of his tongue.

I'm surprised when he lets go of one of my legs, but a finger slips inside me. Then another.

He pumps me at the same time he sucks and rolls his tongue. That's all it takes.

I fall off the edge he's kept me balanced on for far too long.

Stars shine behind my closed eyes, and I gasp to breathe. This is unlike any orgasm I've had before—since all the ones pre-Rocco were self-induced.

My body is heavy and satisfied, but nothing could make me feel as good as Rocco's weight pushing me into the bed—his bare chest pressed to my bare skin. I'm in such a haze, I didn't realize he lost his pants. The barriers between us become fewer and fewer as our days together add up. The only thing separating us are his thin boxers.

Every inch of his long, hard cock is pressed to my sex. I'm still sensitive, so when he grinds into me, my body shudders as he wraps me up in his arms and rolls us to our sides.

And this is where we settle—me naked and Rocco almost naked. He's got one hand on the back of my head and one on my ass holding me tight to him. I'm still trying to catch my breath against the skin of his neck.

"That's a first for me," I whisper.

He tenses. "We need to talk about that."

I snuggle into him farther. He's so warm. "What's there to talk about? I just told you that was a first."

He fists my hair and gives it a little tug until our gazes lock. Despite him still holding me tight to his hard cock, his expression is dead serious. "Are there any other firsts you've yet to experience?"

I wet my lips, not sure if I want to have this conversation. In a way I do. I want to tell him everything, even about the things where there isn't much to tell. But he also flipped out on me because of our pasts and family.

"Teagan," he bites my name. "Answer me."

My post orgasmic haze quickly clears. I narrow my eyes. "You don't get to demand I do something and expect me to jump."

He hikes a brow. "So you're still a virgin."

Not a question. A statement.

"I didn't say that."

"You didn't say *anything*," he stresses. "If that was a new experience for you, and you're not a virgin, then you had a shitty lover."

"Lover?" I wince. "Yeah, I would not exactly call him that."

He lets me go long enough to roll me to my back. His narrow hips fit like a glove between my legs, and I drag my feet up his sides just to feel his rock-hard ass with the tips of my toes.

I've wondered what it felt like so many times.

Look at me now.

My fingers are jealous of my toes.

He props himself on his forearms. "Having this conversation with you naked beneath me was not on my bingo card, but now I need to know, or I'll go crazy and never sleep. What exactly would you call this asshole?"

I trace his full bottom lip with the tip of my finger. "Technically, I guess he was my first. But it was just once, and it wasn't good. It was so fast, I'm not even sure it happened. I definitely didn't come. I've wondered if it even counts."

An expression washes over his face that's a mix of horrified and angry. "Are you fucking kidding me?"

I grip his shoulder. "Do you really think I would lie here naked and kid about something like that?"

He looks away from me and stares at the wall behind my bed. His jaw is tense, and I think a muscle in his cheek just twitched.

"Rocco?"

His gaze returns to me with an exasperated exhale before he rolls. The next thing I know, I get something else new with Rocco. He's flat on his back, and I'm sprawled naked on top of him. His hands slide down my back and land on my ass. "I don't know what to say other than I'm pissed."

I tuck my messy hair behind one ear and look down at him. "Why?"

His grip on my ass tightens. "Was this shitty experience after our first kiss and before our second?"

"That's one way of putting it. I like to refer to that time as *hell week*, but it dragged on for two years. I've also named that time in my life the *dark ages*." I can tell his patience is thinning. "And yes. It happened during the dark ages."

"Fuck me," he mutters.

I shake my head. "No. That didn't happen, hence the dark ages. It was my time in hell. Why are you pissed?"

He drags his hands down my hamstrings and yanks my legs up his sides. "I'm pissed you had such a shitty experience, you're not even sure if it counts. And I'm pissed at myself that I gave in and left you alone when you asked me to. I just tasted you for the first time and now I'm pissed about everything. Your first time could've been me. Fuck, it should've been me."

I like this position, so I press down on his semi-hard cock. "I agree."

His hands return to my ass for a firm squeeze. "That doesn't make me any less pissed."

I rock up and down against him. He's back to a full-on erection, which makes me smile. "That's your problem, not mine."

When he narrows his eyes, it happens so fast, I'm not sure which was more shocking, the sound or sting.

His right hand leaves my ass long enough to return for a sharp spank.

I gasp and exclaim, "What was that?"

He doesn't answer, but he does lift his hips to press into my sex as he rocks me up and down his length.

Then, he smiles.

"Rocco." I bite his name, but I don't pull away. My sex spasms where he's pressed.

He keeps moving me, rocking me up and down his cock. "You liked that."

"You spanked me." I state the obvious. "Why would I like that?"

He reaches farther with one hand and dips his fingers between my legs. "Because you're wet again. Really fucking wet."

He's right.

So, so right.

Even so, I'm not about to admit it. "You have no idea what I like."

His smile swells. "Neither do you. But I'm willing to test the waters so I can figure it out."

"You're impossible."

"And you like a little kink," he quips. "Who knows, maybe a lot. You've just never had anyone to help you figure it out, since you may or may not be a virgin."

"I'm not a virgin," I exclaim.

"If you say so."

I drop my face back to his neck. He continues to knead my ass. If anything, his touch is firmer than it's ever been.

"I'm tired," I lie.

He continues what he's doing and starts to drag his fingers from my clit to my ass. "Then you should go to sleep."

"I can't sleep when you're doing this. And I can't sleep on you. We'll both get hot."

His lips slide to my ear. "You're already hot."

"I thought you were pissed?" I say, trying to focus on anything other than how good this feels.

"I'll always be pissed about that. But I've decided to set that aside and give you something new."

I lean up to look into his eyes. "What would that be?"

He flicks my clit. "You're going to come again, but you're going to do all the work, and I'm going to watch."

All the oxygen leaves my body. "No."

"Yes." My clit gets another swipe. It feels so good, I press down on him for more. "You'll sleep better. Come on, baby. Move."

His finger finds my clit again, but not for a flick. It's a ghost of a touch.

A tease.

I want more, so I move.

I groan when I come into contact with him.

He angles his face to the side of my head. "Good, baby. Just like that. Do it again. Do it for me."

His words make me wetter.

Praise from Rocco. My brain goes back to when I would do anything just to win a smile. But this...

This is so much more.

I rock again and have to move farther to find his touch.

This feels different. I'm in control, rocking up and down on his cock while frantically trying to find his touch. I arch my back and spread my legs wider. I'm desperate and move faster to find it.

That's when he does it again.

I gasp.

Another sharp sting, this one right on my sex.

This time he doesn't move his hand. Instead, he massages away the sting. I'm left with red-hot desire.

"Fuck, you love that," he growls in my ear. "If I don't come just watching you, it'll be a miracle. Don't stop, baby."

I can't form words, but I do know what I want.

What I need.

I move.

Every time I do, I find his touch. I move faster and harder, feeling him lift his hips into me.

I'm about to fall over the edge once more, when I get another spank. This one harder, sharper, louder.

Right where I needed it.

I come immediately.

And Rocco takes over.

He thrusts his hips into me as his strong hand cups me between the legs. His fingers work my clit as I come and come and come. With the second coming so soon after the first, this one feels different.

But I'm not the only one breathing hard.

Rocco's thick arm angles up my back. His hold on me is strong yet desperate.

That's when a groan like I've never heard rumbles through the small space and vibrates against my chest.

His hold between my legs tightens as he presses his cock into my body. I feel him pulse against me as his body jerks.

We both came together.

And, still, no sex.

Not officially, anyway.

His body is a machine. For years, I've watched him play college football. Walk around in swim trunks. There was the one time I saw him lifting weights at Micah and Evie's.

So when every tense muscle in his body gives in to what we experienced together, it's like he collapses beneath me.

Exhausted.

Spent.

Sated.

I haven't lost his touch, but his hold that was absolute

moments ago is loose and relaxed. Still, his hand that spanked me three times doesn't leave my ass.

I rise and fall on his chest as he works to catch his breath. "Fuck, I lost my load in my underwear. I think I was in middle school the last time that happened. What the hell are you doing to me, Teagan?"

I nuzzle my nose into the crook of his neck. I'm just as depleted as he is. Maybe more. I've had two orgasms to his one. "That's because of your stupid no-sex rule."

At my words, he's not relaxed any longer.

His hands take my face and he pulls me up his body.

Then his mouth claims mine.

His tongue plunges in my mouth. He tastes as good as ever mixed with the scent of me.

I love it.

His lips are bruising and firm. He never breaks our connection as he rolls me to my back. This kiss isn't like our first or our second.

It's different.

Rocco is hungry.

He kisses me in a way I didn't know possible.

When he finally slows, we're both breathing hard again. I open my eyes when his forehead tips to mine.

In all our time together, I've never seen this look in his eyes.

"I won," I whisper.

He frowns but says nothing.

"The kiss," I go on. "You gave in first. I didn't have to beg. So I won."

"Baby." His breath blankets my face on an exhale. "I'm the winner. And I hit the fucking jackpot."

Something warm blooms inside me.

And it wraps itself around my heart.

19

GHOST

Teagan

I frown when I look at the caller on the screen. What in the world could he need already?

I answer the call and put it over Bluetooth. "We've barely been on the road for twenty minutes. Do you need a bathroom break already?"

"I like the sight of you from behind, but not like this," he says. "This is going to be the longest trip of my life."

"You interrupted my crime podcast to tell me you like my ass?"

His answer is immediate. "I do love your ass. Especially in your new underwear."

"And to think it was just last week that you were grumpy about my graduation panties."

"I'll buy you all the panties."

I sigh and look out at nothing but highway, blue skies, and two days of travel ahead of us. "My podcast was getting to the good part, you know."

"I figure we have two days on the road and two years to make up for. There's a lot to talk about."

I grab my lip balm as I talk. "You want to make up for two whole years? That's a lot of talking."

"It'll keep you alert."

I sigh. "Okay, should we start with the day after you broke my heart by pushing me away?"

"Hell, no." I hear the frown in his tone. "I want to start with your quasi virginity."

"Of course you do," I mutter. "I have no desire to talk about that."

"You can't break something like that to me when you're naked and not expect me to ask about it. I want to know who the asshole is who left you questioning your virginity."

"My virginity is not in question, Roc. I'm not going to lie, I regret it. It was just…" I cringe thinking back on the horrible experience. "It was bad. We'd been seeing each other for a few months. I think he even knew how bad it was. It made everything awkward. Sex should make a good thing better, right?"

"It will with me," he states.

"So confident," I mutter. "But what about your rule? I may never know."

"Oh, you'll know. I just need to get you to commit first."

"Rocco—"

"Which is something else we need to talk about," he interrupts. "Are you moving to New York because I'm moving back to Miami?"

"Confident and presumptuous."

"Tell me," he demands. Rocco the talker strikes again.

I don't say anything. This is the last thing I want to fess up to.

He keeps going. "Not that we were around at the same time since you made it your life's mission to avoid me prior to last week, but do you remember when Brax and Landyn announced they were pregnant again?"

"How could I forget? The group chat was nonstop for two days. I finally had to put it on silent so I could get anything done."

"Landyn called me right after that. She said it was my turn, that she and Brax wanted me to be the baby's godfather."

"That wasn't a surprise. Everyone knew that was coming," I say. "They've been saying it for years."

"Saying and doing are two different things, Teag. This isn't just about it being my turn. This is more. And it's a big fucking deal."

I shake my head like he's sitting next to me having this conversation. "I know where you're going with this, and you're wrong."

"It doesn't matter if I'm right or wrong. The fact they chose me cements me in the family."

"You were cemented into the family the day you saved Landyn. She's said it. Brax confirmed it."

"It's not the same. My point is, I take that shit seriously. It might be a gesture that most people take for granted and show up at birthday parties and shit, but that's not going to be me. I need to be there. Hell, I want to be there. I want this kid to know it can count on me for more than just gifts and gum. There's nothing I want more than to be better than where I came from."

My eyes prick with tears behind my sunglasses. "You've never had to try, Roc. Everyone sees that but you. You know how protective my parents are. Do you think they would've let you live with us if they didn't trust you?"

"That doesn't matter," he goes on. "The reason I'm telling you this is to explain why I want to be back in Miami. Hell, it's not even a want. I'm desperate for it."

I change lanes to pass a car that's going far below the speed limit and glance into my rearview mirror. Rocco is right there—two to three car lengths behind me—not letting me out of his sight. It doesn't matter that I'm driving the speed limit and he never does. He hasn't complained once.

"I'm not blaming you for wanting to be back." I know where this is going. And after the recent turn of events between Rocco and me, I'm more confused than ever about moving to New York. "You deserve to be back in Miami. I've heard the agents talk. I know how hard you work. You've made a name for yourself, and you did it on your own. And I know them asking you to be the godfather is a big deal, because I know what it means to Brax and Landyn—especially Landyn."

The line goes silent when he doesn't respond. I wish I could look into his eyes right now. This is the side of Rocco not many people know. Brax and Landyn and my parents understand it best. I've witnessed it secondhand. If I were to guess, Micah and King know of it because there are no secrets in our little found family.

I mean, there is one secret, and it had better stay that way for the time being.

I decide to take a chance and step into the uncomfortable. "That night when I kissed you the first time and caught you so far off guard, you pushed me away ... I might've been younger and on the wrong path and tipsy, but I wasn't young and stupid. It wasn't a spur-of-the-moment thing. For as long as I can remember, I've compared every guy who came into my life to you. And it's because you're you. Everything about you is good, Rocco. I wish you could see yourself the way everyone else sees you." And then more quietly, I add, "The way I see you."

"You don't know what it's like. I've got a fucking ghost on my heels, reminding me who I am every waking minute of the day. Hell, it reminds me of who I'm not more than anything else. That's the worst. It doesn't matter how much I try, I can't shake it."

I probably shouldn't ask, but I can't help it. I need to know. "Do you feel that way when you're with me?"

"Baby," he huffs, almost like it's the most stupid question

anyone has ever asked. "Brax and Landyn moved me across the country with them. Your parents moved me into their house. Micah pretty much handed me the opportunity to go to college on a silver platter. King treats me like an equal, which I do not deserve. But nothing, and I mean not one fucking thing, has made me feel less deserving of anything in my life than the thought of making you mine. It consumed me for two years."

A single tear streaks my cheek, and I don't bother wiping it away. I'm too mesmerized by Rocco's confession mixed with the endless highway in front of me to respond. It doesn't matter how consumed I am by the man he's become. All I see is the boy in a man's body who came to live with us all those years ago.

The one who felt the need to earn every meal he ate.

The one who never had his own bedroom until my parents gave him one.

And the one who felt so uncomfortable if anyone showed him kindness—let alone love—I thought he was going to run away from our family forever.

But he was also the same one that would do anything for anyone.

"You deserve everything," I say on a whisper that I hope he can hear. "You definitely deserve better than me shutting you out just because I didn't get what I wanted at a time when I'd lost my way. You didn't deserve that. I'd do anything to go back and change it if I could."

"Fuck," he mutters. I can't tell if that one word is from anger or frustration. "See that next exit? Pull off."

I hit my brakes, because the next exit isn't in miles, it's right in front of me. "Why?"

"Do it, Teag. Get off the damn highway," he demands.

I flip my signal and veer to the right. We're in the middle of nowhere. The only thing off the highway is an abandoned gas station. "There's nothing here. Why are we stopping?"

He doesn't answer.

He disconnects our call.

I pull into the parking lot that hasn't seen a car in years if its desolate state is anything to go by. A faded *closed* sign hangs crooked in the window, as if anyone would be mistaken about this place being open for business. I put my car into park in the middle of the lot.

Rocco pulls in behind me and is out of his car faster than me. When I glance in my side mirror, all I see is his large frame stalking toward me like a police officer on a mission who just pulled me over.

I unlock my door and reach for the handle, but he gets to me first. The next thing I know, my door is open, and Rocco is pulling me from the driver's seat. He plucks the sunglasses from my face and tosses them haphazardly into the car.

"What are you—" I start, but don't get another word out.

He claims my face as his hands span my jaw and cradle my head.

He consumes me.

His body presses mine to the side of my car. The metal is hot on my skin from the bright summer day, but it's nothing compared to his desperation. I taste it as his tongue spears my mouth and feel it where his hips press into my belly.

I have no choice but to grip his forearms and hang on. Whatever this is, I'm here for it. Because this is different.

Ever since Rocco pushed his way into my life uninvited, it's been everything from angsty to passionate. He's been demanding and generous. And, per his stupid rule, there's been no sex, but that doesn't mean they haven't been the hottest experiences of my life.

Yet, this is something new.

Rocco breaks his kiss and tips his forehead to mine. His eyes are closed, and his wide chest rises and falls with heavy breaths.

I squeeze his wrists. When his eyes open, I see it—the difference between this kiss compared to any other intimate interaction we've had.

This is raw.

His fingers press into my scalp where he still holds me. "You're one of the few people in this world off-limits to me. You're also one of very few who know the old me and the new me. The fact that you're standing here in my arms feels as taboo as it does perfect. I should focus on the fact your dad might kill me, or the fact the agents will have his back, or I could just be an asshole and enjoy it while I can since it's a secret. But all I can do is think about how you're about to slip through my fingers, and it will be my own damn fault."

I have to squint since the fiery ball in the sky bears down on us. "You really carry the weight of the world on your shoulders, don't you?"

There's a tick in his jaw. "Move to New York and that will for sure be the case."

That thought makes me sick to my stomach—both the move and his guilt.

"I didn't know this was going to happen. I'll admit it—my move to New York was pure self-preservation. The thought of living in the same city as you was painful. I knew I wouldn't be able to take it."

His grip on my face tightens. I have a feeling he's about to revisit the same argument he's touched on more times than I can count, but I'm saved by the bell.

Or his cellphone.

He lets go of me, pulls it from his pocket, and frowns when he reads the screen.

"Who is it?" I ask.

"Brax." He sends it to voicemail and turns back at me. He

braces both hands on the roof of my car behind me, boxing me in. "Stay."

My mouth gapes. "Excuse me?"

"Don't go to New York. Stay in Miami. Be there for Sammie and her baby. For your parents." He leans in closer and gives me the heat of his body again. "But for more than anything, stay for me."

I put my hands to his sides. "Rocco—"

His cell rings again.

"Dammit," he grits.

I have no desire to have this conversation in the summer heat. "He seems insistent. You'd better answer that."

He shakes his head and touches the screen almost violently. He greets one of his best friends in the world as if he interrupted a meeting discussing State secrets. "You're fucking needy today. What do you want?"

Rocco

"Maybe we need a code word or a bat signal since we'll be working together. Sometimes I call with important shit. I've texted you five times and called three. Answer your damn phone."

I've been too wrapped up in baring my soul to Teagan in hopes it will make her rethink her move. Hell, I'm not above begging. That will come next.

It was easy to ignore him.

I don't move away from Teagan. I want to get to the hotel I

booked for us tonight in the Florida panhandle, but the thought of getting closer to Miami brings the reality of this ending.

Which is what brought me to my new low of begging her to stay. I even emotionally guilted her with her sister and new baby.

"I have news," Brax states gravely. "And you're not going to like it."

Teagan grips my shirt, and her expression looks like a question mark. I shrug and look over her head at the abandoned building behind her that looks like it's from another era. "Did someone die?"

"Not exactly," Brax says. "In fact, it's more like the opposite."

"You know, I am dealing with a lot of shit at the moment. I don't appreciate the riddle."

"Sorry, man. Maybe I should've had Landyn call you. I'm not great with this stuff." He pulls in a deep breath. "It's your father."

I step away from Teagan, turn to the side, and freeze. "What about him?"

"I've kept tabs on him. I have ever since we were in with the Marinos. Later, I did it for you. I wanted to make sure he never touched your life again, especially when you were younger."

I drop my head and stare at the weeds growing up through the cracks of the parking lot. Useless weeds, thriving in a shithole environment. Not unlike me before Brax and Landyn dragged me out of the shithole I was barely surviving in.

"Roc, I don't know what to say, other than I'm sorry. I haven't looked into the details yet, but it sucks to tell you your father has been released. Not even on probation. He's out. Free and clear."

I drag a hand through my hair and grip the back of my neck. "Fuck."

I feel hands on me. Her touch isn't familiar at this point. That's how new it is. How new we are. She wraps me up from behind and presses her cheek to my spine. She doesn't even know what's going on, but she knows it's bad.

"How the hell did he get out early? And when did it happen?"

"Like I said, I just found out. I'll reach out to my contacts in California and find out what I can. But it was the week before last. I've checked on his status about once a month since the beginning. I feel like shit I didn't know sooner."

I grab Teagan's hand and pull her to my front as I speak. "Why should you feel like shit? I didn't even know you were keeping tabs on him. I've looked him up once or twice over the years, but really, it's all I could do to forget about him."

"I get that." Brax says as Teagan looks up at me with worried eyes. "Let me find out what I can. I'll get back with you. When will you and Teagan roll into town?"

"Late tomorrow afternoon. How's Landyn?"

"She's nesting, which means I'm cleaning shit nonstop. The sooner you get back the better. She can focus on you for a change."

I don't tell him that I refuse to clean anything, because he knows I'll do it. I've never said no to Landyn. "See you soon. Teagan and I made a stop. We need to get back on the road or we'll never get there."

"Take care of her. I'll let you know when I find out anything on your father."

Oh, I'll definitely take care of her. "Will do."

I disconnect the call and pull Teagan tighter to my chest. "Change of plans. Fuck Miami and fuck our jobs. We're moving to Canada."

She rolls her eyes. "What happened?"

I lean down and press my lips to hers. "The un-fucking-believable. If I get into it now, we'll never leave. I'll call you."

"Two years to catch up on, huh?"

"And more, baby. So much more."

20

YOU'LL PAY

Rocco
Fifteen years ago

"Rocco Monroe, do you solemnly swear or affirm that the testimony you're about to give will be the truth, the whole truth, and nothing but the truth, so help you God?"

I look from the book in the guy's hand to the judge.

"Go ahead," the judge nods to the guy standing in front of me in a uniform. "We need your answer for the court record."

It's all I can do not to look across the room at him.

I swallow hard and nod. "Yeah. I do."

"Have a seat, Rocco," the judge orders. He's the same guy who's asked me two million questions. I think he's trying to make sure I'm not whacko crazy.

"Your Honor, the defense objects to the boy as a witness. He—"

But the judge bangs his gavel. "Overruled. I interviewed him myself. He's sound and capable."

I stare down at my hands as I violently wring my fingers in knots. The guy from the table across from Dad stands and moves in front of me. Hell, he told me his name, but I can't seem to remember it. "Hi, Rocco."

I have to clear my throat. "Hey."

"I'm going to keep this short. We'll get you out of here as fast as we can, okay? I only have a few questions."

I shrug. It's not like I have a choice but to be here. Not really. Mom's brother told me I had to if I wanted to live with him. The only other option was foster care. He told me no one would want someone my age, and I'd end up in a boys' home. I know he's right. It happened to a guy at school last year.

"Okay," the guy goes on. "Do you know that man sitting at the table over there?"

I refuse to look across the room. We caught sight of each other when I walked in, and that was bad enough. If Dad could kill me with his eyes, I'd for sure be dead right now.

An addition to the family gravesite. If there was one.

I don't look away from the guy in the suit talking to me. "Yeah. He's my dad."

The guy stuffs his hands in his pockets. "What's your dad's name, Rocco?"

I swallow hard. The sound of his name on my lips sounds like sandpaper. "Rodney. Rodney Monroe."

"Thank you for making that clear for the court. Rocco, I'm so sorry about the loss of your mother. Can you tell us where you were the night she died?"

That's easy. I'm never at home. It's the most miserable place on earth. I'd give anything if I weren't there that day.

Telling the truth isn't the norm for me, but I just swore on the Bible I would. I've never even touched a Bible. But I don't need that kind of bad karma. And the guy talking to me now prepped me that if I told the truth, there's a good chance I'd never have to see Dad again.

That's something I could be down for.

"I was at home."

He nods. From the expression on his face, it looks like he thinks that's the saddest thing he's ever heard.

I'd go with gross, but I guess to someone who looks like they could be on TV, it could be sad.

"I see," he goes on. "Were your parents at home that night?"

I don't look away from him. For some reason, the pounding in my chest gets louder in my ears. "Yeah."

"Can you tell me what happened that night?"

I do what he told me to do when he acted like he gave two shits about me, which he doesn't. There's no reason for him to give two, let alone one.

"They were high." Like they always were.

"I see. Anything else?"

"They were fighting." Like they always did.

"Do you know what they were fighting about, Rocco?"

"No. But they always fought. No different than any other day."

"Then what made this day different?"

I look down at my hands to see blood. Fuck. I cut myself with my own thumbnail and didn't even feel it.

I wipe the blood away on my worn jeans and sit on my hands to make myself stop.

"Rocco, can you tell me why that day was different from any others?"

"He started pushing her around. But that always happened."

"I see," he says. "What happened then?"

My stomach turns at the thought of it. I can't puke in here. I could care less who sees me or has to clean it up. But there's no doubt Dad will laugh in my face if I do.

"I tried to stop it."

Fuck.

Don't puke.

Don't puke.

I swallow hard.

"Have you ever tried to stop it before?"

I shake my head. "No. I was too small. He was too big."

The guy nods and pauses like he's in a damn movie or something. "Can you tell me what happened next?"

It's all I can do not to squirm on my hands. "He came after me."

"Is that the first time that happened?"

I shake my head. "Nah."

"How old are you, Rocco?"

Something about the way he asks me that makes me want to stand up for myself. I don't need anyone feeling sorry for me. "Fourteen—fifteen next month."

"Did your father hit you?"

"He tried." I sit up a bit taller. "But I'm faster." And there's the bit that he was high, but I already said that.

"That's good." Fucking great. Another sad smile from the guy. If I throw up, I'll just throw up on him. At least he won't look like he feels sorry for me. I fucking hate it when people feel sorry for me. That seems to be a common theme since the big event. "What happened next?"

Well, damn. It's my turn for the stupid pause. "It pissed him off. Like bad. Worse than normal. Like he had something to prove. He went at Mom worse than he ever has. I tried to push him off, but I guess I'm not that big."

"It's okay, Rocco. You're fourteen."

I say nothing, but the desire to wring my fucking hands again crawls over my skin like spiders.

"What happened next?" he pushes.

I do what I need to do to not go to a boys' home. I tell the truth but do it in as few words as possible to get the hell out of here. "She fell. He grabbed her head. By the time he was done banging it on the floor, she wasn't moving and there was blood everywhere. That's when I ran out."

He nods slowly before glancing at the judge. "That will be all."

The guy goes back to his table. I have no one else to focus on and can't help but look at Dad arguing with his guy—lawyer, whatever he is. Their whispers are loud and angry. The guy is jabbing his finger into the table, and Dad leans in to get into his face.

I turn to the judge and frown. He's about to say something, but Dad's guy beats him to it and juts to his feet. "No questions, Your Honor."

"Goddammit," Dad yells. Papers fly off their table, and Dad throws himself back into his chair like he's throwing a fucking baby fit.

The next thing I know, the judge turns to me. "That'll be all, son. You can step down."

Son.

No one's ever called me that before. Hell, I doubt anyone's put me and that word in the same thought.

What I do know is I'm ready to get the fuck outta here.

I stand and stuff my hands into my front jean pockets so no one can see what I did to myself. The lady in charge of me stands in the middle of the aisle waiting to usher me out, probably to Mom's brother. I did what he told me to do. I told the truth, and I did it in front of Dad.

If he doesn't go to prison forever and then some, I might die.

I stalk as fast as I can without running, but when I pass Dad's table, the last thing I hear before I leave the courtroom are his words.

"You'll pay for this, boy."

21

BEFORE THE OBSESSION

Rocco
Present time

"Where do you think your dad will go?"

I look from the water to Teagan. "Let's get something straight. He is not my dad. You have a dad, I do not. A dad and father are two very different things."

She gives me a sad smile. As much as I hate sad smiles on anyone, I can't hate anything on Teagan. "Sorry, you're right. But do you know where he'll go? He's been in prison for fifteen years."

I shake my head. "No fucking clue. I'm going to find out though. It was my testimony that put him away. And he's not the kind of guy to be reformed. If I had to guess, he'll come looking for me."

"Do you think he knows you were a cop and now an agent? He'd be stupid to try to find you, let alone do anything to you, right?"

"Baby, he killed my mother in front of me while he was high. I can't imagine that he all of a sudden found his softer, gentler side in prison. If he does try to find me, I doubt it will be to apologize." I let go of her hand and wrap my arm around her neck to pull her in for a kiss. "For someone who lives and breathes unsolved crimes, I didn't think you'd be so optimistic."

"Only when it comes to you. Your past made me sad from the first day we met. I only want the best for you. Wishful thinking, I guess. You said yourself you have a ghost on your heels—I know it's your father."

She's right. And the fact she knows everything about me is yet another reason my obsession with her has swelled into an emotion that is borderline unhealthy. The things that have gone through my mind to keep her in Miami...

We continue to walk this stretch of beach. We drove all day. When I told her I booked a room on the beach, her face lit up like it was Christmas morning, and I made all her dreams come true.

I do shit for people all the time. I might complain, but when someone needs something, I'll bend over backwards to make it happen. But the look on her face when all I did was book a basic-but-clean room on the beach?

I had no idea that would make me want to do it over and over again. But here I am, wondering where I can secretly take her next.

But not to fucking New York City. Once I get her to Miami, I have no desire for her to take a step north without me.

That's becoming a personal problem. Once this secret isn't a secret any longer—and I know it won't be since I'll be the one shouting it from the rooftops—I'll be sure to catch shit from every male in my small circle.

"I'm done talking about my fucking father. I want to talk about something else."

"You weren't kidding when you said you wanted to catch up for the last two years."

We talked for hours on the drive, all through dinner, and there hasn't been one peaceful pause to enjoy the sound of the surf.

"That's what you get when you shut me out for so long." I stop, catch her hand, and pull her around to face me. "I want to talk about your parents."

She rolls her eyes. "I don't. They were happy on my graduation day because it's basically a requirement of being a parent. But I know they're mad about me moving to New York. And now you're on my case too. Can we just go back to Miami and celebrate my niece or nephew? Is that too much to ask? Sammie upped the drama in her life to the next level. She deserves her moment in the spotlight."

"I have no doubt Sammie will get all the attention she wants. But your move to New York has put me on the clock. I decided I'm going to talk to your dad about us."

Her eyes widen. "No, you're not. You can't. I won't allow it."

I knew I'd get this reaction. I shrug. "You can't stop me."

She pushes away and throws her arms out wide. "What are you going to do? Sit him down and tell how I was almost arrested for underage drinking in New Orleans, that you had to bail me out, that I threw myself at you like an unashamed, love-sick puppy, and that you turned me away because of him? But now you regret it and have decided to rock his daughter's world with all sorts of earth-shattering orgasms? Oh, and I forgot about the fact you and him will probably team up to try to get me to quit my dream job."

I lick my lips. "Don't make me horny by talking about orgasms. I want to see the sunset with you before we move on to that part of the evening."

She ignores everything I said about the orgasms. "Listen to yourself, Roc. You cannot talk to my dad about your intentions like this is some historical romance. I don't give a shit what my parents think about who I'm with. Hell, if you wanted to do this two years ago, I probably would have been your biggest cheerleader. But I did what you told me to do that night. I grew up and got my shit together."

"I've been thinking about that," I say.

"I've spent the last two years trying not to think about it."

"Life is funny," I note. "Despite our ages, we met as kids and couldn't have been more different. Then we were friends. When I pushed you away, I became obsessed. You got pushed away and talked yourself into hating me. Now I'm giving you life altering orgasms and you're begging me for sex. Not bad, if I do say so myself."

She takes a step forward and tries to give me a playful swat on the chest. "You're so full of it."

Between the news of my father and our impending arrival back in Miami where we'll never get another moment alone, I want nothing more than to be here.

Now.

With her.

I hold my arms out, hike a brow, and dare her to come at me as I wiggle my fingers. "You just want to be full of me."

Her eyes widen before they narrow just as fast. "Oh, you did not just say that."

"Baby," I drawl and lick my lips. "You're lying to yourself if you deny it any longer. If you want me, come and get me. I dare you."

There's something about being obsessed with someone you know inside and out before the obsession starts.

I know her.

I know what makes her tick.

I know what drives her and makes her crazy and what pisses her off.

And she proves that she might be a woman, but she still can't turn down a challenge.

She comes for me.

It might've been years ago, but I was a wide receiver. My job was to catch the ball, but I also had to outrun, outsmart, and outmaneuver the defense. Sometimes, that meant running. Other times, that meant footwork.

Teagan ran track. She's fast and athletic as she chases me through the sand.

I turn and dart to the side.

She follows with ease.

I sidestep.

She might be two steps off, but she recovers.

She still can't get me.

"Rocco," she yells for me.

I turn and run backwards three steps until she closes the distance. When she's within a couple steps, I stop and dip just enough.

I don't know what her plans were when she caught me, but I make sure they don't happen.

When we collide, I grab her by the waist and lift. We both go down on the sand—me first and her on top. My back and shoulders take the brunt of our fall.

She grips my shoulders and braces to hang on. I roll before we come to a stop. I'm on top of Teagan. Her hair is a dark wave on the light sand, and her wild expression is stark compared to the calm sea.

"There," I say as my hips find the most perfect place they've ever experienced—between Teagan's legs. I press my swollen cock into her pussy and don't give a shit that we're on a public beach. "You caught me. Nicely done."

"I hardly caught you." She's still breathing hard. "You caught me, and you know it. You played D1. I ran for a small, private college. They don't compare in the slightest."

"We're both athletes," I say as I press my cock into her pussy. "You're also hard-headed and refuse to give in to your wildest desire ... me."

She puts her feet to the sand and lifts her hips. "It's the other way around, Roc. I've given in to everything you've allowed. You're the one holding out on the experience we both want." Then she throws my words back at me. "You're lying to yourself if you deny it any longer."

That sobers me. I brush a few grains of sand that are sticking to her cheek before I put my lips to hers. This isn't playful or heated.

This is different.

I roll again until she's resting on top and I'm the one in the sand, but never break our connection. Every minute like this with her cements something deeper in my gut. Her mouth moves with mine. It's like we're the only ones in the world, with just the ocean to keep us company as background music.

I fist her hair and give it a gentle pull. When she looks down at me, I tell her the truth. "I'll never deny anything when it comes to you. I've had two years. As much as I hate to admit it, the best thing you ever did was set up that meeting with Robichaux. I'm pissed I gave you the space you wanted for as long as I did."

She shakes her head. "You've only ever said no to me once. And when I look back on it, I needed the time to grow up. Become me. Figure out who I am on my own."

My hand slides down her back and lands on her ass. "And you did that at twenty-two. It's taken me almost thirty years."

"Our birthdays are next month. Maybe it will be a different kind of celebration this year." Instead of pushing away to get up, she scoots down my body far enough to rest her cheek over my heart. "Can we watch the sun set and not talk about what's next? All I want to think about is this."

"Okay."

"Rocco?"

I drag my hands through her hair. We're a mess and both covered in sand, but neither of us care. "Right here, baby."

"Please don't talk to my parents. Not yet. I need to figure out what I'm going to do about New York on my own."

I look from the surf to the sky as the weight of her body sinks into mine. "It sucks for me, but I can't say no to you."

She lifts her head far enough to press her lips to my heart before settling back in. "Thank you."

Tomorrow by this time, we'll be back in Miami. We'll have to pretend this isn't a thing.

Until she's ready.

22

A WATERMELON AND A BAGEL

Teagan

Rocco Monroe entered my life again the day I stepped out of my comfort zone and met with Jules Robichaux. So much has happened.

My car, my apartment, an undercover operation where I pretended I was Rocco's girlfriend, Rocco got his arm sliced open...the list goes on.

That's not even the good stuff.

The good stuff includes no clothes, orgasms, and soul-wrenching conversations.

And then there's the fact his father is a free man.

Throughout everything, Rocco and I have been pretty much inseparable.

"Are you ready for this, baby?"

I put my car in park and glance into my rearview mirror. Just like he has been since the moment we left my apartment, Rocco is at my back. I don't look away from him as I talk over my Bluetooth.

"No. Now that we're here, I'm not ready. I want to go back to the beach. Or my studio. Hell, I'll go back to New Orleans."

He shakes his head but doesn't make a move to get out of the car. "Me too. But babies are being born, I have a new job, and you have decisions to make."

I lean my head back, shut my eyes, and don't say a thing. That very decision is weighing on me like an anchor.

The next thing I know, the call clicks off and Rocco raps twice on my window. I pull in a deep breath, turn my car off, and unlock my doors. I can't sit out here all day. I load my arms with as much as I can from my front seat and console.

Rocco opens my door and looks down at me. "What are the chances anyone is watching us right now? I want to kiss you one more time before I'm forced to treat you like I do everyone else."

I climb out of my car loaded down with trash and bags. "You know how many cameras are on the house, with audio no less," I whisper. "I'd say the chances are bigger than slim. Don't you dare kiss me."

He pulls a bag from my hands and doesn't push it. He steps back a safe distance and gives me the amount of space one would for a friend.

Ugh.

A friend.

Kill me now.

"This is going to suck," I grumble like a petulant teenager. "Let's go."

He steps aside so I can lead. We go straight to the front door of the house Rocco and I have both called home since the day we moved in. Sure, we've had our own places when we moved away, but this has always been where we return.

Today feels different.

I'm about to reach for the handle when the door flies open in front of me.

I stutter to a stop.

Rocco runs into my back and wraps a hand around my hip to keep from bowling me over.

"Surprise!"

It's shouted in unison so many times ... I have no idea how many people just screamed at us.

"You're back!"

"Welcome home!"

"It's about time!"

"Today is the best day ever!"

"You're late. We've only been waiting for two hours. Can you get in the house and shut the door? It's hot. Some of us are creating brand new humans. We're tired and want to get this over with."

That last one was Sammie.

But it's the other woman creating a human who beams at us and wraps her arms around me quickly so she can move onto Rocco.

"You're home! I missed you so much. I'm sorry I missed your graduation." Landyn goes on and on before letting me go so she can wrap her arms around Rocco. "I didn't think this day would ever arrive. Quite literally the best day ever. I might cry."

Rocco hugs her back as best he can while carrying my things. "Don't cry. That's got to be some bad juju for my godchild."

Landyn beams.

Sammie rolls her eyes.

My mom moves in and takes Landyn's place. "You're home. You're both home. I can't remember the last time I've been this happy."

When she lets me go, I realize the party isn't small.

It's not just Brax and Landyn. Micah, Evie, King, and Goldie and all their kids are here too.

Everyone is here.

Mom juts her arms high in the air. "It's a graduation party slash welcome home party slash birthday parties since you both turn another year older in the next couple weeks. With two babies on the way, I figure if we can get everyone together once to celebrate everything, all the better."

"Three birds, one stone," Rocco states. "Efficient, Annette. I like it." Then he turns to me. "Will you be here when you turn twenty-three, or will you have to celebrate by yourself in the Big Apple?"

I open my mouth to answer, when really, I'd rather kick him in the shin, but my dad interjects. And he does it with a margarita. "Your favorite. We couldn't stay long enough to celebrate, but this is your party. Drink up, food is in the kitchen, and the table is set. Let's eat!"

"I'm starving," Sammie spouts.

I turn to my sister and take her in. Sammie is taller than me with more curves when she's not pregnant than I could ever hope for. My mom always said it wasn't our height that made us completely different children, it was what's on the inside.

I haven't seen Sammie in months. As grumpy as she is, she's beautiful. She might be frowning, but she's doing it while glowing. And her hair might be thrown into a messy bun, but it shines bright. And if someone saw her from the back, you'd never know she was about to give birth. She's all belly. Her dress is a bodycon from two years ago.

I move into my sister and cup her swollen belly in my hands. "You look beautiful. Just beautiful."

She chomps a bite from the stalk of celery she's holding. "That's good to know, because shit's about to get ugly."

Evie gives me a hug before turning to Sammie. "It won't be ugly. It will be beautiful. At least, that's how you'll look back on it."

Sammie rolls her eyes. "I'm about to push a watermelon out of a bagel. If that's beautiful, then I have zero desire to be even remotely cute." She holds her hand up and makes an O with her fingers. "Zero!"

Well, Sammie has officially ruined bagels for life. Even thinking about a schmear of cream cheese makes me want to gag.

Evie looks contrite as she bites her lip, but she doesn't try to convince Sammie that anything else is beautiful.

Goldie comes in, wraps her arm around Sammie's shoulders, but turns to me. "If you want to work while you're home, I'll always need you at The Pink. Consider it an open offer."

I worked at The Pink the first summer I was home from college. It's an enormous mansion and venue on Biscayne Bay, and it's all Goldie's. I was a server for parties one summer. It was a great job.

"Thanks, Goldie. I'll see if I have time before I have to leave. I've been saving for my place in New York. It will be smaller than the studio I just moved out of but four times the rent."

"And to think she could live here," Mom butts in. "I'm just saying."

"Well, look at that," Evie says and motions across the room to the men. "Rocco has been in town approximately two-point-three minutes and the guys are already monopolizing him and talking shop."

I'm grateful for the excuse to gaze across the room. Rocco is holding a beer like the rest of the guys, but they don't look like they're talking about work. None of them look like they're enjoying their topic of conversation. And I've been around them long enough, when they talk DEA, they eat that up. They could talk about cases day and night.

This is not that.

This is different.

This feels ... personal.

Brax is standing square in front of Rocco with the rest flanking him. Rocco looks about as happy as he was when he caught me trying to work undercover to figure out where Heath Hayes is."

I can't take my eyes off him, and I don't give a shit who sees.

He pulls in a deep breath and stares at an invisible spot on the wall while Brax talks nonstop.

"He doesn't start until next week," Mom says when she comes to stand beside me. She hands Sammie a glass of water. "I wish they'd just relax and let Rocco enjoy his family for once."

His family.

That's a concept.

Especially after learning about his father yesterday.

I'd bet all the contents in my car that Brax isn't talking about a case or drugs or his newest target.

I bet Goldie doesn't realize what's going on. Her husband, King, stands there with a grave expression on his face as their toddler, Bale, is sacked out on his chest.

Landyn is the only woman in their huddle. She can't tear herself away from Rocco now that he's home. She stands with the men glued to Rocco's side, arm in arm. Her head rests on his shoulder.

I guess news hasn't traveled to the entire group yet, which is hard to believe.

I know what they're talking about. It's not a wiretap or cartels or interdictions.

"It's not a case," I mutter, not able to take my eyes off Rocco. I don't need to be in the conversation to know what they're talking about. It's etched in Rocco's incensed expression. I hate that look on his face. "It's about his father."

The women turn and gape at me.

Even Sammie is surprised.

But it's my mom who is the most astonished. "His father?"

When I realize she doesn't know, I turn to her and reach for her hand.

Rocco's gaze angles up. Like a magnet, it finds mine without having to search. I roll my lips and bite my bottom lip.

Mom turns to me. "What's going on?"

Shit.

But even with the tone and look Mom throws at me, I can't look away from him.

I'm not sure how I know, but I know. Whatever is going on in that huddle on the other side of the room, shit just got worse than it was before we got home.

What was supposed to be a welcome home party and celebration of everything under the sun turns dark the moment I answer.

I turn to my mom and tell her the truth, even though I know it will hurt her. Rocco isn't hers, but she loves him like he is.

"His father was released from prison," I say, glancing back at Rocco. He's not upset or worried. Rocco is pissed. "He's free."

Rocco

Who knew I had the capability to turn a party into a funeral.

It seems Brax kept the details about my father between us. But that all changed when he got a call a couple hours ago with the details of his release.

It seems my father's new attorneys spun bullshit into gold and convinced a judge that my testimony was coerced. That my uncle pressured me into saying what I said.

Witness tampering.

It's the truth, I guess. But that doesn't make my testimony any less truthful.

Rodney Monroe killed my mother.

Was Rachael Monroe a good parent?

Fuck, no.

But he killed her all the same, and I watched him do it. The memory lives rent free in my mind. It doesn't matter how much I wish I could wipe it clean from my brain, I can't.

My testimony was thrown out, and the decision was overturned. The guilty verdict was nullified, his record expunged, and he can't be tried again.

Landyn rests her head on my shoulder. "I don't understand how this could happen after so many years."

"That's not all," Brax goes on.

"Great," I mutter, but can't take my eyes off Teagan. She looks from me to Annette. I can see the drama unfolding by the moment. Everyone knows.

"I'm working with my contacts in California. Rodney Monroe purchased a car from a used lot five days ago. He put a small down payment and had a friend co-sign since he has no credit. He was issued a temporary tag. I've got the make and model, but that's it."

"Not to underestimate your father," Micah starts. "But do you really think he'll come looking for you?"

"I don't give a shit if he does. In fact, I hope he fucking finds me."

Landyn looks up at me. "You don't mean that."

"I fucking do."

Tim, always the voice of reason, holds out a low hand. "Let's just take a step back. Micah could be right. He's breathing free air for the first time in fifteen years whether he deserves to or not. He can't be stupid enough to throw that away by coming after you with retribution."

"That's generous of you," I say. "But he would, and he will. If there's anything that flows through his veins, it's vengeance."

"Maybe so," King pipes in. "But finding you will be like a needle in a haystack. You're unlisted and have kept yourself off social media. You probably turn up on old stats from college ball and cases that made the news in New Orleans. Your name was in the papers for Evie's drama. The chances of him having the means to get here and finding you are two very different things."

I shake my head. "I wish I were that optimistic. There are no plates registered to his car. We have no phone number to ping. I'll be looking over my shoulder until I figure out where he lands."

Annette makes her way across the room with Teagan on her heels. The happy from having her daughter home just minutes ago is gone. She looks from me to Tim and demands, "What are you going to do about this?"

Tim puts his arm around his wife. "I love that you think I'm that powerful. I can't overrule a judge, and I can't find a person who's untraceable. Rocco will be diligent."

"Roc will be fine, Annette," Brax adds. "We know he's out. We'll stay on top of it."

"That's it?" Landyn asks. "We're just going to hope to stay on top of it?"

Brax pulls Landyn from my side and puts his arm around her. "That's cute you think you're a part of the *we*."

The group has now congregated around me, and I fucking hate it.

It's like Teagan senses it or hates it just as much as I do and says, "There's nothing we can do right now. I thought this was supposed to be a party. Roc and I have been on the road all day. I'm hungry and I'm sure he is too. Can we forget about this for tonight?"

I look at Annette. "They're right. There's nothing we can do. I'm starving."

She finally gives in. "I guess. Dinner is ready. Let's get the kids fed so we can sit down and focus on what we came here to do."

"See?" Teagan plasters a fake smile on her face. "Let's celebrate."

"Yes," Sammie deadpans. "I'm starving even though I don't know how I can fit anything into my stomach. This baby is kicking every organ in my body like a soccer ball, but hey, I can eat a taco."

"I don't like this *it'll be fine until it's not* approach to the problem, but I am hungry." Landyn rubs her belly. "I had back-to-back clients this afternoon and haven't eaten since lunch."

"Let's eat!" Teagan says with too much enthusiasm for anyone in the room, even though I know it's fake.

Annette finally gets with the program and ushers everyone to the kitchen.

Teagan's gaze hangs on me for a beat before she swings Brax and Landyn's daughter, Baylee, into her arms and heads for the food.

This is just any other holiday or celebration.

And there's nothing I can do other than pretend I'm not fucking pissed or falling in love.

My control and emotional detachment have taken a flying leap out the window.

I hardly recognize myself.

23

TEACH ME

Rocco

Everyone left hours ago.

Teagan has defied every lie she told me about being excited to move to New York. She's been by Sammie's side, looking through the mountains of shit that must be needed for a new baby. Annette has no chill on a normal day, but when she's about to become a grandmother, she's lost her mind.

While they were doing that, I talked to Taylor for an hour. He's been a busy guy back in New Orleans. He managed to get a tracker put on Robichaux's car along with the wire. Jules hasn't mentioned Stella, Heath, or Mack Crowder on the wire once, which means he's moved on to new targets.

Taylor is all over that, and Jules has no clue he's one step closer to being arrested for human trafficking.

The agents do their best to keep work and family separated since they started having kids. After everyone calmed down about my father, the murderer, living and breathing a free man, nothing more was spoken about it. I have a few more days until I report to the Miami division, which means I can keep the details of this case to myself for a few more days. But that doesn't mean I'm not working on it.

I am.

And I hope to hear back tomorrow.

That was all enough to distract me from having to pretend Teagan and I are not what we've become. It was easy while I was talking to Taylor, and she was busy with Sammie.

But now the house is dark and quiet. The family of four plus me are under one roof again for the first time in two years. I've never once been here and thought about Teagan the way I do now.

It's fucking hard.

I grab a pair of boxers and head across the hall to the bathroom. Maybe a shower will help me sleep.

I'm grabbing a towel from the hall closet when I hear the click of a doorknob.

I don't even have to turn to see who it is. I know.

She's standing in the threshold to her room across the hall from mine. The low light from a lamp shines from behind her. She's wearing nothing but a thin tank and a pair of panties.

Panties I bought her.

Her nipples are hard and visible through the thin fabric. The tank is so small, the skin of her midriff peeks at me.

Her gaze feels tangible. It was just this morning that we woke tangled in one another before I put my mouth between her legs and gave her two orgasms. It was all I could do to keep her hands off my dick, but I did.

Knowing she would be off limits to me when we got here, it might've been one of the hardest things I've done.

She bites her lip before glancing up and down the hall. Then she looks back at me as she silently pulls her door shut behind her. Not even a click.

It takes her two seconds to get to me. Her light touch lands on my bare chest, drags down to my abs, and farther down to the elastic of my gym shorts where she tucks a finger and runs it under the band.

I don't give a shit who's asleep down the hall. She doesn't have to beg or say a word. At this point, I'd follow her anywhere.

Currently, the bathroom.

I switch on the light and lock the door behind us. My gaze drops to her perfect ass. The slip of material disappears between each perfect globe. I can't take my eyes off her as she reaches in the shower to turn on the water.

To muffle the noise.

Smart.

No wonder her grades were so good.

When she turns to me, her arms cross at her waist. The tank hits the floor right before her panties do. Not uttering a word, she kicks them to the side as her fingers return to my abs right before her lips touch my pec.

"Rocco, are you going to make me beg?" she whispers against my skin before she looks up to me. "Because I will, even though it seems like a waste of time."

I capture her face between my hands and bring it to mine. I devour her mouth as her hand lands on my dick. She slides it down and cups my balls through my shorts.

I've never wanted to throw away my own convictions more than I do now.

She slides her hand up and into my shorts.

I'm commando.

The moment she realizes, her slim fingers wrap around me for a squeeze.

That's it.

I break our kiss and let go of her long enough to push my shorts to the floor. Her eyes go straight to my cock for the first time and widen.

She licks her lips.

I take her by the hand and pull her into the shower with me. If we're doing this down the hall from her parents and sister, I need all the white noise I can get. I pull her under the water but keep going. Her back is pressed to the tile wall, and I'm pressed to her. My cock is long and hard as all my blood rushes south. I press my hips into her stomach when all I want is her pussy.

But then she surprises me.

Her hands land on my hips, and she pushes me away. Her eyes go straight to my cock again, like she can't get enough. Without looking away from her target, I wonder if I've died and gone to heaven.

She drops to her knees.

Water drips down my chest as I stare down at the woman I can't get enough of. Until now, it's been me doing the giving. This is a memory I'll happily be willing to burn on my brain forever.

She looks up at me, and I think she's about to whisper something when her lips part, but she says nothing. Her tongue sneaks out to taste me, dragging the tip along the vein on the underside of my cock.

I suck in a breath and put a hand to the tile wall to brace.

Her hands come to the front of my thighs to hang on when she whispers, "Is that okay?"

Is that okay?

Fuck.

When I don't answer, she keeps whispering, "I've never done this before. But after today, I want to do something for you."

I run my fingertips over her bottom lip. "I have no fucking idea what I did to deserve you."

She licks a drop of water off her top lip. There hasn't been anyone in two years but my fist. And I haven't touched my cock since she's come back into my life. After only having my hand for two years, when I had the real thing next to me, I knew my hand wasn't going to do it.

I only want her.

Seeing her kneeling before me is almost more than I can bear.

Her tits rise and fall with shallow breaths. "Will you teach me what you like?"

Yes, it's official.

I've fallen off a cliff from reality. I'm dead. If I never wake up, I've lived a full life.

At least I will after Teagan Coleman sucks my cock.

"Put your arms behind your back." My voice is deep but low. I wait and watch, as her small tits jut out when she does as I say. I drag the head of my cock over her bottom lip. "Suck. But just the tip."

I watch as her full pink lips close around me. I cup the back of her head with one hand as I guide myself with the other.

I force myself to breathe deep and slow and will time to stop so I can enjoy this as long as possible.

"Use your tongue, baby. Circle the tip." She does. "Fuck. I'm not sure what I'm getting off on more. The feel of your mouth on me or the sight of my cock disappearing between your lips."

At my words, she sucks harder.

It's all I can do to keep my eyes open so I don't miss a second.

With my cock in one hand, I fist her hair with the other. I'm in total control as I press into her mouth. Her eyes widen and peer up at me, but I don't stop. I go slow, inch by inch. She can't take all of me, but it's not for a lack of trying.

She likes it.

"No, baby." I give her hair a tug and shake my head. "I'll control it."

She stills.

"Suck," I demand and slide in farther. "And enjoy it."

Her eyes fall shut as I feel the tip of my cock hit the back of her throat.

"Good girl," I croon. "So fucking good."

I let go of my cock to stroke her face, brush the water away from her eyes, and guide myself.

She sucks. Licks. And strokes me with her tongue. She finds her stride, and I silently vow to never let her go.

I push in and out. We find a rhythm. That is until I can't control my breathing and feel my balls tighten.

No way am I going to come in her mouth the first time.

I pull out. She's so surprised and was sucking so hard, there's a pop when my engorged head exits her swollen lips.

"Did I do something wrong?" she exclaims on a whisper.

I shake my head and angle my cock toward her chest. "No, baby. That was so fucking good."

My breathing is shallower than hers as I pump my cock. She's still got her arms behind her back as I brace myself on the wall. It's all I can do to stay silent when my cum decorates her tits.

Her eyes flare as she looks from her chest to me. It's the last thing I see before I tip my head back to the ceiling and close my eyes.

Damn.

I come and come and come.

Like it's been years of torture.

I guess it has been. Specifically, two. But that's on me.

I feel her hands grip my thighs before she stands and presses herself to me. She wraps her arms around me, and we're glued to each other with my cum. I want to wrap her up and keep her here forever.

Instead, I peel her away from me and turn her. I press her hands to the tile and put my lips to her ear. "Are you going to come for me?"

She nods and turns her face enough to catch my gaze. "Please. I'm so ready after that. That was the hottest thing I've ever done."

I wrap an arm around her, and my fingers dip straight into her pussy. I pump in and out of her before giving her clit any attention. When I nuzzle her wet skin with my nose and keep talking, her head falls back to my shoulder. "You're so fucking wet, baby, and it has nothing to do with the shower. You liked the taste of my cock, didn't you?"

She shifts her legs farther apart to give me more space. "I love everything with you, Roc. And all I wanted to do was make you forget reality for a short moment. I was nervous."

I don't take my time. I press my front to her back and circle her clit with enough pressure. She was already primed. It doesn't take long.

Her body shudders in my arms as she comes. I hold her tight to my chest when I feel her legs weaken. Her jaw goes slack, and I'm forced to take her mouth to quiet her moans.

Her limbs are weak, but I turn her to me and wrap her in my arms. I shift us so her back is in the warm water and put my lips to her ear. "How am I going to sleep without you tonight?"

She doesn't answer but sinks into me deeper.

"I knew this was going to be hell, baby. This is so fucking stupid. We're adults. Come to bed with me. I can't let you go after that."

I get a weak squeeze and a nod against my chest.

I press my lips to the top of her head. "Thank God. Let me get you cleaned up."

I grab the body wash and give us both a quick rubdown before turning off the water. We share the towel, I put on clean boxers, but she doesn't bother with clothes and wraps the towel around her.

Before I open the door, I tip her head to mine for a deep kiss. "I don't know how long I can go on like this. We need to figure it out."

For once, she doesn't argue with me. That might be the most progress I've made with her so far.

I don't let her go. "We'll go to bed and talk it out. It won't be anything you don't want. But I don't want this to end, and you don't either. It took us too long to get here to fuck around any longer. I'm not willing to waste any time when it comes to us."

She catches her lip between her teeth.

This is it. She's giving in.

Maybe it's being home.

Maybe it's my cock.

I'm not one to question the magic. I'll take her however I can get her.

I can't help the smile that swells on my face as I unlock and open the door.

I put my hand to her ass and give her a push.

Teagan gasps.

I look over her head and see what she sees.

Shit.

Eyes the same color as Teagan's are focused on us. She points a finger between the two of us. "Um, excuse me. What in the actual fuck is going on here?"

Teagan takes a step backward into my chest.

Sammie's eyes bug out of her head when her stare drops to my hand wrapped around Teagan's hip.

Teagan whispers, "I can explain—"

"No fucking way," Sammie bites.

"Quiet," I hiss, but don't let go of Teagan. This is not what I need. I had Teagan right where I wanted her and now this.

But Sammie is Sammie and doesn't shut the fuck up or lower her voice for that matter. Instead, she stares straight at me. "You're fucking my sister? We grew up together!"

That's it. Teagan steps out of my hold and grabs her sister by the wrist. "Would you shut up? You're going to wake Mom and Dad."

Sammie can't stop glaring at us. "Well, I'm pretty sure they're going to want to know about this."

"Don't you dare," Teagan warns in a menacing whisper. "We know what we're doing. We have a plan ... sort of. We just need some time to—"

Sammie gasps again.

"What?!" Teagan hisses.

Sammie looks down.

Water drips down her legs.

"Oh my gosh!" Teagan isn't whispering or hissing any longer. "Your water broke!"

Sammie looks up at Teagan and forgets all about me. A horrified expression takes over her face. "It's coming. Holy shit, Teag. The baby is coming. I'm not ready."

Teagan looks her sister in the eyes. "You are ready. You can do this. You're going to be the best mom." Teagan turns to me. "Get dressed."

She doesn't have to tell me twice. I sidestep around the baby juice on the floor and go straight to my room.

I don't even get the door shut when I hear Teagan yell, "Mom, Dad! The baby is coming!"

And there go my plans for the night.

24

EMOTIONAL DIATRIBE

Rocco

Tim paces.

He's been pacing for hours.

Annette and Teagan have been in the birthing suite with Sammie since we got here. Sammie kicked her dad out when they went through the whole vaginal statistical exam, and he never returned.

Smart man.

Since then, Teagan has come out periodically to give us updates. This has included more vagina stats as well as generic Sammie stats. Based on both, I'm glad I'm here and not in there.

But for real, when the baby is here and the dramatics are over, society needs to come together and agree that when it comes to some information, too much is not okay.

That includes vaginas that you are not up close and personal with on a regular basis.

Bagels have already been ruined for me for life. We need to agree to stop.

Thank goodness no one mentioned donuts.

A dramatic trip to the hospital and now sitting around waiting for hours has made for a long night after a long day. I recline back as far as I can without sliding onto the floor in this very hard chair. My eyes are closed, and I'm imagining being wrapped up in a naked Teagan rather than my back turning into another pretzel. This is worse than the corner of my sofa.

"You know, this isn't the way I envisioned this stage of life," Tim says, breaking into my naked thoughts about his youngest daughter.

I suck in a deep breath and force myself to an upright seated position. "Sammie will be better off on her own. Her boyfriend seemed like a tool."

"I have no doubt she'll be better off without him. I secretly hope he doesn't come crawling back."

"No offense, but given her temperament lately, I doubt that will happen."

Tim tips his head, as if he doesn't want to agree, but does. "True. Even so, I hate to see her alone. I don't want that for any of you. Life is hard enough. To go it alone is … well, it makes everything harder."

I lean forward to rest my elbows on my knees and stare at the floor. Most of the time it feels like second nature to be included in the Coleman family.

Then, every once in a while, Tim or Annette say something like that. Effortlessly including me in a wish for their kids. Hell, I wasn't even a kid when I moved in with them, no matter what Teagan says about my emotional state at the time.

"And then there's your father," he says on a turn.

No comment. What the hell is there to say? My father will try to wreak havoc on my life or he won't. If he does, I'll take care of it.

Whether I do that through the legal system or on my own will be determined.

The legal system failed me once. I'll be more than happy to take care of it on the side.

I'm not sure if he's delirious from lack of sleep or emotional about the state of his family, but Tim doesn't need me to help further this conversation. He's doing a bang-up job all by himself.

"I can't imagine how you feel knowing he's out. Especially after some asshole judge released him based on your testimony. This is a scenario I never thought would happen. Annette and I know we have an unusual relationship with you. We have no claim to you. We're not your parents. But I've got to tell you, Roc, nothing's pissed me off more than knowing Rodney Monroe is free. And not even because he wants some type of retaliation for your testimony. I know you can handle yourself. It's about me, which is fucking crazy. Like he's going to duel me to win the role of your father."

There's something to know about Tim Coleman. He's not a verbose man. Still, you always know where he stands on any issue.

His emotional diatribe is unusual, to say the least. Sammie being in labor and having a grandchild must have Tim all up in his feels.

I stand and move into the path he's wearing in the waiting room. When I put a hand up, he stops in front of me.

"You've got a lot going on," I start. "Sammie, the baby, Teagan moving. I get it. Brax and Micah treat me like a younger brother. King treats me like an equal. But if there's one thing you and Annette can count on, it's that no one in this world has treated me like a son other than the two of you. You're having a moment, but that's the last thing in the world you need to worry about."

Emotion washes over his features that were already plagued by exhaustion, both the physical and emotional kind.

He puts a hand on my shoulder and gives me a squeeze. He even leaves it there for a long moment.

The universal guy substitute for a hug.

"What's going on?"

We both turn to see Teagan standing at the opening to the hall. Her eyes are wide and she's glaring at me.

I'm quick to answer. "Nothing."

"We were having a moment," Tim amends.

"What about?" she snaps.

"My father." I glare back so she'll stop with the inquisition. "How are things going..." I wave my hand around. "Back there?"

She rubs her face, and I realize she's crying. "Not good. She's not progressing. She's pushed for the last hour and a half ... but nothing. They're taking her for a C-section."

This time, it's my turn to give Tim the shoulder squeeze. He looks like he needs one.

"Shit," he hisses.

"I know," Teagan goes on. "She's emotional and exhausted. She can have one person go in with her since the father isn't here. She picked Mom. You can go back and see her if you want, but be quick. They're prepping her."

Tim looks from Teagan to me and then heads back to the birthing suite without another word.

Teagan waits for him to get out of sight before coming straight for me. She buries her face in my chest as I wrap her up and put my lips to the top of her head. "She'll be fine—the baby will too. There's no way they won't be fine. Sammie won't allow it."

"I know. It's just hard to watch her go through this." She lifts her head to look up at me. "I really thought you told Dad about us."

I shake my head. "I figure Sammie will do that after she has the baby. She's not going to miss the opportunity to rat us out. Something like that is right in her wheelhouse."

"True." She wraps her arms around me one more time before letting go.

"I'm not anxious to be ratted out by your sister. We need to claim the upper hand. Once the baby comes and we know everyone is okay, it's time to have a talk with Tim and Annette."

She nods in agreement just in time for Tim to return.

He looks more emotional than he did before. I think we're beyond shoulder squeezes.

"She's going to be fine. The baby's going to be fine. Women do this all the time," he says, as if he's talking himself into it.

Teagan goes straight to him, wraps her arms around her father, and gives him the real thing. "You're right, Dad. They'll both be perfect."

25

FIGURATIVE ORGASM

Rocco

The doors part. I walk outside to fresh air and a new day. This was not a call I could take in front of anyone.

"It's about time," I say.

"You sent me a needle that I had to find in fucking Africa of all places. Do not bust my balls, Roc. I get enough of that from Uncle Sam."

"I don't know why you're searching an entire continent. I narrowed it down to a country. And not even a big one."

"Right. Nigeria. They're super-duper cooperative when someone like me makes a phone call. Do you think I got to where I am today by my smooth-talking personality and rugged good looks alone? I'm an investigator, dammit. Don't marginalize me. It hurts my feelings."

"For fuck's sake. Did you find Heath Hayes or not?"

"Let's back up a moment. You, my young, handsome friend, have uncovered a network so large and broad, I have the fucking CIA eating out of my hand and shocked that I can be even more amazing than I was last week. I love it, and I love you for it. To be honest, I might be taking a little credit for the whole thing. But I want to know how you found it."

I've known Cole Carson since I was on the other side of the law as a prospect in a motorcycle club. He was the reason Brax was able to go undercover in the cartel as deep as he did. Cole pops up from time to time and is a good man to have in your corner. He can do shit we can't when it comes to investigations outside of the country.

And if Cole Carson is a good contact to have, his wife is even better. Bella Carson is as badass as they come. She is former MI6 for the British government, but now she works for a private organization that contracts with the CIA. That organization doesn't care what the law is when it comes to getting shit done.

Cole is tight with Brax. Really tight. But he's also worked with Tim, Micah, and King. I took a chance on calling him on my own. It was a first for me. When I made the call last week, Cole was downright giddy to hear from me.

Fuck the State Department for not helping the Hayes family. It seems all I needed was a friend at the CIA.

I look out at the parking lot of the hospital and answer as blandly as I can. "I had a tip."

"Well, no shit," he drawls. If I had to guess, he's reclined in his office at Langley and just propped his feet on the corner of his desk. "I'm going to need more than that if you want me to spill all the beans in the whole damn pot. And let me tease you, my beautiful friend, it's a big pot."

I drag a hand down my face and try not to yawn. We didn't sleep at all last night. "I'm not sure I can tell you."

He lowers his voice as if someone is eavesdropping when I know that's not the case. He's probably on one of the most secure lines in the country. "I'm the CIA, Roc. If you don't tell me, I can find out. But since you're trying to get an elderly man out of a

Nigerian prison, I have better things to do with my time. You know I'm a softy at heart. The Hayes man is as old as my dad when he died. Now that I've figured out the big picture, I want to get that man home to his family."

"What's the big picture?" I demand.

"Tit for tat."

"Is this what it was like when the rest of the guys worked with you? I'm tired, Cole. I haven't even been back in Miami for twenty-four hours. Tim's oldest daughter went into labor last night. We've been at the hospital, and I haven't slept in over a day."

"No shit? How did I not know Tim was going to be a grandpa. Boy or girl?"

"Girl. It got dicey, but everyone is okay."

"A girl." I hear a smile on his face. "That's great. I'll tell Bella, and we'll send something."

"Can we get back to Heath Hayes?"

"Jules Robichaux," Cole states. "That guy is a slimy fucker. I had to have Bella dig deep on him so I didn't throw any red flags poking around within our borders. He's connected all over Africa. The bigger organization I uncovered has multiple Robichauxs all over the US, and the Hayes man is one of many. And when I say many, the number is not insignificant. There, I gave you something. I want to know how the DEA found Heath Hayes. He didn't once come into contact with anyone you work with while he was still in the US."

"Robichaux's name popped up on multiple cases for the last year, but he was careful—until he had an unusual meeting in public. I got wind of when and where it was going to take place on a wire and was able to sit and listen in public without a warrant." I pause, recounting the big event that finally got me to this point with Teagan. "But I wasn't the only one undercover that day. There was a woman who was working with the Hayes family to get him home." I pause before adding. "An investigative journalist. She'd already done the work on Robichaux. I took it from there because they were targeting her in a way that was not good."

"A female investigative journalist," he drawls. "And one who's not afraid to meet someone like Robichaux. That is fan-fucking-tastic. And when you hear just how big this is … well, let's just say I had a figurative orgasm. I want to meet this journalist. You know how I feel about a badass woman. I'll be in Miami tomorrow. It's been a hot minute since I've seen the gang. Everything is arranged."

"Wait," I say, wondering how I'm going to keep Teagan's name out of this. "She's a journalist. I'm not sure she wants her name out there."

"I'm the CIA, Roc. Do you think I'm going to rat her out to the bad guys?"

Shit. "I'll talk to her. See what she says."

"No offense, but if she's willing to work with the DEA, she'll wet herself over me."

"I know for a fucking fact that won't happen," I bite.

"Whoa. Do I sense a bit of possessive jealousy in your tone? Would this woman be *your* woman?"

"It's complicated, Cole. Really fucking complicated at the moment. I'm not going to make her meet with the CIA if she doesn't want to."

"Not to worry. I will make sure the CIA protects your journalist-lover's identity. I'll call Tim and set the whole thing up. I know he's got the new grandbaby, but when he hears what you've done with this case, he'll think he's died and gone to heaven."

I'm not afraid to tell Tim that I'm falling in love with his youngest daughter.

I am, though, not excited to tell him that Teagan met undercover with someone like Robichaux. Not only that, but that I took her back in myself.

"Like I said," I go on. "I'll have to check with her—"

"It's all set." Cole Carson proceeds to take over the situation. "I'm booking my flight now. Man, it's like a family reunion. Get some beauty sleep, Roc. You're going to need it."

And with that, he hangs up on me.

"Dammit," I mutter to no one but myself.

Of all the ways this could have played out, this is not the script I would have chosen.

Wait until Teagan hears about this.

Teagan

It's official.

I'm in love.

I cradle the perfect pink bundle in my arms as Sammie naps.

Marley Teagan Coleman.

When Sammie announced her name, I might've fallen into a puddle of emotions. Sammie said she wants her daughter to be smart and brave and strong, and if a middle name could give her the juju to be as smart as her aunt, even better.

When I came into the room and saw Sammie and Marley together for the first time, I knew right then and there, Sammie would be okay. She might be taking on this parenting gig alone, but that doesn't mean she won't be the most amazing mom ever. I could see it the way she looked at her newborn daughter.

Love.

Patience.

Devotion.

This might be exactly what Sammie needs. She has no idea

how strong she is or what she's capable of. I have a feeling Marley will bring out the best version of her mother.

With a cap on her head and swaddled in a blanket, my niece is a work of art. Skin the color of Sammie's and a full head of dark hair. Ten fingers and ten toes. She's only a few hours old and gets better with every moment that passes.

Mom and Dad went home to shower and change clothes. Rocco opted to stay in the waiting room since they were still getting Sammie settled and she was nursing for the first time.

All things Rocco said he didn't need to be a part of.

I texted him when Mom and Dad left to let him know it's safe to come in and meet Marley.

There's a light knock on the door before it pushes open.

He's here.

His gaze flits to Sammie before turning to me and my niece.

Rocco moves silently into the room, but his stare never wavers from us as he takes the seat next to me on the hard sofa. His hand lands high on my thigh and gives me a squeeze.

"She's perfect," I whisper before going on, "Uncle Rocco."

He shakes his head with a smirk. "I'm not sure whether that's good or creepy given the status of you and me."

"Only good. You're Uncle Rocco to all the kids, right?"

He shrugs. "I guess I am."

"Good practice," I whisper without looking away from my namesake, even if it is in middle name only. "After everything Sammie has been through, it's hard to believe she's finally here." I look up at Rocco. "Do you want to hold her?"

He shakes his head. "Later. I'm enjoying looking at you with a baby at the moment."

My stomach does a flip, but I don't have a chance to refute him, beg him to give me a million little baby Roccos, or ask if that means the sex embargo has been lifted.

"You two can babysit all you want, but you're not stealing my baby. I worked too hard to make her."

We both look over at Sammie who's staring at the three of us. She proves going through labor and having an emergency c-section hasn't tamed her in the least.

"And just so you know, it's going to take a minute for me not to throw up a little bit when I see you two together, but I'll get there." Her gaze turns to a fiery glare when she turns it to Rocco. "My sister has been in love with you for as long as I can remember. If you fuck her over, you'll have to deal with me."

I'm not sure if Sammie would intimidate any other man, but Rocco doesn't cower.

He laughs at her.

"I'm not going to fuck over your sister. I'm doing everything I can to get her to stay with me."

"Well, I just gave her a niece. She has a namesake, so she's bound to be a part of her life. The only way you'll be able to top that is if you knock her up." Sammie tips her head where she's reclining in her hospital bed. "Actually, that might be fun. You should do that. It'll take the attention off me. Perfect Teagan knocked up by our foster brother."

Rocco loses his playful smirk, and his expression turns grave. "I don't care that you just had a baby. Don't ever fucking say that again."

"I figured out how to push Rocco Monroe's buttons. Point taken." Sammie's smile swells into a huge grin. "By the way, if you don't tell Mom and Dad soon, there's no telling what will happen. I'm hormonal. It might slip."

"I have a feeling nothing would make Rocco happier." I turn my attention back to Marley. "I'm not talking to either one of you. My focus is on Marley. I don't want to miss a moment of her first day. Go back to sleep, Sammie. She'll be hungry soon, and Mom and Dad will be back. You need to rest while you can."

Sammie winces as she tries to get comfortable. She must be exhausted, because she doesn't argue.

Rocco scoots closer until our sides are glued and stretches his arm out behind me. When he starts playing with the ends of my hair, Sammie yawns and says, "This situation is going to take me some time to get used to."

I smile at Sammie.

Rocco presses his lips to my temple.

"Yeah, I'm going to need a minute," Sammie mutters as she closes her eyes.

Marley yawns and squirms in my arms before settling back into her nap.

Rocco

"I'm exhausted," Teagan says. "I'm going to go home, take a real shower, and go straight to bed."

I bring our entwined hands up and press my lips to the top of her hand. "My bed. Your parents will be here for the rest of the day. I'm not wasting the opportunity to sleep next to you."

She smiles through a yawn. "You won't have to ask me twice."

I pull her to me for a kiss on the lips this time as we walk to my car. "We haven't even been back a day, and I'm sick of hiding this. We were going to talk last night and never got the chance. Decisions need to be made."

I think she's about to answer me when I hear my name. "Rocco?"

I stop and turn but don't let Teagan go.

Shit.

"And Teagan."

I pull Teagan tight to my side.

Evie Emmett stands before us dressed for work. She's in a patterned dress that barely hits her knees and heels with her hospital credentials hanging around her neck.

"Rocco and Teagan," she repeats our names together, like she's trying them out together for the first time. "Well, this is an interesting development."

"It is," I agree.

Teagan says nothing as she slinks into my side like she wants to disappear.

"So." Evie hitches a foot and puts a hand on her hip. She studies us like we're an unusual virus that she's trying to treat. "Am I the only one who doesn't know about this?"

"No. You're definitely not the only one," I say.

"Huh." She smiles and can't stop looking between the two of us. "Is this new?"

"Yes," Teagan spouts.

"No," I answer at the same time.

"It's no wonder that I'm confused if you two can't agree on that," Evie says. "If I'm not the last to know about this, who else knows? Or should I ask, who doesn't know?"

"Sammie knows," I say.

"And Marley," Teagan amends. "And you. But that's it."

"Yes, sweet Marley. That's why I'm here."

Teagan finally relaxes. "She's beautiful."

Evie smiles. "I can't imagine she'd be anything less. I can't wait to meet her and check on Sammie. Sounds like she had quite the night."

"It was rough," Teagan says. "But my parents are up there. If you could not mention this." She motions between the two of us. "We'd appreciate it."

Evie frowns. "Is this a secret?"

"It was," I say. "But we're about to fix that."

Evie steps forward and pulls Teagan in for a hug. "Don't keep it a secret for long. Life is too short. I'm just glad you're both back." She takes a step back. "Oh, wait. You're moving to New York. How is that going to work?"

I roll my eyes as Teagan clams up.

"I see," Evie says. "Well, I won't say anything to your parents today. But that's all I can promise. I don't like secrets."

No, Evie wouldn't like secrets. That's understandable given what she went through before she met Micah. Hell, it's how she met Micah.

"We'll take care of it," I promise.

Evie beams. "A new baby and new love. This is the best day ever."

And with that, what I assume are pricey shoes click on the pavement and take her into the hospital.

Teagan and I stand here, frozen to our spots.

She faceplants in my chest, and I bring my hand up to the back of her head. "You okay, baby?"

"No." The word is muffled in my chest. "Not really."

"You'll be fine," I promise. "But now our conversation might be a little bit different than we planned. And I have a feeling we've just been put on the clock."

26

UNDER DURESS

Rocco

Today at 10:47 AM
Brax Cruz added Rocco Monroe to the conversation.

Brax – What the fuck?

Brax – Rocco!

Brax – You'd better fucking answer.

Micah – I'm just going to put it out there that we've known Teagan since she was in diapers.

King – Would you assholes chill? Do you really think he's going to fuck her over? I mean, you'd better not fuck her over, Roc. I don't think you would, but it's our duty as uncles to say it.

Micah – He's not going to answer. Evie said they were up all night.

Brax – This is not the time to sleep. We have shit to discuss.

King – They're not going to stop, Rocco. You might as well answer.

Micah – For what it's worth, Evie threatened me and told me I'd better not do anything to fuck this up, so I'm only here as moral support for Brax, who somehow feels responsible, which I do not get. I'd also like to add that my wife said, and I quote, "They are adorable! So freaking cute! I love them together!!!" Yes, she even included all the exclamation points.

Me – You fuckers always find a way to wake me up. And for the record, I'm not adorable or cute.

Brax – Great. You're alive…for now. Until Tim finds out.

King – You really think Tim is going to be pissed? He loves Roc like a son. He might be happy about it.

Micah – Look at King, all sunshiney and shit. Tell Goldie nice work. She's really rubbed off on you.

King – I was also threatened by my wife not to do anything to mess this up. So, there's that. But I'm going to say it again—Roc isn't going to fuck her over.

Brax – This is sure to blow up into a massive event. And for the record, when did this little secret affair start?

Me – That's a long story. Maybe when you don't sound like you're going to try to kick my ass, I'll tell you.

Brax – Oh, I could kick your ass if I wanted to.

Me – Mm-kay.

Micah – He just Mm-kay'd you, Brax. The group chat would be way more entertaining if Rocco didn't keep leaving.

King – I don't understand why Brax is so pissed.

Me – I'd like to know the same thing.

Brax – For one, Landyn is hurt that you didn't tell her.

Me – I didn't tell Landyn because she would've told you, and you would've told everyone. This same thing would've happened, just sooner.

Brax – Just a warning, she's going to be calling you as soon as she finishes up with her client.

Me – The only reason I'm texting you old men is because my phone was about to vibrate off the nightstand. I'm definitely not answering the phone. Teagan is asleep.

King – Welp, there's your answer.

Micah – I'm just ... not sure how I feel knowing baby Teagan is having sex.

King – OMG.

Brax – Shut your mouth! We've known her since she was a toddler!

> Me – I agree with Brax. Shut your mouth. In fact, I'd like you all to shut the fuck up. I'm leaving the damn chat.

Micah – Wait! Don't leave. We want to help.

King – I can say for certain, I don't want to help with anything. I'm not that sunshiney.

Brax – Same. But honest to God, Landyn will kill me if I don't.

> Me – I don't need anyone's help.

Micah – Don't speak so soon. You'll need help with Tim.

Brax – I just got off the phone with Landyn. Just so you know, you made my pregnant wife cry.

King – Oh, shit.

Micah – Wow. That's not good.

> Me – Why in the hell is she crying?

Brax – All I know is, when she texts, you'd better answer.

Damn. She's fast.

I switch over to my private thread with Landyn.

Landyn – You and Teagan?

> Me – Yes.

Landyn – Why didn't you tell me? You know what, it's okay. It's okay. I mean, it's not. I don't get it, but I still love you.

Me – I'm sorry. I didn't know how this was going to shake out. I had to keep it quiet for Teagan's sake. The future is still uncertain.

Landyn – You mean New York?

Me – Yes. You're not going to chew my ass about fucking over Teagan? That seems to be the theme of the day.

Landyn – Roc. It's me.

Me – What does that mean?

Landyn – It means, I'm your person, and I'll always have your back. I do want to know one thing…

Me – What's that?

Landyn – Are you happy?

Me – I love her. I haven't even told her yet, but I love her. I've just decided, if she goes to New York, I'm going to have to find a way to follow her.

Landyn – I'm crying.

Me – I heard. And I got yelled at for it.

Landyn – I just got you back. You can't move to New York. But I get that you'll follow her anywhere. I did the same thing with Brax. The only thing I've ever wanted for you is to be happy.

Me – I am. And I'll be happier when everyone quits yelling at me.

Landyn – I hope Teagan understands how lucky she is.

Me – I'll do anything for her.

Landyn – I know you will. And I'll be here for whatever you need. Love you, Roc.

Me – Right back at you.

Landyn – I'll take care of Brax and make sure he manages Tim. Go be happy.

Me – Thank you.

I switch back to the shit-show thread.

Me – I'm done. I don't need anyone's help. There's nothing I want more than Teagan. Get on board or don't. I don't give a shit. I'll take care of Tim. I'm tired, and I'm leaving the chat. Again.

Brax – Wait.

Me – Seriously?

Brax – Is this for real?

Me – Do you think I'm an asshole and a masochist? Yes, it's for real. I'll do anything for her.

King – I told you so.

Micah – Damn. I feel as old as King.

King – Fuck you.

Brax – I'm on the phone with Landyn. She's still crying by the way.

Me – Yeah, she told me.

Brax – Happy tears.

> Me – I'm leaving the damn chat. Feel free to talk about me after I'm gone.
>
> Me – Oh, one more thing, Cole Carson will be in the office first thing tomorrow morning. See you then.

Brax – What?

Today 11:21 AM
Rocco Monroe left the conversation.

I barely have a chance to shut my eyes when it starts all over again.

Today 11:27 AM
Goldie Jennings added Rocco Monroe to the conversation.

Goldie – I might be putting the cart before the horse here, but I started planning your wedding. It's going to be epic!

Landyn – These damn hormones. I can't stop crying, and now you're talking about their wedding. I have a color and cut in five minutes. I'm not sure how I'm going to manage.

Evie – Wait until you see them in person. They're perfect. I'm not sure how we didn't see it before. The wedding pictures will be stunning.

Goldie – Roc, are you there?

> Me – Under duress.

Goldie – Sorry. I just had to tell you how happy I am. And about the wedding. It's all on me.

Me – You do know we're not engaged, right?

Landyn – But you love her. And you just told me you'd do anything for her. It's just a matter of time.

Evie – He loves her! I didn't know for sure, but I thought so. I could see it.

Goldie – I'm just saying, Roc, you need to plan accordingly. I'll block off some prime dates on the calendar. After hurricane season for sure—probably late fall so the weather is nice and you're not sweating bullets for pictures on the beach.

Me – Um, I don't know what to say.

Landyn – Thank you?

Goldie – No thanks needed! The next generation is getting married.

Evie – Oh, I didn't think about it that way.

Me – I'm not that much younger than you. I'm definitely not the next generation.

Goldie – But Teagan is. Soooo…

Evie – OMG, she's right. Rocco is our generation, but Teagan is the next generation…

Me – Are you kidding me with this shit?

Landyn – Let's not think about it that way.

Evie – And let's definitely not mention the crossing of the generations to Tim. Micah promised me he'd help with that.

Landyn – And Brax is on board. Well, he wasn't, but he is now. I made sure of it.

Goldie – King has been on board since the get go. He thinks it's great.

Evie – That's because your age gap is bigger than theirs. How do you think I feel? Hardly a day goes by that Micah doesn't remind me that he landed an older woman.

Me – As "fun" as this is, I was up all night at the hospital. You women are as bad as your husbands.

Goldie – Don't make me break out the video of you dancing at the senior center.

Evie – Oh, please do. That's a classic.

Landyn – I think he has enough on his plate. We love you, Roc.

Goldie – So much love all around. I'm giddy.

Evie – Their babies will be beautiful. Can you even?

Me – Stop. Just stop.

Evie – Marley is perfect. And that's all Sammie's genes, not the asshole. I can't imagine what we'll get with Rocco and Teagan.

Landyn – Our family is growing by the day. We need all the weddings and babies.

Goldie – I've got to go. I have a meeting at The Pink. Roc, I've got your back, you need to do your part. Figure out her ring size.

Me – That's it. I'm done.

> Evie – Why wait? I mean, it's you and Teagan.

> Landyn – We only want the best for you. And keeping it all in the family is even better!

> Me – Why would you say that? Now you made it creepy.

> Landyn – LOL. You know what I mean.

> Me – Goodbye. And do not add me back just to torture me again. It's not cool.

Today 11:39 AM
Rocco Monroe left the conversation.

27

UNBRIDLED

Teagan

Sometimes you reach a certain point of exhaustion that when you wake up, confusion blankets you as to where you're at or what time of day it is.

That's me right now.

But when a hand wraps around my hip and lips touch the skin below my ear, I might not know what time it is, but I know exactly where I am.

I'm back in my childhood home.

But I'm across the hall from my own room.

In Rocco's bed.

But most notable about our current situation, I'm naked.

In Rocco's bed.

And Rocco is naked too.

It's official. The best thing I ever did in life was pretend to be Stella Hayes.

Rocco's hand slides up the center of my body as he presses his very hard cock into the crack of my ass.

"Good morning," he murmurs against my skin.

I tip my head back to give him more access. "Is it morning?"

"I have no fucking idea." He nips my earlobe. "I also don't care."

"I don't either."

"I've been waiting for you to wake up."

I arch, pressing into his erection. "I can tell."

His hand engulfs my breast and he twists my nipple. An electric shock shoots south, landing between my legs.

His hands and mouth move on me. My skin is sensitive under his touch, and I'm not tired any longer.

I'm hyperaware of his every move.

His hand slides down my body and dips between my legs where he cups my sex possessively. Strong fingertips dip into me before giving my clit a teasing swipe.

"You're so fucking wet, and you just woke up."

I am, but I'm not about to agree to that out loud. It's obvious.

"Oh … Rocco."

"You like that," he states. Not even a question. My body is one big tattle tale. "I'm going to make you come so hard, it's good no one is home."

Yes.

Yes, yes, yes. I'm down for that.

One hand works my nipple and the other my clit. Then he wedges his muscled thigh between my legs to part me.

"Yes."

Shit. That was out loud.

"You're so damn sweet. I don't know how I got so lucky to be here."

"It's always been you, Roc." The magic he's spinning between my legs must be a truth serum. "I've never wanted anyone but you."

"Then it's official. I'm the luckiest asshole on the planet."

He doesn't waste time. His fingers are deft and skilled, and my body so in tune to him, I wonder if this is meant to be. I have never once believed in kismet or serendipity.

But this could convince me.

It doesn't take long, and he doesn't make me work for it. It's all him controlling me. His fingers part me farther and his knee lifts toward the ceiling. I'm open and ready for whatever he'll give me.

My clit is swollen and wanting. Another two circles, and I can't take it any longer. I fall. My body quakes as he holds me in his strong arms, cradling me against his chest. And he's right. I'm not quiet.

But then I lose his touch altogether.

I'm rolled to my back, and he covers me with his body. When his hips fall between my legs, there's nothing I want more than for him to stay here.

Forever.

He rubs the underside of his hard cock against my clit. I'm wet and so, so sensitive. The only thing I have the mind to do is focus on how close he is.

How close we are.

The slightest movement and thrust, and we'll be one.

One.

I've wanted this for so long.

"You say the word, baby. I'm ready to make sure your virginity will never be in question again."

My eyes fall shut. I'm still recovering from my orgasm. We're pressed together everywhere it matters but one. His lips hit my collarbone where he sucks but not hard enough to leave a mark. My hands trail up his sides until they land on his wide shoulders. "Yes."

That's all it takes. With one angle of his hips, I feel him at my sex. The tip he demanded I suck before he took over and fucked my mouth.

"Roc," I murmur. "I'm not on birth control."

He never takes his intense gaze off me as he sinks inside me, inch by delicious inch, despite what I just said. "I know, baby."

Oh God. Why is that hot?

Feeling him inside me.

Inching.

Stretching.

He sucks in a breath, like he's trying to control every cell of his being. "I'm not taking you for the first time with anything between us. I'll get a condom. But when I fill you for the first time, the only thing I want you to feel is me."

"Yes." I can't believe I'm agreeing to this. My sister just became a single mom today. But, hell, this is Rocco. "I want this. I want to feel you everywhere."

He looks into my eyes, and with every fiber of his being, says, "I'll never leave you, baby. You're mine."

And with one strong thrust, he fills me.

To the root.

Then he takes my mouth. A kiss filled with such emotion and pent-up sexual tension—I've never felt anything like it.

I'm completely consumed by Rocco Monroe in every way possible.

My lips feel swollen when he breaks our kiss.

But he doesn't move.

Not even an inch.

And even though I'm only a quasi-virgin, I do know that sex involves movement.

A lot of it at times.

Sometimes even aggressively.

"Roc?" I whisper.

"Mmm," he hums.

My fingers press into the skin of his shoulders. "Is everything okay?"

"Just…" He pauses. "Fuck, you feel good."

I relax and let my body get used to the size of him. Being taken by him.

I love it.

"Rocco?"

His tone is tense. "Yeah, baby."

I tip my face so my lips brush his ear. "You're worth everything I've been through to get right here."

I feel him exhale, and he finally moves. I groan when he pulls out halfway and pushes back in. "I don't deserve you. For a million reasons, I'll never deserve you."

He pulls out and pushes back in once more. His hand fists my hair, and he groans as he pulls all the way out this time.

He reaches over to the nightstand, yanks out the drawer, and produces a condom.

I feel empty when his body leaves mine.

Until he sits back on his knees. Then I get something I never dreamed of. A view of Rocco rolling a condom on his cock. And as much as I hate that there will be anything between us, I do enjoy the show.

When he returns to me, he hooks my knee under his elbow, spreading me wide.

His forearm rests by my head, and he brushes the hair away from my face as he sinks into me to the root again. His eyes never waver from mine. This time he moves. Not fast, but not slow.

I've never experienced anything so intimate. So personal. So connected—and I don't mean on a physical level.

I put my feet to the bed and lift my hips for more.

He thrusts harder.

He does it again.

And again.

When we connect, it's new and beautiful and life changing. It hurts, but it doesn't. I can't even rationalize it—all I know is it feels amazing. I'm going to want more of this, and this isn't even over.

And that's before Rocco really moves. For a man who prides himself on control, this is something I won't soon forget.

His body moves with abandon. Every muscle in his body is taut, and his skin is covered in a light sweat. I even smell us. We're a delicious scent of sex and angst.

When he starts to pound into me, a feeling flows through me like a second orgasm, but better.

No, not better. Different. But definitely just as good.

I lift my hips again, and that spurs him on. He moves fast and hard and with no rhythm.

Rocco is out of control. Unleashed. Unbridled.

And it's all for me.

Something foreign washes over me. I arch my back and take everything Rocco gives me.

He wraps an arm under me and holds me tight. One, two, three thrusts, before he plants himself deep inside me.

My body becomes one with the bed.

And Rocco becomes one with me.

I work to catch my breath and realize Rocco is doing the same. We're sticky. I have no idea what time it is other than the sun is up, and we will for sure be expected to people today.

All I want to do is roll into Rocco and sleep for the next week.

Our heart rates finally return to the healthy zone when he pushes to a forearm and looks down at me. "I'm going to deal with this condom. Do not move. I want to be right back in this spot."

My smile is lethargic. "So demanding."

He bumps the tip of his nose on mine. "Be right back."

Rocco proves to be a man of his word. I don't take my eyes off his beautiful body. Tan, muscled, and his cock is still half-hard bobbing as he crawls back into bed on top of me.

He's more careful about giving me all his weight this time and kisses me. "I've come to a decision."

My eyes widen. "That's quite a statement."

Resting on one forearm, he doesn't seem languid or relaxed like I am. He keeps talking and straight up blows my mind. "I'm done begging. If you feel strongly enough about going to New York, I'll follow you. I don't know how I'll make that happen. If I have to quit the DEA and find a new job, I will. It's just a job. Nothing is more important than you."

I forget about any post-sex haze and gape at him. "Are you kidding? You've worked too long and too hard to get where you are. And you love your job. You can't quit."

He shakes his head. "I'm done asking you to stay. You've worked hard. I'm not the only one who deserves to have a dream job. I'll follow you."

Tears prick my eyes. "You would do that?"

He doesn't say a thing. He leans down and presses his mouth to mine. This is different than all the ones before it.

This kiss is laced with desperation.

And since we're fused naked to one another, I feel it in every muscled plane of his body that touches mine. This is just as intimate as what we just experienced together.

He pauses and tips his forehead to mine. He's tense...

No.

He's the most intense I've ever seen him. Especially when he should be relaxed.

"Roc—" I start, but he interrupts me.

"I love you."

I suck in a small breath.

His gaze washes over my face before it catches my eyes and stays there. "I think I've always loved you in some way. When the agents brought me into the family, everyone accepted me. But they did it because they're good people, and because they felt sorry for me. But you were different. You didn't feel sorry for me—you just accepted me."

I bring my fingers up to trace his jawline. "You intrigued me in a way no one ever has. I didn't know anyone like you. And you were always nice to me."

He shakes his head. "You were Tim and Annette's daughter. I had to be nice to you."

I nudge him with my toes. "You just told me you loved me, and you're going to ruin that by telling me you had to be nice to me?"

He smirks.

"But you were nice to everyone."

"Now who's ruining the moment?" he teases.

"You love me." I try the words out for the very first time. "Rocco Monroe loves me."

He kisses me, slow and soft. "And I'll follow you anywhere. Letting you go is not an option. I don't care what the agents say, what Sammie thinks, and especially your parents. I want to spend the rest of my life with you. I'll make sure you're nothing but happy."

Tears pool in my eyes. "I can't remember not loving you. Even when I tried to hate you, I loved you. Trying to hate you was the worst feeling in the world."

"I'm sorry, baby. I needed time." He tucks his arm under me and rolls. I'm on top and his hands go straight to my ass. "Reconciling the idea of you like this compared to the awkward, lanky girl who grew up across the hall was a lot. I am not some creepy-ass old man, and that's how I felt. But once the idea was planted, there was no looking back."

I smile through my tears. "Can we not talk about moving or following each other? I wish we were back in New Orleans or Mississippi. There's too much going on here. I just want a minute to enjoy this. You love me."

He leans up and presses his lips to mine. "And you don't hate me."

I shake my head. "I could never. And, trust me, I tried. It wouldn't stick when it comes to you."

He puts a hand on the back of my head and tucks me into his broad chest. He's warm and comfortable. The idea that this is my life—my forever—is overwhelming.

"Let's just hope Tim and Annette don't hate me."

I smile against his chest. "I don't care what they think."

"That's easy for you to say," he mutters. "By the way, while you were sleeping, I got a text from the guys. They all know. No one in this family can keep a secret. That means everyone knows but your parents. We need to get in front of that before it blows up in our faces."

"I'm glad they know. And I thought you were going to give me a minute to enjoy this. Can we please not talk about my parents while we're naked?"

He sighs. The way he pulls his fingers through my hair is so soothing, I might go back to sleep.

"One more thing," he adds.

I yawn. "As long as you don't mention Tim and Annette."

"I have a meeting tomorrow morning with the CIA. Since you're the mastermind who connected Robichaux to a worldwide drug distributor and human trafficking ring, you're expected to be there."

Rocco barely filled me in on the way home about the Hayes case. We were too distracted by running into Evie, he didn't give me all the details.

I push up on a forearm to look down at him. "They want me there?"

"Yep. And your dad and all the guys will be there too. So, you know, it should be fun," he deadpans.

I lower myself back to his chest and settle in. "I refuse to think about that until tomorrow."

"Avoidance," he mutters. "Not the strategy I'd recommend, but since you're naked, I'll play along."

I press my lips to his pec. "I love you."

He pulls in a deep breath and holds it for a dramatic pause before releasing it. I'm not sure, but it feels like he's letting those words sink in like I did his. His lips touch the side of my head when he says, "Go back to sleep, baby. Reality will slap us in the face soon enough."

Unfortunately, he's right.

Soon enough comes way too fast.

28

BLOODY CHUFFED AND BADASS SHIT

Rocco

Getting my shit together when it comes to Teagan at the same time Sammie had a baby could not have worked out any better. Tim and Annette are solely focused on their oldest daughter and newborn granddaughter.

As it should be.

I can't lie, not having their attention has been a gift. It's better than college football, the draft, and the biggest game of the year all wrapped into one. That's how good it's been.

But I have a feeling that's about to change.

Tim and Annette have been at the hospital most of the time since Marley was born. Teagan and I went back last night. When her parents were out of the room, Sammie promised us she'd keep the news of *us* to herself, which is not like Sammie.

Motherhood agrees with her.

At this point, it's choosing the right time to talk to the only parental figures I've ever had. But since the woman I just made sure isn't a virgin any longer is their youngest daughter, I'm anxious to get that conversation over with.

Oddly, I'm not dreading it.

I'm fucking excited about it.

When that's checked off the list, Teagan and I can focus on what comes next. It's up to her. I'm not looking forward to quitting a job and career I love, but I'll do it. New York is a big place, and I'm a hard worker. I'll find something.

But we're on the clock.

I'm set to close on a house not far from Brax and Landyn. If I have to back out of that, it needs to happen soon.

Not to mention, I'm ready to get on with my life with Teagan. I've waited almost two years. Who knows … maybe I waited longer than that.

Nothing has felt as good as this.

As right.

As effortless.

Even though it's been a lot of fucking effort. She's worth every bit of it.

"Roc, everyone is staring at us," Teagan whispers.

She's not wrong and does everything she can to twist her hand out of mine. Most people in this building know who Teagan Coleman is. I don't officially start reporting to the Miami Division until next week, but that doesn't mean there aren't some who know me too. I was a Miami PD cop for three years and the personal project of the infamous fab three plus Tim.

I don't whisper. "Trust me."

"This seems like a bad idea. The DEA can be worse than old church ladies spreading gossip."

I grip her hand tighter. "This is not gossip. This is happening."

Her eyes widen, mortified. "Well, okay. If you want my dad to find out about us through the drug-agent grapevine, then so be it.

At least we won't have to find an opening to tell him. It'll be done for us when this spreads like wildfire."

I don't slow down as I lead her through the halls of the building I know like the back of my hand. I've been here with the guys and Tim as much as I was at the precinct. "I'm not sure what you're worried about. I'm the one who's tying myself to Tim Coleman's youngest daughter. That's not the best look. It screams creepy old man. I'm going to have to ignore the chatter and ribbing until it dies down. It's none of their business. If I don't ignore it, I'll probably have to kill someone. The next month or so will definitely test my control. But this—" I bring her hand to my mouth for a kiss. "Is like ripping off the bandage. Quick and painful, but it'll be done."

"You're crazy. And you're dragging me down with you."

I lean in to put my lips to her ear. "Is that like you going down on me? Because I'm hard for that anytime you're in the mood."

Her face warms with a beautiful flush.

I reach up to tuck her hair behind her ear and nod to the door on the left. "This is us. Prepare yourself. This will probably be unlike any meeting you've ever been to."

I don't give her a moment to respond. I push the door open to the conference room. Four men who were in light conversation turn to us.

Two are amused.

One is downright ecstatic.

And the last drags a hand down his stress-lined face.

That would be Brax.

He needs to get over himself.

"Another one bites the dust." CIA Officer Cole Carson claps his hands once, making Teagan jerk from the shock of it. "What you didn't tell me is that your contact slash love interest is also Tim Coleman's youngest daughter. Had I known that I would've been here last night! This is the best thing since Brax and Micah went to blows over Brax hooking up with a mafia princess."

Brax proves he is not in the mood and points to Carson. "How many times do I need to tell you to quit calling her that?"

Cole stuffs his hands in his pockets and glances at Micah. "But she was."

Micah shrugs.

Brax fumes.

King stares at me with a smirk. "Goldie was right. Here in the flesh, you two might as well be a walking billboard for The Pink. I hear your wedding will be on the house."

"Um, what?" Teagan sputters.

I glare at King before turning to her. "Nothing. I'll explain later."

Cole beams. "I hear wedding bells ringing right here in the hallways of the DEA."

Micah gives Brax a shove. "Man, get over yourself. It'll blow up when Tim finds out, but you know they'll love it in the end."

Brax turns to his best friend and frowns. "I don't like being in the middle of drama. It's stressful as fuck. Tim has always had my back. I've been loyal to him. The fact that I'm in the know about this and haven't told him is not cool. I have a daughter—hell, I could have another one next month. But my wife is best friends with this guy." Brax motions to me and rolls his eyes before he turns his attention to Teagan. "We're happy for you. Seriously, we are. We know Rocco isn't going to do anything to fuck this up. He wouldn't do that to anyone. But this is an unusual situation."

Micah slaps Brax on the back. "Other than Brax lying to Landyn about his true identity when they were married, we're learning that our boy here doesn't deal well with keeping secrets."

Cole rubs his hands together. "I want to know who's going to blows today."

"No one is going to blows," I assure him.

"I'm not taking sides if they go to blows," King adds. "Goldie will kill me."

I look down at Teagan. "That won't happen. I promise."

"Oh, I'd never allow that. I think my dad will be surprised, but he'll get over it. He trusts you with everything," Teagan says.

"*Everything* is different when it's your daughter," Brax amends.

"As fun as this is, can we please get to why we're here? I have information I think everyone will like, especially Teagan."

"Why Teagan?" King asks.

Cole turns to me. "They don't know?"

"They don't know what?"

We all turn to the door. Tim stands there staring at us.

"Well, hello, gramps!" Cole bellows. "Congratulations. I hear she's a beauty. I love babies."

"Thanks." Tim frowns and turns to his daughter. "What are you doing here?"

Teagan is standing close to me. No matter how much I want to, we're not touching. Tim's reaction is to her being here, not to her being here with me.

Yet.

Brax, Micah, and King all look as perplexed as Tim. I'm about to open my mouth to explain before Cole demands the podium like he usually does, but Teagan speaks first.

"So, do you remember how I was volunteering for A Life for Justice? Well, one of my cases crossed paths with Rocco's. That was before either of us moved. When we realized we both had the same goal, we teamed up."

"Teamed up," Micah echoes in a way that makes me want to punch him in the face. "They sure did."

"When did this happen?" Tim demands. "And why didn't I know about it before now?"

"Not too long ago," I offer. "You've been busy with Sammie."

Proving he can't keep his mouth shut for long, Carson jumps in.

"Your daughter is fan-fucking-tastic at what she does. Not only has she cracked an international human trafficking ring, it opened the doors to a drug distribution pipeline that spans so far and wide, it has my supervisors sporting wood." He looks at Teagan. "Sorry, but it's true."

"It's fine," Teagan says.

Tim doesn't think about the human trafficking or the international drug ring, and keeps his attention focused on his daughter. "I thought you were just working on cold cases."

Teagan bites her lip and shrugs. "That's true. This is a case where a man has been imprisoned for something he was tricked into doing. An elderly gentleman."

"In a Nigerian prison," Cole adds and stresses the word Nigerian for effect. "And not a good one. But really, are any of them good? I've located him, by the way. You're welcome."

Teagan's eyes widen.

"Exactly," Cole agrees and points to Teagan. "And I hear you are the badass who went undercover to lead us to where we are now."

Tim gapes. His happy aura from becoming a grandfather flies out the window. He holds a hand out low and glares at me. "So, let me get this straight. You took my daughter undercover to locate an elderly man in Nigeria because it's tied to your case?"

"No way," I answer with a partial lie. "We stumbled upon each other. The first time was all on her. I was doing surveillance on the target and saw Teagan. I moved in when I realized it was her so she wasn't doing this by herself. There was some car trouble and then a little break in. Look, it doesn't matter how we got here. The rest fell into place."

"I'd say so," Micah mutters.

King nods like he's seen the light. "Now it's all coming together."

Tim explodes. "A break in?!"

"Dad, I swear, I was fine. That wasn't a big deal. Nothing was taken." Teagan takes a step toward Tim and tries to calm him down. "Since then, Rocco and I have worked together."

Brax lets out an audible exhale.

Seriously, when the fuck did Brax start breathing so loud?

Either these men are always this dramatic, or Tim doesn't notice because he's too focused on his daughter. "Why am I just learning about this?"

"I'm just putting it out there, we're just finding out about this too," Brax states.

Great. Now Brax is a suck ass.

Teagan motions around the room. "Obviously, I didn't think it would turn into this. I didn't expect it to be tied to the DEA let alone the CIA. I planned to find out where Heath Hayes was and tell his family. That's it."

Tim drags a hand down his face and finally looks like he's had two sleepless nights. "Teagan, you have no idea what the hell you're doing."

"I'd beg to differ," Cole spouts. "We all had to start somewhere."

Tim narrows his eyes at Cole. "Shut the fuck up. She's not a secret agent. She's a journalist—not to mention she's my baby. She is not doing this shit."

"Dad—"

There's no way I can sit here and let Teagan sit through this—not when she's worked as hard as she has. I step in and position myself at her back. I'm not touching her, but I am close. "Calm down. Teagan has been working with the Heath family for months. It would've taken multiple wires and countless affidavits to get where she got. She was never in any danger, even when I found her working on her own. She's smart."

Tim doesn't have a chance to respond, because Teagan beats

him to it. She twists and nudges my chest. "After all this time, now you'll admit I was never in danger?"

I try to bite back my smirk. "For the most part."

She shakes her head and smiles. "You're a piece of work."

I shrug. "Can you blame me?"

"Well, not now. But then, yes. I totally blamed you. You were such an ass."

"It always starts out with an asshole, doesn't it?"

We all look at Cole. He's wearing a wolfish grin.

"What?" he acts affronted. "I'm just saying, I think we've all been the asshole at one point. And look at us now ... every single one of us is living the dream. Welcome to the club, Roc."

"What club?" Tim exclaims before he turns his attention to his daughter. "What the hell is he talking about?"

Teagan takes a step back. Whether she means to or not, her back collides with my chest.

And whether I mean to or not, my hand wraps around her hip.

It's instinctual and deliberate.

Tim's gaze turns to a glare when it shifts from his daughter to me. "What the fuck."

Well then.

Not a question.

A statement.

Teagan leans into me farther, and her hand wraps around mine where I hold her tight.

"Dad—" she tries again, but this time he interrupts her.

"No." He shakes his head. "No fucking way. When did this happen?"

Teagan tenses against me.

Tim's glare shoots daggers at me and raises his voice. "Answer me, dammit."

"Dad, stop it. It hasn't been that long—" Teagan starts.

"It's been building," I interrupt. "Trust me, I did everything I could to ignore it. I even tried being the asshole Cole described. That was almost two years ago."

Tim's eyes widen. "Two years?!"

"Only two years," I stress. "She was twenty-one at the time. Or almost."

"Fuck me," he growls as he turns a one-eighty. He can't stand to look at me.

Damn, that cuts deep.

"Dad," Teagan whispers.

I don't take my gaze off her father. The man who didn't have to take me into his home when he did. The man who trusted that I wasn't some asshole kid in a man's body when I slept down the hall from his young girls.

"Tim," Micah calls for him. "This is Rocco. You know he's not going to hurt her. He'd never do that to you."

Tim shakes his head, but just stares at the floor.

"I don't have a daughter," King adds. "But if I did, I couldn't ask for a better man for her."

"I knew this would happen," Brax mutters.

I give Brax my best *why-the-fuck-are-you-stabbing-me-in-the-back* look.

He doesn't even acknowledge me.

Tim turns to Brax. "You knew about this and didn't tell me?"

Brax crosses his arms and focuses on Tim. "I'm the one who brought Rocco into the fold. I'm the one who vouched for him all those years ago when the rest of us were in limbo moving across the country together. I'm the reason he's here."

Now I'm pissed.

I haven't done shit to deserve any of this. Teagan is a damn adult. We don't need anyone's blessing.

Maybe it's good she's moving to New York. All of a sudden, I'm not upset about quitting my job.

My normally level and calm temperament starts to crack. "I

don't need anyone's approval but Teagan's. She's a grown-ass woman and has been for years. I respect you, Tim. You know I do. Maybe more than anyone. If you cut me out because Teagan chooses me ... well, I'm not going to lie, that'll kill me. Until now, this family has been my life. I'd do anything for any of you. But if you make me choose—"

"Rocco, don't say that," Teagan whispers as she turns. She wraps her arms around my waist and tucks herself to my side.

"I knew this was going to happen. Look, I have a daughter. I get it." Brax crosses his arms and looks around the room before zeroing back on Tim. "What I'm saying is that I trust Rocco with my life. Hell, I trust him with the most important people in my life."

Damn. It took Brax long enough to get on board, so I say, "Tim will accept me or he won't. I don't need anyone's help."

Brax holds a hand up to me but doesn't turn away from Tim. "The day that man saved Landyn's life, I knew I could trust him. That was more than a decade ago. I've never once regretted my decision."

Tim turns back to face the group and every year of his life is visible in his expression.

He's obviously had a week.

But that doesn't mean I'm going to stand here and be treated like some lowlife.

I've proven myself to this family over and over.

"I love her," I announce to the room. "And since you all know me better than anyone, you know saying that does not come easily or naturally for me. But when it comes to Teagan, it was easy. That's how right this is."

As soon as I utter those words, the air thickens. Teagan wraps me up tighter. Her words, though, are for her father. "I love him, Dad. I always have. This is what I want. And if it makes you feel any better, I made the first move when I hit on him two years ago."

"Holy shit," Micah mutters.

King lets out a low whistle.

Cole leans toward me and whispers in the loudest voice, one that only Cole Carson could achieve, "Nicely done, young man."

Brax, who was late to the party to have my back, rolls his eyes.

Tim rubs his temple like a migraine has taken over his brain.

"Tim," I call for him.

When he opens his eyes, he doesn't look like he wants to kill me. He's resigned.

I can deal with that.

But his next question surprises me. "You love her, and she loves you. Did you get her to stay in Miami instead of moving to New York?"

Teagan bristles in my arms. "Dad!"

His question doesn't bother me in the slightest. "Not yet, and I've stopped asking. If she wants to go to New York, I'll follow her."

"Whoa," Micah bursts. "You just got here."

I look down at Teagan and tip her face to mine. "If you want to chase your dreams, I'll chase you. But we'll do it together."

"That is so damn sweet," Cole says.

"I already knew this," Brax adds. "Landyn told me."

"Well," Tim demands, glaring at his daughter. "What are you going to do?"

Teagan tips her face to me and all I see are the endless dark eyes I've become obsessed with. "I only took that job because there was no way I could live in Miami knowing you were here."

I bring my hand up to cup her cheek and lower my voice. "Baby, I knew that. I was trying to help you save face and not tell anyone that you hit on me first and that I was the reason you were moving to New York."

She sighs. "That's why I love you."

I don't give a shit where we are or who's watching. I lean in and press my lips to hers. "Does this mean you're staying?"

Tears pool in her eyes. "Yes. *We're* staying."

"This is too much," Tim says. "I need some time to get used to this. If your mom knows and I didn't know, I'm going to be even more pissed."

Teagan doesn't let me go but turns to Tim with a smile. "She doesn't know. Let me tell her."

Tim goes on. "You'd better call her the moment we leave here. Is there anything else I don't know? I'm not happy about the secrets."

I'd like to remind him that Sammie hid her pregnancy from them for the first four months to take some pressure off us, but I figure now is not the time.

King slaps me on the back. "Told you everything would be okay."

"I felt good about it from the get-go," Micah adds.

Brax is the only one to speak the truth. "I did not feel good about anything. I'm just glad it's all over. I'm with Tim, secrets stress me out."

"Again," Micah drawls. "Your wife didn't know your real name, for what, a year?"

Brax frowns. "A few weeks. And we're well past that."

"This is one of the best days ever. I feel like I've been here for all the big moments. I wish Bella could've witnessed this. She'd be *bloody chuffed*," Cole announces, mimicking his wife's British accent. "I feel like a part of the family. Can I be the crazy cousin from the boonies? Don't make me say goodbye after this case is wrapped."

"This case," Tim echoes. "Can we get to that please? I'd like to be briefed before I retire. Sammie and Marley are coming home this afternoon. And we still need to deal with this." He waves his hand around at Teagan and me. "When they tell Annette."

"The case," Cole announces. "We're about to take down a shit-ton of motherfuckers that cross continents. Who's in?"

I think it's safe to say the agents are sick of relationship and family drama. They're ready to take down some motherfuckers—internationally and domestic.

"Finally, something I can control," Tim mutters.

"Fuck yeah," Micah pipes.

"Every day, all day," King agrees.

"Finally, some badass shit." Brax looks downright relieved. "Let's do this."

29

MESSIER

Teagan

I spent my fair share of time volunteering for A Life for Justice. Before I met the Hayes family, my cases were simple and as basic as a pumpkin spiced latte the first week of September.

I've overheard Dad and the guys talk about their cases from time to time. I could tell they did their best not to bring up work when their families were around.

Sometimes they just couldn't help it. I loved listening and learning. Who knows, maybe that's why I became intrigued with unsolved cases.

But the intricacy of this boggles my mind.

He wasn't kidding about multi continents.

We've been here for almost two hours. We've conferenced with Rocco's old partner in New Orleans, Taylor, and three of Cole's CIA assets across the world. It's turned into a simultaneous worldwide takedown.

Jules Robichaux is connected to the African Cartel Federation. Apparently that name wasn't easy to find. They usually refer to themselves as simply *A* throughout most communication.

That is unless you have assets all over the globe like Cole Carson.

The Federation pays for mules to be brought in and used to transport heroin, cocaine, and meth. And not only through airports the way they use people like Heath Hayes for. They're huge in ports across the continents.

I guess the elderly are unsuspecting, unless they are unlucky and get caught. Like Heath, they aren't told what they're carrying. He was simply promised a payout and return plane ticket in the end.

Brax, Micah, and King are impressed. And that's not easy given the kind of work they've done in the past. The more my dad learned, the more he mentioned his tension headache setting in. And the more he learned about Robichaux, the more upset he was with me. It was like Rocco in the beginning all over again. But unlike the man I plan to spend the rest of my life with, I doubt Dad will come around like Rocco did and admit I was smart and not at all unsafe during my initial meeting.

Whatever.

Dad stopped looking at Rocco and me like he wanted to throw up.

Progress. Especially since I still need to tell my mom.

But if anyone loves Rocco more than me and Landyn, it's Annette Coleman. I have a feeling she'll have the exact opposite reaction as Dad.

So the plan is set. A multi-continent takedown. I wish we were back in New Orleans for the action, but there's no way to get there fast enough. It's happening soon.

But there's still one thing that hasn't been addressed.

Like, the biggest thing. I've sat back and waited. Cole Carson was on a roll with the operational plan. I wasn't going to be the one to interrupt.

But they're wrapping this up, and I refuse to leave this room until I know there's a plan.

My dad starts piling papers as the guys shut their laptops.

This is my last chance.

"So, I have to know." Everyone in the room turns toward me. "This is all great. I'm impressed. In awe. But what about Heath Hayes? He's the reason I investigated Jules Robichaux to begin with."

Cole stuffs his laptop in a bag and powers down his cell.

"Oh, shit," Dad mutters. "I know what this means."

Everyone in the room does the same. I turn to Rocco and frown.

"I've never been an agent for this, but this means shit's about to go off the record."

Cole looks at my dad. "Are we good to talk here or should we go somewhere else?"

"We're good," Dad says.

Cole nods and turns to me. "My wife, Bella, is a baddie—like you—just with more experience under her belt."

Dad turns to Cole. "Can we just stick to the case here? I'm still coming to terms with today. The thought of Teagan becoming a Bella Carson will push me over the edge."

"Now I want to meet your wife," I add.

"Bella used to be MI6," Cole says.

I'm a journalist. Or that's what I want to be, since I'm basically unemployed. Now that I agreed to stay, I need to find another job. I'm really good with reporting what's already happened. I have no desire to be any type of agent—secret or otherwise.

Cole keeps talking. "Now she works for a private organization in the States. Her associates have special and varied skills. Extraction is not normally their thing. They're usually..." Cole pauses and tips his head, looking for the right word. "Messier. Anyway, I work with her organization from time to time. I need them, they need me—it all evens out in the end."

I focus on one word that matters in his discourse. "Extraction?"

Cole nods but answers carefully. "Basically."

The men around the room look mildly impressed. But then again, I think it takes a lot to impress them, whereas it doesn't take much for me.

But it sure as hell requires details.

"Look, I'm new to this," I explain. "Don't assume I can read between the lines. And I don't want to assume Heath Hayes will soon be a free man if that's not true. Are you saying your friends are going in to get him?"

Cole narrows his eyes and looks like he's solving a complicated calculus problem in his head. "I feel like there's a good chance you're safe to read between the lines. But when it comes to things like this, nothing is a sure thing. I'll know more in a few hours."

My jaw goes slack. I can't help but gape at the news. "Are you serious? Hours?"

"Like I said, my wife's associates and I do each other favors. This is a biggie, but I could tell it was important to Rocco when we spoke. I called in the favor. That Nigerian prison was not going to release Mr. Hayes. It just wasn't going to happen. Even though he was taken advantage of—"

"Elder fraud," I butt in. "That's what I called it in my thesis."

Cole nods. "See there? A badass in training."

"Thanks, Cole," Rocco says from where he stands close behind me. Even though he's played a part in orchestrating this operation, he never separated himself from me. A lot of that time, he's touched me in some way. The fact that my dad knows about us, and it's settled that we're staying in Miami, I feel a peace I haven't felt in a long time.

Cole beams. "I'm always happy to visit my weird cousins in Miami. You guys are always an entertaining bunch."

Dad picks up his things. "Are we done? I need to get back to the hospital. I have the car seat with me."

I move away from Rocco for the first time since our secret was blown into a million pieces and wrap my arms around my dad. "Thank you."

He returns my hug with a sigh. "Not sure why you're thanking me. It seems you didn't trust me enough to tell me things you should have."

I press my cheek to his chest. "Thank you for not flipping out worse than you did."

He presses his lips to the top of my head like he's done my entire life. "That's the worst *thank you* I've ever gotten."

I smile because I know he's giving me shit. "Love you, Dad."

"Love you, too, Teag." Then he dips his lips close to my ear and whispers only for me to hear. "Only want you to be happy, baby. He'd better make you happy."

I hug him tighter. "He does. He really does."

"He's a good man. I've always known that. I was ... shocked."

I pull away far enough to look up at him. "I'm relieved that you know."

He kisses my forehead. "Go tell your mom. I doubt she'll have the same reaction I did."

My smile might break my face. "I hope you're right."

I know he's right.

I feel a tug on the back of my shirt.

"Let's go," Rocco says. "If we tell Annette sooner rather than later, she might not kill me. I have a couple more days off until I officially report. I've got a couple stops I want to make while we wait on news about Hayes."

"I'm back on the next flight to D.C. This could've been done over a conference call, but these visits really feed my soul. I love the comradery," Cole says.

We both say goodbye, Rocco does the handshake thing all around, and we leave the way we came in. He holds me close, and I realize I don't care what anyone thinks.

I'm ready to shout my new reality from the rooftops.

Rocco

ANNETTE SCREAMS.

She actually screams.

What's happening in front of us couldn't be more different than Tim's reaction back at DEA.

Sammie scoffs from her reclining chair where Marley is cradled in her arms. "I know Teagan is your favorite and Rocco isn't far behind, but you do have a granddaughter now. You're going to wake her."

Annette throws her arms around Teagan while talking to Sammie. "I don't have favorites. I love everyone. And if we tiptoe around the baby, she'll never sleep. Trust me, if she can sleep through chaos, you'll thank me later."

"Do you hear that, Marley? Your granny wants you to sleep through a fireworks show," Sammie says in a baby, sing-songy voice even though her daughter is fast asleep.

Even with tears in her eyes, Annette turns to Sammie. "I don't care if you are postpartum. If the word granny is muttered in this house again, there will be hell to pay."

Annette turns to me. I almost have to catch her when she

throws herself into my arms. "I'm so happy. I love you like you're mine, Roc. But you're not. Not really. I was always afraid when you settled down, I'd lose you. I love you. And, if it's possible, I love you more for Teagan. You two are made for each other. I've thought that for years."

"I literally gave her a grandchild, and she can't stop going on and on about how perfect Teagan is," Sammie complains. But when I look over, she's doing it with a grin on her face and turns back to the bundle in her arms. "Are you going to be as perfect as your Aunt Teagan? Of course, you are. In fact, you'll blow your aunt out of the water, that's how perfect you are."

I kiss Annette on the cheek before she lets me go. "I'm glad you're happy."

"Glad?!" Annette exclaims. "This is the best thing since grandbabies!"

Sammie rolls her eyes.

We had to rehash the whole thing for Annette. As much as I want to shout to the world that Teagan is mine, I'm also ready to move on.

Move forward.

And that means moving out of this house with Teagan sooner rather than later.

"As much as I'd like to stand around and talk about how much everyone loves me, we have an appointment."

Teagan turns to me. "What appointment?"

I look to Annette. "We'll be back. Let me know if there's anything you need while we're out."

"Just some sleep and peace and quiet," Sammie calls.

"We'll be here settling in," Annette adds. "You're going to miss the girls. Landyn and Goldie are bringing dinner soon. I can't wait to tell them about you two!"

We need to get out of here.

I grab Teagan's hand. "Don't wait on us to eat."

"Don't worry," Sammie deadpans. "I'm eating for two. I'm not waiting on anyone."

I've got Teagan in my car and we're pulling out of the drive. "I don't want to be here when Annette learns she was the last to find out about us."

"She's got too much to think about to hold it against us for long." Teagan buckles up and turns to me. "Where are we going?"

I turn south. "I want to show you something."

"Are we going to Brax and Landyn's?"

"No. In fact, I've had about enough of everyone. I'd kill to get you alone. Which is why this can't happen soon enough."

"What can't happen?" she demands.

We've been driving for almost fifteen minutes, which is nothing in this city. It's not far from Tim and Annette's. It's also only twenty minutes from the DEA.

I pass the BMW parked on the curb and pull into the drive.

"Are we visiting someone? Because it would've been nice to know so I could mentally prepare for more socializing. It's been a long few days."

"Don't worry, Teag. You can put your social battery on hold. It's just you and me."

She meets me at the back of the car and whispers. "Then who's that?"

"My realtor." We watch a woman walk to us who's around the same age as Annette. Her heels click on the driveway as she makes her way to us. I take her hand. "Thanks for arranging this, Sarah. I know you're busy."

She flips off her sunglasses and shoots us a smile. "No problem. I've already unlocked the front door. I have to make some calls. I got an offer on one of my listings. Since the house is empty, I'll work in the car while you do your thing. I just called the title company. We're all set to go for next week."

Teagan tugs on my hand as she takes a better look around. "This is your new house?"

"Not yet," I say.

Sarah smiles, probably thinking about her commission. "It will be next week."

"Come on." I lead Teagan to the front door. "I'll show you. Though, it won't take long. It's not big."

I push the door open and hold out a hand. Teagan enters first. The lights are out and the place echoes when I shut the door behind us. I stand back as she looks around and moves from the small family room to the smaller kitchen.

She says nothing as she looks around on her own. There's no reason for a tour. It might be bigger than anything I've ever had, but it's nothing compared to the home where our bedrooms are across from each other. She peeks in each room, the guest bath, and finally the primary suite.

The floors aren't in bad condition, but the kitchen and bathrooms have seen better days. There's not one thing modern or new or fancy in the place.

She pulls back the faded curtains and peeks out to the backyard. It's nothing but grass. And that's not thriving either.

"I have no idea how to take care of a yard other than to mow it," I say. She turns back to me and crosses her arms. "But I'll figure it out. I'm sure the agents will be more than happy to tell me how to do everything. Other than Micah. They've got gardeners and shit."

She motions to the window. "It's a big yard."

I shrug. "Smallest house in the neighborhood with the biggest yard. Sarah said it's a no brainer if I'm willing to put in the effort to fix it up."

Teagan turns in a slow circle, as if there's anything to look at besides four bland walls and wood floors that are faded here and there.

I flip my key ring around my finger. "I'm going to gut the place even though I have no fucking idea what I'm doing."

She turns to me and hugs herself across her middle. "You have the internet. And the agents."

"They never disappoint."

"I have a feeling you'll figure it out just fine on your own," she goes on. "You're smart like that."

I smirk. "That's quite the vote of confidence. I appreciate it."

"I'm sure Landyn will give her opinions on … stuff."

I shake my head. "I don't want Landyn's opinion. I want yours."

Her tongue sneaks out to wet the crease of her lips. "I've never decorated anything other than my childhood bookshelves. I doubt you want your new home littered with crime fiction and random journals stuffed here and there. Plus, this place is like a mansion compared to what I'm used to living in. You said yourself I've become a minimalist out of necessity. I wouldn't know what to do with all your space."

"I don't care what's in the space as long as you're in it."

Her fingertips land on her lips as if she doesn't know what to say. Or maybe it's to keep herself from blurting out what we're both thinking.

She stays silent.

"Teagan, do you like it?"

She states the obvious. "It's yours."

"I haven't closed yet. I'll lose my earnest money, but I can back out."

"It doesn't matter if I like it."

"It'll be yours someday," I say before I amend. "Ours. And that someday will be sooner rather than later."

"Ours," she echoes. "That's a quick turn of events."

"Quick?" I have to manage myself so the word doesn't come out angry. "This is the antithesis of quick. I've known you for over a decade. Like an idiot, I spent the last two years trying to talk myself out of standing right here. This is the least quick thing I've done in my life."

She's in the middle of the room, and I'm boxing her in from my spot at the threshold.

She doesn't break our gaze. "Right back at you. I'm here, and I'm staying in Miami. But now I'm an unemployed graduate and have to start over on my job search. You have a career and you're buying a house. I need to get my shit together."

"Do it here."

She sucks in a breath. "Roc—"

I shake my head and shut her up. "I want you, Teag. I don't want to date you. When I come home from work, I want to know that we'll meet back in the same spot every day, no matter what. Hell, I want to see your shit in every corner of this house."

"You moved me out of my apartment. You know I don't have a lot of shit."

I shake my head. "Even better. That means I can move you in one trip. There will be TVs, though. Plural. That's nonnegotiable."

"I won't have anything to contribute. You know, financially. Or even a TV."

"I've got the TVs covered. I might not be a billionaire or a millionaire or anything-aire. I'm just me, and I only want you. I'll play catchup with the traditions later. But I told you there's been no one but you for two years, even if you were only a fantasy. Every house I looked at, I pictured you in it. The fact that you're here right now is nothing short of a miracle or the result of two years of manifestation."

She does her best to bite back a smirk. "You manifested me?"

"I didn't do a very good job since you came back to me during a meeting with Robichaux."

All of a sudden, she puts her hands on her hips and hitches a foot. "Do I need to remind you, that you never would have *mani-*

fested me had I not given into my childhood crush turned adult obsession?"

I shrug. "It would've happened eventually."

"All I'm saying is that you cannot take credit," she waves a hand between the two of us. "For this. *This* is because, as Cole Carson says, I'm a lady badass."

"Is that right?"

"It's the truth. Cole said so, and he's the CIA. He knows all the secrets. So I guess it depends on if there's room for two badasses in your new house."

"If you promise not to go undercover without telling me, I'll make room."

Her smirk swells. "Will there be consequences?"

My smirk doesn't swell, but my cock does. "Do you want there to be?"

"Hmm ... maybe."

I push off the door jamb and stalk the short distance to her. "Baby, don't make me hard in a house I don't own yet with my realtor sitting outside. Especially when we go home to a houseful of family and a newborn. I'll be lucky to sneak into your room tonight. There will be no consequences until we move into this house."

She doesn't have a choice but to look up at me when I pull her to me with my hands on her ass. "Does this mean if I move in that I don't have to buy you a housewarming gift?"

I give her ass a squeeze and wonder what panties she's wearing. "This is housewarming enough. I don't need anything but you."

"And a TV," she amends.

"That goes without saying." I grip her ass and lift. She yelps but wraps her legs around my waist. "Is that a yes to eventually moving in or a yes to moving in with me on closing day?"

She runs her hands up the back of my neck. "If those are my only options, then I guess it's a yes. The sooner the better."

I put her back to the wall and press my cock into her pussy. "I want to fuck you, but I don't have anywhere to do it in the middle of the day. I can't wait until the keys are ours."

She leans in and kisses me. "Did you really picture me in this house?"

I sober. "I pictured you everywhere, baby. In every part of my life. I also kicked my own ass daily for fucking things up with you when I did."

Her gaze roams my face, and nothing has ever felt so right. "We're here now. Nothing will come between us again."

"Never again. I won't allow it." I press into her and return her kiss. "Now you've made me hard, and I'm going to have to walk out of here in front of my realtor."

She traces my bottom lip. "I'll sneak into your room tonight. We'll have to be quiet."

"This will be the longest week ever."

"And I have to break it to my dad that I'm moving in with you. I hope he lives through the next week."

"This can't start soon enough, Teagan. I've waited a lifetime for just a sliver of happy. Getting the whole damn cake and eating it too is something I never thought I'd get."

I watch her beautiful face light up and realize I'd do anything to see this same expression for the rest of my days. "I love you, Rocco Monroe. You're proof that dreams really do come true."

30

FAIRYTALE

Teagan

Calling your future employer to tell them that you finally allowed yourself to fall in love, and they're going to have to find someone else to fill the job they hired you for because you aren't moving across the country after all ... well, it sucks.

Beyond sucks.

But I did it.

Rocco and I also told my mom that I'm moving in with him as soon as he closes on his house. Then, because I'd had enough, I begged her to tell Dad.

She agreed.

Sammie announced she is officially the favorite child, even if it only lasts a day or two.

Rocco had some errands to run, and I came to my room to pack.

What else am I going to do?

Well, look for a job, I guess.

I frown when my cell vibrates with a call.

No one ever calls me but my parents. Not even Sammie.

Everyone in my life knows that unless someone is dying, I'm strictly a text girl.

I have no idea who it is, but it doesn't even say Unknown Caller. It doesn't say anything other than incoming call.

I send it to voicemail.

Two minutes later, I get a text.

> Unknown – Teagan-the-baddy-Coleman. Answer your phone.

What the heck?

This goes against everything I am. But curiosity also runs through my veins.

> Me – Um, who is this?

> Unknown – I have news you're going to want. On Heath Hayes.

Oh, wow.

My phone immediately rings again, and this time I can't connect the call fast enough.

"Hello?"

"Thank you for answering. Uncle Sam doesn't exactly give us Caller ID."

"Sorry. I can't help it. I don't answer calls without a name. You have news about Mr. Hayes?"

"I'm well, thanks. Got home safely. The wife and kids are thriving. Even the damn cat is living its best life. The Virginia countryside is as peaceful as ever. I'm happy."

I frown. "Um, that's great."

Cole sighs. "Conversation is a lost art."

"I can converse all day long. I'm just very anxious to know if Mr. Hayes is okay."

"The target has been extracted. He's with my contact on a private jet, and they just landed in Spain."

I drop my face into my other hand as tears spring to my eyes.

"Teagan?"

I force myself to swallow over the lump in my throat and squeak, "Yeah?"

"Are you okay?"

I shake my head like he's in the same room and can see me. "No. I'm not okay."

"I'll sit here and wait until you're ready to hear the rest."

My manners fly out the window when I sniff too loud. "There's more?"

"There is."

"Oh, shit. I don't like the sound of your voice."

"They stopped in Barcelona to fuel up. My contact said Mr. Hayes wasn't doing well. My guy, Jarvis, is trained as a medic but didn't want to chance flying across the pond if Mr. Hayes needed further care. They're at the hospital now."

I climb off the floor and forget about everything in my closet. "The hospital? What's wrong with him?"

"Let's just say he wasn't well cared for in prison. I'll let you know when I know something."

"Thank you, Cole. Thank you for getting him. I'm so relieved he's out of there."

"No worries," Cole says. "Consider it an early wedding present."

I freeze.

"Excuse me?"

But he's gone. The line goes dead.

I dial a number that I haven't called in I don't know how long. Probably since before I lost my mind and decided to use a hand-me-down fake ID at a sketchy bar on the outskirts of the French Quarter.

Rocco and I have hardly been apart since we were reunited in the lounge of The Hotel Monteleone. There's been no need to text him, let alone call him. He does all the calling.

He picks up on the first ring. "You miss me."

I smile. "I missed you for two years. We've been apart for an hour and a half, and I've been packing the whole time. Missing you hits different after knowing what two years feels like."

"Baby." He lowers his voice. "Quit making me love you more. My heart can't take it."

I fall back on my bed and stare at the ceiling fan whirling above me. "Will it always be like this?"

"Like what?"

"Like a fairytale. Like if I blink, this will be ripped away from me forever."

"I hope so. That means I'm doing my job."

I close my eyes and let the cool air fan my face. "See? Fairytale."

"Thanks." I hear him talking to someone in the background before returning his attention to me. "Did you just call to tell me you loved me? Because if so, I'm here for it."

"No. Cole called me. Did you give him my number?"

"He's the CIA. He could probably listen to your calls if he wanted to. Not that it would be legal, but it doesn't change the fact he could do it. He definitely doesn't need to ask for your number."

"Oh, wow."

"What did he say?"

I sit up and get to the point of the phone call. "Cole's contact was able to get Mr. Hayes, but he's not well. They stopped in Barcelona for fuel and took Mr. Hayes to the hospital."

"That's not good."

I listen to Rocco start his car. "I need to update Stella. She needs to know her father is out of Nigeria. But I also don't want to worry her when we don't know anything. I guess I'm just calling to let you know. Have you heard from Taylor?"

"No. I know he's busy so I'm going to wait for him to call me. But I'm getting antsy. I'm never not a part of the action."

"I'm going to call Stella. I just wanted to let you know what was happening. And that it was exciting that Cole called me. He even called me a baddy."

"You were that day in The Monteleone."

I roll my eyes. "Whatever. I'll talk to you later."

"Teag," he calls before I hang up.

"Yeah?"

"Love you, baby. I'll never get tired of saying it."

I might melt into a puddle of gooey feelings. "I love you too."

"And I need to find a way to muffle you tonight when you sneak into my bed."

"That is not at all romantic!" I exclaim. "Kind of hot, though."

He laughs. "I'm getting a call from Taylor. Talk soon."

Rocco muffling my moans while my parents, sister, and new niece sleep down the hall should not excite me.

But then again, I am surprised by what excites me when it comes to Rocco.

That gives me an idea.

I want to surprise him.

I grab my purse and keys. I'll call Stella on my way to the mall.

Rocco

"Dude, I'm in the middle of a takedown. I'm a little busy. When I text you, fucking answer me."

"You're welcome," I say as I merge onto the freeway. "I handed you the case of a lifetime. Do you have everyone yet?"

"Oh, it's a fucking shit show." Taylor is not his cool and easygoing self. His stress is off the charts. "We hit the door of one of the houses where Robichaux lives like every third day, or some shit like that. Anyway, we followed him there. We busted down the door, but he has himself barricaded in the center with one of his prostitutes."

"No shit?"

"Not one shit. Zero shits," he bites as fast as a boomerang, talking ten times faster than I've ever heard during the three years we worked together. "It's a standoff. We're bringing in a negotiator. We have ten others in custody. They were easy since they were at work at the Parish Tax Assessor's Office. We went in, read them their rights, and hauled them off. We got three more who ran from the house where Robichaux is barricaded."

"Nice work—other than the barricade."

"That's not why I'm calling," he says.

I hear his comm radio crackle in the background. I'm patient while he gives directions to stand down and wait for the negotiator.

"I'm back and have to make this shit quick. I wish I had time to deliver this news gently, but I don't."

"You're making me edgy. What the hell is going on?"

He inhales an audible breath before he puts it out there. "It's your father. He called the Division after your last day. When I called the office about the negotiator, the clerk who answers the general calls asked if Rocco's dad ever got hold of him. Dude, he's out of jail. Did you know?"

"Fuck," I hiss. I grip the steering wheel so tight, my knuckles turn white. "I found out recently. Brax has been keeping tabs on him."

"Big bro has your back. Lucky man." The radio crackles again. "But this is what you need to know. Daddy Monroe sweet-talked the southern lady on the phone who likes to chat with everyone. I guess he acted like you two were close. He asked for you to begin with, then told the clerk he wanted to surprise you with a gift for your new house. It took her about ten seconds to realize she fucked up after she told me this and I freaked the fuck out on her. She's in deep shit with the Division for giving out personal information. But dude, she told your old man you transferred to Miami. And that's not the worst part."

"No," I growl. "She didn't..."

"She did. She gave him your forwarding address. Did you give them the Colemans?"

I should be relieved.

But there's nothing to be relieved about.

"No." My gut tightens as I think about it. "I gave the office my new one. The house I'm closing on next week."

"Oh." Taylor exhales with relief. "That's good. You've got a week to figure that shit out then. Or burn the house down. One of the two."

I drag a hand down my face, thinking about being there today with Teagan. There's a decent chance he wasn't there.

But there's always a chance he was.

"Dude, did I lose you?"

"No, man. I'm here. Thanks for the heads-up. You're one of maybe three people in the New Orleans Division that even knows about my old man. Appreciate you."

"Hey, the negotiator just rolled up. I'll call you."

"Stay safe and let me know," I say.

"Later."

I disconnect and exit the highway to turn around. My appointment will have to wait.

The last words Rodney Monroe ever uttered to me ring through my head.

"You'll pay for this, boy."

Those fucking words.

They've haunted me for years. But today, they have a much different meaning.

And I'm not taking any chances.

31

BOY

Teagan

"We just got these in," the clerk says as she checks me out. "They're gorgeous, and the color will compliment your skin tone beautifully."

"Um, thanks."

I've never shopped for sexy anything before, let alone lingerie. Wearing thongs doesn't count. That's just underwear. Who wants panty lines anyway?

Buying lingerie is a whole new experience, but so is a salesclerk complimenting me on how I'll look in it.

I'm not sure why that seems weird.

I take the receipt and tiny bag, because let's be real, what I bought is *tiny*. It's also a little itchy, but I doubt I'll have it on for long once Rocco sees me in it. I'll probably be too nervous to realize how itchy it is.

I leave the store and side shuffle the slow mall walkers when my phone rings.

I connect the call as fast as I can, so I don't miss it. "Cole, do you have news on Mr. Hayes?"

Cole gets right to it. "He's dehydrated and malnourished. His heart rate is high, but they think that's from lack of fluids. They're going to keep him overnight to monitor him because of what he's gone through. An extraction is never easy. Jarvis is one of the best there is and took a local team in with him. He said Hayes wasn't expecting it—thought he gave him a heart attack when he broke in and took him."

I stop in my tracks. "Wow. I don't know who this Jarvis is, but that's impressive."

"Let's not tell Jarvis that. His head is big enough as it is."

A call beeps in, and I pull the phone away from my ear to see who it is.

Rocco.

Who misses whom now?

I'll call him back.

Two people mutter at me for stopping traffic, so I start moving again. "How is everything else in Nigeria?"

"Fantastic," Cole belts. "It's not done yet, but we're getting there. I think when all is said and done, we will have put a big dent in a global network of motherfuckers, and that's if we don't dismantle it. Just for shits and giggles, I threw in the travel agent who booked the flights. We found out they were sliding her cash under the table to pay off airport security to let as many mules through as they could. Grandpa Hayes was one of the unlucky ones."

I listen as I walk past the food court. I don't remember the last time I've been at the mall and not had cinnamon pretzel bites with icing dip, but not today. The last thing I want is to be bloated when I put on my tiny lingerie. No pretzels for me today. "That's amazing."

"And we're not done," Cole keeps going as another call beeps in.

Damn. It's Rocco again. He's going to turn me into a phone talker.

But Cole doesn't stop for anyone. "We've started to follow the money and drugs. My asset in South Africa connected your friends with the Gray Hatchet. This group is bigger and more organized than most cartels south of the border. The amount of motherfuckers we're dealing with keeps adding up."

I tell him the truth. "I'm shocked. I had no idea."

"One thing leads to another, right? Sometimes it's like digging for fossils, and other times it's like dominoes and everything falls into place. All because you located Grandpa Hayes."

"I couldn't have done it without Rocco. I just located Robichaux. Rocco got all the information from him."

"Working with the love of your life is special. I told Bella all about you. She loves your tenacity and wants to meet you."

I can't keep the smile off my face. "I really want that to happen."

"I promise, it'll happen. If not sooner, we'll see you at the wedding."

I stop again, and this time I get bumped by a stroller. "Um, that's the second time you've said that to me."

"Sorry," he pipes without sounding at all sorry about anything. "All in time. We'll get you and Bella together sooner rather than later."

I put thoughts of a wedding out of my mind. It was hard enough buying itchy lingerie.

Another call beeps through. "Goodness. Is there anything else? Rocco has called three times."

"New love. I remember those days. He's impatient. Tell him I said hi."

"I will. Thank you so much. I don't know what I'd do without you. I can't wait to call Stella back and give her the good news. She'll be so relieved."

"What I wouldn't do to see it myself. It's probably best I'm not there. I'd have to make an excuse for the tears. I love a happy reunion. They get me every time."

I walk through the sliding doors into the hot, muggy day. "Me too. Thanks again."

"We'll talk soon."

I disconnect the call and hit go on one of Rocco's many missed calls. It barely rings once before he answers with a vengeance. "Fuck, baby. Why haven't you answered my calls? Where are you?"

I walk across three parking lanes. "I was packing and decided I'd make a quick trip to the mall. Then I was on the phone with Cole again. Guess what? They're keeping Mr. Hayes overnight, but he should be released tomorrow."

"That's great. But where are you?"

"I told you, I'm at the mall. What's the emergency?"

"Come straight home," he bites. "I got a call from Taylor. It's about my father."

There's something about his tone that puts me on edge. I pick up my pace and beep the locks on my car. "What about him?"

"I don't want to get into it now, other than to say he knows I'm in Miami. I have no idea where his mind is at, but I know he's been looking for me. The whole thing has me on edge. And I don't know if it's him being out and knowing where I am or that you've hardly been out of my sight since New Orleans. I fucking hate that you're not with me. Everything feels off."

I open my car door, climb inside, and lock myself in. "I'm safe in my car. Doors are locked. Do you feel better?"

"I'll feel better when you get home. If I weren't on the opposite side of town, I'd come to you."

I put him on Bluetooth and back out of my spot. "I can't lie, your father knowing where you are freaks me out too. But I'm on my way home. And I have a surprise for you."

His tone barely changes. "Oh yeah? Is it a rake or lawn mower? Because I'm going to need those."

"I'll keep the rake in mind, but you forgot I'm unemployed with no job prospects as of this morning. You're going to have to buy your own lawnmower. It's not in my budget."

He finally sounds like he's calming down. "Then I'll just have to settle for whatever you got me. Are you going to tell me?"

"No." I can't keep the smile out of my voice. "But I'll give you a hint. It's small—very small—and shows a lot of skin."

Rocco doesn't have a smile in his voice. "Don't tell me you bought a bikini. I'll go mad when you wear it around other people."

"First of all, I'll wear whatever bikini I want to wear. But no, it's not a bikini. You will be happy because it's for your eyes only."

"Damn. Will I get to see it tonight?"

"If you can manage to sneak into my room to have silent sex."

"Silent sex ... for my surprise, I can make that happen."

I'm about to turn onto the ramp to go home before I switch lanes and change my mind. "Goodness, the highway is gridlocked. I'm taking the back way home. I forgot how miserable the traffic is here at this time. Maybe I should find a remote job so I don't have to drive in this every day."

"Find something that makes you happy, baby."

"Do you realize how much we talk on the phone? My mom always complained that you weren't a phone talker when you were at college."

"I think we can agree that I can't get enough of you. You've turned me into a talker. I'm more surprised than anyone. Don't change the subject. I want to know what you got me. In fact, if you could describe it in great detail, even better."

I take another turn. "Sorry, big guy. You're going to have to wait. I told you too much. Maybe let your imagination run wild. Anticipation is everything, right?"

"I don't need anything else to make me wild but you."

"We just need to wait for everyone to go to sleep and hope that my newborn niece isn't up all night—"

But I can't finish my thought.

A scream rings out inside the car at the same moment my entire dash explodes.

"Teagan?" Rocco calls for me. "What happen—"

But I lose the call.

It feels like I lose him too.

The airbags don't even deflate when I realize the muffled scream is my own.

The side of my face is on fire. My arms burn.

There's no steering the car. Hell, there's no seeing out the windows. The car skids across the earth below me. Just when I think I've come to a stop, another full force hit collides from my side.

The tail end of my car spins before coming to a stop.

It takes all the energy in my body, but I try to push the airbags from my face. I've never been claustrophobic, but I can't breathe.

My chest won't work.

My head spins, and I see nothing but stars.

Then...

Then.

It's like I've woken from anesthesia when I hear glass shatter.

"There you are."

I force myself to breathe in much-needed oxygen and try to look to the side.

The pain ... my neck, back, shoulder. Hell, everything hurts.

When I turn, I see him.

I only recognize a hint of the man from old newspaper reports. No one has ever shown me a picture, especially not Rocco. I had to find them myself. It was the beginning of my obsession with crime.

Rodney Monroe.

Murderer.

He killed his wife—Rocco's mother.

And he did it in front of his son.

I'd know him anywhere, even though he looks much different than his mugshot from fifteen years ago. He's aged well beyond his years. Seems prison will do that to you.

"Rocco?" I call, praying something in my car still works.

"Rocco? Who does he think he is? He's Ricky. He'll never be anything more," Rodney growls.

Ricky?

He goes on. "Let's see what that boy is willing to do. He's a fucking pig. Saw you with him today. I have a feeling he'll come for you, you little bitch."

"No!" I scream. "Someone, help! Help!"

I might have taken the back way, but this road isn't desolate.

Rodney yanks my door twice to wrench it open.

When he reaches in, I start to slap, hit, and punch. I scream. I do everything to cause a scene. But that's when something sharp hits my leg.

I gasp and look down.

A needle.

"Oh shit," I muster.

I feel something surge through my body before my head feels so heavy, I can't hold it up with my neck.

"There we go," he says from far, far away. "Let's get out of here."

And my bright, sunny, happily ever after...

... goes dark.

32

HELL

Rocco

Hell.

I thought I'd been there fifteen years ago when I saw my father kill my mother.

Then the universe decided to up its game when I had to sit on the stand across from him and recount what I saw.

I even made a quick trip the day the MC decided to take back their tat with a blow torch.

At least I thought those days were hell.

It has nothing on today.

Today is a dark fiery pit of flames.

And I'm burning from the inside out.

Teagan's car is surrounded by police units. They were already swarming the place when I got here. I didn't know exactly where she was, but I had an idea. It wasn't hard to find the exact location since a handful of calls came into nine-one-one at the same time. They all reported the same thing.

Teagan's car was hit from behind and then the side. That was right before a man pried her door open and dragged a limp woman from the car.

A man tried to stop him, but it seems Rodney Monroe is just as savage as ever.

From witness accounts, he threw Teagan in a car like a rag doll and tried to run over the man trying to save her.

And no tags.

No fucking tags.

Just a make and a model that's too common, but it does have a busted front end.

"The lieutenant briefed me. Units are canvassing the area. They're checking the closest street cameras too," Brax says. His expression is grave. He was the first person I called after nine-one-one. Micah, King, and Brax showed up almost at the same time.

But Tim...

I couldn't call him. I made Brax do it.

His daughter was hurt and taken.

Because of me.

I can't think about Tim or Annette. I hate myself enough as it is.

I thought I could have something good. I gave into my selfish fucking nature ... nature I'm sure I got from *him*.

I've tried all my life to not be *him*.

Then I gave in to temptation.

And Teagan paid the price.

I turn to the men and force my voice to work. "I've got to get her back. I can't stand here and wait for someone else to do something."

Micah shakes his head and clamps a hand on my shoulder. It doesn't feel warm or comforting. He's doing what he can to restrain me without tackling me to the ground. "That's a bad fucking idea, and you know it. Let the PD do their thing. You know how good they are. You were one of them."

"He's right," King agrees.

"We stay here," Brax states, like they get to collectively decide my whereabouts. "We stay together."

I shrug Micah's hand off me and explode in their faces. "I can't stand here and do nothing!"

That's when a car tears down the street and screeches to a halt next to us.

It's Tim.

"Fuck," I hiss.

"Well?" Tim yells as he jogs up to our group. "What the fuck are they doing to find her?"

I drag my hands over my head and turn in a slow circle.

King catches Tim up on the search.

If you can call it that.

I'm about to turn, fall to my knees, and beg Tim to forgive me, when my cell rings.

"Oh my God," I growl. "It's her."

I connect the call. "Baby? Are you okay? Where are you?"

I hear a laugh.

That maniacal laugh.

The same one that would ricochet through the shack of a house I grew up in. The same one that heckled me after he beat the fucking daylights out of me or my mother. He enjoyed it so much, he'd laugh while doing it.

"*Baby*," he mocks. "You're a fucking pussy for this girl, aren't you? Well, boy, I can see why."

"Where is she?" I demand.

Four sets of incensed eyes bore into me. I take the phone away from my face and put it on speaker.

"I'm in my room." It sounds like he's reclining in bed when he goes on. "She's asleep next to me. Sweet thing, Ricky. You really leveled up in life."

I pinch the bridge of my nose and wish it were possible to reach through the phone to strangle him.

"Where is she?" I repeat. I can't help myself. The thought of Teagan at his mercy makes my control slip through my fingers. "Where the fuck is she?"

With a fierce expression that tells me to shut the fuck up, Brax gives me the palm of his hand, but Micah and King step away and get on their phones immediately. We need to ping her line to see where it hits. Tim looks as stressed and as angry as I feel.

I take a deep breath.

"You want her?" His voice is low. "You gotta come and get her. But it'll cost you."

"What do you want?" I spit, willing to do anything to get her away from him. "Anything. Name it but do it fucking fast."

"I lost fifteen years 'cause of you," he seethes. "I've got nothing. Not a fucking thing to my name. I want money. Cash. And you'd better come by yourself. If you don't, the girl is as good as dead. And I'm not gonna kill her. I'll find someone who wants her. Either you pay up, or I'll find someone else who will."

"Done." I don't think about anything besides her. I don't care what he demands. "Tell me when and where. But a warning, old man, if I get there and Teagan has so much as a scratch on her, I'll kill you myself."

There's that laugh again.

But this time, his tone turns evil.

"I've got your girl, Ricky. I'm the one with the negotiating power. I can do whatever the fuck I want until you get here. How's that for motivation?"

Fuck.

Teagan

My eyelids are so damn heavy.

A hand moves across my body.

Fingers brush through my hair. But there's nothing familiar about it.

Not one thing.

I try to stretch my legs. I thought my eyelids were heavy. Everything is heavy. I can't move.

"There you go. Wakey-wakey. We're leaving soon."

Everything comes rushing back.

The lingerie. Talking to Rocco. Plans to move into his new house. Needing a job.

The accident.

And Rocco's father.

Rodney Monroe.

I push through the haze and peek through my lids. I'm on a bed. And Rodney is stretched out beside me. His evil eyes bore into mine.

"It's wearing off," he utters in a low gruff tone. "And just in time. I'm about to make a trade. We'll see how my boy comes through."

My body won't cooperate with my internal freak out. I try to push his hand away, but when I do, his touch becomes harder.

Insistent.

Sadistic.

I pull in a breath and swallow over the sandpaper that is now my throat, but I don't utter a word. I can't believe he had the nerve to wonder if his *boy* will come through.

Rocco will come through. I have no doubt.

I just hope it's in time.

Only adrenaline could give me the push to move my body. When I roll away, his hand that was firm on my head grips into a fist.

He pulls me to a stop.

My stomach roils from whatever he shot me up with. The only other thing I can focus on is the pain screaming through my skull.

"Don't even think about it," he growls in my face. His foul breath washes over me. Old cigarettes and sin permeate my space. No wonder I want to throw up all over him. "This is what's going to happen. You're gonna get up and walk out to my car like nothing's wrong. I had to make excuses to the manager when he saw me carrying you in here. Told him you were drunk off your ass and needed to sleep it off. Then we're meeting Ricky. If you make one wrong move or do anything to fuck this up, it's not going to go well for you. You'll never see him or your fucking family again, got it? You can kiss your cushy life in that big house goodbye."

I have no idea how he found me. But he knows where we live. All I can think about is my family ... and Marley, who's only a few days old.

My voice is rough and weak, but I know what I have to do. I'm not sure which smells worse, him or the bed I'm lying on. "Just take me back to Rocco. Please."

His grip on my hair loosens. "How about that? I took you for a fighter. I have a feeling you'll do exactly as I say. My boy is lucky."

He's right and he's wrong. I'll cooperate until I don't have to, because I am a fighter. I'll do anything I need to get back to Rocco and my family.

I have to catch myself as I wobble when I push myself to my

feet. I'd rather be upright and woozy than in that damn bed with Rodney Monroe.

33

I SEE MYSELF

Rocco

There was no time for an op plan, but this is no normal operation.

This is Teagan.

I've never been a part of anything that felt like this.

Raw.

Desperate.

Final.

However this ends, there will be a finality to it that cannot be reversed. I'll die before it doesn't go my way, and that's saying a lot.

I've lived my entire life in fight or flight mode. Done everything I've had to do to survive. Only one time did I fall on the sword and put someone else before me. That was Landyn.

I was a kid.

I'd do it again and fight to the bitter end.

If it comes to that today, it will be tragic for my whole world.

And it'll be my fault.

My only saving grace is that we pinged her phone, which

proves my father was, and always will be, an idiot. We know she's in the vicinity.

Teagan is close, and I'm going to get her back.

I'm not new to this part of Miami. I was a cop and SWAT officer and spent a lot of time in this neighborhood.

I'm a sitting duck waiting on this damn call. He's late, which is not a surprise. Hell, he was always late or a no show for everything. Even when I was younger and he liked to pretend to the rest of the world that he gave a shit. That was before I discovered he didn't give a shit what anyone thought.

He was a no-show in life.

Unless he was creating havoc.

Night has set in, and the criminals usually are out to play by now.

But not tonight. I haven't seen one.

My cell rings and Teagan's name flashes on the screen. I connect the call immediately. "You're late."

"Wanted to make sure you'd show up. And I had to make sure you didn't have the place surrounded since you are a pig these days."

I look around to see where he might be. "I want to talk to Teagan. If you want me to hand over my life's savings, I need to know you're going to pay up."

"You're just going to have to trust me."

"You're late to your own deal. I've never trusted you—it's hard to go downhill from there. Let me talk to her."

I hear the phone shuffle, and he growls in the background, "Say something, dammit."

My insides tighten when she cries out in pain before calling my name. "Roc!"

Fuck.

"She's still breathing."

This can't be done soon enough. "Get her here, and I'll give you the money."

"We're on our way." He disconnects the call immediately.

I scan my surroundings and do what I always do. It never fails.

I see myself. How it could have been.

The night before I graduated from the DEA academy, I found a moment alone with Brax and Landyn. I thanked them for pulling me out of the hellhole I was born into.

Both of them looked at me like I'd grown a second head. Brax told me all he did was open a door. I was the one who walked through it.

Landyn did what she always does when it gets emotional. She threw herself in my arms, held on tight, and told me she loved me.

That was the day I told her she was the first person to feel that way about me.

She cried.

Brax told me he's never seen anyone cry more happy tears over someone than his wife had for me. Then he said he should be jealous, but he did it with a shit-eating grin on his face.

Standing here, knowing what Teagan has gone through because of me, I've come full circle.

And I don't fucking like it. This was the point I never once wanted to circle back to.

Something catches my attention. Turning onto the street is the car that was described by every witness at the scene of the crash. It comes around the corner on a wing and a prayer. The bumper hangs off the front corner, and it's scratched to hell and back with the paint from Teagan's car.

My fucking father. He'll rot in hell for what he did to her. It might not be in the op plan, but I'll make sure of it.

I'm in the dark corner of the parking lot where the floodlight is out on the lamp pole. I stand at the hood of my car with my duffle gripped tight in my hand.

His brakes complain when he comes to a stop and throws it in park. My gut clenches when I see her dark hair in the passenger seat. My father doesn't waste any time, though it does take him some effort to climb out.

It's the first time I've laid eyes on him since I left the courtroom after driving the final nail into his coffin.

From his expression, you'd think he hates me as much as I hate him.

Not possible.

Besides his face that ages him well beyond his years, he looks fit. Even healthy.

Must be the lack of drugs in prison.

He's struggling to get out because of Teagan.

I take a step forward before I stop myself. He's dragging her out of the car. She struggles as he twists her arm to fucking manhandle her.

She cries out in pain when she tumbles from the car to the pavement. Even through the shrouded darkness, I can see that she's wearing the same thing she was when I kissed her goodbye at her parents' house this morning, but she's not wearing shoes. And since she came from the mall, I know it's not her own doing.

Her hair is a mess, and she looks exhausted.

Exhausted, but relieved the moment my gaze locks on her.

My father yanks her to his side like she's a ragdoll and not the woman I plan on making my wife as soon as fucking possible.

She whimpers.

My heart shatters.

He focuses his evil stare on me. It doesn't feel any different than it ever has. "Ricky, we're reunited. And what do you know ... you turned out ... fucking normal."

I want to tell him that he turned out to be the biggest ass on the planet, but I don't take the time. Instead, I tilt my head to Teagan, never taking my eyes off him. "Let her go."

He shrugs as he gives Teagan a jerk in his tight grip. "What? After all this time, that's it? You don't want to catch up?"

"The only thing I want is her." I hold up the duffle. "Come get your money."

He narrows his eyes. "Unzip it. I want to see."

I turn my gaze to Teagan as I unzip the bag and rip it open. He studies the contents for the short time I allow. Instead of waiting for him to ask me to count it for him, I zip the bag and give it a short toss. It lands closer to me than him when I demand, "Let her go."

He doesn't.

He proves he's just as much of a jackass as ever and will never go away on his own.

When he reaches behind his back, I tense. He pulls out a gun and loses what little control he pretended to maintain.

I need to get her away from him long enough for them to take a shot.

He aims the weapon straight at me. "You think I turned into an idiot in lockup?"

What he doesn't know is I thrive when I'm trying to be the exact opposite of him. My tone is calm and even. I take three steps toward them, putting the money closer to me. "I don't have to think anything. Here's what I know ... I'm a federal agent. I worked for Miami PD for three years. You just kidnapped the daughter of a respected, well-liked, and well-known agent."

Teagan trembles and doesn't take her eyes off the gun.

My father's anxious eyes dart between me and the money.

I close the distance between us by another slow and steady step and keep talking. "If you think I came here by myself, then who's the idiot now? Put the fucking gun down."

His face turns red, and even in the darkness, I see a vein pop on his temple. He screams, "I'm your fucking father! You put me away for fifteen years!"

I take another step and ignore his words. My only focus is her. "Let her go."

Teagan screams in pain from where he squeezes her.

He tightens his grasp on the gun. Even through the shadows, I see his finger flirt with the trigger. "I'll kill you, boy. I'll fucking take you down for what you did to me."

"No!" Teagan screams.

Teagan

I SEE IT.

In all this time, I didn't think he'd do it. Not with witnesses.

Vengeance must be rooted deeper than his will to live free. Rodney Monroe is proof.

I've barely looked away from the gun. He might be pointing it at Rocco, but he's been all show and no threat. His index finger has never touched the trigger.

Until now.

"No!" I scream and twist my arm. I've been compliant and passive this whole time. But not anymore. I can't live without Rocco.

I reach around with my free hand, grip his shirt, and pull.

"Teagan!" Rocco calls for me, but I don't stop

I pull and yank. I claw and jerk in every way I can. Rodney and I both tip to the side just as Rocco lunges forward.

I hit the ground when the gun goes off.

"Dammit!" Rocco yells.

Rodney lands on top of me, but our scuffle doesn't stop. Deep voices come out of the dark as boots hit the ground.

Rocco wrestles with his father, but Rodney doesn't let go of me. The weight of him is too much, pressing me into the pavement.

Voices rise and echo through the night. It's chaos.

"Get the fucking gun," Brax orders.

Rodney cries out in pain.

Micah joins the fray. "Roc, no!"

"Teagan!"

Dad.

They're all here.

All of the sudden, the mass that felt like the weight of the world on my shoulders is gone.

I scream when I'm pulled from behind.

"Baby, it's me."

Dad.

"You're okay. I've got you."

"Rocco?" I crane my neck around to look for him.

Then, I hear the gun discharge for a second time.

The sight in front of me ... God.

I slump in my father's arms, and my tears flow.

34

NORMAL

Rocco

My breath is shallow and heavy.
 I have to work for it. I was a DI athlete and still work out. I never find it hard to breathe.

Brax pries the gun from my hand. It takes me a second, but I allow it even though I can't focus on anything.

"I need EMS, stat," King orders. He rattles off our location right before he gives the rundown of what just happened.

"Rocco!"

I blink.

Fuck, that stings.

"Is that his blood?"

I look up where I'm ass to the pavement just in time to see Teagan drop to her knees by my side.

Her expression turns to horror when she sees my forearm.

"You've been shot," she whispers, right before she turns to her father and screams, "He's been shot! Do something!"

I bring up my good arm and place my hand on the side of her face to make her look at me. "I'm fine."

"You're not fine," she cries. "He shot you. You're bleeding."

I hold my arm up and look at the bite that's been taken out of my flesh. "I'll be fine. I need some stitches. Baby, get up. I can't sit here."

Cops come out of the woodwork where they were close for backup, and more units descend on the scene where my father is crumpled, dead on the ground, and blood seeping from beneath his body. And I thought I didn't want anything to do with him when he was alive. Turns out, I feel the same way about him dead.

I don't want to be anywhere near him, and I sure as hell don't want Teagan near him. If I could talk everyone into letting me take her away right now, I would.

She scrambles to her feet, and I follow. I walk her away from the scene, even though she's only focused on me. It doesn't bother her in the slightest that my father is dead, and I'm the one who made it happen.

She plasters herself to me and holds on tight. I wrap her up in my good arm.

Good arm.

How many times have I referred to it as that?

"Teag, I need to get something on his arm to stop the bleeding," Tim says as he tries to pry his daughter from me.

Neither of us are having it.

I bury my face in her hair and don't let go.

"Okay, then," Tim mutters. I'm pretty sure it's a dirty golf towel, but he wraps my arm and holds it firm while I hold his daughter and focus only on her.

"Baby, are you okay? Did he hurt you?"

She shakes her head against my chest. "I'm okay. He drugged me with something, but that's it. I'm better now. I can't believe you were shot."

I shake my head. "Same arm. Third time's a charm, right? That's got to be it."

She looks up at me with tears in her eyes. "Don't you dare jinx it."

I lean down and press my lips to hers. "I'm so sorry. I didn't think I was going to be able to get to you. I was out of my mind."

"You two are something." Brax stands next to us shaking his head. "And if you think you were going out of your mind, I just talked to Landyn. She insists on meeting us at the hospital."

"I need to call Annette," Tim says. Teagan and I turn toward him. "I think we've had enough excitement in this family. We need to go back to normal and boring like we've always been. I can't handle this."

"Dad?"

Tim sighs and never lets go of the pressure on my arm when he looks down at his youngest daughter. "Yeah?"

"I'm moving in with Rocco."

I give her a squeeze. "That could've waited until later."

Tim's eyes fall shut. He looks like he's praying for patience.

"Next week," Teagan adds. "When he closes on his house."

Tim opens his eyes and gives us a slow nod. "Is there anything else?"

"I'm going to marry her," I say.

Teagan beams up at me. Her dark eyes glint with tears. Happy ones. This time it's my turn to get a squeeze.

"Soon," I add without looking away from her. "Very soon."

"I'll let Goldie know," King pipes in. "She'll be all over it. You won't have to do a thing."

Brax disconnects a call and turns to us. "Robichaux is in custody. They're wrapping things up across New Orleans. I gave Taylor the condensed version of what just went down. He'll call you later."

"One less thing to worry about," I say.

"Is there anything *else*?" Tim stresses. "Normal. I just want normal."

Micah crosses his arms and rocks back on his heels as he surveys the situation. "If Rocco marrying baby Teagan is normal, then we really don't need any more drama."

"No more drama," I promise.

What I don't add aloud is that the ghost of my past is going to stay right where it belongs.

Six feet under.

35

RUSSIAN ROULETTE

Rocco

I grip both of Teagan's wrists in my hand and press them into the mattress above her head.

Her dark eyes shine up at me as she shifts under my weight. Her feet are flat to the bed, and she lifts her hips to find my cock.

She loves it.

I just love her.

And every time we're like this, it's like a dream I didn't think would ever be possible.

Because she's Teagan Coleman.

But also, because I'm Rocco Monroe.

Someone like her isn't supposed to be with anyone like me.

The last week and a half have dragged on like a never-ending purgatory.

I was investigated and cleared for the shooting of Rodney Monroe. It was procedure, but it still pissed me off. I was ready to move on.

Teagan and I made a last-minute trip back to Mississippi and she got to meet Heath Hayes in person. He's getting stronger and healthier every day, and he came to tears when he wrapped his arms around the woman who put the plans in motion to bring him home.

And between it all, we've had enough silent sex to last a lifetime. At least we didn't have to sneak around. After what happened with my father, there was no separating us. No one questioned it. Not Tim, especially not Annette, and certainly not Sammie. She's in her own world. Nothing has ever suited her more than being a mom, even though she's a single one. She's surrounded by family, and that's all they need.

And Teagan made it clear after that dark day. She only needed me.

I drag my hand down her body and do what we've been doing more and more of every day.

Playing Russian roulette with my sperm.

I slide into her bare.

Until today, it's been a silent conversation.

I'd hike a brow.

She'd bite her lip and nod.

And when her body formed to mine, we'd savor it. Every time, just a little longer.

Another moment.

One more thrust.

Her eyes fall shut, and she tips her head back. This is like the others, but with words. "This is risky, but I love it. I shouldn't love it this much, but I do."

She opens her eyes when I slide out and in one more time.

Not hard.

Not unbridled.

When I put on a condom, it's all of that.

But when we're like this, it's different.

We're focused on each other. I'm in full control. She gets to enjoy.

And learn.

I'm here for that.

This is the first time we've talked aloud about our little game that gets pushed farther and farther every time.

I want this.

Hell, I want everything with her, and it can't happen soon enough. But her being okay with playing around bare and being ready for all the things that I am is very different.

I closed on the house this morning and the movers delivered what little I own in this world. It took fifteen minutes for me to carry all of Teagan's stuff from her car. She has a hell of a lot less than me.

Nothing is unpacked and the only thing set in place is the bed we're on.

Our bed.

I slide in balls deep and stay here. When I press my lips to hers, I force myself to breathe deep, be steady, and focus. This is against human nature. My body wants nothing more than to let go, take her just like this, and set my sperm free to do its thing.

"I might just love this more than you do," I say against her lips.

Her small tits brush my chest

She started her job search again. And she's young. I know she wants this, but that doesn't mean she's ready.

I let go of her wrists and reach over to the nightstand. When I open the drawer, I bypass the condoms even though I shouldn't.

Instead, I grab the small box I've been saving for today. There's no way we're sleeping in this house one night without getting this done.

I flip open the box with one hand and nudge the slim piece of gold onto the tip of my index finger. It barely fits over my nail, but I know it will fit her. Annette helped me with the size right after I told Tim my plans.

Since we're connected as one, I feel it around my cock and everywhere else when I raise my finger for her to see.

She tenses, squeezing me in all the right places.

Focus, Roc.

"Marry me."

Her eyes flare right before they glaze over with unshed tears.

I go on. "It's not a question because there's only one acceptable outcome to this scenario. Once you opened my eyes to what could be, there's been no one but you. Love your heart, baby. Love your mind. I love you inside and out. I sure as hell don't deserve you, but I want everything with you."

"It's perfect." She touches my hand and runs the tip of her finger over the small diamond before gazing back up at me. "You're perfect."

"We're perfect," I amend. "And I'm ready to start our lives together."

Tears run down her temples as she nods. "I can't believe this is real."

I take the ring and slip it on her left ring finger. I stare at it for a moment before turning back to her. "It's real." I pull out and push back in. "Very real."

As much as I don't want to, I pull out. By the look on her face, she'd said yes to anything I ask, but that's a conversation for a different time and place. I make the quickest work of a condom yet and slam back into her.

"We need an alternative," I say through a groan. "I'm good with whatever you want. But the condoms have to go."

She lifts her hips as I take her, doing what she can to meet every thrust.

I take her left hand in my right one and thread our fingers. I bought the best ring I could afford. Feeling it on her finger where it will stay for the rest of our lives does something to me.

I slowly lose control in the only way I love to—when I take her.

Teagan.

Mine.

Now and forever.

EPILOGUE

Four months later
Rocco

Teagan leans into me and whispers, "I feel so out of place."

My hand goes to the small of her back and my lips to her ear. "You think you feel out of place? Baby, I never knew this would be a reality for me. It feels like we stepped into an alternate universe. And I've never, as in fucking ever, let anyone else carry my bags before. I don't recognize myself."

We follow the porter to the check-in desk.

The Manor at Winslet.

Though, it's not a manor in the sense it used to be when it was built more than a hundred years ago.

Reginald Benedict Winslet, III.

He's a Brit who settled in the U.S. to hit it big in the gold rush. Reggie came from old money that funded his search for new money back in the day. He created such a stir in the region when he built this place that an entire community developed around him simply because everyone thought he knew something they didn't. They wanted new money too. They even named the town after him.

Who doesn't want money—new or old?

Spoiler alert, no gold for Winslet. He had no fucking clue what he was doing.

At least that's what the internet told me when I searched this place.

But the manor still stands today and looks like it sits in the English countryside and not in the red, white, and blue.

Now it's a resort overlooking Winslet Lake at the base of the mountains. It's posh, booked out for eons, and so expensive, I doubt there's another human on the property in my tax bracket—other than maybe the cabana boy.

If there is one. Taking in the place while riding up the long drive in the limo that picked us up at the airport, the cabana boy might have his own assistant.

"Welcome to The Manor at Winslet. My name is Felicity. I see you're checking in. Your names?"

Teagan's face lights up like it has every time someone asks that question since the big event two days ago. "Mr. and Mrs. Rocco Monroe."

The woman behind the counter smiles and types at the speed of light into her sleek computer. "Ah! Honeymooners. Congratulations on your marriage. I see you are special guests of Bella Carson."

"There's no other way we'd be here," I tell her the truth.

"I'll say," the woman agrees, but for different reasons. "We're booked out for the next year, but Mr. Donnelly will do anything for his sister."

"Mr. Donnelly?" Teagan asks.

"The owner. He bought The Manor a couple years ago, brought it back to its old glory, and made it into a resort." Felicity stops typing and leans toward us to speak in a whisper. "Mr. Donnelly always keeps a few rooms on the side for occasions like this."

"So that's how Bella and Cole got a room." Teagan looks up at me. "I hope they got the family discount. We'll need to send them an extra special thank you note when we get home."

"Here you go." She hands us two key cards, as if I'm going to let Teagan out of my site the entire time we're here. I take the keys and Teagan takes a folder. "And this will tell you all about Winslet. I do hope you enjoy our little bit of heaven on earth."

I plan on keeping Teagan in bed and ordering room service the entire week.

Teagan starts to flip through the marketing material before I can pull her away from the desk. Her inner investigative curiosity comes out. "I want to see it all. Thank you!"

Well, never mind being in bed for a week. I guess we're going to see it all.

I claim Teagan's hand and move to the elevators. "Heaven on earth. That's quite a claim."

She reads while we walk. "I can't believe Cole and Bella gifted us an entire honeymoon. That's on top of our wedding at The Pink. I know it wasn't a huge wedding, but Goldie really went overboard."

I press the button. "Welcome to my world where my found family goes above and beyond to make up for the fact my given family is fucked up enough to fill an entire season of Dateline."

She tucks the folder under her arm and leans into my chest. "They love you."

I lean down and press my lips to hers. "They love us."

Teagan is about to say something when the elevator dings and the doors part. I have to pull Teagan back so we're not run over by a short blonde wearing a getup that looks like she's late to a tennis match.

And she's pissed about it.

"Come back here." A tall, dark-haired man in a suit stalks after her but pauses when he sees us. His greeting hits us in an irritated British accent. "Oh, hello. Welcome to The Manor. Enjoy your stay."

Then, he's gone.

I give Teagan a little push, and the porter joins us in the elevator with our luggage.

"Heaven on earth, my ass," I mutter. "Looks like they're in hell."

We exit on the top floor, and the porter asks for my key card to open the door. Before he pushes the door open, he turns to us. "The honeymoon suite."

"Oh my gosh," Teagan gasps as she walks in. "This is the most gorgeous place I've ever seen."

I follow up her gasp with a low whistle. She's not wrong, and I don't give a shit about stuff like this.

"I changed my mind," Teagan says as she pokes her head into the bedroom before going to the glass doors that look out over the lake, and beyond that, the mountains. "I don't care what there is to do or see in Winslet. I could stay right here all week."

That's something I agree with. And I'm ready to start as soon as possible.

I pull a couple of twenties out of my money clip and hand them to the porter. "Appreciate it."

When he gives me a ceremonious bow before leaving, I decide room service is the way to go.

Teagan opens the doors to the balcony. Mild, dry air hits us, the exact opposite of what we're used to in Miami. Usually, I'd take in the beauty surrounding us, but all I see is my new wife.

My wife.

Damn. I like the sound of that.

I go to her where she stands on the veranda looking out over the countryside and press my lips to the skin below her ear. "I don't care where we are. I love you, Mrs. Monroe."

She turns in my arms to gaze up at me. "This is just the beginning. I can't wait to see what life brings us, hubby."

"We're the shit." I smile. "It's going to be epic."

♥♥

Fifteen years later
Teagan

I GO to our dresser to find the earrings. I've worn them for every occasion like this one, though I didn't think I'd get another opportunity like today.

We decided long ago we were good with two. A boy and a girl. What more could we want?

Gray came along the year after we were married. We tried to wait, but then we realized we didn't know what we were waiting for.

When you start off as friends, have a little hiatus as enemies, and then go straight to lovers, waiting for anything is painful. We felt like we'd waited a lifetime.

We were ready to get on with life—and that meant babies.

Lettie came two years later.

We thought our family was complete.

The universe had other plans.

Rocco is the dad every man should strive to be. He changed diapers. He walked our babies through the night when they were sick. He never misses an event. But what he really loves to do is coach. It doesn't matter the sport.

He even volunteers to coach teams that our kids don't play on.

Not everyone has a dad who will invest time in them. Rocco sure didn't. But he had coaches who poured themselves into him when he was little.

That's how this started.

When Gray and Lettie got older, Rocco took on a football team of second graders. It was their first year to play tackle. It was a shit show—at least that's how Roc described it—except for Vince. That little guy gave new meaning to pee-wee tackle in the game of football.

And it wasn't because he knew the game or was exceptionally big or tough.

It's because he had so much pent-up aggression.

Rocco recognized it. He saw himself in Vince.

Vince would walk himself to practice with bruises that weren't from the game Rocco loves so much.

They were from his father.

It was horrifying.

Child protective services got involved. I was beside myself with worry for the child.

But Rocco was not worried.

My husband was beside himself with anger.

We had to do something. The day Vince was removed from his home was the day we became emergency foster care parents. Vince spent two days with a stranger before coming to live with our family.

We went from a family of four to a family of five in a matter of days with no planning.

That was three years ago.

Today, we won't be foster parents any longer.

I put on the same earrings Rocco gave me before I had Gray. They're diamond studs. They're small, but their meaning is so big it fills my heart. I only wear them for special occasions.

When Gray was born.

When Lettie was born.

And today.

The last three years weren't easy, but that doesn't mean they weren't life changing. I even guarded my heart when it came to Vince. I was afraid to love him too much in case this day didn't come.

Because I knew if it didn't, I'd be heartbroken in a way I'd never recover.

"Are you ready? We're going to be late."

I look into the mirror as Rocco stalks into the room. Our gaze never breaks through the reflection as he fits his chest to my back.

I clasp the last stud and pull in a deep breath. "Why am I nervous? He's been ours since the day we brought him home to live with us. Nothing will change after today."

He shakes his head. "Everything will change after today. Trust me. I know what it feels like to have no one want you."

I pull in a breath. It's everything I can do to keep my tears at bay. Rocco has told me everything over the years. How it felt to not have anyone make a commitment to him. He was a legal adult when Brax came into his life. But the agents and my parents were the first people who invested in him because they wanted to, not because they had to.

He'll never forget the day he came to live with my family.

I'll never forget that day either.

It was life changing for both of us for different reasons. Giving that to Vince is as much for him as it is for Rocco.

Full circle.

Cathartic.

And today is the day we make Vince ours.

Rocco's hand snakes up my side, over my shoulder, and into my hair. "You're wearing your baby earrings."

I smile. "Well, we are birthing a child today ... in another form. It's still the same."

He presses his lips to my temple. "It is the same."

Then he brings his other arm around, the one he was hiding behind his body.

I gasp when I see them.

An enormous bouquet of dahlias.

"You remembered." I take the bouquet and turn in his arms.

"Did you really think I'd forget?"

I shake my head. "I didn't know what to think. I have all the emotions without the pregnancy hormones. I don't know how to feel about anything."

When I moved in with Rocco all those years ago, I was determined to make his desolate backyard a beautiful space. Rocco did the grunt work, but I planted the seeds. It seems I didn't have a natural green thumb. I killed a lot of flowers, but not the dahlias. They never died on me, so naturally, they became my favorite.

We moved to a bigger house after we had Lettie. I miss that garden, but when something works, it's best to stick with it. I planted them in our new house the first season we were there.

When a big event hits our family, Rocco always brings me flowers.

And they're always dahlias. After all, they symbolize a strong bond and everlasting love between two people. Nothing could be more meaningful for us.

I beam up at him. "You found purple."

He shrugs. "It's Vince's favorite. I figure it fits."

I push to my toes and press my lips to his. "Thank you."

He gazes down at me like we have all the time in the world, which we don't. We need to be at the courthouse in an hour. "Best mom in the world."

I shake my head. "Best parents. We're the shit."

A grin takes over his beautiful face. "Yeah, we are. Are you ready to have another kid?"

"Lead the way, Roc. I'll do anything with you."

Rocco

Today is the day.

And everyone is here for it.

To think the whole thing started when I was an MC prospect and moved in with the cartel.

Landyn tucked me under her wing and never let go. It took me a bit to get on board, but her idea that the bigger the better when it comes to family finally wore off on me.

I've never told anyone this. Not even Teagan—and I tell her everything.

But the first time I saw a bruise on Vince, I knew he'd be ours. I was determined.

There was no way I could sit back and let that happen. It's bad enough he put up with it for eight years. I know what it's like. I wasn't going to let it go on.

I had to break the cycle.

"This is a big group. Not very many adoptions bring in this kind of crowd," the judge says as she smiles straight at Vince. "Not everyone has a family this big to celebrate their big day."

Vince hardly ever sits still, and today is no different. He's almost bouncing in his seat when he twists his body to look at the crowd behind him. He turns back to the judge. "My new family is big! I'll have lots of aunts and uncles and cousins, but just one grandma and grandpa."

The judge focuses on him and him alone. "They're very lucky to have you. Don't you forget it."

Vince nods as his legs bounce and swing in his chair where he sits between Teagan and me. Gray and Lettie are standing right behind him.

Beyond them is … everyone.

Tim and Annette.

Sammie and her family.

Brax, Landyn, Brian, Baylee, and my goddaughter, Brenna.

Micah, Evie, Chase, Zane, and Hannah.

King, Goldie, and Bale.

Family.

I couldn't live without them.

The judge picks up a pen and scribbles on two pieces of paper.

This time when she looks up, she addresses the group. "Congratulations on your new grandson, nephew, brother, and son." Then she looks directly at Vince. "Welcome to your new family. You're officially a Monroe."

The room bursts into applause. Gray picks up his brother the way he does every day when they roughhouse. Vince cackles and proceeds to hug and be hugged by everyone.

I let him do what he wants and go straight for my wife. When I pull her to her feet, she's in tears.

Happy tears.

She nods and grins up at me through her dark teary eyes. "You're so lucky I hit on you all those years ago."

My smile turns into a grin. "You couldn't help yourself."

She shakes her head.

I pull her to my chest and whisper into her ear. "Best life ever, baby. Best life ever."

ACKNOWLEDGMENTS

The moment I created Rocco Monroe in book one of The Agents, I knew he needed a happily ever after. He grew up, matured, and this is his time. I hope I did him justice. His story broke my heart while writing at times, but it was him who put it back together.

I love Teagan as an adult. She's a woman who knows what she wants and doesn't stop until she gets it. May we all have a little bit of Teagan in our souls.

Well, I did it again to Hadley Finn. I asked her to edit my raw words. How many deadlines can a book have? Hadley continues to be a cheerleader, my editor, and my friend. I wouldn't be able to do the without her.

Annette, thank you for your daily support and friendship. You go above and beyond what any PA should. I'm blessed to have you in my life.

Carrie and Beth, you are the best proofreaders around. I'm not sure what I did to deserve you. Thank you for always having my back.

Emoji read this book in under twenty-four hours. That's a record. And can we all say a collective *thank you* to my hubs for the kickass playlists? He did it again.

Michele, thank you for reading chapter by chapter, like you always do, and being patient. You have permission to demand words from me faster from here on out.

MSB Design – Ms. Betty's Design Studio absolutely killed it

with the covers for The Agents. Betty, thank you for your patience and knowing exactly what this book needed more than I did.

I don't hand out many ARCs these days, and it's for a reason. My review team is the best. Thank you for always wanting my words and crazy love stories.

And finally, thank you to my Beauties for hanging with me on a daily basis. There are anywhere between 362 to 363 days a year I do not release a new book. That's a lot of time to talk about things other than new releases. You make every day bright and happy.

All my love,

BA xo

ABOUT THE AUTHOR

Brynne Asher lives in the Midwest with her husband, three children, and her perfect dog. When she isn't creating pretend people and relationships in her head, she's running her kids around and doing laundry. She enjoys cooking, decorating, shopping at outlet malls and online, always seeking the best deal. A perfect day in Brynne World ends in front of an outdoor fire with family, friends, s'mores, and a delicious cocktail.

- facebook.com/brynneasherauthor
- instagram.com/brynneasher
- amazon.com/Brynne-Asher/e/B00VRULS58/ref=dp_byline_cont_pop_ebooks_1
- bookbub.com/profile/brynne-asher

Made in the USA
Monee, IL
30 August 2024